By Barbara Taylor Bradford

TO BE THE BEST
ACT OF WILL
HOLD THE DREAM
VOICE OF THE HEART
A WOMAN OF SUBSTANCE

TO BE THE BEST

BARBARA TAYLOR BRADFORD

TO BE THE BEST

Large-Print Edition
Doubleday
New York London Toronto Sydney Auckland

This Large-Print Edition contains the complete, unabridged text of the original Doubleday edition.

Published by Doubleday, a division of Bantam Doubleday Dell Publishing Group, Inc., 666 Fifth Avenue, New York, New York 10103.

Doubleday and the portrayal of an anchor with a dolphin are trademarks of Doubleday, a division of Bantam Doubleday Dell Publishing Group, Inc.

The Production Review Committee of the NATIONAL ASSOCIATION FOR VISUALLY HANDICAPPED has found this book to meet its criteria for large type publications.

DESIGNED BY PETER R. KRUZAN

Library of Congress Cataloging-in-Publication Data

Bradford, Barbara Taylor, 1933–
To be the best.

I. Title.
PS3552.R2147T6   1988   813'.54   88-3813
ISBN 0-385-24579-3

FOR BOB
who is.
With my love.

CONTENTS

PROLOGUE

To be on my team, you've got to be the best.
And to be the best, you've got to have character.
Emma Harte in *A Woman of Substance*

Paula left Pennistone Royal just before dawn.

It was still dark as she eased the car out of the tall iron gates and turned left, heading for the moors. But as she came up onto the road which cut through the Pennine Chain of hills, the sky was already beginning to change. Its blurred mass of anthracite grays was giving way to amethyst and pink and a cold and fading green, and on the far horizon the first rays of the sun shimmered like shards of silver against the dark rim of the moors. It was an eerie hour, neither day nor night, and the silent spacious moors seemed emptier and more remote than ever. And then unexpectedly there was a sudden burst of radiance and that crystalline light so peculiar to the north of England filled the entire sky and day finally broke.

Paula rolled down the window and took a deep breath, then leaned back in the seat, relaxing as she pushed the car forward at a steady speed. The breeze that blew in was cool, but then it was always cool up here on the "tops" whatever the time of year and hardly the right place to gauge the weather. She knew it would be a scorching day again, and she was glad she had set out for Fairley early.

It was the end of August when the heather always blooms in Yorkshire and the wild, untenanted moors were glorious. Grim and daunting for most of the year, they were breathtaking in their beauty this morning, a sea of violet and magenta rippling under the wind, rolling ahead as far as the eye could see. On an impulse Paula stopped the car and got out, glancing around, filling her eyes. The landscape was awesome . . . stunning. She felt her throat tighten with emotion. Grandy's moors, she murmured, thinking of Emma Harte. I love them just as much as she did . . . as my own daughters, Tessa and Linnet, have grown to love them too.

Paula stood for a moment by the car, savoring her surroundings, looking and listening. She could hear the sharp trilling of the larks as they soared and wheeled high on the clouds and in the distance was the tinkling of water as a little beck rushed down over rocky crags, and on the cool and lucent air were the mingled scents of heather and bilberry, wildflowers and bracken. She closed her eyes briefly, remembering so many things, and then she lifted her head and looked up. The inverted bowl of a sky was China blue and filled with white puffball clouds and brilliant sunshine. The beginning of a pretty day, she thought, smiling inwardly. There is nowhere like the moors when the weather is beautiful, nowhere in the whole world. It was a long time since she had been up here. Too long really. My roots are here, just as Grandy's were, she thought, lingering a moment longer, the memories flooding her fully, carrying her back . . .

Abruptly, Paula turned away, got into her Aston Martin DB 2-4, and drove on, following the winding moorland road for another hour until it finally started its descent into the valley below, and Fairley. Because it was so early, the village still slumbered. The streets were entirely deserted. Paula parked in front of the ancient gray stone church with its square Norman tower and stained-glass windows, then she alighted, went round to the passenger door, and opened it. She had wedged the cardboard box on the floor near the seat, and now she lifted the vase of summer flowers out of the box and closed the door with her knee.

Carrying the vase with both hands, she pushed through the lych-gate that led into the cemetery adjoining the church.

Her steps carried her down the flagged path until she came to the far corner, secluded, bosky, infinitely still. Here, near the ancient moss-covered stone wall and shaded by a gnarled old elm tree, were a cluster of graves. For a while she stood staring at one headstone.

Emma Harte was the name engraved upon the dark green marble, and below were the dates *1889–1970.*

Eleven years ago, Paula thought. She died eleven years ago today. Whatever has happened to the time? It has spun away from me so fast . . . it seems like only yesterday she was alive and vigorous and running her business and ordering us all around in her inimitable way.

Moving closer to her grandmother's grave, Paula bent down, placed the flowers on it, then straightened and stood motionless with one hand resting on the headstone, staring out toward the distant hills. There was a reflective look in her eyes, and she was lost for a moment in the sweep of her thoughts.

I've got to do something, Grandy, something drastic you wouldn't like. But I'm certain you'd understand my reason . . . that I want to create something of my own. If you were in my position you'd do exactly the same thing. I know you would. And it'll come out right. It must. There is no room for doubt.

The striking of the church clock split the silence like thunder, made Paula start, and brought her out of her reverie with a jolt.

After another moment or two she turned away from Emma's grave and let her eyes roam over the other headstones. They came to rest on David Armory's, then moved on to regard Jim Fairley's . . . her father . . . her husband . . . who had lain here for ten years. They had both been far too young to die. Sadness struck at her with such sharpness she caught her breath in surprise and her heart filled with an old familiar ache. She steadied herself, spun around, and continued along the path, clamping down on the pain and sadness the memories engendered in her. She reminded herself that life was for the living.

Paula broke her rapid pace only once, when she passed the private plot which stood close to the church. Encircled by iron railings, it was filled with the graves of Jim's forebears . . . Adam and Adele . . . Olivia . . . Gerald. So many Fairleys . . . just as there were so many Hartes buried here. Two families whose lives had been entwined for three generations . . . bound together in a bitter feud . . . and in love and hate and revenge and marriage . . . and finally in death. Here they lay, together in their eternal resting place under the shadow of the windswept moors, at peace at last in this benign earth . . .

As the lych-gate clicked behind her, Paula straightened up, threw back her shoulders, and hurried to the car, a new determination in her step, a new resoluteness in her expression. There was so much ahead of her, so many challenges, so much she had to accomplish.

She got into the car and settled herself comfortably for the long drive ahead of her.

The tape was on the passenger seat where she had placed it earlier that morning in readiness for the journey. After slipping it into the player in the dashboard, she turned up the volume. The strains of Mozart's *Jupiter* Symphony filled the car . . . rich, melodious, so full of spirit and vivacity and, for her at least, a soaring hope. It was one of her favorites. Tessa had bought the tape for her a few weeks ago. It was the latest recording. Herbert von Karajan conducting the Berliner Philharmoniker. Paula shut her eyes, letting the music wash over her, thrilling to the first movement . . . *allegro vivace* . . . it made her feel . . . uplifted.

8

PROLOGUE

A moment passed, and then another, and she opened her eyes finally, turned on the ignition, and coasted down the hill, making for the Leeds-Bradford Road, which would lead her onto the M1, the motorway going south to London. She swung onto it thirty minutes later and saw at once that the traffic was light. There were only a few stray cars on the road and no trucks at all. If she was lucky and continued to have a clear run, she would be sitting behind her desk at Harte's in Knightsbridge within four hours.

Picking up speed, Paula roared ahead, her foot hard down on the accelerator, her eyes fixed on the road.

The symphony swelled to a crescendo, fell away, rose again, enveloping her in its beauty, transporting her with its magic. She experienced a surge of real happiness. Her mind was vividly alive. She could see the months ahead very clearly, knew with a sureness that thrust deep into her soul that she was right in everything she intended to do.

She increased her speed. The Aston Martin flew forward along the motorway as if it had wings and were airborne. She was enjoying the feel of this superb piece of machinery under her hands, enjoying the sense of control she felt . . . . control of the car, of herself, of the future.

She had made her plan. *Her master plan.* She intended to execute it as soon as possible. It was watertight. Nothing could possibly go wrong . . .

LOVERS
&
STRANGERS

Call no man foe, but never love a stranger.
Stella Benson

Be not forgetful to entertain strangers:
for thereby some have entertained angels unawares.
The Bible: Hebrews

My true-love hath my heart, and I have his,
By just exchange one for the other given:
I hold his dear, and mine he cannot miss,
There never was a better bargain driven.
Sir Philip Sidney

1

Paula walked into her private office at the London store with her usual briskness, and after removing several folders from her briefcase, she sat down at the antique partners' desk in the corner. It was precisely at this moment that she noticed the buff-colored envelope propped against the antique porcelain lamp.

Marked PERSONAL, it had apparently been hand-delivered, and she recognized the writing at once. She felt a small shiver of pleasure. Eagerly, she reached for the envelope, slit it open with the gold-and-jade paper knife, and took out the folded piece of paper.

The note was boldly penned.

Meet me in Paris. Tonight, it said. *You're booked on Flight 902. British Airways. 6 p.m. I'll be waiting impatiently. Usual place. Don't disappoint me.*

Paula frowned. The tone was peremptory, commanding, and implicit in his words was the assumption she would go. Mild irritation at his high-handedness flared and diluted the flush of pleasure she had experienced a second before. Of course she wouldn't go. She couldn't. She must spend the weekend with her children as planned, *wanted* to spend it with them, in fact.

Still clutching the note, she leaned back in the chair and gazed into space, thinking about him. Bossy . . . conceited . . . those were the adjectives which sprang into her head. They were certainly appropriate. A trace of a smile surfaced, flickered on her mouth. She was suddenly amused by the invitation and sorely tempted to accept. Admit it, you'd love to spend the weekend in Paris with *him.* But then you'd love to do a lot of things you constantly pass up, a small voice at the back of her head reminded her. And she smiled again, though this time with wryness, a hint of regret even, knowing that she could never be indulgent with herself. Perish the thought! Duty had to come first. That little rule of Emma Harte's had been inculcated in her since childhood, although sometimes she wished her grandmother had not been so thorough. But Grandy had schooled her well, had taught her that wealth and privilege also meant responsibilities, and that they had to be shouldered without flinching, no matter what the cost to oneself. And since she was now thirty-six, almost thirty-seven, her character was hardly likely to change at this stage in her life.

Paula sat up, slipped the note back into its envelope, sighing under her breath as she did. A romantic interlude in her favorite city with that very special and exceptional man was infinitely appealing but decidedly not possible. No, she would not go to Paris for a weekend of love and intimacy and pleasure. Instead, she would go to her children and be a good mother. Her children needed her. After all, she had not seen them for two weeks. On the other hand, she had not seen him either . . .

"Damn and blast," she muttered out loud, wishing he had not sent the note. It had thrown her off balance, made her feel unexpectedly restless, and at a moment in time when she could not afford to have distractions of any kind. The months ahead were going to be extremely complicated, and they would be crucial months.

And so she would phone him later, tell him she was not coming; she must also cancel the airline reservation he had made for her. On second thought, perhaps she ought to call British Airways immediately.

As she reached for the telephone it began to ring.

She picked up swiftly, said, "Hello?" and glanced at the door as her assistant, Jill, hurried in with a cup of coffee.

"Hello, Paula, it's me," her cousin Alexander was saying at the other end of the phone. "I came into the Leeds store looking for you, only to find that on the *one* day I'm up here, *you're* in London."

"Oh Sandy darling, I *am* sorry to have missed you," she exclaimed, then covered the mouthpiece, murmured her thanks to Jill, who placed the coffee in front of her, smiled, and disappeared.

Paula went on, "Were you in Yorkshire last night?"

"Yes. I got in around six-thirty."

"I was still at the store, Sandy. You should've called me. We could've had dinner."

"No, we couldn't. You see, I had to get out to Nutton Priory as early as possible. My estate manager's going off on holiday today and we had a lot to go over." Alexander paused, cleared his throat. "You were at Grandy's grave this morning . . . those *are* your flowers, aren't they, Paula?"

"Yes," she said, her voice growing softer. "I went there very early, before driving to London."

"I was close on your heels." He laughed faintly. "I suppose we just weren't meant to meet up today. Well . . . my loss."

Paula loved her cousin dearly and thus was sensitive to his moods. She had caught something odd in his voice, a nuance that disturbed her. "Sandy, do you have some sort of problem?" she asked quickly. "Do you want to talk to me about anything?"

There was only the slightest hesitation before he exclaimed with a certain firmness, "No, no, not at all! I merely thought it would be nice for us to lunch together, I haven't seen you for weeks. I realize you've been busy . . . however, I do miss our tête-à-têtes, old thing."

Paula had been listening attentively, straining to catch that peculiar inflection she had noticed a moment ago, but now it was absent. His voice sounded perfectly normal—well-modulated and controlled, as it always was.

She said, "Yes, I miss them too, Sandy, and it has been a bit hectic for me this summer, what with all the flying to the south of France and back, and staying ahead of the game with the business. And look here, whilst I have you on the phone there's something I've been meaning to say to you for ages." She took a quick breath, and her voice was a trifle sterner when she continued, "I'm terribly cross with you, Alexander. You've hardly spent any time with us at Cap Martin this year, and it is *your* house for God's sake. Besides, I do think you—"

"You're not the only person who works for a living!" he shot back curtly, then added, in a rush of words, "I've had a lot on my plate, too, you know, so please, Paula darling, don't nag. Emily's become quite the expert at that technique. *She's* beginning to get on my nerves."

"Your sister thinks you don't get enough relaxation. She wants you to take it easy, enjoy life a bit more. And I happen to agree with Emily. Wholeheartedly, I might add."

Ignoring these comments and her reproachful tone, Alexander said, "I expect you're going down to the villa this weekend, aren't you?"

"Yes. I'm catching the nine o'clock plane to Nice tomorrow morning, returning early on Monday. Sandy! I've just had a wonderful idea! Why don't you come with me? You'll enjoy it, you know you will, and the children will be so thrilled to see you. So will Emily."

"I really do have to be at Nutton Priory for the next few days. Honestly I do, Paula. I'd love to join you, but there's far too much that needs my attention on the estate. Look, let's have lunch on Tuesday." His voice was suddenly eager.

"Oh God, I *can't,*" she groaned. "I'm taking the Concorde to New York first thing on Tuesday morning, and at the end of the week I'm flying from New York to Sydney. I'll be gone for the whole of September."

"Oh. I see."

His disappointment communicated itself to her so acutely, she exclaimed, "Why don't we make a date now? For October." As she spoke she opened her engagement book, flipped the pages. "How about the first Wednesday in the month?"

"I'm sure it's fine, but let me look at my pocket diary. Hold on, Paula."

There was a clatter as he put down the phone.

Paula lifted her cup, took a sip of the hot coffee.

A moment later, Sandy was back on the line, his voice bright and chipper. "All free and clear, darling. I'll see you in October then. And I'll be looking forward to it."

"Oh so will I! And Sandy . . ."

"Yes?"

"Take care of yourself."

"I will, and you do the same, Paula. My love to everyone at the villa."

After they had hung up, Paula sat drinking her coffee, frowning, and staring at the telephone, her mind on her cousin.

She felt a pang of genuine regret for having let the summer slide by without putting more pressure on him to come to the Riviera with them. On the other hand, would her insistence have done any real good? Most likely not. After all, Emily had been relentless with him since Easter, using all of her not inconsiderable wiles and doing everything in her power to persuade him to join them at the Villa Faviola. He had flown down twice, but only for brief stays and then only to please his sister. This had been quite evident to both her and Emily.

Still, she could not help feeling guilty now, recognizing that she had neglected Alexander of late. There had been so much to cope with this past year; so many things had encroached on her free time, interfered with her various friendships. Sandy had been a casualty of the merciless work ethic she had adopted for herself. Poor Sandy, she hadn't had time for him, that was the sad truth, and she admitted it freely.

Perhaps that was why he had sounded strange. No, that was not the reason at all. The peculiar inflection in his voice, which she knew she had not imagined, had been tension pure and simple. No, it had been strain. Or anxiety?

Yes, that was it. *Anxiety.* And it had alerted her to something . . . to trouble.

As she came to this realization, Paula thought, with a sinking feeling: *Everything's not right with Sandy.*

A curious unease took hold of her. It was an odd sensation, one that made her sit up in her chair, and she held herself tensely, worriedly asking herself what could possibly be wrong. Frowning again, she ran things through her mind at the speed of light. There could be nothing amiss at Harte Enterprises. Emily would have known and would have told her. Sandy's health was good. He certainly had no financial problems. And even though he was not wooing anyone special—according to Emily, who knew everything about everyone in the family—he did not appear to lack for female companionship whenever he felt the need of it. His social life was not spectacular. But then again, this seemed to be his preference, the manner in which he chose to live his life these days.

He must often be lonely though, she mused, wishing for the hundredth-or-so time that Sandy had remarried.

After Maggie's death in the avalanche at Chamonix he had been grief-stricken and inconsolable for so long. Then slowly he had pulled out of it, had regained his self-possession, and painstakingly, he had put himself back together. But it was as if he had assembled all of the pieces of himself in a new and wholly different pattern. He had not seemed quite the same ever again.

The avalanche affected us all, Paula reminded herself, thinking in particular of her brother, Philip. He had also been skiing on the mountain that day. But he had been the one family member who had lived . . . the sole survivor. And then there was her mother, who had lost a husband. And *I* lost a father; and my children lost a father. Yes, the avalanche wreaked havoc on the entire family. It damaged us, changed us, and irrevocably so. Each one of us has been decidedly odd ever since . . .

She began to laugh under her breath. And *me* most of all, she thought, as she endeavored to shake off that sense of unease she had felt about her cousin a moment ago. Wasn't she being overly imaginative, perhaps? After all, she and Sandy had been close as children, had remained close over the years. If there truly *was* something troubling him, he would have confided it to her on the telephone. I'm being irrational about this, and unaccountably so, she decided, and made a resolute effort to dismiss her worries about Alexander.

Her gaze came back to the papers on her desk.

The quickest of glances told her there was nothing particularly urgent to be dealt with, and she was relieved. Problems that arose on Fridays usually had a way of impinging on her weekends —and ruining them. This did not matter so much in the winter, but in the summer, when the children were home from their respective schools for a long period, it was distressing for them. They treasured their weekends with her, guarded them jealously, and resented any intrusions on their time, just as she did.

Once she had read the morning's mail and a memorandum from Jill, which detailed suggested structural changes in the Designer Salon, she checked the pile of purchase orders, then reached for the telexes. All had emanated from the New York store and were signed by her American assistant, Madelana O'Shea. They had come in late last night and only one required an answer.

Pulling a yellow pad toward her, Paula began to draft a reply. When this was done, she opened the thickest of the folders she had brought with her from Yorkshire and took out the top sheet of paper. It was the only thing which interested her at this moment. On it were the salient points of her master plan. A single sheet of paper . . . but it was the key to so much . . . the key to the future.

Within seconds she was so immersed in her work, so busy making additional notes on the pad, that all thoughts of her cousin Sandy fled. But months later Paula was to recall this day only too well. She would remember her uneasiness about him with great clarity and vividness, and she would fervently wish she had paid more attention to her intuition. Most of all, she would bitterly regret that she had not pressed him to confide in her. Knowing about his problems would not have enabled her to change the inevitable outcome, but at least she could have revised her travel plans. In so doing she would have been able to help him, simply by being there for him whenever he needed her.

But on this scorching morning in August of 1981, Paula had no way of knowing any of this, and that sense of impending trouble—a foreboding almost—which she had experienced earlier had already been squashed by the force of her will. Also, like her grandmother she had the enviable knack of pushing everything to one side in order to concentrate on her business priorities, and this she now did. Head bent, eyes riveted on the page, she fell deeper and deeper into her concentration, as always so totally absorbed in her work she was oblivious to everything else.

Twenty minutes later, Paula finally lifted her head, stapled her notes together, and put them in the folder along with the single sheet of paper; she then locked the folder in the center drawer of her desk for safekeeping over the weekend. Half smiling to herself, satisfied that she had thought of everything and was prepared for any contingency, she sat holding the key for a split second longer before placing it carefully in her briefcase.

Pushing the chair back, she rose, stretched, walked across the floor, feeling the need to move around. Her body was cramped, her bones stiff from sitting—first in the Aston Martin and then here at her desk. She found herself at the window and parted the curtains, looked down into Knightsbridge below, noticed that the traffic appeared to be more congested than ever this morning, but then Fridays were usually wicked in the summer months.

Turning, Paula stood facing the room, a look of approval washing over her face. From her earliest childhood days she had loved this office, had felt comfortable within its confines. She had seen no reason to change it when she had inherited it from her grandmother, and so she had left everything virtually intact. She had added a few mementos of her own and photographs of her children, but that was the extent of it.

The office was more like a drawing room in an English country house than a place of business, and this was the real secret of its great charm. The ambiance was intentional. It had been created by Emma Harte some sixty-odd years earlier when she had used valuable Georgian antiques and English oil paintings of great worth instead of more prosaic furnishings. Classic chintz fabrics on the sofas and chairs and at the windows introduced glorious color against the pine-paneled walls, while antique porcelain lamps and other fine accessories lent their own touches of elegance and distinction. The decorative look aside, the room was spacious and graceful, and it had a beautiful old Adam fireplace which was always in use on cold days. The office never palled on Paula, and she was delighted when people entering it for the first time exclaimed about its beauty and uniqueness.

Like everything else she did, Grandy got this room exactly right, Paula thought, walking across the threadbare but priceless Savonnerie carpet, drawing to a standstill in front of the carved pine fireplace. She gazed up at the portrait of her grandmother which hung above it, painted when Emma had been a young woman. She still missed her, quite intensely at times, but she had long drawn comfort from the feeling that Emma lived on in her . . . in her heart and in her memories.

As she continued to stare at that lovely yet determined face in the portrait, she experienced a feeling of immense pride in Emma's extraordinary and most singular achievements. Grandy started out with nothing and created one of the greatest business empires in the world . . . what incredible courage she must have had at my age. *I* must have her kind of courage and strength and determination. *I* must not falter in what *I* have to do . . . my master plan must succeed just as her plan did. Paula's mind raced, leaped forward to the future, and she was filled with excitement at the thought of what lay ahead.

She returned to her desk, realizing she must get on with the day's business.

She flipped on the intercom. "Jill . . ."

"Yes, Paula?"

"My things *were* brought up from the car, weren't they?"

"Some time ago, actually, but I didn't want to disturb you. Do you want me to bring everything in now?"

"Please."

Within seconds Jill's bright auburn head appeared around the door and she hurried through into Paula's office, holding aloft Paula's garment bag in one hand, a suitcase in the other. Jill was tall, well built, an athletic type of young woman, and she appeared to manage these items with the greatest of ease.

"I'll put these in your dressing room," she said, disappearing through the door leading to this adjoining area as she spoke.

"Thanks," Paula murmured, and when her assistant returned to her office, she went on, "Sit down for a minute, would you, please, Jill? I'd like to go over a couple of things with you."

Jill Marton nodded, took the chair on the other side of the desk, sat watching Paula through warm and intelligent brown eyes. Jill had worked for her for over five years and she never ceased to admire her, forever marveling at her extraordinary energy and stamina and drive. The woman opposite her was a powerhouse, not to mention astute and inspired and frequently daring in business. Jill had never worked for anyone like her. Those at the store who had known the legendary Emma said that Paula was a chip off the old block. Jill suspected this was the truth, that the traits she so admired in her boss were inherited from the famous founder of the Harte chain. Yes, it's all in the genes, Jill thought, continuing to observe Paula surreptitiously.

"Ah, here it is . . . your memo about the

Designer Salon," Paula said, picking up the piece of paper she had been searching for on the desk.

Jill sat up straighter in her chair, looked at Paula with alertness. "I hope it makes sense to you," she said.

"It does indeed. Your recommendations are excellent. I've nothing to add. You can put the structural alterations into work immediately and make the other changes as well. They'll do wonders for the salon, Jill."

On hearing this compliment Jill felt vivid color staining her neck and cheeks, and with a flush of pleasure she took the memo which Paula had slid across the highly polished surface between them. She said, "I'm so glad you approve," and beamed.

Paula returned her smile. "Send this telex to Madelana later, and here's the morning mail . . . nothing important, as you already know. You can deal with it easily. I've initialed these purchase orders." She tapped them with a bright red fingernail, then asked, "Now, did any of last week's advertisements come up from the art department yet?"

Jill shook her head. "But they'll be on your desk immediately after lunch. I spoke to Alison Warren earlier, and they're almost ready."

"Good. And speaking of lunch, did Michael

Kallinski confirm? Or let you know where I'm supposed to meet him?"

"He called a bit earlier. He didn't want me to bother you, since you'd just arrived when he rang. That's why I didn't put him through. He's picking you up at twelve-fifteen."

"Oh." Paula looked at her watch, rose and walked over to the dressing room, paused at the door, glanced down at her wrinkled cotton pants. "In that case, I'd better change. I want to go out onto the floor, check a few things before Michael arrives, and I don't have too much time. Excuse me, Jill."

"Of course." Jill scooped up the papers on the desk and headed to her own office. "Let me know if you need anything."

"I will," Paula said, closing the door behind her.

The dressing area had been the filing room in Emma's day, but Paula had revamped it, adding floor-to-ceiling closets with mirrored doors, excellent lighting, and a dressing table. She sat down at this, freshened her makeup and brushed her hair, then she slipped out of the shirt, pants, and sandals she had worn for driving from Yorkshire.

Within seconds she was dressed in the clothes she had brought with her in the garment bag: a black silk shantung suit, designed especially for her by Christina Crowther, classically simple, tailored, and smart, worn with a white silk camisole, dark, sheer stockings, and high-heeled black patent pumps. The jewelry she added was equally simple but effective: A three-strand pearl choker with a diamond clasp at the front encircled her neck, and large *mabé* pearl studs ringed with diamonds glittered on her ears.

Staring at herself in the mirror, eyeing her reflection critically, Paula decided she liked the way she looked. The suit was crisp and businesslike without being overly severe and was therefore perfect for the store; it was also chic enough to go to lunch at an elegant restaurant. And no doubt they would be going somewhere smart. Michael always took her to the best places.

The staff elevator whizzed her down to the main floor.

Paula crossed the jewelry department and headed in the direction of cosmetics and perfumery, looking about as she did.

The store was crowded this morning.

But then it was generally thronged with shoppers from the moment it opened its doors at ten until it closed them at six. Over the decades it had become a famous landmark in London, and people from all over the world flocked through its great portals, to walk around its renowned halls and simply *look* as well as to buy the merchandise.

Paula loved the bustle, the activity, the crowds, the high-pitched buzz of the voices, so many of them foreign, the excitement that seemed to hang in the very air. She usually experienced a small thrill when she returned after an absence, however short it had been, and this morning was no exception. The Yorkshire shops were important entities in the chain, just as those in Paris and New York were, but this was the flagship store, and the one she loved the most.

Emma Harte had opened it in 1921.

In three months they would be celebrating its sixtieth anniversary. And what a celebration she had planned. It would be a tribute to her grandmother, one of the greatest merchant princes who had ever lived, as well as a salute to sixty years of superlative retailing and a record unchallenged by any department store, in any city, in any country in the world. Harte's of Knightsbridge was the best. The only one of its kind. A legend.

A sense of exhilaration at being back on this very special territory, her favorite bit of turf, brought an extra spring to her step as she walked into Perfumery and drew to a stop.

Eagle-eyed as always, she stood seeking out

imperfections but found none. This pleased her. The area had recently been redesigned under her close supervision, and even though she said so herself, the results were smashing.

Glass panels etched in the manner of Lalique, many mirrors, masses of chrome and silver accents, crystal chandeliers and wall sconces . . . all these elements combined to create a shimmering effect that was stunning. The scheme made the perfect backdrop for the eyecatching displays of cosmetics, perfumes, and beauty products. Opulent, glamorous, inviting, the department was designed to lure women into spending tons of money, and it had succeeded brilliantly, just as she had known it would when it was still on the drawing boards.

Good merchandising and marketing, that's what it's all about, Paula commented to herself, moving on briskly, making a detour through lingerie on the way to the Rayne-Delman shoe salon. She was reveling in her morning walk through her store . . . the finest department store in the world. It was the seat of her power, her strong citadel, her pride and joy. In fact, it was everything to her.

2

For the second time that morning the portrait of Emma hanging in Paula's office was undergoing a close and fixed scrutiny.

The man who had just drawn to a standstill in front of it was in his late thirties, fair-haired with light blue eyes and a summer tan. He stood about five feet eight, but appeared taller because of his lean, trim build. Also, his clothes added to the illusion of height. He wore a white shirt and a burgundy silk tie, and his dark blue suit, made of the finest imported raw silk, was so flawlessly cut, so unerringly tailored, it hung on him perfectly, obviously a work of art from Savile Row.

His name was Michael Kallinski and he stood

examining the alluring face captured in oils on the life-sized canvas, his eyes narrowed in concentration as he ruminated on the formidable Emma Harte.

It suddenly struck him as quite curious that a woman who had been dead for over a decade— eleven years to this very day to be exact—was always spoken about as if she were still alive, and by most people at that, not merely her immediate family. He supposed that someone of Emma's charisma and brilliance, who had made such a vivid and powerful impact in her lifetime, *would* be on the short list for immortality. After all, the dent she had made on the world—in her personal relationships, in international business, and through her many philanthropies—was enormous.

Michael stepped back, tilted his head to one side, trying to ascertain how old Emma had been when she had sat for this portrait. Most probably in her late thirties, he decided. With her chiseled features, flawless complexion, reddish-gold hair, and those extraordinary green eyes, she had been a great beauty as a young woman, there was no doubt about that whatsoever.

Little wonder his own grandfather had been madly in love with her those many years ago, and ready and willing to leave his wife and chil-

35

dren for her—according to Kallinski family gossip, at any rate. And from what he understood from his father, David Kallinski had not been the only man to fall under her mesmeric spell. Blackie O'Neill had apparently been bewitched by her, too, in their youth.

The Three Musketeers. That's what Emma had called them—his grandfather, Blackie, and herself. In their early days together, at the turn of the century, they had been considered an unlikely trio . . . a Jew, an Irish Catholic, and a Protestant. Seemingly they had not paid much attention to what people thought of them or their friendship, and they had remained close, almost inseparable, throughout their long lives. And what an unbeatable trio they had proven to be. They had founded three impressive financial empires which straddled half the world and three powerful family dynasties which only went from strength to strength with the passing of time.

But it had been Emma who had been the real mover, the doer and the shaker, always pushing ahead with vision and enterprise, the two men following her lead. Anyway, that was the way his father told it, and Michael had no reason to disbelieve him. And he knew from his own experience of her that Emma had been absolutely unique. As far as the younger members of the three clans were concerned, she had certainly left her imprint on each one of them, himself included. Her indelible stamp, his father called it.

Michael smiled to himself, remembering exactly how Emma had been thirty-odd years ago . . . rounding them up as children and carting them off to Heron's Nest for the spring and summer holidays. They had called her "The General" behind her back, and the house in Scarborough had been affectionately referred to as "the army camp." She had put them through their paces and instilled in them her own philosophy of life, had taught them the meaning of honor and integrity, the importance of the team spirit and playing the game. And all through the years of their growing up she had given unstintingly of her love and understanding and friendship, and they were better people now for having known her then.

A look of love washed over his face, and he touched his hand to his forehead, giving the portrait a small salute. She had been the very best . . . just as her granddaughters were the best. A rare breed, the Harte women, all of them, and most especially Paula.

The sound of the door opening prompted him to swing around quickly.

His face lit up at the sight of Paula.

"I'm sorry to have kept you waiting!" she exclaimed, looking apologetic, hurrying forward to greet him.

"You didn't, I was early," he replied, going to meet her in the center of the floor. He gave her a huge bear hug, then held her away, stared down into her face. "You're looking wonderful." He glanced over his shoulder at the portrait, then brought his gaze back to hers. "And you're beginning to resemble *that* legendary lady more than ever."

Paula groaned, gave him a look of mock horror as they drew apart.

"Oh God, Michael, not you too! *Please.* There are enough people who call me the Clone behind my back without *you* giving voice to the idea." She shook her head. "That's all I need from a dear friend . . ."

He burst out laughing. "I sometimes think you're all clones, actually. The lot of you . . . Emily and Amanda, as well as you." He swiveled to face the portrait. "And when was that painted, by the way?"

"In 1929. Why?"

"I'd been trying to figure out how old Emma was when she sat for it."

"Thirty-nine. It was started and finished just before her fortieth birthday."

"Mmmm. I guessed as much. And she *was*

38

beautiful then, wasn't she?" Not giving Paula a chance to reply, he went on, with a small grin, "Do you realize that you and I would have been related if David *had* left my grandmother Rebecca and run off with Emma?"

"Let's not get into all that history today," she said with a light laugh, moved rapidly toward the desk, sat down, and added, "Anyway, I feel as if we are, don't you? Related, I mean."

"Yes."

He followed her across the room, seated himself in the chair facing her.

There was a brief silence, then he remarked quietly, "Blood might *not* be thicker than water as far as some families are concerned, but it is when it comes to the three clans. Our grandparents would've killed for each other, and I think their kind of loyalty has been passed down to our generation, hasn't it?"

"I should say so—" She cut herself short when the phone rang, and she reached to answer it. After saying hello and listening for a second she put her slim, tapering hand over the receiver, explained, "It's the manager of the Harrogate store, I'll only be a minute."

He nodded, sat back in the chair, waiting for her to finish her call, quietly studying her as he had studied the painting only a few minutes before.

Michael Kallinski had not seen Paula for over two months, and because he had been away, her uncanny resemblance to Emma had struck him more forcibly than ever when she had walked in. Her coloring was different from Emma's, of course. Paula had hair as black as pitch and eyes of the deepest darkest blue. She had inherited Emma's clear, finely wrought features, though, and the famous widow's peak, which was extremely dramatic above those large eyes set wide apart. With the passing of time the two women seemed to merge more and more, to become identical, to him at least. Perhaps it had something to do with the expression in Paula's eyes these days, her mannerisms, her pithiness, the way she moved—swiftly, always in a hurry—and the habit she had of laughing at her misfortunes. These characteristics reminded him of Emma Harte, just as her attitude in business did.

He had known Paula his entire life and yet, oddly enough, he had not really known her until they were both in their thirties.

When they had been children he had not liked her one little bit, had considered her to be cold, standoffish, and indifferent to them all, except for her cousin Emily, that roly-poly pudding of a child whom she had forever mothered, and

Shane O'Neill, of course, whom she had always striven to please.

Privately, Michael had called her Miss Goody Two Shoes, because she had been just that, a child who appeared to have no faults whatsoever, one who was always being clucked over, praised, and held up as an example to them by their respective parents. His brother Mark had had his own name for her . . . Paragon of Virtue. He and Mark had secretly laughed at her, made fun of her behind her back, but then again, they had scoffed at *all* the girls from the clans, had never wanted to spend time with them, had preferred to be roistering around with the other boys. They had banded together with Philip, Winston, Alexander, Shane, and Jonathan, who had been their boon companions in those days.

It was only in the last six years that he had come to know Paula and he had discovered that this shrewd, hardworking, and brilliant woman hid a deep emotional side behind her cool air and her inbred refinement. The aloof manner was merely an outward manifestation of her shyness and natural reserve, those traits he had so misunderstood in childhood.

Discovering that Paula was quite different than he had believed her to be had come as something of a shock to him. To his astonishment, he found she was so very, very human.

She was vulnerable, loving, fiercely loyal, and devoted to her family and friends. Terrible things had happened to her over the past ten years, devastating things which would have felled most other people, perhaps even destroyed them. But not Paula. She had suffered deeply, yet had found strength from adversity, had become a most compassionate woman.

Since they had been working together they had drawn closer, and she was his staunch supporter in business and an ally in every way, whenever he needed one. It occurred to Michael now that he would not have been able to cope with his messy divorce and his dreadful personal problems without Paula's friendship. She was always willing to listen to his woes at the end of the phone, or make herself available for a drink or a meal when the going really got tough. She had cornered a special place in his life, and he would be forever grateful that she had.

For all her success and sophistication and self-confidence, there was something about Paula—an endearing little-girl quality—which tugged at his heart, made him want to do things for her, want to please her. Frequently he went out of his way to accomplish this, as he had in New York recently. He wished the interminable phone call from the Harrogate store would come to an end so that he could impart his news.

42

Suddenly it did.

Paula put down the receiver, made a little moue.

"Sorry about that," she apologized. Leaning back in the chair, she went on, in an affectionate tone, "It's lovely to see you Michael . . . and how was New York?"

"Terrific. Hectic. I was up to my neck with work, since our business is going well over there right now. Still, I also managed to enjoy myself, even had a few weekends out in the Hamptons." He leaned closer to the desk. "Paula—"

"Yes, Michael?" she cut in, eyeing him astutely, alerted by the urgency in his voice.

"I think I may have found it . . . what you've been looking for in the States."

Excitement flew onto her face. She sat forward slightly, her eagerness only too apparent. "Private or public?"

"Private."

"Is it for sale?"

"Isn't everything—if the price is right." There was a hint of mischief on his face as he held her eyes.

"Come on, don't tease me!" she exclaimed. "Is it actually *on* the market?"

"No, it isn't. But what does that mean in this day and age of the takeover? The owners can be approached . . . it doesn't cost anything to do that."

"What's the name of the company? Where is it? How big is it?"

Michael chuckled. "Hey, steady on, I can only answer one question at a time. The company is called Peale and Doone and it's in the Midwest. It's not big, only seven stores . . . suburban stores. In Illinois and Ohio. But it's an old company, Paula, founded in the 1920s by a couple of Scotsmen who settled in the States and at first dealt only in Scottish imports. You know, woolen goods, tartans and plaids, cashmeres and the like. They extended their inventory during the forties and fifties. But the merchandise is supposedly stodgy and the company's in the doldrums, management-wise that is. Quite solid financially, or so I've been led to understand."

"How did you hear about Peale and Doone?"

"Through a lawyer friend who's with a Wall Street law firm. I'd asked him to be on the lookout for a chain and he heard about this company through a colleague in Chicago. My chap thinks they're ripe for a takeover."

Paula nodded. "Who holds the stock?"

"The heirs to Mr. Peale and Mr. Doone."

"There's no guarantee they'd sell, Michael."

"Correct. On the other hand, often stockholders don't *know* they want to sell until they're actually approached to do so."

"That's true, and it's worth investigating further."

"You bet it is, and although this chain is small, it might well be perfect for you, Paula."

"It's just a pity the stores are in the boondocks," she murmured, and with a grimace, thinking out loud. "Big cities like Chicago and Cleveland would be more my speed."

Michael gave her a sharp stare. "Look here, with your flair and expertise you can easily put your own special cachet on any store *anywhere,* and you *know* that. Besides, what's wrong with the boondocks? There's plenty of money to be made out there."

"Yes, you're quite right," she answered quickly, suddenly realizing she may have sounded ungrateful after the effort he had made on her behalf. "Can you get some more information, please, Michael?"

"I'll ring my friend in New York later in the day and ask him to pursue this further."

"Does he know you were inquiring about retail chains for *me?*"

"No, but I can tell him if you like."

Paula said very briskly and firmly, "No. I think not. At least not for the moment, if you don't mind. It's better no one knows. The mention of my name could send the price skyrocketing. *If* there's going to be a price, that is."

"Point well taken. I'll keep Harvey in the dark for the time being."

"Please . . . and thank you, Michael, for going to all this trouble for me." Her smile was warm, sincere, as she added, "I really do appreciate it."

"I'll do anything for you Paula, anything at all," he replied, his eyes filling with affection for her. Then he glanced down at his watch. "Oh, it's getting late! We'd better be going," he announced and promptly stood up. "I hope you don't mind, but the old man's invited himself to lunch."

"Of course I don't mind," she said, her voice rising slightly. "You know I adore Uncle Ronnie."

"And the feeling is mutual, I can assure you." He threw her an amused look. "The old man dotes on you . . . he thinks the sun shines out of you."

She picked up her black patent bag and moved across the room. "Come on then, let's go. We don't want to keep him waiting, do we?"

Michael took her arm, escorted her out of the office.

As they went down in the elevator he could not help thinking about his father and Paula, and their special relationship which had developed over the past few years. The old man treated her like a beloved daughter, whilst she seemed to revere him. Certainly she behaved as if he were the shrewdest man alive, which, of course, he was. Dad's become her rabbi, Michael thought suddenly with an inner smile, and also a substitute for her grandmother. Not surprising that some people considered their friendship peculiar and were jealous. Personally, he applauded it. Paula filled a void in his father's life as he did in hers.

3

Sir Ronald Kallinski, chairman of the board of Kallinski Industries, walked across the impressive marble lobby of Kallinski House at a leisurely pace.

Tall, slender, and a man of dominating presence, he had black wavy hair, heavily frosted with white, and a saturnine face. He had inherited the eyes of his father David and his grandmother Janessa Kallinski; they were of the brightest cornflower blue and seemed all the more startling because of his weatherbeaten complexion.

Renowned for never appearing ruffled or disheveled, no matter what the circumstance, he was always perfectly groomed and elegantly attired. This morning he was wearing a charcoal gray three-piece suit with an impeccable white shirt and a pearl-gray silk tie. Although he was almost seventy, he was in such robust health and was so vigorous for his age he looked like a much younger man.

As he strolled through the vast entrance foyer, he nodded graciously to several people who recognized him, and paused to admire the Henry Moore reclining figure in the center, which he had commissioned from the great English sculptor who also happened to be a Yorkshireman born and bred. Sir Ronald was as proud of his north country origins as he was of his Jewish heritage.

After a brief moment of contemplation in front of the imposing piece of bronze, he continued on his way, pushed through the swing doors, and stepped out into the street. He drew to an abrupt halt after taking only two steps, recoiling as the intense heat hit him. He had not realized how hot the day had become.

Sir Ronald could not abide heat of any kind. Upstairs in his executive suite, a series of handsomely furnished rooms spanning the entire top floor of the giant office complex bearing his name, the atmosphere was icy cold, thanks to the air conditioning that was permanently turned up high and the well-shaded windows. This area of Kallinski House was generally referred to as "Antarctica" by those who occupied it with him. Doris, his secretary of twelve years, had grown used to the freezing temperature by now, as had other executives who had been with him for more than a year or two, and none of them bothered to complain anymore. They counteracted the chill simply by wearing warm sweaters in their offices. Even in winter, Sir Ronald kept the executive suite and his various homes as cold as he possibly dared without eliciting violent protests from staff, family, and friends.

Earlier that morning he had contemplated walking to the Connaught Hotel; now he was relieved he had changed his mind and had ordered his car up from the garage. It was sizzling out here, and oppressive, hardly the kind of weather for sauntering through the busy streets of Mayfair.

His chauffeur had spotted him the instant he had emerged from the building and was already standing stiffly to attention next to the back passenger door.

"Sir Ronald," he said, inclining his head respectfully, and opened the door wider.

"Thank you, Pearson," Sir Ronald responded

with a half smile, stepping into the burgundy-colored Rolls Royce. "The Connaught, please."

The car pulled away from the curb and he settled back against the seat and stared absently ahead. He was looking forward to lunching with Paula and Michael. He had not seen her for several weeks and his son had been in New York for over two months and he had missed them both . . . in different ways.

His son was his good right hand, his alter ego, and his favorite. He loved his younger son, Mark, very much; but Michael had a special hold on his heart. He was never quite sure why this was so. How could one explain these things? Sometimes he thought it was because his son was very much like his own father. Not that Michael *looked* anything at all like David Kallinski, being so much more Anglo-Saxon in appearance with his fair complexion and blondish hair. It had to do with a similarity of character and personality, and just as Sir Ronald had enjoyed a marvelous camaraderie with his father until the day of David's death, so did he now with his son. It had been thus ever since the boy's childhood, in fact, and he noticed Michael's absences most acutely these days, was frequently lonely when his firstborn was traveling.

As for Paula, she was the daughter he had

never had, or rather, the surrogate for the daughter who had not lived through her childhood. Miriam, their second child, born after Michael and before Mark, would have been thirty-four this year, if she had not died of encephalitis at the age of five. How they had grieved, he and Helen; they had not understood why she had been taken from them at such a tender age. "God works in mysterious ways, His wonders to perform," his mother had said to them at the time, and only in old age had he come to terms with *that* extraordinary belief.

Paula was the smartest woman he had ever known, except for Emma, and he appreciated her sharp and clever mind, her quickness, her business acumen. But she could also be very female at times and he missed her femininity as much as he relished his role as her sounding board and, on occasion, her advisor. He had a lot of admiration for Paula. She was a good mother as well as a successful executive. Hers was a hard road and she trod it most adroitly, rarely ever stumbled.

He wished his daughter-in-law were half as practical and down to earth as she was. The trouble with Valentine was that she lived in another world. She was a bit flighty, and forever discontented. Nothing was ever *enough* for her, or ever *right,* and he understood only too well

Michael's feelings. His son's frustration had grown to monumental proportions over the years and the inevitable explosion, when it had come, had been violent. He had not been surprised. He had never approved of Valentine as a wife for Michael, not because she was a *shiksa*—differences in religion scarcely mattered to him—but because she was so shallow, unworthy really. He had always known this, but how did one tell such a thing to a young man in love? In any event, the divorce agreement had been concluded finally, after much bitter wrangling and the exchange of vast amounts of money. Michael, most fortunately, had succeeded in getting what he wanted—a decree *nisi* and joint custody of his three children, the boy, Julian, and the two younger girls, Arielle and Jessica.

A smile softened Sir Ronald's stern face as he thought of his little granddaughters. If only Helen had lived to see them, it would have made her so happy. But his wife had died eight years ago. He had never stopped missing her, and when he had been given his knighthood by Harold Wilson in 1976, his joy had been tempered by sadness because Helen was no longer with him.

This singular honor had come as a genuine surprise to him. He had never asked for nor sought a title, nor had he tried to buy one by making heavy donations to charity. He *was* philanthropic, and he had his favorite causes, had contributed generously to medical research and the arts, but this had been done discreetly and without fanfare.

To be on the Prime Minister's honors list was flattering, and especially since everyone knew the title had been earned and was therefore deserved. Kallinski Industries was one of the largest and most successful conglomerates in Great Britain, and as such it not only provided much-needed jobs for thousands but was a major exporter of British goods abroad. Ronald Kallinski had devoted his life to bringing the company to its present dominant position, and he was proud of his accomplishments. So was his country apparently, since this was the reason the knighthood had been bestowed upon him.

Sir Ronald was enormously proud of his title. He was not the first Yorkshire Jew to be knighted; others had been singled out by grateful prime ministers over the years . . . men like Montague Burton and Rudolph Lyons. But nevertheless he prized the honor, as if he *had* been the first, and most especially when he contemplated the Kallinski family's early history, thought of his grandfather Abraham fleeing Russia and the pogroms in the last century, settling in the ghetto in Leeds, and eventually opening his tailoring shop in North Street. That little factory turning out piece work for the John Barran Company—the first ready-made clothiers to start in Leeds after Singer invented the sewing machine—had been the beginning, the nucleus of the billion-pound empire that Kallinski Industries was today.

On the morning of his investiture his one regret had been that Helen, Abraham, his father David, Emma, and Blackie had not been present to share his pride and happiness. The four old-timers in particular would have appreciated the significance of the ceremony at Buckingham Palace, truly understanding how far the Kallinskis had risen since Abraham, the young refugee from Kiev, had first set foot on English soil at Hull in 1880.

The Rolls Royce came to a sudden stop in Carlos Place.

Sir Ronald shook off his thoughts, leaned forward, addressed his chauffeur: "Please pick me up around two-thirty, Pearson," he said as the uniformed doorman outside the Connaught Hotel stepped up to the car, opened the door for him, helped him alight.

They "Sir Ronalded" him to death as he went from the front steps to the dining room, and a faint smile touched his eyes as he was shown to the table his son had reserved. Five years ago he had wondered how he would ever get used to being addressed by his title. But he had—and in no time at all.

After he had ordered a dry sherry, he took a sip of the iced water a waiter had placed before him, then sat back to wait for Paula and Michael.

Sir Ronald did a double take.

Paula and his son were heading across the restaurant in his direction, and she looked so much like Emma at a comparable age it was quite amazing.

He realized, as she drew closer, that she was sporting a new hairdo, and that it was this which underscored her already-pronounced similarity to her grandmother. Her dark glossy hair had been cut short in a sort of sleek bob. It was chic and obviously of the moment, and yet to him it had the look of the 1930s. It brought to mind the film stars of his youth . . . and the elegant Emma he had known and admired as a boy.

He rose, took Paula's outstretched hand in both of his, shared her broad and loving smile, kissed her cheek. They exchanged affectionate greetings, seated themselves next to each other, and at once started chatting animatedly.

Michael went to the other side of the table,

took a chair, motioned to the waiter. After Paula and he had ordered aperitifs, he asked for the menus.

Turning to Paula, he said, "You're always in such a hurry, so let's order . . . then we can relax."

"Why not?" she laughed and took the menu from the captain.

The latter hovered next to the table, explaining the specialties of the day, and making his own recommendations. After a cursory glance at their menus, Paula and the Kallinskis followed the captain's advice. All three asked for the cold poached salmon and cucumber salad, and Michael ordered a bottle of Sancerre.

The aperitifs had materialized in front of Paula and Michael whilst they had been ordering lunch, and once the captain had disappeared, Sir Ronald raised his glass. He looked directly at Paula. "To the memory of your grandmother."

"To Emma," Michael toasted.

Paula smiled at them both. "Yes, to Grandy."

They clinked glasses, sipped their drinks.

After a moment, Paula said, "I thought you'd remember what day it is today, Uncle Ronnie."

"We both remembered!" Michael exclaimed.

Sir Ronald remarked, "How could anyone forget the passing of such a great woman. And she'd be so proud of you, my dear. You've never let her down, and you've held her dream wonderfully well."

"I hope so, Uncle Ronnie . . . I've certainly endeavored to guard everything she built . . . and make it stronger."

"And you have," Sir Ronald said, regarding her warmly. "You're as much of a genius at retailing as Emma ever was. You've displayed a great deal of vision over the years, and I can only commend you on everything you've done with the stores."

"Thanks, Uncle Ronnie," Paula said, smiling, enjoying his approval.

"And I second everything Dad says," Michael declared emphatically. He took a sip of his Cinzano Bianco, then winked at her over the rim of his glass.

Paula's violet-blue eyes filled with laughter. "You're prejudiced, Michael. Actually, you both are."

Sir Ronald settled back in his chair, said in a more confidential tone, "One of the reasons I invited myself to lunch is to seek your advice, my dear."

Paula's curiosity was instantly piqued, and she quickly asked, "But how can I possibly advise *you?* Why, you're the wisest person I know, Uncle Ronnie."

He made no response to this remark. It was almost as if he had not heard it. A preoccupied expression invaded his face; he took a sip of his sherry, then gave her a long and careful look. "Ah, but you can advise me, Paula. About Alexander. Or to be more precise, you can give me an opinion." Sir Ronald briefly paused, before asking, "Do you think Sandy would sell Lady Hamilton Clothes to Kallinski Industries?"

This was the last thing Paula had expected to hear, and she was taken aback. She stared at Sir Ronald without speaking for a moment. "I'm quite sure he wouldn't," she said at last in a surprised voice. "That division is far too important to Harte Enterprises. And to Harte stores, for that matter."

"Yes, it had great value to Sandy, and to you too, of course, since the Lady Hamilton line is made exclusively for Harte's," Sir Ronald said.

Michael interjected, "He may want to unload it, Paula—for the right price, and to the right people. Let's face it, Sandy has been terribly overburdened ever since that family debacle, when he fired Jonathan and Sarah. He and Emily really have their hands full, and they have to work awfully hard running Harte Enterprises—"

"Oh, I don't know," she cut in swiftly, "they seem to manage quite well, Michael."

"In any case, we'd be prepared to pay top money for that division," Michael added, determined to get his point across.

"I'm sure you would," Paula replied evenly, "and I'm just as sure Sandy wouldn't even consider it, no matter what you offered." She looked from the younger Kallinski to the older, rapidly and with quickening interest. "*Why* do you want to buy Lady Hamilton Clothes, Uncle Ronnie?"

"We'd like to have our own women's fashion division," Sir Ronald explained. "And to supply your stores with women's ready to wear in much the same way we supply your men's clothing, and to sell to your boutiques in the hotels. Just as importantly, we wish to start to build up a strong export line."

Paula nodded slowly. "I see."

"Obviously, we wouldn't sell the women's fashions in countries where you own retail stores," Michael pointed out. "We're thinking of trading only in Common Market countries—"

"Excluding France," Sir Ronald interrupted, "since you have a store in Paris."

"Oh I know you'd never do anything to damage my business, that goes without saying," Paula murmured. "And I can see why you'd like the acquisition, Uncle Ronnie, it makes a lot of sense."

She glanced at Michael. "But *you* know how

conservative Sandy is, and bound by tradition. Those are just two of the reasons Grandy gave him control of Harte Enterprises. She knew it would be safe in his hands because he would never do anything to *weaken* its basic structure. Such as selling of a very, *very* profitable division," she finished dryly, but her mouth twitched with sudden amusement.

Both men laughed.

"Touché," Sir Ronald said.

"Yes, I do know *exactly* what kind of person Sandy is," Michael acknowledged, shifting in his chair. "And that's why I suggested to Dad that we got your reading on the matter first."

At this moment the waiter arrived with the food, and Michael changed the subject. The three of them chatted about inconsequential things for the next few minutes, and once they had been served, the *sommelier* poured the chilled white wine for Michael. After tasting it, he nodded approvingly. "It's excellent," he said to the wine waiter, who immediately proceeded to fill the other glasses.

Sir Ronald and Paula sipped their wine and both of them commented on its fresh dry taste and lightness, and then Sir Ronald put his goblet down. *"Bon appetit,"* he said, and picked up his fork and cut into the poached salmon.

"Bon appetit," Paula and Michael responded almost in unison.

They ate in silence for a while, but at one moment Paula swung her gaze between the two Kallinski men, and asked curiously, "Uncle Ronnie, Michael, why don't you simply start your own women's clothing division? Certainly you've got all the necessary resources."

"We thought of that, my dear," Sir Ronald admitted. "But quite frankly we'd prefer to buy a well-established brand. So much easier, you know. And it would save us an enormous amount of time—and money, of course, in advertising and promoting a new product."

"And surely there must be lots of manufacturers who would jump at the chance to sell to Kallinski Industries!" she exclaimed.

"I'm perfectly certain there are." Sir Ronald gave her a pointed look. "But I'm interested in Lady Hamilton Clothes because it was founded by Emma and my father all those years ago. He had a soft spot for the company long after he sold his shares to your grandmother, and so do I." Sir Ronald smiled wryly, and finished, "I must admit, I do feel rather sentimental about it."

Paula placed an elegant, beautifully manicured hand on Sir Ronald's arm, squeezed it affectionately. "But Alexander has no reason to sell that division . . . at least, not one *I* can think of, Uncle Ronnie. His sister's been running it successfully for a number of years now." Her arched black brows drew together in a small frown. "Besides, what would she *do* if he sold Lady Hamilton? Amanda would be out of a job, and Sandy would always take that into consideration. You know how he fusses about her."

"She need not necessarily be out of a job," Michael was quick to announce. "Amanda's terrific at what she does. She'd remain with the company and run it for us."

Paula made no comment. She toyed with the cucumber salad on her plate, suddenly acknowledging to herself that if Lady Hamilton were ever up for grabs Sandy ought to sell it to the Kallinskis. In a way they were entitled to it.

Sir Ronald dabbed his mouth with his napkin and ventured, "I'd like to pose a hypothetical question, Paula."

"Of course." She looked at him alertly, wondering what was on his mind now.

He said, "Let us just suppose that Alexander did want to sell Lady Hamilton, was anxious to do so, in fact. *Could he?* Or would he have to go to the other shareholders, get their agreement?"

"Oh no. There's only Emily, and she would

go along with anything her brother wanted to do. She always has, you know."

Puzzlement flickered in Sir Ronald's eyes and he leaned back in his chair, regarding Paula thoughtfully. After a second, he said slowly, *"Only Emily . . .* But surely you told me several years ago that Sarah and Jonathan still owned their shares in Harte Enterprises, even though they were thrown out of the company because of their shoddy behavior."

"That's perfectly true, they do. They draw their dividends, receive the company reports and balance sheets, but they have no power whatsoever. But then, neither does Emily, now that I think about it."

Sir Ronald appeared to be more baffled than ever.

Recognizing this, Paula said, "Let me clarify things for you, Uncle Ronnie, and for you too, Michael."

Father and son nodded and Sir Ronald said, "Please do, my dear."

"My grandmother left fifty-two percent of Harte Enterprises to Sandy. The remaining forty-eight percent was split three ways among Emily, Jonathan, and Sarah, who each received sixteen percent. As chairman of the board and majority stockholder, Sandy can do virtually anything he wishes in the company, or with it, for that matter. This is the way Grandy set it up. Whilst she wanted all four of them to draw income from the company, she knew Sandy must have absolute power to prevent any bickering among the four cousins. She felt Sandy had earned, and also deserved, the bulk of the shares in her privately owned company. She gave total control to him because she knew that he would always abide by her wishes."

"Ah, yes, I can see the sense in everything your grandmother did." Sir Ronald never failed to be impressed by the late Emma Harte's clever strategy. He went on, "As usual, Emma was shrewd—and most prudent, I might add. Certainly Sandy has guided Harte Enterprises through some rough periods and done admirably well in the past few years."

Quickly Michael said, "Look, Paula, I know you're adamant about Sandy not being interested in selling, and perhaps you're right. At least about his attitude at present. But he may well change his mind and decide to pare down Harte Enterprises . . . one day in the future . . ." Michael paused. There was a speculative expression on his face as he added, *"No?"*

Paula could not help smiling at his dogged persistence. "So you'd like to talk to him anyway, explain that Kallinski Industries are standing in the wings, if ever he decides to get rid of

Lady Hamilton Clothes. Is that what you're trying to say?" she asked with a laugh.

Michael nodded. "That's exactly it. You
wouldn't object if Dad did have a word with
him, would you, Paula?"

"No, of course not. There's no harm in letting
Alexander know about your interest in the division." She swung to the older man. "Are you
going to Yorkshire this weekend, Uncle Ronnie?"

"Yes, I am, my dear."

"Then why don't you drive over to Nutton
Priory, and have a chat with him. He's always
much more relaxed when he's in the country."

"I think I shall do that," Sir Ronald said.
"And my thanks to you, Paula, you've been
most helpful."

Michael flashed her one of his engaging
smiles. "Yes, thanks, we really do appreciate
your input." He sipped his wine and his light
blue eyes grew thoughtful and after a moment
he asked, "By the way, just out of curiosity, is
Sarah Lowther still married to that French
painter? Or don't you hear anything about her
anymore?"

"Obviously not directly, since I kicked her
out of the family along with Jonathan," Paula
murmured, the gaiety on her face instantly fading. "But there was a piece on Yves Pascal in a

French magazine about six months ago . . .
Paris Match, I believe. Anyway, amongst the
many photographs was one of Sarah and Yves
and their five-year-old daughter, Chloe. Seemingly they live in Mougins in the Alpes Mari-
time. They own an old farmhouse; that's where
he has his studio. He's known as the *enfant terrible* of French art, and he's become very big,
immensely successful."

Michael said, "He's a damned good painter
actually, although his work's not my cup of tea.
Having been raised on the school of French Impressionist painting, all this ultra-modern stuff
leaves me utterly unmoved. Give me Monet,
Manet, Sisley, and van Gogh any day of the
week."

"Absolutely," Paula agreed.

"And talking of Sarah, whatever happened to
her partner in crime, Jonathan Ainsley?" Michael stared at Paula, frowning. "Is he still lurk-
ing in the Far East?"

"I believe so, but not even Sandy knows for
sure," Paula said, her voice low and unemo-
tional. "Friends of Emily's reported seeing him
in Hong Kong, and then Singapore on another
occasion. Jonathan's dividends and the balance
sheets of Harte Enterprises go to a firm of ac-
countants here in London who handle his business seemingly." She made a sour face. "Just so

long as he doesn't show up in England, that's all that matters to me. As Emma would have said, *good riddance to bad rubbish.*"

"Christ, yes!" Michael began to shake his head wonderingly. "I've never been able to understand why he did what he did. He was such a fool—bloody stupid if you ask me. He had everything going for himself and he threw it all away."

"Perhaps he believed he would never get caught," Sir Ronald ventured to Michael. "But then I'm sure he hadn't bargained for this one here." He glanced at Paula through the corner of his eye, patted her arm, and finished with a chuckle, "He met his match in you, my dear, no doubt about that whatsoever."

Paula attempted to laugh with him but it came out sounding forced and artificial, and for a moment she did not trust herself to speak. She was hating this discussion about Jonathan Ainsley, her cousin, her deadly enemy of long ago.

Michael pressed, "And so nobody in the family knows what he's doing for a living?"

Paula stared at Michael through eyes grown bleak and flat. She gave him a long and careful look, and pursed her lips, a habit she had picked up from her grandmother years before. After a split second, she said with a certain pithiness, "Jonathan Ainsley doesn't have to *earn* a living, since he receives a very sizable income from Harte Enterprises." There was a small pause before she thought to add, "And nobody's ever bothered to find out about his personal or business life . . . because none of us *care* what's happened to him." Now frowning in perplexity, and pinning Michael with her vivid blue gaze, Paula asked testily, "Why the sudden preoccupation with Jonathan anyway?"

"I don't know, I haven't thought about him in years, and now, unexpectedly, I'm riddled with curiosity," Michael admitted with a rueful grin.

"I'm not." Despite the warmth of the Connaught dining room, Paula shivered. She had never forgotten the last words Jonathan had spoken to her . . . *I'll get you for this, Paula Fairley. Sebastian and I will bloody well get you,* he had screamed, shaking his fist at her in the most ridiculous way, like the villain in a Victorian novel. Well, Sebastian Cross could not "get her" since *he* was dead. But Jonathan would if he could. Sometimes she had nightmares about her cousin, nightmares in which he did her terrible harm. He was certainly capable of it. Capable of almost anything. She knew that from their childhood. Once, a few years ago, she had confided her fears in Sandy, who had laughed and had told her to dismiss Jonathan from her mind. Sandy had reminded her that Jonathan was a bully and, like all bullies, a coward. This was true; nevertheless, she had never been able to expunge the memory of the day Sandy had fired him. It was only too easy to recall the baleful look in Jonathan's eyes, the mask of hatred contorting his face, and instinctively, ever since then, she had known he would always remain her unremitting enemy until the day they buried him. Ten years had passed and she had not set eyes on him again, none of them had, in fact, and yet deep down inside her was this small kernel of fear.

Suddenly becoming aware that Michael and Sir Ronald were watching her, were waiting for her to say something, she turned toward Michael. Adopting the lightest of tones, she said, "Master Ainsley turned out to be a bad penny, and the least said about *him* the better."

"Quite so, my dear, quite so!" Sir Ronald muttered. He had grown conscious of the change in her demeanor whilst they had been discussing Ainsley and he decided it would be wise to change the subject. And so he said with a rush of genuine enthusiasm, "I received your invitation to the dinner dance you're giving for the sixtieth anniversary of the store, Paula, and I'm looking forward to it immensely. Now, tell me more about the other celebrations you've planned."

"Oh I'd love to, Uncle Ronnie, I have some really special things coming up—" She cut herself off as the waiter drew to a standstill at the table. "But perhaps we should order dessert first," she went on, accepting one of the menus being thrust at her.

"Splendid idea, and I do recommend the sorbets," Sir Ronald said. "It's really far too hot for anything else, isn't it?"

Paula nodded. "I think that's what I'll have. Michael will you join us?"

"Only coffee for me."

As the waiter went off with their order, Michael's eyes swept over Paula appreciatively. He grinned as he remarked, "It seems to me *you* can eat anything and never put on an ounce . . . I'm afraid I have to watch myself these days."

Paula shook her head and laughed with him. "Oh I don't know, you're trim enough, Michael."

Swiveling to face his father, she now picked up the conversation where they had left off a moment ago, and launched into a recital about the forthcoming events to be held at the Knightsbridge store later that year.

Michael had settled back in his chair, toying with his wineglass. He was only vaguely listening to Paula.

His mind remained focused on Lady Hamilton Clothes and the endless possibilities the company held for them, *if* they were lucky enough to buy it back from Harte Enterprises. Amanda Linde, Sandy's half sister, had been creating the line for a number of years now, and in his opinion she was a far better designer than Sarah Lowther had ever been. Her clothes were easy and comfortable to wear, and yet they had a special kind of elegance because she always managed to give them a touch of the Harte class. Her designs would sell as well in other Continental countries as they did in France, of that he was quite certain.

Sir Ronald and Paula continued to chat about her celebratory plans for the store's anniversary. Their voices were a faint murmur, barely audible against the buzz of the lunchtime crowd in the busy restaurant.

The waiter came back and served the dessert, poured the coffee.

Michael picked up his cup, further ruminating on the talented Amanda. If they bought Lady Hamilton, whether now or in the future, she would have to remain as head fashion designer and managing director. That was an imperative. If she was in any way reluctant to stay on, to work for them, he would have to come up with some special inducements—

Paula's sudden laughter reverberated on the warm air, cut into his myriad thoughts. It was a full, throaty, curiously sexual laugh and it caused Michael to lift his head swiftly.

He glanced across the table at her. She was spooning sorbet into her mouth. A small glob of it clung to her upper lip and she licked it off with the tip of her tongue and went on eating. He watched her, fascinated, and as he did he experienced the most extraordinary physical attraction to her. His reaction unnerved him. Michael held himself perfectly still in the chair, dropped his eyes, and stared into his coffee cup.

When he eventually looked up she had finished the sorbet and her face was averted as she responded to something his father had just said. He blinked, not understanding himself at all. He must be mad to think of Paula in this way.

Brilliant sunshine was pouring in through the window immediately behind her and it encircled her with shimmering light, brought her into focus as if she were under a pinspot on a stage. Her coloring appeared to be more vivid than ever . . . the black hair, the violet eyes, the incomparable skin touched with a faint tan like the golden bloom on a summer peach. How vibrantly alive she was at this moment . . . and how very sexual.

Michael, who had never felt anything but fraternal affection for Paula, was filled with a fierce desire to make love to her. He took a steely hold of his feelings, which had flared so suddenly, and lowered his head, fearful that something would show in his face, that his eyes would betray his lust for her. *Why?* he asked himself. Why do I want to take her to bed *now* after knowing her for so many years? He gazed intently at the small vase of flowers in the center of the table, his face unreadable as he endeavored to quell his emotions.

Sir Ronald was saying, "And I shall be in Paris next weekend, Paula, en route to Biarritz, and if you're going to be over there, visiting the Paris store, perhaps we could dine together."

"No, I won't be in Paris next weekend—" Paula began, and came to an abrupt halt. "Oh damn!" she exclaimed, sitting up jerkily in her seat, frowning, remembering the note on her desk. She had forgotten to cancel the Paris airline reservation which had been made for her for later in the day.

"Is something wrong?" Sir Ronald asked in concern.

"No, no, it's nothing," Paula assured him, making a mental note to telephone British Airways the minute she returned to her office. "I forgot to do something before lunch, but there's no problem, really there isn't, Uncle Ronnie."

Michael, who had managed to extinguish his erotic thoughts about Paula, gave his father a puzzled look. "Why are you going to Biarritz at this time of year, Dad? The season's over."

"Yes, I know it is . . . but I'm going to look at an Imperial Russian Easter Egg by Fabergé," Sir Ronald announced with obvious pleasure.

He beamed at them both. "My art dealer in Paris has a client in Biarritz. A very old lady. A White Russian. She is apparently ready to sell her jeweled egg at long last. And quite naturally, I want to get there first, before the American publisher Malcolm Forbes or any other serious collector hears about it and snaps it up before I do. You know how extremely rare the Fabergé eggs have become." Sir Ronald peered at his watch, clucked to himself, and before Michael had a chance to comment, he rapidly went on, "And that reminds me, I have an appointment at Wartski's in fifteen minutes. Kenneth Snowman recently acquired a cigarette box which belonged to Czar Nicholas the Second. It's by Perchin, one of the greatest of the Fabergé designers, and I promised I would pop in to see it this afternoon."

"I'm delighted for you, Dad, and I hope that you manage to get both items," Michael said with real sincerity, knowing how important collecting these beautiful objects had become to his father. What had begun as a vague hobby had turned into a grand passion. The Kallinski Fabergé Collection was renowned, and was frequently on exhibition with the Sandringham Collection, which had been started by King Edward VII and Queen Alexandra, sister of the Czarina Marie Feodorovna, later added to by Queen Mary and now owned by Queen Elizabeth II.

Michael smiled at his father. "Since you're in a hurry, I'd better get the bill, Dad," he said, and motioned to their waiter.

Sir Ronald glanced at Paula. "If you wouldn't mind dropping me off at Wartski's first, my car can then take you back to the store, my dear."

"Thanks, Uncle Ronnie, that'll be lovely."

"Michael, can I give you a lift too?"

"Oh no," Michael said, suddenly having no wish to be around Paula any longer than was necessary today. "Thanks anyway, Dad, but I prefer to walk."

4

She went to Paris after all.

It was a sudden decision, made when she returned to the store at three o'clock. She had picked up the phone and begun to dial British Airways, ready to cancel her reservation, when she had changed her mind and had let the receiver drop back into its cradle.

It had been a scramble then to finish her work and stuff several silk dresses into the garment bag and get out to Heathrow to catch the six o'clock plane. She had made it with ten minutes to spare and the flight had been smooth and fast with the wind behind them and exactly one hour and five minutes after takeoff they had landed serenely at Charles de Gaulle Airport.

Her luggage had come through without much delay and she had passed customs quickly and with no fuss, and now she sat comfortably in the back of the chauffeur-driven car he had sent to meet her, being whizzed toward Paris and their rendezvous.

For the first time since lunch at the Connaught with the Kallinskis earlier in the day, Paula began to unwind. And as she did she realized that it had not been such a sudden decision to come here . . . she had known from the first moment she had read his note that she would go to him, hadn't she? Hadn't it been a *fait accompli* even then? Of course it had. But, very simply, she had not wanted to admit this to herself and so she had clouded the issue with thoughts of duty and responsibility.

Paula leaned into the corner of the seat and crossed her long and shapely legs, and a smile flitted across her face as she recalled something her grandmother had said to her many, many years before. "When the right man beckons, a woman will always go running to him, no matter who she is, no matter what her responsibilities are. And no doubt you'll fall into that same trap one day, just as I did when I met your grandfather. You mark my words, Paula,"

Grandy had remarked in her knowing way. As usual, Emma had been correct.

The smile lingered on Paula's face as she turned her head to glance out of the window. With the hour's difference in time between London and Paris it was now nearly nine and already growing dark.

The car was leaving the Boulevard de Courcelles at a good clip, following the other traffic through the Étoile without slowing, and as it whirled at a dizzying speed around the Arc de Triomphe, that giant monument to a nation's valor, Paula cringed. She wondered how all these fast-moving automobiles, being driven as if they were in a miniature Grand Prix, would make it safely without crashing into each other and creating a major disaster. That seemed to be almost an impossibility.

But suddenly their car was free of the traffic jam, jostling bumpers, screeching tires, and madly hooting horns, and was pulling onto the Champs Élysées, and she caught her breath in delight as she usually did upon seeing this glittering avenue.

Whenever she returned to Paris she remembered the very first time she had come here and all the other times after that, and there was always something of those times caught up in her feeling for it. Memory and nostalgia were woven into her love for the City of Light, her favorite city, the most beautiful city in the world. It was full of evocations of the past and of all those who had been with her and who had made those occasions so very special: Grandy, her mother and father, her brother Philip, Tessa, and her cousin Emily, who had been her dearest companion on so many trips when they had been girls.

He was very much bound up with her remembrances of Paris, too, and in a short while she would be seeing him and she made up her mind not to spoil the weekend by worrying about the children or having regrets that she had changed her plans to be with him instead of them. That would not be fair, and anyway, she had always considered regrets to be pointless and a waste of valuable time.

They were on the Rond-Point now and ahead she could see the Egyptian obelisk built in the reign of Ramses II and transported from Luxor to rest in the immense rectangle of floodlit stone that was the Place de la Concorde. How spectacular the sight was . . . a breathtaking scene that was forever etched in her mind. She felt a sudden thrill of pleasure at being back here, was glad she had told the chauffeur to take the longer route to the hotel.

But within a matter of minutes they were entering the Place Vendôme, that quiet gracious square of perfectly proportioned buildings designed in the reign of Louis XIV, and coming to a standstill in front of the Ritz, and Paula was alighting and thanking the chauffeur and asking him to deal with the luggage.

She moved swiftly through the grand and elegant lobby, down the seemingly endless gallery filled with display cases from Paris shops, making for the Rue Cambon section of the hotel—known as *côté Cambon,* just as the other side where she had entered was called *côté Vendôme.* When she reached the smaller lobby she took the lift to the seventh floor and ran the length of the corridor to his suite. She found she was taut with excitement when she reached the door. It was slightly ajar, in anticipation of her arrival, and she pushed it open, went in, closed it softly, leaned back against it, catching her breath.

He was standing behind the desk, his jacket off, the sleeves of his white shirt rolled up, his dark tie dangling loose around his neck. He was talking on the telephone and he lifted a sunburned hand in greeting, his face lighting up at the sight of her. He paused in what he was saying into the receiver, listened carefully to his caller, and finally said in a low rapid tone, *"Merci, Jean-Claude, à demain,"* then hung up.

They moved toward each other at precisely the same moment.

As she passed the small Louis XV table holding a bucket of champagne and two crystal glasses she gaily twirled the bottle resting in the ice and said in a light voice, *"You* were sure of yourself, sure I'd come, weren't you?"

"Of course," he said, laughing, "I'm irresistible."

"And so terribly modest."

They met in the middle of the room, stood facing each other for a split second.

Quickly she said, "I almost didn't . . . I was worried . . . worried about the children . . . they need me—"

"Madam," he said, "your husband needs you too," and reaching out he pulled her into his arms. He bent down and kissed her deeply on the mouth and she returned his kiss, clung to him, and he held her hard and very tightly for the longest moment after they stopped kissing.

"Oh Shane," she said at last against his chest, "you have me."

"Yes, I know I do," he answered. And then with a deep chuckle he drew away from her, held her by the shoulders, and looked down into her face upturned to his. He shook his head slowly.

"But you're always surrounded," he continued, the residue of laughter clinging to his mellifluous voice. "By children and relatives and secretaries and staff, and I can never seem to get you alone for very long, or have you entirely to myself for a while these days. And that's why I decided early this morning, when I was flying up to Paris for a meeting with Jean-Claude, that we were going to have this weekend together. *Without* our usual encumbrances. A bit of private time for us, before you leave for New York. We're entitled to that, aren't we?"

"Yes, we most certainly are." Paula gave him a small, rueful smile. "Coming in from the airport I vowed I wouldn't say anything about the children, and I've only been here a few minutes and already I've—"

Shane gently placed his hand over her mouth. *"Sssh!* I know how much you wanted to see the kids before going away, and you shall."

"What do you mean?" she asked, giving him a puzzled look.

"Tonight and Saturday belong to us, and then on Sunday morning Kevin will fly us down to the Riviera to spend Sunday and Monday at the villa with the brood. You'll have to go to New York one day later, that's all. On Wednesday instead of Tuesday. Okay?"

"Oh darling, yes, of course! What a marvelous idea and how lovely of you to think of it, to think of pleasing them as well as us," she exclaimed.

He grinned at her. "They're my kids, too, you know."

"But you've been coping alone with them for the last two weeks and you must have had your fill of them by now."

"Only too true . . . in some ways. On the other hand, they've really been looking forward to seeing you, and I don't want them to be disappointed, or you to think I'm an *entirely* selfish sod. So, I'm prepared to share you with our offspring . . . After all, you are going to be gone from us for five or six weeks."

Paula gazed up at him, loving him. "Yes, I am . . ." She paused, hesitated, then asked softly, almost tentatively, "How's Patrick? Is he all right, Shane?" A worried frown knotted her dark brows together and her clear blue eyes turned cloudy and apprehensive.

"He's wonderful, Paula, and as happy as a sandboy enjoying every minute of the day and having lots of fun," Shane reassured her, his tone very positive. "Please, darling, don't *worry* so much." He put his hand under her chin, tilted her face to his, and added, "Patrick manages very well, really he does."

"I'm sorry, Shane, I know I fuss about him, but he's such a little boy and so diffident . . .

and different. And the others can be so boisterous at times, and I'm always afraid he'll get hurt
when he's out of his usual environment . . ."

She let her sentence trail off, not wanting to
express the thought that anything might ever
happen to their firstborn child. Patrick, who was
seven, was slow, retarded actually, and she
could not help being concerned about him when
he was not under her sharp and watchful eyes.

Although Shane was equally protective of
their son, he was constantly—if gently—chastis-
ing her for being overly anxious. Deep down,
she knew Shane was right and so she tried very
hard to control her anxiety, to treat Patrick as if
he were perfectly normal, like his five-year-old
sister, Linnet, and his half-brother and half-sister, Lorne and Tessa, the twelve-year-old twins
fathered by Jim Fairley.

Shane, observing her carefully, understanding
her complex feelings about Patrick, said with a
confiding smile, "I haven't mentioned this to
you before, but Linnet's become a real little
mother while we've all been down at the villa.
She's taken Patrick under her very small but
very loving wing and, actually, without you
around, she's even turned a bit bossy. And you
know how Lorne is with Patrick . . . he adores
him. So all is well, my darling, and—" Shane
broke off at the sound of knocking, exclaimed

"Entrez," and moving away from Paula, he went hurrying to the door as it was being pushed open in response to his command.

A genial-looking porter came in carrying her garment bag and small suitcase, and Shane dealt with him briskly, showed him through into the bedroom, told him where to put the luggage and tipped him.

Once they were alone again, Shane strode over to the table, began to peel the metal paper off the champagne cork.

"Listen," he said, "enough of the kids. They're absolutely fine with Emily and Winston."

"Yes, of course they are, darling."

A moment before, Paula's thoughts had swung to their youngest child, and now she started to chuckle and her eyes crinkled up at the corners in amusement. "So Linnet's *true* character has finally emerged, has it? I always suspected that that daughter of ours had inherited a bit of Emma's imperiousness, that she also had the makings of a general."

Shane glanced up, pulled a face, rolled his eyes heavenward. "Another general in the family! Oh my God, I don't think I can stand it! Oh well, I suppose *all* of my women compensate for their bossiness by being so easy on the eye." Winking at her, he said, "And by the way, Emily sends her love. When I rang her earlier this evening, to tell her I'd sidetracked you to Paris, that we wouldn't be at the villa until Sunday, she was tickled to death about our weekend alone together. She thought it was a smashing idea, and she says you're not to be concerned about a thing. Now, how about a glass of this marvelous stuff, before we get ready for dinner?"

"That'd be lovely, darling."

Paula had seated herself on the sofa whilst he had been dealing with the porter, and she kicked off her shoes, curled her legs under her, and sat back, watching him.

It did not matter whether they had been apart for four days or a fortnight, she was always a little startled when she saw Shane after an absence and overwhelmed by the sheer physical presence of him. It had much to do with the force of his personality—that extraordinary charisma he possessed—as well as his height and build and natural dark good looks. Sixteen years ago, at his twenty-fourth birthday party, Emma Harte had said that Shane O'Neill had an intense glamour, and this had never been truer than it was today. He was the most dazzling of men.

Shane had celebrated his fortieth birthday this past June and he was in his prime and looked it.

He had a powerful physique with a broad back and massive shoulders, he had stayed lithe and trim, and his sojourn in the sun with the children had given him a deep tan. There was a touch of gray at his temples now, but curiously, this did not age him. Rather, in combination with his bronzed complexion, the gray seemed to underscore the youthfulness of his strong and virile face. And in contrast to his hair, there was not a strand of gray in his mustache, which was as coal black as it had always been.

I've known him all of my life and it's never changed, this extraordinary feeling I have for him, Paula thought, continuing to quietly observe him. He's the only man I've ever loved. The only man I will ever want . . . for the rest of my life . . . my husband, my lover, my closest friend.

"Hey, Beanstalk," he said, using his childhood nickname for her as he walked across the room. "You're a million miles away." He handed her the glass of champagne, sat down next to her on the sofa, and gave her a quick quizzical glance.

"Just daydreaming," she replied, clinking her glass to his when he held it out.

He leaned into her and fastened his eyes on her face. "Emma would've approved of this weekend of ours . . . she was a thorough-going romantic, just as I am."

"Yes, that's very true."

"She was on my mind earlier today and for the obvious reasons," Shane went on, "and it suddenly struck me how quickly the time has passed since her death. It's frightening, really, the way the years have sped by. It seems like only yesterday that she was ordering all of us around—"

"I was thinking *exactly* the same thing when I was at the cemetery this morning!"

Their eyes met. They exchanged slightly startled glances and then smiled knowingly at each other. This frequently happened, the shared thought when they were apart, or when they were together, the sudden voicing by one of them of a sentiment that the other had been about to express.

As a small child, Paula had believed Shane had the ability to read her mind and that he knew her every thought, and she still believed this. But it no longer surprised her; they were too much a part of each other now and she took their closeness for granted and considered it perfectly natural that they were on the same wave length.

Looking across at him, she said in a voice that rose slightly, as if she were suddenly surprised,

"It doesn't seem possible that we'll have been married for ten years in November, does it?"

"No . . ." He lifted his hand and touched her cheek lightly. "But we have, and every single day I've been your husband has been meaningful to me, and I wouldn't have missed one of them, not even the really bad days. Better to be with you, no matter what the circumstances, than without you."

"Yes, I feel the same way," she said and her eyes signaled her deep and abiding love to him.

Shane returned Paula's unwavering gaze and the expression in his brilliant black eyes echoed the one in hers.

A silence fell between them.

It was a compatible and harmonious silence, one of those quiet interludes they often shared when they discovered words were not necessary to communicate their feelings.

Paula sat back and sipped her drink and unexpectedly thought of what it would be like to be without him, and she felt herself shriveling inside, appalled at the idea. It was Shane who gave true meaning to her existence. He was the substance of her life, her rock, and he was always there for her, just as she was for him. She was glad he had devised this weekend, that they had this bit of special time together before she went off on her business trip to the States and

Australia. She smiled inwardly, thinking of the clever and masterful way he had planned the interlude for them, adoring him for it.

Shane, studying her, became aware that the tensions of the day were slowly ebbing out of her face, and this gladdened his heart. He frequently worried about her, knowing how hard she worked, but he never interfered. She was like Emma. Protesting about her unremitting schedule would only be a waste of *his* breath and an irritant to *her.*

He eased his large frame into the corner of the blue velvet Louis XVI sofa, settled back to enjoy his drink; he, too, was finally able to relax, to let go for the first time since leaving the villa that morning. From the moment he had stepped off the O'Neill corporate jet, until Paula's arrival in the suite, he had been busy with Jean-Claude Soissons, the head of O'Neill Hotels International in France. But he had no intention of letting business intrude any further, either tonight or tomorrow, which was why they were not staying at the hotel he owned in Paris. Whenever he wanted Paula to himself, to spend some quiet private time with her, he always took a deluxe suite at the Ritz where he knew no one would disturb him.

Now, as Paula had done a moment before, he turned his gaze inward, contemplating the next thirty-six hours and the joy they would derive from being together—and completely alone.

There was something very special between these two.

It had always been there, even as children, this spiritual oneness, this closeness, this bonding together, and what had begun in infancy had come to full flower with their sexual union as adults.

For a period of time, during Paula's disastrous marriage to Jim Fairley, Shane had been at odds with her, but the bond between them had never *really* been broken. When they had patched up their friendship and had subsequently become lovers at long last, they had been profoundly shaken by the strength and force of their physical passion for each other. But they had recognized how right it was, knew they had always been meant to be together in this way, and they felt whole and complete for the first time in their lives.

Shane realized how utterly worthless his liaisons with countless other women had been, and at once understood that without Paula his life would be meaningless; Paula finally knew that Shane was the only man she had ever loved, saw how empty and loveless her marriage to Jim was, and acknowledged that to continue to live this lie would be like killing herself. And she accepted that she must end the marriage if she was to save her life—and keep her self-respect and sanity.

Expecting to meet opposition from Jim, Paula had, nevertheless, been staggered by his vituperativeness and the spiteful way he had behaved once he knew she wanted a divorce. They had battled, locked horns, reached an impasse.

In the middle of one of their worst crises, Jim had done a bolt to Chamonix for a winter holiday with her parents at their rented chalet. Paula had been furious with him for going skiing at such a crucial time in their lives. And then he had been fatally struck down on Mont Blanc by the avalanche that had decimated the family, and she did not have to worry about getting a divorce anymore because she was suddenly a widow at the age of twenty-six.

Jim's death had come between Paula and Shane, and she had sent him away out of her great and terrible guilt. But eventually she had come to her senses and had found her true self again. She had gone to him, had told him she wanted to spend the rest of her life with him, and they had been reconciled immediately, for Shane O'Neill had never stopped loving her.

Two months later, with Emily and Winston

Harte as their witnesses, they had been married at Caxton Hall registry office in London.

And they both knew deep in the innermost recesses of their hearts that they had finally fulfilled their destiny.

The antique ormolu clock on the white marble mantelpiece began to chime loudly.

Paula and Shane both started in surprise and glanced across at it, and Shane exclaimed, "Good Lord, it's nine-thirty already, and I booked a table at the Espadon for quarter to ten. Can you get ready in fifteen minutes, darling?"

"Yes, of course," Paula said, putting down her glass, stretching, then smothering a yawn behind her hand.

Shane stared hard at her and scowled. "You're terribly tired," he said in concern. "How thoughtless of me to expect you to go downstairs to the restaurant. It's a hot bath for you, my girl, and immediately. We'll have a snack from room service tonight."

"Don't be silly, I'm fine," Paula began and paused, yawning again. "Well, to tell you the truth, it has been a long day," she admitted. "Perhaps you're right about eating in the suite."

"I know I am."

As he spoke, Shane stood up, reached down, took her hands in his, and pulled her to her feet.

He laid his arm around her shoulders and propelled her toward the bedroom door. "I wish I'd
canceled Kevin's weekend off and sent him with
the plane to collect you this evening—"

"I'm jolly glad you didn't cancel it!" Paula
cried, giving him a sharp, almost reproving look.
She was fond of Kevin Reardon and was aware
that the pilot's devotion to them frequently
caused him to neglect his personal life. "Kevin's
been looking forward to his girlfriend's birthday
party tomorrow night for weeks now. Anyway,
he made a good messenger, didn't he? It *was*
Kevin who delivered your note to the store this
morning, wasn't it?"

"Yes, it was." Shane grinned as he proceeded
to bundle her into the bedroom. "Come on, get
undressed and take a hot bath, and whilst you're
relaxing I shall order supper. What do you
fancy?"

"Oh anything you like . . . I'll leave it to
you, darling."

"How about a picnic . . . with some of your
favorite things? And another bottle of bubbly."

Paula laughed gaily. She said, "If I drink any
more champagne I might *just* pass out."

"That's permissible," Shane shot back. "You
have your husband here to look after you."

"True. And a very special husband at that."
She stood on tiptoe, kissed his cheek.

Shane's arms went around her and he caught her to him for a moment, tightening his grip, kissing the top of her dark head, and then he let go of her abruptly, stepped away from her.

"I'd better be a good boy and go and order supper, otherwise you never know *what* might happen. After all, I have been deprived of you for two whole weeks, and I don't mind telling you, I've missed you like bloody hell, my love . . ."

"Oh Shane darling," she said slowly, very softly. "Yes . . . I know what you mean . . ."

It was the inflection in her voice, the sudden longing flaring on her face that made him instantly take a step forward.

She reached out her hand to him.

He took it.

Their clasped hands tightened and they moved into each other's arms swiftly. He bent his face to hers, seeking her mouth, and felt the sudden hotness of her cheeks, and the knowledge that she always wanted him as much as he always wanted her aroused him, made his heart begin to clatter erratically. They kissed, a long deep tantalizing kiss, and he let his tongue explore her mouth, and she did the same; then their tongues lay still, and they shared a feeling of the most profound intimacy.

Paula was suddenly trembling in his arms and

together they swayed on their feet as if they were intoxicated, and of course they were—with each other—and then they half stumbled, half walked in the direction of the bed, their arms still wrapped around one another.

Shane stripped her of her clothes.

She went and lay down on the bed, waiting for him, and her eyes never once left his face as he flung off his shirt and trousers. As she watched him intently she was hardly able to contain herself, wanting him so much, and when she saw how excited he was she felt a shiver trickle down her spine.

And as Shane stared back into those violet eyes turning inky black with longing for him, he was possessed by such a violent desire for her it sent the blood rushing to his head and made his heart begin to pound against his rib cage. He felt dizzy and light-headed as he walked across to the bed and stretched out beside her.

Pushing himself up on one elbow, he bent over her, looked down into her face.

She gazed up at him.

Their eyes locked and held for the longest moment of the most intense and adoring communion, and then he touched her cheek with two fingers, moving their tips across her brows, her eyelids, her nose, and onto her mouth; slowly he traced the outline of her lips and parted them and rested his fingertips against her tongue. She sucked on them and the sensuality of this little act inflamed him, made the fire leap through him. Immediately, he crushed his mouth to hers. It was hard and insistent and their teeth grazed and he kissed her with mounting passion, and as he did he moved his fingers away from her lips, slid them along the elongated line of her lovely throat. They did not linger there, but moved on to fondle her voluptuous breasts, then slipped farther down to flutter lightly across her flat concave stomach until they were finally resting between her thighs.

Shane began to stroke her lovingly, languorously, in slow motion, and with such tenderness he seemed hardly to be touching her at all. But he could feel the velvet softness of her increasing and he continued to stroke, to explore, until his fingertips came to nestle against that precious part of her that was the fountainhead of her womanhood.

Instantly, Paula twisted herself into him, bringing her body closer to his, her slender hand reaching out for him, and she began to caress him as delicately as he was her. Shane felt his hardness growing as she unexpectedly moved her hand with greater rapidity and he had to bite back a cry as he began to throb under her touch. He grasped her wrist, stilled her hand, and then he intensified the pressure of his fingertips and she tensed, and held her body rigid. He explored further, slipped deeper into the velvet folds of her, and as he did he heard a strangled cry in her throat.

He leaned over her satin-smooth breasts, very taut and upright, and savored the hard, erect nipples with his mouth, first one and then the other. She started to gently undulate under his expert fingers, his loving mouth, and she sighed and murmured his name softly, over and over. Now her hands went out to him again, were strong and hard on the nape of his neck and in his thick hair, and they suddenly moved on to grasp his wide shoulders as her excitement accelerated.

Paula stiffened and gasped. She was filling with an exquisite warmth. His touch quickened, became ever more nimble and deft, and she cried out in her excitement, "Shane, oh Shane, my darling husband, I love you so much!" And he said against her throat, in a voice thickened by desire, "You're my true love, Paula, my own true love. Come to me, my darling, so that I can take you to me." And she gasped again and said, "Yes, oh yes," and gripped his shoulders more tenaciously than ever.

Shane thought he was going to explode as she

opened up to him like an exotic flower unfolding soft lush petals, moaning his name and shuddering. He was unable to contain himself, and he moved onto her, took possession of her swiftly, raging with the same kind of molten heat that was suffusing her.

He lost all reserve and she was as unrestrained as he. Her arms went around him and were full of strength as she held him to her. And he pushed his hands under her body and lifted her to him and they cleaved together, were joined, became one.

As Shane thrust deeper, lost himself completely in her and in the joy of her, he suddenly thought, *I want to make her pregnant tonight. I want another child.*

This idea, unexpected as it was, sent such thrills surging through him he moved against her violently and she responded with unbridled ardor, matching his passion equally, and they quickly found their own rhythm as they had all through the years of their marriage. But for Shane, tonight was suddenly like the first time they had ever made love and in an instant the years fell away. He was back in Connecticut, in the barn he had once owned, taking her to him as he had yearned to take her during the years of her marriage to another man, loving her as he had never loved any other woman, as only he and she were meant to love.

And then he was reaching up . . . reaching into the light . . . the light was surrounding him . . . she was at the center of the light . . . waiting for him . . . his dreamlike child of his childhood dreams. And she was his now. Nothing, no one, could ever separate them again. They belonged together for all time, into eternity. He felt weightless . . . he was soaring higher and higher . . . rising up into that timeless light . . . floating into infinity. And he was carrying her with him, holding the world in his arms, calling her name, just as she called his.

And together they crested on waves of ecstasy in the golden shimmering light . . . were blinded by it and then could see . . . and oh the blessed peace of it . . .

Shane woke up abruptly.

He moved his head to the right and looked at the bedside clock. In the dim light he could see that it was almost five.

Paula slept soundlessly by his side.

He braced himself on one elbow, bent over her, touched her face lovingly, but very lightly, so as not to awaken her from her exhausted sleep, and lifted a strand of hair away from her eyes. Then he settled down again, stretched out on his back, and closed his eyes, but before many minutes had passed he decided he was not going to fall off again quite so easily, or as quickly as he had just imagined he would. He was suddenly wide awake. Still, he had slept very deeply for the past few hours, as he always did when he was with Paula, as if he were more content and at peace when she was in his bed. Well, of course he was.

He turned over onto his side, made an arc of his body around hers. She was his whole life, and now, lying next to her in the darkness, adoring her in the silence of his heart, he wondered if he had made her pregnant. Weeks ago they had agreed she should stop taking the pill.

Tonight he had planted his seed in her and he prayed that the seed had taken hold and would come to flower as a child . . . a true love child conceived at the height of passion and spiritual joining. He stifled a sigh, thinking of Patrick. He loved his little boy with a deeply tender and protective love, but he could not help being sad that their firstborn was not normal. He dare not let Paula perceive his feelings, for fear of underscoring her own pain. They were never far from the surface and yet, somehow, he always managed to conceal his sorrow from her.

Instinctively, Shane lifted his right arm, put it around her, drew closer, burrowed his face in her fragrant hair, overflowing with his love for her. He closed his eyes again, let himself drift into sleep. Yes, he thought, now is the time for our next child. And he wondered, as he finally dozed off, if that was the real reason he had sidetracked her to Paris.

LOVERS & STRANGERS

5

The Villa Faviola was situated in the town of Roquebrune-Cap-Martin, approximately half-way between Monte Carlo and Menton.

It stood in its own small park at the end of the little peninsula of Cap-Martin, sheltered by pines at its back, with its many tall windows facing out toward the sea.

Built in the 1920s, it was a lovely old house, sprawling, airy, and gracious, with a curving driveway bordered by pines, spacious green lawns that swept down from the terrace past the swimming pool, up to the edge of the rocky promontory and the glittering Mediterranean Sea beyond.

Its exterior walls were painted a soft melon, but in a tone so pale it was almost sand, and the canvas awnings shading the windows were of a deeper melon, partnered with shutters of pristine white.

A wide terrace stretched along the side of the house facing the sea. Made of white stone and marble, it appeared to float gracefully above the verdant gardens where flowers grew in riotous color and fountains sparkled in the shimmering sunlight. Scattered along the terrace were several round white-metal tables topped by melon-colored parasols; matching white chairs, swing-sofas with sun-awnings, and chaises all had cushions of cream. Because only these soft integrated tones had been used, nothing jarred the harmonious flow of pale color across the lovely facade.

The Villa Faviola had been purchased by Emma Harte in the late 1940s, just after the end of the Second World War, and it was she who had originally created the gardens surrounding the house and intersecting the lawns. But in recent years, Paula had enlarged the flower beds and borders. She had planted a wide variety of small flowering trees, shrubs, and exotic plants, cultivating the entire park to its present beauty —and a magnificence that was renowned along the Côte d'Azur.

Inside Faviola its cool, lofty rooms were filled with lovely filtered sunlight and furnished with a simple yet distinctive elegance. Charming old French Provincial pieces made of dark woods or bleached oak were mingled with vast sofas, comfortable chairs, chaises, and ottomans. Occasional tables held small pots of African violets, pink and white cyclamen, and the latest magazines and books.

Floors of highly polished parquet and rose-veined cream marble were either bare or were covered here and there by old Aubussons and plain rugs of cream wool. Throughout the house, colors were pale and cool. Cream, vanilla, and white predominated, flowed over the walls, were repeated in the fabrics that fell at the windows, covered sofas, and chairs; accent colors were variations of melon and peach and sand. And there were touches of *café au lait,* that lovely milky brown that was so typically French.

Spilling vivid color into these monochromatic-toned rooms were romantic, lyrical paintings by such noted contemporary French artists as Epko, Taurelle, and Bouyssou and huge Baccarat crystal urns overflowing with a great abundance of flowers and foliage from the gardens.

But none of the rooms were so imposing or so grand that guests and children were intimidated and felt they were in a museum. On the contrary, Emma had designed the house as a vacation home, one to be lived in and enjoyed, and it had an easy grace that was all its own. It also happened to be one of those houses that had always had a warm, welcoming atmosphere, and there was a lovely serenity about its sundrenched rooms and the inviting pine-shaded park with its glorious gardens.

Alexander Barkstone owned Faviola, having inherited it from Emma along with its contents —with the exception of the Impressionist art, which his grandmother had bequeathed to Philip in Australia. But Sandy rarely came to the villa, preferring his country estate in Yorkshire. It was mostly used by his sister Emily and her family, his cousins Paula O'Neill and Anthony Dunvale, and their respective spouses and children. Occasionally his mother, Elizabeth, and her French husband, Marc Deboyne, came down from Paris for long weekends, usually when the season was over.

But of all of them, it was Emily who loved Faviola the most—and with an enduring passion.

As a little girl some of the happiest times of her childhood had been spent at the villa with her beloved Gran, and she had always believed it to be an enchanted and magical place. She knew every cranny, every corner, of every room on every floor; every inch of the park and the garden and the beach below the rocky promontory. After she had married her cousin, Winston Harte, in June of 1970, they had flown down to the Riviera for their honeymoon and the first two weeks of their life as man and wife had been spent at the villa. The lovely carefree days and romantic evenings were so blissful, Emily's deep feelings for Faviola were only intensified, and ever since then the villa had been her haven which she could escape to at odd times during the spring and winter, either alone or with Winston, and always in the summer months with their children, Toby, Gideon, and Natalie. She had never grown tired of it and she knew she never would; she thought of the villa as the most perfect place in the world to be.

But in contrast, Sandy's visits to the house had grown fewer and fewer after his wife's death; in 1973, recognizing how much Emily loved the place, he had asked her to take over from him, to supervise its general management. He had been relieved and happy when she had promptly and enthusiastically agreed.

Inevitably, Emily had put her individual stamp on Faviola over the years, but she had not tried to turn it into a replica of an English country house. Instead she had retained its Gallic flavor in every possible way, and if anything she had even enhanced the predominantly Provençal feeling with her inimitable touches. But as involved with it as she had become in the last eight years, Emily never considered the villa to be her own, never once forgot that it was the property of her brother. And yet it *was* hers in a certain sense, because of the time and the care and the great love she constantly lavished on it, and certainly everyone thought of Emily as *la grande châtelaine* of the Villa Faviola.

When Emma Harte was living, the day-to-day running of the villa had been in the capable hands of a local woman from Roquebrune, one Madame Paulette Renard. Engaged by Emma in 1950, she had moved into the pleasant and roomy caretaker's house in the private park—known as *la petite maison*—and had looked after the Harte family with unfailing care for the next twenty years.

But with Emma's death in 1970, Madame Paulette had decided the time had come for her to retire and she had handed over her responsibilities and her keys to her daughter, Solange Brivet, who wished to leave her job as the housekeeper at a hotel in Beaulieu. Madame Paulette was a widow, and the Brivets and their children had been living with her in *la petite maison* for a number of years, and so there had been no great upheavals or sad good-byes. And since it was only a short walk across the vegetable garden to the villa, Madame Paulette was always on hand to give her expert advice or air her considerable knowledge.

Over the past eleven years, the management and running of Faviola had become something of a Brivet family affair. Solange's husband, Marcel, was the chef, two of their three daughters, Sylvie and Marie, were the maids, and their son, Henri, was the butler and, as Emily put it, "our general factotum *par excellence,*" while Marcel's nephews, Pierre and Maurice, were the gardeners. These two drove over from Roquebrune in their little Renault every morning, bringing with them another Brivet, Cousin Odile, who worked in the kitchen as assistant to Marcel, and it was Odile who carried with her the huge basket of breads from her mother's *boulangerie* . . . fresh *croissants* and *brioche,* which Marcel served warm for the family's breakfast, and *baguettes,* those long French loaves with a hard crust which the children especially loved.

Madame Solange, as she was called by everyone, had been trained at the Hotel de Paris in nearby Monte Carlo, and she ran the villa in the grand Riviera style, rather in the manner of a great hotel, with efficiency, meticulous attention

110

to detail, and with the same kind of loving devotion her mother had expended before her. And in all the years she had been employed, she and Emily had worked together in harmony, with rarely, if ever, a cross word.

The phrase, "Thank God for Solange," was forever on Emily's lips, and she was muttering it under her breath on this Monday morning in August as she hurried into the kitchen, stood in the center of the floor, glanced around, and nodded to herself, looking pleased.

They had had their annual, end-of-the-summer dinner party last night, but no one would have known it from the look of the large, old-fashioned kitchen. As usual, the hanging pots and pans sparkled, the wood countertops were scrubbed to gleaming white, the terra-cotta tile floor shone, and everything else was spotless and back in its given place.

Solange must have really cracked the whip to get everything so ship-shape for this morning, Emily thought, recalling the mess in the kitchen the night before, after the last of their guests had finally departed. Smiling to herself, she took a glass from the cupboard, went to the refrigerator, poured herself some Vichy water, and carrying the glass she walked back through the pantry, across the dining room, and out of the French doors onto the terrace, the clicking of

111

her sandals the only sound on the warm, still air.

Emily was always the first one to be up and about every morning, sometimes as early as dawn.

She treasured this private time before the family awakened and the staff started to arrive. She liked being entirely alone to enjoy the gentle quiessence of the silent slumbering house, to savor the early morning smells and colors of the Mediterranean landscape.

It was also her hour for reviewing the paperwork she invariably brought with her, making notes for her secretary in London, whom she phoned several times a week, working out the day's menus, and planning activities for the children. But frequently she just sat quietly on the terrace, glad to have a few moments of solitude and introspection before the excitement of the day began and a horde of children descended on her, dragging a kind of chaos in their wake.

It was not so bad when she had only her own three to cope with, but when Paula's four and Anthony's three children were at Faviola, often bringing with them a number of young guests, it was rather like having an unruly juvenile football team underfoot. But Emily had her own system and she managed to control them far better than anyone else. It was not for nothing the children called her "The Sergeant Major" behind her back.

Now, taking sips of Vichy as she walked, Emily went up to the edge of the terrace and leaned against the balustrade, looked out across the gardens to the sea. It was a dark metallic blue and choppy, and the sky that surged above it was a curdled cloudy gray that seemed ominous.

She hoped the weather was not going to change again, as it had last week when the mistral, that dry north wind that blew down out of the Rhône Valley, had brought several days of mean weather with it. Without exception, all of the children had been restive, moody and difficult. Solange had immediately blamed the mistral, reminding Emily that this wind usually disturbed everyone's equilibrium. Emily had agreed, and they had both been relieved when it had finally blown out to sea. The weather had changed for the better—and so had the children. They were much calmer, almost their normal selves again. Even Emily felt more at ease. She had been edgy and irritable during those dull, incredibly windy days; she now had to admit there was probably a lot of truth in what Solange—and the locals—said about the mistral and its peculiar effect on people. She glanced at her watch. It was only twenty minutes past six. By nine o'clock the sky would be a perfect cerulean blue, the sun would be out, and the sea would be as still as a pond, she decided, as always the eternal optimist, as her grandmother had been before her.

Turning away from the balustrade, she stepped up to the table where she had laid out her papers earlier, and sat down. As far as work was concerned, her immediate priority was her impending trip to Hong Kong to buy merchandise for Genret, the import-export trading company she ran for Harte Enterprises. She opened her diary, glanced at the dates in September she had tentatively selected some weeks ago. She flipped the pages backward and forward several times, carefully studied her schedule, penciled in the changes she now wished to make; then she began to scribble a note for Janice, her secretary in London, outlining her new itinerary.

A few minutes later, Emily almost jumped out of her skin as a strong cool hand came to rest firmly on her shoulders. She started up in her chair and swung her head swiftly, her eyes wide with astonishment. "My God, Winston! You mustn't creep up on me like that! *So silently.* You scared me!" she cried.

"Oh, sorry, darling," he apologized, then bent over and kissed her cheek. "Good morning," he added as he walked across the terrace and leaned against the balustrade, where he stood regarding her lovingly for a moment before proffering her a warm smile.

Emily smiled back. "And tell me, what are *you* doing up so early? You're usually dead to the world until ten o'clock at the earliest."

Winston shrugged his bare shoulders, put the towel he was holding on the balustrade. "I couldn't sleep this morning. But it's always the same with me, isn't it, Em? I mean, on our last few days here I seem to want to cram everything in, enjoy every single second, just like the kids."

"And as I do, too."

"Yes, that's true . . . you do love this place so. But then it loves *you,* Emily . . . why, you're positively blooming."

"Thank you, kind sir," she said.

He eyed the glass in front of her. "I suppose that's water you're drinking . . . aren't you going to make coffee?"

Emily shook her head. "No, Winston, I'm not," she said very adamantly. "Because if I do, I'll also make some toast and I'll butter the toast and put jam on it and then I'll eat it, and when Odile arrives at seven, with all that scrumptious stuff from the bakery, I'll have another breakfast, a *second* breakfast, and you know perfectly well that I've got to watch my weight."

"You look pretty terrific to me, Mrs. Harte,"

he said with a chuckle and leered at her. "I don't half fancy you."

"Honestly, Winston, at this hour!"

"What's wrong with this hour? It's still very early . . . come on darling, let's go back to bed."

"Oh don't be so silly, I've a thousand things to do this morning."

"So do I," he remarked lightly, giving her a pointed look, leering again. Then his face changed suddenly, and he leveled a swift appraising glance at her, liking what he saw. Emily was now thirty-four and, in his opinion, one of the prettiest women alive. She was blonder than ever and brown from the sun and her brilliant green eyes, so identical in color to his own, sparkled with a vivid intelligence and a *joie de vivre* that were uniquely hers. She was wearing a lime-green-and-pink cotton shift over her bikini, looked impossibly young and fresh and delectable this morning.

"Winston, you're staring. And very *rudely*. What's wrong?"

"Nothing. Just admiring you, that's all. And thinking that you look like a delicious ice cream . . . and good enough to eat."

"Oh pooh!" Emily laughed, but her neck turned bright pink and she dropped her head, stared at her engagement book intently.

There was a tiny silence.

Winston swallowed a smile, both amused and pleased that he could still make her blush after eleven years of marriage, but then that was his Emily and he adored her for her girlishness, her femininity, and her softness. Odd, he thought, that she can be so tough in business and yet she has such a soft edge to her in her personal life. Like Paula, of course, and Aunt Emma, when she was alive. It was just this dichotomy in their natures that made the Harte women so original. He had known that for a long time.

Emily raised her head. At once, she saw the contemplative expression on her husband's face and asked, "And what are you thinking about *now?*"

"I was just wondering what all this is in aid of this morning?" Winston murmured, strolling over to join her at the table. He flopped down in the chair opposite and held her eyes as she looked across at him.

"What do you mean?" she asked, puzzled.

"Why are you going at the work hammer and tongs today, when you'll be back in London at the end of the week? It hardly seems worth it, love."

"I'm not working, actually, I'm trying to figure out the dates for my buying trip to Hong Kong and Mainland China," Emily explained.

"If I leave on the tenth of September, instead of the sixth as I'd planned, I'd still be there when Paula breaks her return journey back to the States from Sydney. We were talking about it yesterday afternoon, and decided it would be nice to have a couple of days in Hong Kong. Relaxing . . . doing our Christmas shopping . . . and then we could fly on to New York together, spend a day or two there before taking the Concorde home to England. What do you think?"

"It sounds good to me, if that's what you feel like doing. I've certainly no objections, I don't have to be in Canada until the first week of October. Presumably you'd be back in England before I left?"

"Yes, of course I would. I've taken your Canadian trip into consideration and planned around it."

"Then it's fine, darling," Winston answered with a smile and stood up, went to get his towel. "Well, if you're not going to take pity on your poor husband and make him a cup of coffee, I think I'll go for a swim before that tribe of fiendish little monsters invades the area and ploughs down everything in sight."

Emily couldn't help laughing at the expression on his face. "Oh I don't know, darling, they're not *so* bad," she protested, feeling the sudden need to defend the younger generation.

"Oh yes they are!" he retorted. "They're ,bloody awful most of the time!" A wide grin glanced across his face. "But I must admit, I do love 'em . . . especially the three that are mine." He kissed her quickly, loped off in the direction of the swimming pool without another word, nonchalantly swinging the towel and whistling merrily.

Emily watched him go, thinking how fit and healthy he looked with his tanned body and face, his reddish hair turned to gold by the Riviera sun. The summer here had done him good. He worked extremely hard running the Yorkshire Consolidated Newspaper Company and its Canadian subsidiaries, and she was always after him to slow down a bit. But he paid not the slightest attention to her, merely commented that they *all* worked like demons, which was true, of course. It was the way her Gran had brought them up. Emma had only disdained slackers; naturally they had all become over-achievers.

How lucky I am to have Winston, Emily mused, settling back in the chair, idly drifting with her thoughts, putting off preparing the menus for that day's meals for a few moments longer.

Sometimes, when she turned her gaze back into the past, she realized she had managed to catch him by the skin of her teeth, understood how easily she might have lost him to another woman.

Emily had been in love with Winston since she was sixteen. They were third cousins. His grandfather and namesake, Winston Harte, had been her grandmother's brother. Although Winston was five years older than she they had been bosom pals as children. But once he had grown up he had hardly noticed her again, at least not as an attractive young woman with whom he might become romantically involved.

He had gone off to Oxford with his best friend, Shane, and the two of them had rapidly acquired reputations as terrible womanizers. Almost everyone had been scandalized by their disreputable antics. *She* had ached with a mixture of jealousy and longing, wishing *she* were one of the girls Winston chased and bedded. Only her Gran had been sanguine. Emma had simply laughed, had said they were merely young bucks sowing their wild oats. But then neither Winston nor Shane could do much wrong in Emma Harte's eyes. She had had a special fondness for them both.

And so Emily had worshipped Winston from afar, hoping that one day his glance would fall on her again. But it hadn't, and much to her profound dismay he suddenly became seriously involved with a local girl, Alison Ridley. At the beginning of 1969 the gossip going around the three clans was that he was about to get engaged to Alison. Emily had thought her heart was going to break.

Then everything had changed. Quite miraculously, Winston had noticed her at the christening of Paula and Jim Fairley's twins in March of that same year. And all because of an incident with Shane which had upset her grandmother. She and Winston had been called into the library at Pennistone Royal and had been grilled by Emma about Shane's feelings for Paula. When they had finally escaped, they had gone for a walk in the gardens to recover from their ordeal, and for some reason Winston had been prompted to kiss her. This action on his part had been as sudden as it was unexpected. Even Emily, loving him though she did, had been as stunned as he by their intense physical reaction to each other as they had sat on the bench by the lily pond, entwined in each other's arms. The world had turned dizzingly and wonderfully upside down for them both.

Winston, in typical Harte fashion, had wasted little time. The moment their affair had begun he had broken off with Alison; shortly thereafter he had asked her grandmother if they could become engaged. Emma had given her consent, thoroughly approving of the match between her granddaughter and her great nephew. One year later, when her Gran had returned from Australia, they had been married in the quaint old church in Pennistone village. Gran had given the most beautiful wedding reception for them in the gardens of Pennistone Royal and her life as Winston's wife had begun. . . . It was the best life any woman could ever want.

Emily sighed with contentment, brought her thoughts back to the present, picked up her pen, and began to write out the menu for lunch. When she finished, she started on the one for dinner, but stopped abruptly as an idea occurred to her. Tonight, she and Winston, Paula and Shane, would drive over to Beaulieu and have dinner at La Reserve. Just the four of them. Without the tribe. That would be much more peaceful. Not to mention romantic. Winston will approve, she thought, and smiled a small secret smile.

6

"You clot! You unbelievably stupid clot! Look what you've *done!* You've splashed my beautiful painting and ruined it!" Tessa Fairley yelled at the top of her lungs, glaring at Lorne, adopting an angry stance, waving the paintbrush in the air.

"The side of the swimming pool is hardly the proper place to set up an easel and start painting," Lorne rejoined loftily, returning her glare. "Especially when everyone's leaping in and out. It's your own fault the watercolor's been splashed. And one more thing—I'm *not* a stupid clot."

"No, you're a stupid *cretin,*" his twelve-year-old twin shot back, then sucked in her breath with a horrified gasp. "Don't do that, Lorne Fairley! Don't shake yourself like that! Oh! Oh! you *rotten* thing. You've spoiled my other pictures. Oh, God, you've made them all *trickly.* Mummy . . . *Mummy* . . . tell Lorne to stay away from my paintings," she wailed.

"I want this," Linnet announced matter-of-factly and snatched Tessa's large yellow sun hat from the chaise near the easel, placed it on top of her bright red curls, and happily marched off, dragging a rubber duck on a string behind her and pushing the hat up as it kept sliding down over her eyes.

"Bring that back at once, you naughty girl!"

When her five-year-old sister paid not a blind bit of notice, Tessa exclaimed to no one in particular, "Did you see that? She took my hat without my permission. Mummy . . . *Mummy* . . . that child's spoiled rotten. You and Daddy have ruined her. There's no hope—"

"Pompous, pompous, Tessa's being pompous, just like Lornie, she's parroting Forlornie," Gideon Harte taunted in a sing-song tone from the relative safety of the pool.

"I won't dignify *that* ridiculous remark," Lorne sniffed, lowered himself onto a mattress, picked up his copy of Homer's *Iliad* and buried his face in the book.

"Bring my hat back!" Tessa screamed, stamping her foot.

"Oh for God's sake, leave her alone," a faintly disembodied voice admonished from the pool, and Toby Harte's reddish-gold head bobbed up over the side. The ten-year-old grinned at Tessa, who was his favorite girl cousin, and then hauled himself out of the water, being careful not to splash her or her paintings, having no wish to incur her wrath. "After all, she's only a little itty bitty *baby.*"

"Not a baby," a muffled voice informed them from underneath the large sun hat.

"And why do you care so much, Tess? It's only a cheap bit of rag you bought in Nice market," Toby said.

"It's not! It's *beautiful!* And it cost me a whole week's pocket money, Toby Harte!"

"More fool you," called out eight-year-old Gideon.

"What do you know about anything, Gideon Harte! You're a *cretin* like my brother."

"Is that the only *stupid* word you know, *Stupid?*" Gideon shouted back and stuck his tongue out at her.

"Brat! Brat!" Tessa yelled at him. "You're a spoiled brat, too!"

"Oh shut up, both of you," Toby admonished

in a bored voice. "Listen, Tess, can I borrow one of your old Beatles' albums?"

"Which one?" Tessa asked, suddenly wary, squinting up at him in the bright sunlight.

"Sgt. Pepper's Lonely Hearts Club Band."

"Oh no, I can't possibly lend you that one! It's become a . . . *classic.* When Auntie Amanda gave it to me, she told me it'd be very, *very* valuable one day. She'd had it since before *we* were even born. But . . . well . . . because it's *you* I'll make an exception, so—"

"Gosh, thanks, Tess," Toby cut in, his freckled face lighting up.

"—you can rent it if you want, it's ten pence an hour," Tessa finished, sounding as magnanimous as she now looked.

"Ten pence an hour! That's highway robbery!" Toby spluttered. "No thanks, Tessa, I'm not going to help you become a capitalist."

"In this family, everybody's a capitalist," Tessa declared smugly.

"Forget it, I'll play my new Bee Gees."

"Suit yourself."

"Aunt Paula. *Aunt Paula* . . . your daughter's turned into a really nasty little sharpie this summer," Toby exclaimed and threw a disgusted look in Tessa's direction.

"Mummy . . . I'm taking my knickers off,

they're all wet," Linnet cried from the depths of the sun hat.

"You see what I mean, Mummy," Tessa sniggered. "She's the only five-year-old *I* know who still wee-wees in her pants."

"I don't! I didn't, Mummy!" a clear voice shrilled as the hat was pushed back and Linnet's round flushed face appeared.

"Auntie Paula, may I have one of these ginger snaps, please?" three-year-old Natalie Harte asked and took one and crunched on it before she was forbidden to do so.

"Mummy! Look at her now! She's *dragging* my gorgeous sun hat in the puddles. Stop it, you little monster. *Stop it!* Mummy, make her stop. *Mother* . . . you're not listening. If you throw that hat into the pool, I'll kill you, Linnet O'Neill! Gideon! Get my hat! Quick, before it sinks!"

"Okay, I will, but it'll cost you plenty."

Tessa ignored this threat. "Wait until I catch you, Linnet," she screamed after the small, plump figure retreating swiftly in the direction of the pool house.

"Mother . . . *Mother* . . . will you *please* tell Tessa to stop screeching like a banshee? I'm getting a frightful headache," Lorne murmured languidly from the mattress where he lay reading.

127

"Auntie Paula, Natalie's eaten *all* of the ginger snaps," India Standish gasped, and turning to her cousin, she added in the most dire tone a seven-year-old could summon, *"You're* going to be *sick.* Horribly, horribly sick, and it serves you right, you greedy little girl."

"Have this, India," Natalie said with a winning smile, pulling a half-eaten chocolate out of the pocket of her sundress, dusting it off, and offering it to the older girl, whom she adored.

"Ugh! *No thanks.* It looks icky!"

"Auntie Paula, there's a dead *something* at the bottom of the pool," Gideon shouted, coming up for air with a splash, triumphantly holding the sodden sun hat aloft.

"Oh my God! Mummy, she's ruined my *expensive* hat. *Mummy,* did you hear what I just said?"

"Where's the dead *something?"* Patrick asked, throwing himself flat on the ground, dangling his dark head over the pool, so that he could peer down into the depths. "Can't see it, Gid."

"I've got to dive for it," Gideon explained, plunging under water again like an agile little dolphin.

"Will you take five pence an hour for *Sgt. Pepper's Lonely Hearts Club Band?"* Toby negotiated hopefully.

"Eight pence . . . *perhaps.*"

"No thanks, Miss Sharpie. You can go and shove it up your . . . jumper."

"Oh Mummy, Mummy, look! A Bird. *Dead,*" Patrick cried. "Oh poor birdie. Funeral. Can we have a funeral?"

"Auntie Paula, please make Gideon get rid of that disgusting, revolting object," eleven-year-old Jeremy Standish exclaimed. "It pongs to high heaven and it's contaminating the air."

"No, it *isn't!*" Gideon glared at his cousin. "We're going to bury it, like Patrick wants, aren't we, Auntie Paula? Auntie Paula, cooee! *Auntie Paula,* we *can* bury it, can't we?"

"*Mummy,* can birdie have a funeral?"

"*Mummy,* I want some dry knickers."

"*Mother,* look at Linnet now. She's waving her knickers in the air. Mummy. Mummy! *Mother!*"

"For Christ's sake, Tessa, stop screaming," Lorne shouted. "How can I concentrate on my Homer with you bellowing in my ears. I'll be jolly glad to get back to school next week and away from you. You're a bloody little pest."

"If Daddy hears you swearing, you'll catch it."

"And who's going to tell him, Miss Tattle-tale?"

"I've never split on you yet, you *moron.*"

129

"If I'm a moron, then so are you, *twin!*"

"Don't bring that smelly disgusting *thing* any-where near me, Gideon, or I'll punch you on the nose," Jeremy threatened.

"Auntie Paula! Auntie Paula! Natalie's being sick! I *knew* she would be," India cried.

"Gideon Harte, I'm *warning* you. Keep your distance or I'll thump you!"

"*Auntie Paula,* tell Toby to let go of me!" Gid-eon screamed. "He's *hurting* me."

"And it's *my* turn next," Jeremy threatened with sudden manic glee.

"Mummy, *Mummy,* make the boys stop fight-ing," Linnet shrieked.

Paula threw down her book and angrily leaped to her feet.

She began to chastise them vociferously, but her voice was drowned out by a series of strange booms that reverberated on the warm air, and as the echoes died away, Paula was able to ask, "What on earth was *that?*"

"The gong," Linnet said.

"*Gong,*" Paula repeated in perplexity, and it instantly struck her how chastened the children seemed.

"What gong? Whose gong?"

Lorne explained, "Auntie Emily's gong . . . she bought it—"

"From the house up the mountain," Tessa

quickly interjected, then volunteered to her still-baffled mother, "The old lady who owned the house died, and there was a sale two weeks ago. We all went with Aunt Emily, she thought we might find some bargains."

"But all we found was the gong," Jeremy muttered.

"Mummy uses it to signal us," Toby said. "One strike means that breakfast's ready, two is for lunch, three is to summon us inside, to get ready for dinner, and—"

"When she bangs and bangs and *bangs,* like just now, it means we're going to *catch* it," Linnet confided and grimaced. "For being *bad.* For something *terrible* we've done."

"I see," Paula said and her shrewd eyes swept over the group of youngsters yet again. It was more apparent to her than ever that each child was suitably intimidated—even the most recalcitrant of them. She turned away to hide a smile, thinking how terribly clever Emily was.

"We're definitely in for it," Lorne muttered, jumping up, edging away.

"You're right," Toby agreed. "Come on, Troops, let's skedaddle before my mother starts giving us stupid chores to do, or worse still, thinks up idiotic activities to keep us properly occupied."

Within the space of seconds, the older children had raced after Lorne and Toby, as always the ringleaders, who were heading at breakneck speed for the steps that led down to the beach below the promontory. Only Patrick, Linnet, and Natalie remained with Paula in the pool area.

Silence finally reigned.

Paula sank gratefully into her chair, delighted to have peace and quiet for the first time that morning. She had done her utmost to ignore them, had remained aloof from their endless bickering—as she had learned to do over the years—at least until Toby and Gideon had started fighting and Jeremy had seemed about to join in the *mêlée.* She couldn't permit that to happen. Anthony and Sally Dunvale's eldest son had not been well, and the last thing his father had said, before leaving for Ireland earlier that morning, was for them to make sure the boy did not overtax himself for the rest of his stay at the villa. Paula knew that if Jeremy went home to Clonloughlin looking as if he had been scrapping with the boys, she and Emily would never hear the end of it from his mother. Their cousin Sally fussed a great deal about her firstborn, the heir to the Dunvale title, lands, and fortune.

Paula took a deep breath, and was about to give her small daughter a lecture about removing her underclothing in public, when she saw Emily hurrying down the path between the lawns.

"Cooee! Cooee!" Emily called, waving.

Paula waved back.

A moment later, Emily drew to a stop and she and Paula exchanged knowing looks. They began to laugh hilariously.

Emily said, "I know it's noisy, but it's *very* effective."

"And *how,*" Paula agreed. "I've never seen them silenced quite so quickly. *Never.* It was an inspired buy on your part."

"Yes," Emily chuckled, "so it's proved. My God, they were kicking up such a racket, I'm surprised you don't have a splitting headache by now. I know I could hardly hear myself think when I was in the kitchen, talking to Marcel about the meals for today."

"Mummy, I've been sick," Natalie announced, going over to Emily, tugging at her shift. "I frowed up."

"Don't talk like a baby, you're a big girl. And it's *threw* up," Emily corrected. She looked down at her youngest child, frowning, and put a hand on her forehead in concern. "Are you feeling all right? Are you better now, angel?"

"I don't know, Mummy."

"It's because she ate *all* the ginger snaps," Linnet said.

"Now, now, Linnet, you know it's wrong to tell tales out of school!" Paula reprimanded sharply, scowling at her daughter. "And let's not forget that you've been very naughty this morning. First, flinging Tessa's sun hat in the pool, and then taking your knickers off in public. I'm terribly cross with you, and ashamed of you, Linnet." Paula shook her head, trying hard to look appropriately angry without much success, but nevertheless, she added, "You've disgraced yourself, and the only reason you haven't been punished *yet* is because I'm still trying to think of a *suitable* punishment."

Linnet bit her lip, adopted a sorrowful expression, and wisely said nothing.

Emily looked from her daughter to her niece and then glanced at Paula. She exclaimed, "Why do I do such stupid things? Such as letting both nannies have the same day off, so they can go up to Grasse to buy perfume. And today of all days—the last chance you have to get a bit of rest before you go to New York on Wednesday. I'm sorry, Paula."

"It's all right, really it is, lovey."

Sighing under her breath, Emily now took hold of Natalie's hand. "Come along, let's go inside and get something to settle your tummy.

And you'd better come along, too, Linnet, for a pair of clean underpants."

"Oh thanks, Emily," Paula murmured, settling back in her chair.

"Lunch is at one," Emily said, "and I've booked a table at La Reserve for dinner tonight. Just the four of us."

"I should jolly well hope so." Paula laughed. "And it sounds absolutely lovely. It's ages since we've been over there . . . it's one of my favorite places."

"Yes, I know," Emily replied, looking pleased as she turned away. She took a couple of steps, stopped, and said over her shoulder to Paula, "Oh by the way, I've got to go into Monte Carlo this afternoon, to pick up a repair from my antique porcelain man. Do you want to drive in with me? I'll only be a few minutes with Jules, and then we could take a stroll around the town and have tea at the Hôtel de Paris . . . watch the world go by for a while, like we used to do with Gran."

"What a nice idea, Emily, yes, I'd like that."

Emily gave her a sunny smile, then bustled her charges forward, half bending down, talking to them as they made for the villa.

Paula watched the three of them go up the path together, the two little girls walking on either side of Emily, clinging to her hands. Linnet and Natalie bore a strong resemblance to each other, could easily be mistaken for sisters since they had both inherited the famous Harte coloring—Emma's red hair and vivid green eyes and English rose complexion. They were dazzling children, really. A couple of Botticellis.

Patrick now came to Paula, stood by her chair, touched her arm, stared deeply into her face. "Mummy . . ."

"What is it, darling?"

"Mummy . . . poor birdie. Gid took it. No funeral now." The child shook his head and looked sad.

"Of course we'll have a funeral," Paula said gently, taking his small, rather grubby hand in hers and looking into his angelic face. His black O'Neill eyes were bright and lively for once, not devoid of expression and vacant as they so frequently were. Her heart lifted with joy to see such life in them today.

She gave her son a reassuring smile, and went on, "I know Gideon will bring the little bird back, and we'll ask Madame Solange for one of her old tin biscuit boxes to put the birdie in, and then after lunch we'll have the funeral. I promise, darling."

Patrick put his head on one side and studied her carefully. "Bury it in the garden?" he asked, and gave her a slow, tentative smile.

"Yes, that's *exactly* what we'll do. Oh darling, *look* who's coming!"

Patrick swung his head, and when he saw Shane approaching, his face lit up and he extracted his hand from his mother's and ran to meet his father.

Paula called out worriedly, "Patrick, do be careful. Don't fall."

Patrick did not answer. He sped ahead as fast as his little legs would carry him, shouting, "Daddy! Daddy! Daddy!"

Shane caught his son in his arms and swung him up high in the air, then placed him on his shoulders, and the two of them laughed merrily as Patrick rode Shane back to the pool area, crying, "Gee-up, gee-up. Nice horsey. Gee-up, gee-up."

"I'm going to take him for a swim. Is that okay, darling?" Shane called. He knelt down and carefully lowered Patrick to the ground.

"Yes, of course," Paula called back.

She sat up straighter, so that she could see the two of them better, shading her eyes with her hand.

Shane jumped into the shallow end of the pool, holding Patrick tightly in his arms, and immediately they began to frolic in the water, still laughing, and shouting with glee, and Patrick's face was bright with excitement and happiness and so was Shane's.

From this distance, her son seemed like any normal seven-year-old; the problem was that he would always have the mind of a seven-year-old. His body would grow and age, but his mental capacities would remain as they were now for the rest of his life. He would never be any different; they had given up hope of that. When they had first discovered Patrick was retarded, Paula had blamed herself, believing she carried some flaw in her genes which had been inherited from her grandfather. Paul McGill had had a legitimate son, Howard, by his legal wife, Constance, in Australia, and the boy, dead now for a number of years, had been retarded. She had so convinced herself that this was the case, she had told Shane she dare not risk having any more children. But Shane had immediately poohpoohed her theory, and he had insisted they see Professor Charles Hallingby, a leading geneticist.

They had both been tested and the results had proved conclusively that neither she nor Shane had passed on any kind of deficiency to their son. Patrick's condition was inexplicable, simply a terrible fluke of nature. Professor Hallingby, having studied their family histories, had pointed out to Paula that her grandfather's son may well have suffered prenatal damage because of Constance McGill's heavy drinking during her pregnancy, a possibility her mother, Daisy, had mentioned innumerable times. She had finally conceded that the professor and her mother could be right. Not unnaturally, the knowledge that Professor Hallingby had imparted had helped to ease her mind. Shortly after, she had conceived again, and when Linnet was born she was a perfectly normal baby.

Paula loved her children equally, and tried not to have a favorite, but deep in the innermost regions of her heart she was aware that Patrick was special to her, that he had a unique place in her affections. There was a terrible fierceness about her love for her afflicted child, perhaps, in part, *because* of his affliction, which made him so vulnerable and dependent.

His siblings also loved him dearly, and took great care with him, and for this she was thankful. Often she thought how heartbreaking it would have been if they had despised him or shunned him, as sometimes happened in families where there was a retarded child. But Lorne, Tessa, and even little Linnet were as protective of Patrick as she and Shane were and, in fact, so were his many cousins. Not one single child in the family had ever made Patrick feel that he was in any way different to them. It was a tragedy that her little Patrick had not been born a perfect child, that he was damaged in the way he was. But Paula recognized that his inherent sweetness and his loving disposition compensated for so many things and endeared him to the family, and certainly he brought out the best in all of them.

An afflicted child is like a bruise on the heart —one never quite gets rid of the aching pain, Paula suddenly thought, and she sighed under her breath and held herself very still, pressing down on her sadness, continuing to watch the two dark heads bobbing around in the water. Her husband, her son. Oh how she loved them both, and with a love that was heart-stopping at times.

It did her good to see how much they were enjoying their nautical games. Shane could be very gentle and tender with Patrick, or roughhouse with him, as he was doing now, and from the joyous shrieks and the whoops of delight filling the air, she knew the little boy was having the best time with the father whom he worshipped. A great rush of happiness filled her to the brim, displaced the sorrow she had felt a moment ago.

Paula lay back and closed her eyes, feeling a measure of contentment, but she lifted her lids almost immediately and sat up at the sound of Winston's voice.

He walked into the pool area carrying a large tray of plastic tumblers, and trotting dutifully behind him was his nephew, Giles Standish, second son of his sister Sally, the Countess of Dunvale. Giles was carefully holding a large jug of lemonade with both hands.

"Bon jour, Tante Paula. Voilà! Ici citron presse pour toi," the nine-year-old Giles said, showing off his little bit of French, as he had been doing all through the summer. He was having special tutoring in the language and made a point of speaking it whenever he could, much to the irritation of the other children, who were not as fluent as he was becoming. But their constant ribbing rolled off his back; he was independent by nature, so he paid no attention and went on speaking French whenever he felt like it.

Giles put the jug down on one of the tables in the shade, and politely stood aside to make way for his uncle.

"How delicious it looks, Giles dear," Paula said. "Just what I need, I'm getting quite parched from this heat. Did your parents get off all right?"

"Yes, but Nice Airport was jammed, wasn't it, Uncle Winston?" Giles said, reverting to English.

"It was bloody awful, Paula," Winston asserted, pouring lemonade into a tumbler and bringing it to her. "Chaotic. I've never seen so many people. Sally and Anthony were thankful they were returning on Shane's private jet, and I must say, that plane's turned out to be a real godsend. I'm certainly glad Emily and I will be able to use it to get the mob back home at the end of the week. Now, Giles, do you want a glass of this?"

"No, thank you very much." Giles glanced around. "Where are Jeremy and India, Auntie Paula?"

"I believe your brother and sister decamped to the beach. With the rest of the troops."

"Oh goody! I bet they're all fishing or looking for *oursins*. I'm going down there too!" Giles squealed excitedly. "Please excuse me, Auntie Paula, Uncle Winston," and so saying he took off, leaping across the grass in great bounds, making for the long flight of steps.

Winston stared after him, and said to Paula, "That kid's got the best manners of the whole bunch of them. If only some of the others—mine in particular—would borrow even *half* a page from his book, I'd be happy." He lowered himself onto a nearby chair, took a long swallow of lemonade, and continued, "Emily told me every single one of them was raising hell earlier."

"It did start to get a bit out of hand, actually, Winston. But Emily finally put a stop to their bickering with that wonderfully effective gong." She glanced at her cousin through the corner of her eye, and chuckled. "Trust Emily to come up with something ridiculous like that. Still, it really works, and I must admit, I wish I had a handle on them the way she does."

Winston grinned. "Don't we all."

7

"I adore old-fashioned hotels, especially when they're in the *belle époque* style and have a grandiose splendor," Emily said to Paula as they turned into the Place Casino in Monte Carlo later that afternoon. "You know, like the Hôtel de Paris here, the Negresco in Nice, the Ritz in Paris, and the Imperial in Vienna."

"Not to mention the Grand in Scarborough," Paula said, laughing, tucking her arm through Emily's companionably. "I can well recall how attached you were to that place when we were little. You never stopped pestering me to take you there for afternoon tea, and you couldn't wait to stuff your fat little face with cucumber sandwiches and cream puffs and scones with strawberry jam and clotted cream," she teased, her violet eyes dancing merrily.

Emily shuddered at the remembrance and made a gruesome face. "My God, all those fattening things! No wonder I've had to work so hard to keep my weight down ever since. Too much ballast as a child, methinks!" She grinned at Paula. "You shouldn't have permitted me to eat like that."

"How could I stop you! I tried very hard to keep you out of the Grand Hotel, using every kind of ruse, even pretending I didn't have any money on me. But you always had an answer for everything, even for that . . . 'Scribble on the bill like Grandma does,' you used to tell me. You were a very enterprising child, you know."

"And so were you."

They both stopped at precisely the same moment and automatically swung to face each other and they shared a smile, thinking of those lighthearted happy days when they were growing up together in Yorkshire and London. There was a brief and loving silence before Emily said, "We *were* lucky, weren't we, Paula? We had such a wonderful childhood, and especially when we were with our Gran."

"Yes, it was the *best,*" Paula agreed. "And she was the *best.*"

They started walking again, lost in their own thoughts as they crossed the pleasant square, heading in the direction of the Hôtel de Paris, which was situated in the far corner, opposite the renowned Casino de Monte Carlo.

It was a lovely afternoon, filled with dappled sunlight and soft white clouds scudding across the azure-blue sky, and there was a refreshing breeze blowing up from the sea. It ruffled the skirts of their summer dresses, puffed them out like tulip bells, and made the white sails on the boats in the harbor billow about, and the brightly colored flags on the masts ripple and dance gaily.

Emily had driven them down to Monte Carlo in her powder blue Jaguar, after a family luncheon on the terrace at the villa, and then the burial of the dead bird in the garden, which everyone had attended, much to Patrick's satisfaction.

Once they had arrived in the Principality of Monaco they had parked the car and gone to Jules et Cie, the antique shop where Emily frequently bought old porcelain, to pick up a Limoges plate Jules had repaired for her. The charming old man had chatted to them at length about antique china and glass, and had shown them his private collection of rare items, and they had browsed for a while before leaving the *antiquaire's* to stroll around the main streets and window-shop on their way to the famous hotel for afternoon tea.

"It's impossibly grand, even a bit ginger-bready, but it's irresistible, at least to me," Emily said, pausing on the pavement outside the Hôtel de Paris, looking up at it, beginning to laugh at herself as they climbed the front steps. Almost instantly the laughter died in her throat, and she grabbed Paula's arm so tightly her cousin winced and followed her gaze.

Heading toward them down the steps was a tall woman with an abundance of flaming red hair and the kind of elegance that was indisputably French. She wore a white silk dress, very chic and severely tailored, with a black-silk rose pinned to one shoulder, black-and-white high-heeled shoes, a matching bag, and white gloves. She carried a black straw picture hat, and she was holding the hand of a little girl of about three years, also dressed entirely in white, who had the same natural, bright red hair. The woman was bending over the child, saying something to her as they moved forward, and she had not seen them.

"Christ Almighty! It's Sarah!" Emily gasped and squeezed Paula's arm again.

Paula sucked in her breath, but she had no

chance to make any response, nor could she and Emily turn around and hurry away.

A split second later their cousin had drawn level with them. The three women were standing on the same step, gaping at each other, and they were so stunned they were utterly speechless, rooted to the spot.

It was Paula who finally broke the uncomfortable silence.

"Hello, Sarah," she said, very quietly, in a soft voice. "You're looking well." She stopped, took a deep breath. "And this must be your daughter . . . Chloe, isn't it?" she added, forcing a smile, looking down at the child, whose upturned face was solemn and filled with curiosity. And Paula saw, on closer inspection, that this was a true offspring of Emma Harte.

Sarah had regained her self-possession, and she gave Paula a look that was deadly. "How dare you speak to me!" she cried, not bothering to sheathe her hostility and loathing. "How dare *you* attempt to make a friendly gesture toward *me*." Leaning closer, she hissed in Paula's face, "You have a bloody nerve, behaving as if nothing happened between us, Paula O'Neill, and after what you did to me, you rotten bitch!"

The undisguised hatred on Sarah's face, and her threatening manner, made Paula recoil in shock and dismay.

"You'd better stay away from me and mine!" Sarah exclaimed, her face turning brilliant red. She looked almost choleric, and her voice was unnecessarily loud and shrill. "And you too, Emily Harte, you're no better than she is," she scoffed, her scarlet lips curling in scorn. "You two turned Grandmother against me, and then you cheated me of what was rightfully mine! You're both *thieves.* Now, get out of my way! Both of you!"

Tightening her grip on the child's hand, Sarah pushed between Paula and Emily, almost knocking Paula over. And she swept on grandly down the remainder of the steps without a backward glance, the child hurrying and stumbling to keep up with her mother, exclaiming, *"Maman, Maman, attendez!"*

Paula had gone cold all over, despite the heat of the day, and there was a queasy feeling in the pit of her stomach. She was momentarily paralyzed, powerless to move. Then suddenly she grew conscious of Emily taking hold of her arm.

Emily said, *"Phew!* That was awful. She's not changed, has she?"

"No, she hasn't," Paula agreed, rousing herself. "Let's go in, Emily, people are staring at us." Paula extracted herself, flew up the steps and through the doors of the hotel, wanting to put distance between herself and those passersby who had witnessed the scene. She was mortified and still shaking inside.

Emily ran after her and found her cousin waiting inside the door, striving to calm herself. She slipped her arm through Paula's and drew her forward into the hotel, saying, "At least we didn't *know* any of those people who were listening and gawking at us, darling, so forget it. Come on, let's go and have a nice cup of tea. It'll do us both good."

Once they had been shown to a secluded table in the lounge area of the vast lobby, and had settled down and ordered a pot of tea, Emily sat back and expelled a great sigh. "What a nasty performance that was," she said.

"Yes. Ugly. And embarrassing. I could hardly believe my ears when she started to shout at us like a fishwife, not to mention the ghastly things she was saying."

Emily nodded and gave Paula a careful look. "Why on earth did you speak to her in the first place?"

"I didn't know what else to do. We were eyeball to eyeball. It was terribly awkward, you know that, Emily," Paula replied, and paused. A contemplative expression settled on her face and she shook her head slowly. "I suppose I've always felt a bit sorry for Sarah. She *was* Jonathan's pawn, and his victim, in a certain sense.

He duped her, used her and her money. I've never really considered her to be wicked like Jonathan. Just rather stupid."

"I agree with you—about her stupidity—but I don't feel sorry for her, and neither should you," Emily exclaimed. She drew closer, continued, "Look here, Paula, you're far too nice, always trying to be fair-minded and compassionate, and seeing everyone else's point of view. That's all very well when you're dealing with people who deserve your concern, but I don't think Sarah does. Stupid or not, she knew it was wrong to back Jonathan, to put up money for his private company. That truly was going against Harte Enterprises—and the family."

"Yes, it was," Paula admitted. "But I still think that in some ways she's more dense than anything else, and I'm sure Jonathan pulled the wool over her eyes."

Emily said, "Maybe he did." She sat back, crossed her legs, and went on, "Don't you think it's odd that we haven't run across Sarah before now. I mean after all, she's been living up the coast near Cannes for about five years, according to that story we saw in *Paris Match,* and Mougins isn't that far away."

Paula was silent.

After a moment she leveled her steady gaze at Emily, and murmured, "What's also kind of odd is that for the first time in years Michael Kallinski was talking about Sarah and Jonathan on Friday and—"

"Why?" Emily cut in peremptorily.

"No special reason, other than his own curiosity. We'd been talking about Lady Hamilton Clothes, as I told you yesterday, so I suppose it was natural for him to inquire about Sarah's whereabouts. Still . . ." Paula broke off, shook her head.

"Still *what?*" Emily pressed.

"I was just thinking that his talking about them was almost prophetic." Paula gave a curious, rather nervous little laugh as she stared pointedly at Emily.

"Gosh, it was! And I hope to God we don't run into Jonathan next. I'm not sure I could survive an encounter with *him* quite as coolly as the one with Sarah."

"I know I couldn't." As she spoke, Paula shivered involuntarily, and she felt the hackles rise on the back of her neck and goose flesh speckle her arms. She sat back in the chair, biting her inner lip, wishing the mention of Jonathan's name would not upset her the way it did.

Fortunately, the waiter arrived with the laden tea tray, and Paula was glad for the distraction as he commenced to place the cups and saucers on the table in front of them and speak in rapid

French to Emily, whom he apparently knew by sight. Paula declined the many delicious pastries being offered, and stole a surreptitious glance at Emily, wondering if her cousin would succumb to temptation.

Emily looked longingly at the cakes, but she also shook her head, and as Paula poured the tea, she said, "Don't think I didn't want one of *everything,* because I did. I could have cheerfully made a meal out of the chocolate eclairs and the vanilla slices, but you saw how I resisted. All for the benefit of my figure. And Winston. He likes me to be svelte, so I've developed a will of iron when it comes to nasty fattening things like cream buns. You should be very proud of me," she finished, irrepressible laughter bubbling up in her.

"And so should Winston," Paula said, also laughing. Their sudden gaiety helped to dissipate the unpleasantness of the scene with Sarah, which still lingered in their thoughts, and it changed their mood, brought them back to normal. Almost at once they began to talk about spending a few days in Hong Kong together next month, and made their plans.

At one moment, between sips of tea, Paula said, "You and Shane are right, Emily, I think I will take Madelana to Australia with me."

"Oh I am glad you agree with us, darling. If

the boutiques really are in a mess, she'll be of tremendous help."

"Yes, that's true, and I think she'll be thrilled to come with me, don't you?"

"Who wouldn't be—it's a marvelous trip, and anyway she's devoted to you."

"She is. It was a smart move on my part, promoting her to be my assistant a year ago. She's proved herself to be invaluable." Paula glanced at her watch. "It's five o'clock . . . eleven in the morning in New York. I'll give her a ring later, explain that I want her to come with me. She'll have her hands full this week, clearing the decks in order to leave with me on Saturday, so the sooner she knows, the better."

"You could call her from here, if you wanted to, Paula," Emily suggested, never the one to waste any time if she could help it.

"No, no, that's all right. I can do it when we get home to Faviola. The six-hour time difference gives me plenty of leeway."

Emily nodded, and then right out of the blue, she said, "I bet you anything that dress she was wearing was a Givenchy."

"I've no doubt it was. Sarah always did have a flair for clothes."

"Mmmm." Emily turned thoughtful, sat looking into the distance for a few moments. Finally, she asked Paula, "Do you think she ever hears from Jonathan?"

"I can't even hazard a guess."

"I wonder what did happen to him, Paula? Where he's living?" Emily said softly, thinking out loud.

"I'd prefer not to know. Or to talk about him, if you don't mind, Emily. You know very well that Jonathan Ainsley's not my favorite subject," Paula answered sharply.

"Oh gosh, sorry, darling," Emily said, suddenly regretful that she had started talking about their cousins again. Changing the subject, she said quickly, "Well, I'd better pay and we'll get off home, so you can call Madelana at Harte's in New York."

"Yes, let's go," Paula agreed.

She was the kind of woman that men looked at twice. And women, too, for that matter.

It was not that Madelana O'Shea was very beautiful. She was not. But she had what the French call *je ne sais quois,* that indefinable something that made her special and caused heads to turn wherever she went.

Tonight was no exception.

She stood outside Harte's department store on Fifth Avenue, patiently waiting for the radio cab she had ordered from her office a short while before. It was eight o'clock on a Thursday and the store was still open. Everyone who hurried in and out stole a glance at her, obviously wondering who she was, for she had style and there was a touch of regality in her bearing.

A tall young woman of about five feet eight, and slender, she had a willowy figure and legs that were long and shapely. Her thick, chestnut-brown hair was shoulder length, worn full and loose around her heart-shaped face. She was a little too bony to be called pretty, but the smooth forehead and high, slanting cheekbones, sharp as blades, gave her the look of a thorough-bred, as did the finely drawn aristocratic nose sprinkled faintly with freckles. She had a wide Irish mouth, with a full, somewhat voluptuous bottom lip, and a lovely smile that filled her face with radiance, but it was her eyes that fascinated and compelled. They were large, widely set, and of an unusual pale gray the color of chalcedony, their marvelous transparency emphasized by the dark brows arched above them. They were highly intelligent eyes, and filled with a determination that could turn steely at times, but there was also laughter in them and sometimes a hidden recklessness.

Madelana had a flair for clothes and wore them well. She looked smart in anything she put on, gave it her own cachet; it might be the way she knotted a scarf, snapped down the brim of a hat, wrapped a length of oriental silk into a unique cummerbund or twisted antique beads around her long and slender neck. And it was this great personal chic in combination with her svelte good looks that made her appearance so arresting.

The evening was stifling, humid as only New York in the middle of summer can be, and everyone seemed worn down and wilted in the oppressive weather as they toiled up Fifth, or stood at the edge of the sidewalk, looking for a yellow cab or waiting to cross to the other side.

But not Madelana O'Shea. Her tailored cream silk tunic, with its simple round neckline and three-quarter-length sleeves, worn over a straight black silk skirt, was as crisp as it had been when she had set out for work that morning, and she looked cool, untouched by the heat, and as elegant as usual.

The burgundy radio cab pulled up in front of the store, and she hurried forward with an ease and lightness of movement that bespoke her childhood ballet and tap lessons. She was limber, and had the agile grace of a dancer, and this, too, was part of her immense appeal.

After opening the taxi door, she put the large Harte's shopping bag on the seat and slid in next to it.

"West Twenty-fourth Street, right, miss?" the driver said, moving off down Fifth.

"Yes, between Seventh and Eighth, in the middle of the block, please."

"Okay, miss."

Madelana sat back, rested her hands on the black patent bag in her lap, her mind racing as it almost always did, no matter where she was or what she was doing.

Ever since Monday afternoon, when Paula had called from the south of France to tell her she was going to Australia, she had felt as if she had been running in a marathon. She had had to complete her current work, cancel her business appointments for the next few weeks, along with the few personal dates she had made, plan ahead for a possibly protracted absence from the store, and select appropriate clothes and accessories for the trip.

And then Paula had arrived in New York on the Concorde, early on Wednesday morning, and had come directly to the store. The two of them had worked like demons for two solid days, but they *had* accomplished miracles, and they would have a relatively normal business day tomorrow, before leaving on Saturday on the first leg of their journey. Tonight she would go over the files of papers she had stacked in the shopping bag and finish working on them, and tomorrow night she would pack.

I'm ahead of the game, Madelana thought

with sudden relief, and nodded to herself, feeling gratified. She glanced out the window, hardly noticing the tawdry glitter and squalor of Times Square with its hustlers and peddlers and drug addicts and pushers and undercover cops and hookers on the make. As the cab slid swiftly through this clamoring rinky-tink wedge of real estate and headed on downtown toward Chelsea, her mind focused on the trip to the other side of the world.

They were going first to Sydney, then on to Melbourne and perhaps even to Adelaide after that, before returning to Sydney, where they would spend most of their time. From what Paula had told her, they had a lot of work to do, and it would be a grueling two or three weeks. But the prospect did not faze her. She and Paula O'Neill worked well together, had always seemed to understand each other right from the beginning, and they were compatible.

It struck her, and not for the first time, how strange it was that she, a poor Irish-American Catholic girl from the South, and an aristocratic Englishwoman, heiress to one of the world's great fortunes and a noted international business tycoon, could be so similar, and in so many ways. They were both workaholics and had boundless energy, were sticklers for detail, disciplined, dedicated, driven, and extremely well or-

160

ganized. In consequence, they did not grate on each other's nerves, or create problems for each other, and they seemed always to be in step. It's like dancing with Fred Astaire or Gene Kelly, she thought and smiled inwardly, liking her analogy.

In the year she had been Paula's personal assistant, she had not put a foot wrong and she did not intend to, not ever, and especially not on their forthcoming trip to Australia. Paula was the key to her future. Her goal was to become president of Harte's store in New York one day, and with Paula's help she would achieve it.

Ambition. She was loaded with it. She knew this only too well, and she was pleased that she was. She considered it to be a plus not a minus. It had goaded her on, helped her to arrive where she was today. Her father had occasionally complained that she was too ambitious. But her mother had merely smiled her lovely Irish smile at him, and behind his back had winked at her and nodded maternal approval and encouraged her at every opportunity.

She wished her parents were still alive. And her little sister, Kerry Anne, who had died at the age of four. And Joe and Lonnie. Her two brothers had been killed in Vietnam. She missed them so very much, just as she missed her baby sister and her parents, and at times she felt as though she had no roots, no center to her life, with all of them gone from her. They had been close knit as a family, and very loving of each other. She considered her losses over the past few years, thought of her sorrow, and her heart clenched. Resolutely, she pushed the pain away.

Madelana took several deep breaths, keeping absolute control of herself and her emotions, as she had taught herself to do after her father had been buried four years ago. Only when he was lying in the ground did her sense of aloneness truly overwhelm her, and only then did she fully comprehend that she no longer had any family left, except for Aunt Agnes, her father's sister, who lived in California and whom she hardly knew.

The cab drew up outside the Residence Jeanne D'Arc. She took the receipt from the driver, said goodnight, grabbed her shopping bag, and alighted. She ran swiftly up the steps and into the building.

The minute she walked inside, Madelana felt herself relaxing.

This place was so familiar and welcoming . . . she had lived here in one of the rooms when she had first come to New York, had stayed for three years. She still thought of it as home, even though she now had her own apartment uptown in the East Eighties.

She crossed the small entrance foyer and turned right, heading for the office.

"Hello, Sister Mairéad," Madelana said to the nun behind the counter, who was in charge of the office this evening. "How are you?"

"Why, Madelana, it's nice to see you, and I'm just fine, very fine indeed," the sister replied, the faint Irish lilt echoing softly in her voice, her rose-apple cheeks dimpling with pleasure. The sister had had a soft spot for Madelana when she had lived here, and she was always delighted to see this lovely young woman who was such a credit to her parents, God rest their souls, and who in every way exemplified her good Catholic upbringing.

"Sister Bronagh's expecting me," Madelana said with a smile, and put the large Harte's bag on the counter, took out a gift-wrapped package, and looked at the sister. "Can I leave my shopping bag with you, please?"

"Of course you can, Madelana. Sister Bronagh said for you to go to the garden. She'll be up to join you in a few minutes. I'll let her know you've arrived." Sister Mairéad beamed and picked up the phone, began to dial.

"Thank you, Sister," Madelana murmured, heading for the small, boxlike elevator that would take her up to the fifth floor and the stairs that led to the roof of the building.

Surprisingly, the roof garden was empty.

Usually in the summer, on pleasant evenings, some of the girls who lived at the residency came up here to chat and socialize with each other, and with the sisters, to share a drink of wine or juice, or read a book or simply be alone.

It was a charming spot, planted with rambling ivy, and there were vines growing on trellis panels, and window boxes of bright red and pink geraniums, and pots of yellow and peach begonias, and the sisters grew vegetables up here. Scattered about were chairs and several small tables, and the atmosphere was inviting and suggested conviviality.

She paused to look at the statue of the Blessed Virgin, surrounded by masses of flowers as it generally was in the summer, recalling how often she had tended the flowers when she had been living here. She had always thought of this spot as an oasis, a lovely patch of green-growing things in the middle of the concrete canyons of Manhattan, and it had given her a feeling of well-being, had nourished her soul.

Gliding forward, she went to one of the tables, put down the gift and her handbag, and seated herself in one of the chairs facing uptown. Straight ahead of her, in her direct angle of vision, were the Empire State and the Chrysler

Buildings thrusting up above the higgledy-pig-
gledy roofs and chimney pots of Chelsea and the
less-distinguished skyscrapers of the city.

Dusk was already falling, and the lavender-
and-gray tinted sky was changing as a deep co-
balt blue seeped in like ink and slowly extin-
guished these paler hues. The lights that washed
over the towers of the two dominating buildings
had been turned on, but the grandeur of the architecture would not be properly visible until
the sky was pitch black. Then these towers
would be thrown into relief, would shimmer
magnificently against the dark velvet backdrop
of the sky, and it was a sight that never failed to
make her catch her breath in delight.

Even in winter, Madelana had enjoyed coming up here when she had lived at the residency.
Wrapped in warm clothes, she had huddled in a
sheltered corner, admiring these two extraordinary edifices and a skyline that stunned with its
unique beauty.

The Chrysler, with its Art Deco sunburst motif on its elegant tapering tower, was only ever
flooded with clear white light that gave it a pristine beauty and underscored the purity of its design, whereas the Empire State changed its colors to suit the season and the holidays. At
Thanksgiving, the two tiers and the slender
tower above were flooded with amber, gold, and

orange; at Christmas with red and green. The lights changed to blue and white for Chanukah and other Jewish holidays, became yellow at Easter, green on St. Patrick's Day, and red, white, and blue for the Fourth of July. And if the Chrysler Building really was the more beautiful of the two, then certainly the Empire State was the most eye-catching when it blazed with a celebratory selection of its rainbow colors.

"Good evening, Madelana," Sister Bronagh called as she walked across to the table, carrying two glasses of white wine.

Madelana sprang up at the sound of her voice.

"Hello, Sister." She hurried forward, smiling, and took the glass being offered to her, and the two women clasped hands affectionately, before sitting down together at the table.

"You're looking extremely well," Sister Bronagh said, peering at her in the gathering dusk.

"Thank you, I feel good."

They touched glasses and sipped their drinks.

"This is for you, Sister," Madelana said, after a moment, and slid the gift across the table.

"For me?" Sister Bronagh's eyes suddenly twinkled merrily behind her spectacles, her face wreathed in smiles.

"That's why I came tonight . . . to bring you the present and to say good-bye. I won't be able to come to your farewell party next week. I'll be in Australia by then."

"Australia! My goodness, so far away, Madelana. But exciting, I think, for you. I'm so sorry you won't be at the party . . . your absence will be noticed. It always has been, when you haven't been able to make one of our little get-togethers. And thank you for the gift, it was thoughtful of you. May I open it now?"

"Of course," Madelana said, laughing, enjoying the sister's obvious delight in the small token she had brought.

Sister Bronagh untied the yellow ribbon, dispensed with the wrapping paper, and lifted the lid of the Harte's silver cardboard box. Underneath the layers of tissue paper were three different-sized toilet bags made of deep blue silk and trimmed with a lighter blue welting.

"Oh, how lovely they are!" Sister Bronagh exclaimed, taking one out, turning it over in her hands, opening the zip, and looking inside. Her small, birdlike face was bright with sudden happiness and she took Madelana's hand resting on the table and squeezed it. "Thank you so much, my dear, they're just what I need."

"I'm glad you like them. I wanted to get you something that was pretty but also useful." Madelana grinned at her. "I *know* you . . . how practical you are. Anyway, I thought these would be perfect for traveling." She rested her elbows on the table. Her fingers toyed with the glass of wine. "When *do* you leave for Rome?"

"On the tenth of September, and I'm becoming excited about going. It'll be a challenge, helping to run the residency over there. It's situated not very far away from the Vatican, and that's an added joy for me, being so close to the Holy See." There was a lovely glow about her as she continued, "I must confess to you, Madelana, I was thrilled when Sister Marie-Theresa picked me to be the one to go."

Madelana nodded. "Everyone here at the residency is going to miss you, though, me included."

"Oh and I shall miss you, too, Madelana, and the other old girls who still come to see me, and the ones living here now, and the sisters." There was a brief pause. A fleeting sadness touched Sister Bronagh's eyes, and they grew moist, and then she cleared her throat quickly, sat up, straightened the collar of her white blouse. She gave Madelana a warm smile. "Tell me about your trip to Australia. It's rather sudden, isn't it?"

"Yes. I'm going on business with my boss, Paula O'Neill. We're leaving for Los Angeles on Saturday morning, and we'll spend the night there, since she thinks we'll both be in better shape if we break the trip instead of flying direct. We take the Quantas flight to Sydney at ten o'clock on Sunday night."

"And how long will you be gone?"

"Two or three weeks, perhaps even four. Paula may have to leave me behind to follow through for her. We're going out there because of the boutiques in the hotels. She's concerned they're not being run properly. The manager has been sick, and her assistant seems to either panic or flounder on alternate days."

"You've done well at Harte's, Madelana, I'm proud of you."

"Thank you. Anyway, my career's very important to me, as you know . . ." Madelana stopped, and there was a hesitation in her manner, and she looked down at her hands resting on the table. Shortly, she went on in a more muted, thoughtful tone, "But working so hard these past few years has also helped me to keep grief at bay, to come to grips with my losses . . ." Her voice suddenly trailed off.

The sister reached out, took Madelana's hand in hers, and there was a sense of comfort in this gesture. "Yes, I know it has. But then so has your great faith, Madelana. Always remember that God has His reasons, and that He never gives us a burden that is too heavy to carry."

"Yes, you've told me that many times before."

Madelana tightened her grip on Sister Bronagh's hand. There was a short silence between them. She lifted her head then, and smiled faintly at this devout and gentle middle-aged woman who had been so warm and loving to her when she had lived here, who had singled her out for special attention.

"I couldn't let you leave for Rome without coming to see you, Sister Bronagh, to thank you from the bottom of my heart for helping me to get through so much pain and sorrow, for making me feel so welcome when I first arrived. You gave me courage."

"No, no, I didn't, Madelana," the sister said swiftly. "The courage was within you, already part of you then. As it is now. And as it will always be. If I did anything at all, it was simply to show you that it *was* there, to make you understand that all you needed to do was to reach inside of yourself, and to draw on it."

"Yes . . . But I'll never be able to thank you enough for all you've done for me. And for all you've taught me—especially about myself."

"You were always very special to me, my child," Sister Bronagh replied in a soft voice. "If I had not chosen this way of life, had not chosen to be in service to God, to do His work, and if I had married and had a daughter, I would have wanted her to be exactly like you."

"Oh Sister Bronagh, what a beautiful thing to say, thank you, thank you so much!" Madelana experienced a sudden rush of emotion and there was the unexpected sting of tears behind her eyes and she blinked them away, not wanting to break down. She realized how much she would miss Sister Bronagh after the nun had departed for her new job in Rome.

Now Madelana said, "Your belief in me has been so important, Sister, it's mirrored the faith my mother had in me. She encouraged me the way you have. I'll try never to let you down."

The sweetest of smiles brushed across Sister Bronagh's pale mouth and she said slowly, to give greater emphasis to her words, "The important thing is never to let yourself down, Madelana."

9

It was a long, hot ride uptown from the residence Jeanne D'Arc to East Eighty-fourth Street, and for the first time that day Madelana felt uncomfortably warm and damp when she finally alighted in front of the small apartment building where she lived.

"Hi, Alex," she said, greeting the doorman breezily as he helped her out of the cab.

The doorman responded in kind, and there was an admiring look in his eyes as he watched her walk rapidly across the sidewalk with her usual ease of movement. She swung into the building before he could rush to open the door for her, and appeared to float across the lobby, her feet hardly seeming to touch the marble as she sped ahead.

She stopped to collect her mail and then took the elevator to the seventeenth floor. The phone was ringing inside her apartment when she put the key in the lock. She hurried in as the phone continued its strident shrilling in the cool silence of the empty apartment.

Snapping on the light in the minuscule entrance hall, she dumped her things unceremoniously on the floor and ran to pick up the nearest extension.

This was on the desk in the yellow-and-white living room, which opened directly off the tiny foyer, and snatching the receiver, she exclaimed, "Hello," only to discover that there was no one at the other end. All she could hear was the faint burring of the dial tone; the caller had obviously disconnected a split second before she had reached the phone.

Oh well, she thought, whoever it is will call back, if it's important, and she dropped the receiver into the cradle with a shrug of her elegant shoulders, then hesitated, pivoted to look at the phone. She was on the verge of picking it up again, wondering if it had been Paula calling her, concerned with some last-minute bit of business. Or about something they had forgotten. It was hardly likely, since it was almost ten o'clock. She immediately dismissed the idea of calling her boss at her Fifth Avenue apartment. That would be an unwarranted intrusion, and anyway, Paula always went to bed early when she first arrived in New York, in an effort to counteract jet lag.

Madelana shivered, becoming aware of the chilly temperature. The air-conditioning had been running at its highest all day, and the apartment was like a freezer. But her body would soon adjust, and she welcomed the coolness after the humidity of the stuffy, airless streets of Manhattan.

She went to retrieve her things, and carried them back to the living room, sat down on the yellow velvet sofa, and glanced at her mail. There was nothing of any importance and she put it on the glass-and-brass coffee table, rose, and went into the adjoining bedroom to change her clothes.

A minute or two later she emerged, barefooted and wearing a long pink cotton caftan, and hurried into the kitchen to prepare a light supper for herself, before digging into the work she had brought home from the store.

The kitchen in her small apartment was long and narrow, and it had reminded Madelana of a ship's galley the first time she had seen it, just a year ago this month. And for this reason she had decorated it in various shades of blue with lots of white and dashes of brilliant red. She had covered the walls with nautical prints, ranging from Boston whalers, nineteenth-century sailing ships, and Mississippi riverboats to ocean-going liners and modern yachts. All were framed in brass, and there were other touches of brass in small accessories; copper molds hung above the stove and the sink, and these added their own sparkle.

At one end, near the window, she had placed a small, drop-leaf table and two bentwood chairs, an ideal spot for a snack. A small window box on the sill was filled with feathery spider ferns, and the kitchen had a gaiety and a charm which owed more to her ingenuity and flair than to the amount of money she had spent.

One of the colorful yachting prints caught Madelana's eye, and she smiled to herself, thinking of her friend Patsy Smith. Patsy was a Boston girl who had lived at the residency at the same time that she had, and two years ago Patsy had invited her to the Smith's summer home in Nantucket for the long Fourth of July weekend. They had done a lot of sailing over those four glorious days, and Madelana had loved every moment she had been on the water. It had been a new and exhilarating experience for her, and much to her amazement she had discovered she had a great affinity for boats and the sea.

Perhaps one day I'll do it again, she thought, turning to the refrigerator, taking out the ingredients for a salad.

The telephone on the wall behind her rang. She reached for it. "Hello?"

"So, you're finally home."

"Oh Jack, hi. Yes, I was—"

"You canceled our date in order to work, or so you said," he interrupted rudely, sourness curling around the edge of his beautiful, resonant voice. "But you ain't been home, kiddo, I've been calling you all night."

Madelana felt herself stiffening at his accusatory tone, and she resented the fact that he had obviously been checking up on her. But she took a deep breath, managed to muster a reasonable tone, to say evenly, "I had to go down to the residency. To see Sister Bronagh."

"I suppose that's as good an excuse as any."

"But it's *true,* and please don't take this attitude with me. I don't like it, Jack."

"You don't expect me to believe that's where you *really* were, do you? Visiting a nun?" He laughed hollowly. "Come on, babe—"

"I'm not a liar," she cut in, bristling with anger. Her voice rose, and she added coldly, "Nor do I appreciate being called one."

He ignored this remark. "Why won't you tell me *who* you were with tonight?"

"I was with Sister Bronagh." She tightened her grip on the phone to steady herself. Her exasperation was running high, her patience growing thin.

He laughed again, this time more sardonically. "Sister Bronagh indeed! Come on, babe, don't start getting holier than thou with me. It's Jack you're talking to. *Me. Jack.* Jack your lover, Jack the big man in your life. But is he the *only* man in your life? That's the question."

She realized then that not only had he been drinking again, but that he was, in fact, quite drunk. Although there was no slurring of his speech, she could recognize the signs these days. He became sarcastic, argumentative, and suspicious of her, and all of his insecurities started to show. And of course he enjoyed baiting her, which only infuriated her further. Jack was a bad drunk. In the last few months she had learned that firmness was the only way in which to deal with him, and that if she adopted the stern posture of a school teacher she could somehow get the upper hand. But she didn't want the upper hand with Jack. She wanted an equal partnership, a balanced relationship in which neither one of them was manipulating or controlling the other.

Sounding crisp and cool, she said, "Good night, Jack. Go to bed. I'll call you in the morning."

There was a sudden silence at the other end of the phone.

She heard him suck in his breath, as if he were taken aback that she was about to hang up on him.

She said again, her voice very firm and colder than ever, *"Good night."*

"Hey, wait a minute, Madelana, how about dinner tomorrow night? A quick, quiet little dinner. At my place. Or yours. Or somewhere in your neighborhood. Come on, say yes, honey," he cajoled, unexpectedly much less hostile, almost contrite.

"You know I can't, Jack. I explained earlier in the week that I have to pack on Friday night. In case it's slipped your mind, I'm going to Australia on Saturday morning."

"That's *right! Of course!* I keep forgetting that you're the little career girl dedicated heart and soul to work. Or should I say *big* career girl. Much more appropriate, no? Ah yes, indeedy, *big* career. *Big* job. *Big* ambitions. But tell me one more thing, babe, is work going to keep you warm in bed on cold nights?" He laughed thinly. "I doubt it. You don't need a *big* career, babe. You need a *big* man. Like me. Listen, I've got a great idea. Why don't I come over right now and—"

"Y'all've had too much to drink, Jack Miller! Why you're drunker than a skunk that's been suckling at the moonshine barrel!" she cried, inadvertently slipping into the idiom of her Southern childhood, as she sometimes did when she was angry or overly excited. "Go to bed," she instructed fiercely, "I'll call y'all in the morning." She replaced the receiver quietly, even though she felt like slamming it down hard. She was humiliated by his attitude toward her, and resentful and angry.

I hate the way he makes me feel these days, she said under her breath, opening the cupboard, taking out a small metal strainer. Furiously, she tore the lettuce apart, dropped it in the strainer standing in the sink, let the tap water run on the broken leaves.

She stared morosely at the wall, her mind intently fixed on Jack Miller.

He's a jerk, she thought, and I'm a bigger jerk for continuing to see him. I've known for weeks that the two of us are not making it together. We're going no place fast. I can't tolerate his possessiveness and his accusations, and the drunken scenes he's been creating lately are insupportable.

She ran her hand through her hair distractedly. And he makes me madder than a wet hen in a thunderstorm. Damn it, why do I take this from him?

Opening a drawer, she took out a sharp chopping knife, but her hands were shaking so much she put it down, for fear of cutting herself.

Leaning against the sink for the longest moment, she endeavored to still her fulminating anger.

It's all over between us.

As this unexpected thought penetrated her brain like an arrow hitting its given mark, she felt her tension lessen. And very slowly the shaking began to subside.

It was true. There was nothing left. At least, not for her. Even her sexual desire for him had diminished. His bad behavior was turning her off ever more frequently. I'll break up with him when I get back from Australia, she decided. There's no point in wasting my time with him. I must get on with my own life. I can't baby-sit Jack Miller, which is what I've been doing for several months now. No, I'd better tell him tomorrow. That'll be much kinder than waiting until I come back. Now, why am I trying to be kind to *him?* That dude's led me a real merry dance of late.

Madelana expelled a wearisome sigh. Jack seemed to want to punish her these days. Or was it someone else he was punishing? Himself, perhaps? He had been out of work for several months, and that was proving extremely hard on him. When he worked he was a different man. A whole man. He stopped carousing in bars with his friends and never touched a drop of liquor.

Poor Jack, she thought, the anger unexpectedly falling away. He has so much. Good looks and charm, talent and even brilliance. But he's wasting it all, letting it drain away down the neck of a bottle. It was the boozing that troubled her; and it was the boozing that had come between them. Invariably, he was full of chagrin afterward, and apologetic, but this did not take the sting out of the way he had behaved, the hurt he had inflicted.

It struck her then that he needed her pity more than anything else. Broadway actor, almost but not quite Star, he was a virtuoso performer who could have made it very, very big if he had wanted, gone to Hollywood, conquered the silver screen as he had the legitimate theater, which was his forte. His clean-cut handsomeness and silver-gilt hair and those marvelous baby blues were arresting and made him exceptionally photogenic. And he even had movie star charisma—when he wished to exercise it. He could have been another Paul Newman, or so his peers constantly informed her. It was always on the tip of her tongue to ask "Then why isn't he?" but she never did. Yes, his friends were most admiring of Jack Miller . . . he was an actor's actor, they said. The best. In the same class as Al Pacino and Jack Nicholson. But to her way of thinking, there was something missing in him, something gone askew in his character. If only he were different of temperament.

It seemed to her that Jack wasn't driven, and certainly he wasn't ambitious enough. Maybe that was the reason he was always jabbing at her, why he resented her career . . . because she had an overabundance of ambition, while he had none. Maybe he had had it once, but he didn't anymore.

Madelana let out a knowing laugh. Jack resented her career because at heart he was a male chauvinist. In his oblique way, he had told her that more than once, hadn't he?

She picked up the knife and began to slice a tomato, and she was gratified to see that her hands no longer shook.

Later, after Madelana had eaten her chicken salad, she sat drinking a glass of iced lemon tea in the living room, aimlessly staring at the television set, not really seeing the mindless movie that was playing, and certainly not listening to it.

Lolling back against the cushions, she realized that she was brighter of disposition, and much lighter in spirit. The constricted feeling in her chest had dissipated, and she had to admit that she was full of relief and felt better because she had finally resolved to terminate her relationship with Jack Miller.

Also in the last half hour, she had come to understand that this decision had not been quite so quick or so sudden as she had previously imagined. She had wanted to cut the cord between them for some time, but she had simply not had the guts to do so before.

She wondered why, wondered if she had stayed with Jack these last months out of the fear of being absolutely alone once more?

Patsy Smith had gone back to Boston to live, and Madelana didn't have too many other close friends in New York. Then again, because she worked so hard and kept such long hours, she had hardly any time for socializing with the few women she knew and liked.

But Jack was a different matter.

Since he was in the theater, his leisure hours started after the ten o'clock curtain had dropped. Their odd time schedules had somehow dovetailed neatly.

Several times a week she had stayed late at the store, or taken papers home with her and worked there, until she had met him at Joe Allen's or Sardi's for supper at eleven. And on other nights he had often come up to her apartment after the show, and she had cooked for him, and he had stayed over; and they usually spent Sundays together at his place on East Seventy-ninth Street.

But when he was not in a play, like now, he wanted to see her every night, regardless of her work. That wasn't possible, and she religiously stuck to her own schedule, refusing to be budged by him, and that was when the trouble started. He loved acting with a passion; in a way, it was the center of his life. Yet he couldn't seem to grasp that her work was just as important to her as his was to him. And thus there was conflict between them.

Patsy had introduced them. She had known him for two years now, and she *had* loved him, and he *was* the one person she had grown truly close to in the time she had lived in Manhattan. In a way, he was almost like family, and perhaps that was why she had continued to cling to him when her deepest instincts had told her to run for her life.

Family, she thought again, turning the word over in her mind, then she swung her head and looked at the framed color photograph on the end table. They were all in it . . . her brothers, Young Joe and Lonnie, herself with baby Kerry Anne sitting on her knee, and her mommy and her daddy. How young they looked, even her parents, and there was such joy and love on their sweet and shining faces. Her family would have been charmed by Jack Miller, would have found him entertaining and likable, because he *was* those things, but they wouldn't have approved of him. Not as a boyfriend for her, at any rate.

Her parents and her siblings had considered her to be unique and great things had been expected of her, especially by her mother, and for as far back as she could remember. "You're the one who's going to go out and do it, mavourneen," her mommy would tell her in that lovely lilting voice that had never lost its beguiling Irish brogue. "You're the clever one, Maddy, the one who's been blessed . . . kissed by the gods, to be sure, me darlin'. Why, you're one of the golden girls, Maddy."

Madelana became motionless, as if turned to stone on the sofa, suddenly hearing their voices echoing in her inner ear, every voice so clear and distinct and individualistic . . . Joe . . . Lonnie . . . Kerry Anne . . . her mommy . . . and her daddy . . .

They were dead, yet she still felt very close to them.

Each one of them had left little pieces of themselves behind in her. They were deeply embedded in her heart, and they were with her all the time. And she had such good memories to cherish and they sustained her and gave her enormous strength.

For a time she drifted off, as if in a trance, traveling back into the past in her mind, but after a short while she roused herself and stood up. She turned off the television, went and got her guitar, and brought it back to the sofa.

Tucking her bare feet under her, she played a few chords, adjusted the strings, then began to strum lightly, thinking of her family, reliving those happy times they had spent together. Each of the O'Sheas had been musically gifted, and they had enjoyed many lovely evenings over the years, playing their various instruments, harmonizing together, or singing solo.

And now, quietly, almost to herself, Madelana started to hum one of the old folk ballads which she and her brothers had sung, and when she finally got the feel of it, found the exact beat she wanted, her voice rang out true and pure in the quiet apartment.

"On top of old Smoky, all cover'd with snow, I lost my true lover, for courtin' too slow. Now

courtin's a pleasure, but partin' is grief, a false-hearted lover, is worse than a thief. A thief will just rob you, and take what you have, but a false-hearted lover will send you to your grave. On top of old Smoky, all cover'd with snow, I lost my true lover, for courtin' too slow."

10

She had arrived in New York shaking the dust of Kentucky off the heels of her silver kid boots.

That was in the autumn of 1977, when she was twenty-three years old. It was probably her wry sense of humor that made her characterize herself as "just a poor country girl, a hillbilly who knows nothing much about anything," since, in point of fact, she was neither.

Her full name was Madelana Mary Elizabeth O'Shea, and she had been born just outside Lexington, in the very heart of bluegrass country, in July of 1954.

She was the first daughter of Fiona and Joe O'Shea and she had been adored from the moment she had opened her eyes to the world. She had two older brothers, Joseph Francis Xavier Jr., so named after his father, who was eleven at the time of her birth, and Lonnie Michael Paul, who was then seven. Both boys fell passionately in love with their beautiful baby sister, and it was a love that never dimmed during the boys' tragically short lives.

Everyone petted and indulged her throughout her childhood, and it was a miracle that Madelana grew up to be so unaffected and unspoiled, and this was due in no small measure to her own strength of character and sweetness of nature.

Her father was third-generation Irish-American, and a Kentuckian through and through, but her mother had been born in Ireland, and had come to America in 1940, at the age of seventeen. Fiona Quinn had been dispatched by her older sister and brother to stay with cousins in Lexington, in order to escape the war in Europe. "I'm an evacuee from the old sod," she would say with a bright smile, her green eyes sparkling, enjoying being something of a novelty amongst her cousins and their friends.

Joe O'Shea was twenty-three in 1940, and an engineer who worked for his father in their small family construction business, and he was the best friend of Liam Quinn, Fiona's cousin. It was at Liam's house that Joe first met Fiona, and he had immediately fallen in love with the tall, lissome girl from County Cork. He thought she had the prettiest of faces and the most dazzling of smiles it had ever been his great good fortune to see. They had started courting, and to Joe's delight, Fiona soon confessed that she reciprocated his feelings and they were married in 1941.

After their honeymoon in Louisville, they set up house in Lexington, and in 1943 their first son was born, just a few weeks after his father had embarked for England to fight the war in Europe.

Joe, who was in the U.S. 1st Infantry Division, was initially stationed in England, and later his unit was part of the Omaha Beach Assault Force that landed in Normandy on D-Day, the sixth of June, 1944. He was lucky and survived this and other Allied offensives in the European theater of war, and came home safely at the end of 1945, proudly wearing a Purple Heart pinned to his battle dress.

Once he had settled down to civilian life in Kentucky, Joe had again gone to work in his father's small business, and slowly life for the O'Sheas had returned to normal. In 1947, Lonnie was born, and with the addition of Maddy seven years later, Fiona and Joe decided it might be wisest not to have any more children, wanting to give as much as they could to the three they already had. Most especially, they were thinking of the cost of college educations for the two boys and Maddy. Joe's father had retired, and Joe had taken over the little family business and was making a decent living. Whilst they were not poor, they were not rich either. "Middlin' comfortable," was the way Joe would put it, and he would always add, "But that's no cause for celebratin', or for bein' extravagant."

Joe O'Shea was a good husband and father, Fiona a tender, loving wife, and the proudest of mothers, and they were a happy family, unusually devoted to each other.

Young Joe, Lonnie, and Maddy were inseparable—"the terrible trio," Fiona called them.

Madelana was something of a tomboy when she was growing up and wanted to do everything her brothers did; she swam and fished in the creeks with them, went hunting and trekking in the hills, always tagging along on any expedition, but invariably holding her own.

Riding was her favorite sport and at this she excelled. She became an accomplished equestrian at an early age, being fortunate enough to work out at various horse farms in and around Lexington where thoroughbreds were trained, and where her father did jobs from time to time.

She loved horses, had an understanding of them. Like her father and her brothers, she was keen on racing, and her greatest thrill was to accompany them to Churchill Downs in Louisville when the Kentucky Derby ran. And it was she who cheered loudest of all when a horse they favored won.

From a young age, Maddy was determined never to be outstripped by her brothers, and they, so adoring of her and immensely proud of her good looks, intelligence, independence, and daring do, forever encouraged her. But their mother, constantly shaking her head at the blue jeans and plaid work shirts, and the boyish, boisterous antics, tried to instill in her more ladylike ways.

"Whatever's going to become of you, Maddy O'Shea?" Fiona would demand, clucking with exasperation under her breath. "Just look at you . . . why, to be sure, anybody could be mistakin' you for a stable lad in that getup, and your friends so bonny and feminine in their pretty dresses. You won't be finding a nice young man to go a-courtin' with, no, not looking like that, you will not, me girl. I aim to enroll you in Miss Sue Ellen's dancing class if it's the last thing I do, so you can be learnin' a bit about deportment and gracefulness and femininity. I swear I will, Maddy O'Shea. Be warned, me girl."

Maddy would respond with a vibrant laugh and a jaunty toss of her chestnut head, for this was an old threat. And she would hug her mother tightly then, and promise to mend her ways, and they would sit down at the kitchen table for a cup of hot, steaming chocolate, and talk and talk their hearts away, and they were never anything but the best of friends.

And eventually, just to please her mother, Madelana did attend Miss Sue Ellen's School for Dancing and Deportment in Lexington, taking ballet and tap. As it happened, she had a natural aptitude for dance, and enjoyed her lessons, and it was here that she quickly learned to move with lightness and elegance, where she acquired the dancer's agile grace that she would never lose.

In later years, when she looked back, Madelana took comfort from the fact that she and her brothers had had such a marvelous childhood. There had been large doses of the Catholic religion rammed down them by their mother, and a good deal of discipline from their father, and they had had to work hard at school and to do chores in the house and yard, but it had been one of the happiest times of her life, and it had made her all the things she was.

193

Nobody was more surprised than Fiona when, toward the end of 1964, she learned that she was pregnant again, and the following year, at the age of forty-one, she gave birth to Kerry Anne.

Although the child had been unexpected, she was loved, and her christening was a happy affair. The only thing that slightly marred their joy that day was Young Joe's imminent departure for his tour of duty in Vietnam. He was a private in the U.S. Army and just twenty-two years old.

Sometimes tragedy strikes a family many times in quick succession, and it is so incomprehensible, so inexplicable, it defies belief. So it was with the O'Sheas.

Young Joe was killed at Da Nang in 1966, one year after he had shipped out to Indochina. Lonnie, who had joined the Marines and was also serving in Vietnam, lost his life during the Tet offensive in 1968. He was twenty-one.

And then to their further horror and heartbreak, little Kerry Anne died of complications following a tonsillectomy, shortly before her fifth birthday in 1970.

Reeling from shock and stunned by their enormous grief, Fiona, Joe, and Maddy cleaved to each other, were barely able to handle their anguish and the pain of their sudden and terrible losses over five short and fatal years. It seemed to them that each new blow was more ferocious than the one before, and it was a suffering they found unendurable.

Fiona was never really to recover, remaining forever after bereft and grieving, but despite this, and even though she needed her only living child by her side, she insisted Madelana continue her higher education at Loyola University in New Orleans, when she became eighteen.

Madelana had set her heart on going there some years before, and her parents had approved of this small college run by the Jesuits. Even so, she was reluctant to leave her parents, in particular her mother, who was so dependent on her, and she was more than willing to change her plans.

But Fiona would have none of it, since it had been a long-cherished dream of hers that Madelana attend college. She knew by this time that she was suffering from cancer, but she and Joe scrupulously kept this devastating news from their daughter.

However, four years later, toward the end, Fiona became so debilitated it was no longer possible to hide the medical facts from Maddy, who struggled through her last few months at Loyola fighting despair and endeavoring to hold sorrow at arm's length. The only thing that kept her going during this excruciatingly painful time was the determination not to let her mother down.

Fiona lived long enough to see Maddy graduate with a bachelor's degree in business administration in the summer of 1976. She died two months later.

"Kerry Anne's going was the last nail in your mommy's coffin," Joe kept saying all through the winter of that year, until the words began to sound like a dreadful litany to her.

Or he would sit and stare at Maddy, then ask, with tears welling in his eyes, "Wasn't one son enough to give to my country? Why did Lonnie have to get massacred too? For what?" And before she could say anything in response, he would add with anger and bitterness, "For *nothing,* that's what, Maddy. Young Joe and Lonnie both died for *nothing.*"

Madelana would take his hand and try to comfort him whenever he talked like this, but she never had any answers for her father, and certainly she had none for herself either. Like the majority of Americans, she had scant understanding of the war they were fighting in Vietnam.

After graduating from Loyola, Madelana had found herself a job in the offices of Shilito's Department Store in Lexington.

Despite her hoydenish ways and lack of interest in feminine things as a child, she had fallen in love with clothes in her late teens, and had recognized that she had a great deal of flair when it came to fashion. Retailing attracted her, and when she had been attending college, she had decided she wanted to carve out a career for herself in this field.

Madelana's job in the marketing department at Shilito's had proved to be challenging, and she had found it stimulating and absorbing as well. She had thrown herself into the work, and divided her time between the store and the family home, where she had continued to live with her father.

Joe had begun to worry her considerably in the early part of 1977, for he had grown more morose than ever, and apathetic, since her mother's death, and unlike her mother, he seemed unable to draw solace from religion. He still continued to mutter to Maddy that his sons had died in vain, and she would frequently find him staring at their photographs on the mantelpiece in the living room, his eyes filled with hurt and bafflement, his face grown painfully thin.

Maddy's heart ached for him, and she did everything possible to take him out of himself, to give him a reason to go on living, but it was to no avail.

By the spring of that year, Joe O'Shea had become a shadow of the handsome, jocular man he had once been, and when he died suddenly of a heart attack in May, Maddy realized, in the midst of her searing grief, that she was not really surprised. It was as if he had willed himself to die, as if he had desperately wanted to join Fiona in the grave.

Once she had buried her father, Madelana began to sort out and settle his business affairs. He had left everything in order and so this task was relatively easy for her to do.

His small construction company had been in the black for a number of years, and she was able to sell the equipment, the materials, and the "goodwill" to Pete Andrews, who had been her father's right-hand man and wanted to keep the business going for himself and the handful of old employees. And though it was wrenching for her, she had also sold the house where she had grown up, along with most of her mother's furniture, and moved into an apartment in Lexington.

It was not very long after this that she had started to understand just how difficult living in Lexington was going to be for her from now on.

As much as her beloved bluegrass country was part of her, in her blood, each day grew increasingly painful. Wherever she went, wherever she looked, she saw their faces . . . her parents, Kerry Anne, Young Joe, and Lonnie. She yearned for them and for the past, and for the way things once were.

Her father's passing had opened up her old grief for the others who had died before him.

She knew she had to get away. Perhaps she could come back one day and rejoice in the past. But now she had to put distance between herself and this place. The heartbreak was too fresh, too potent, and her emotions were far too near the surface for her to draw any kind of solace from the memories of her family.

Only through the passing of time would her pain lessen, and only then would she be able to draw a measure of comfort from her remembrances, and find peace in them.

And so Madelana made the decision to move to the North, to go to New York City, to start a whole new life.

She was very brave.

She had no job, knew no one, had no contacts, but at least she had a roof over her head when she arrived in Manhattan. This had already been arranged for her before she had left Lexington.

The Sisters of Divine Providence, a teaching

order of nuns from Kentucky, and one of the first such orders to be founded in America, maintained a residency in New York. Rooms could be rented at a nominal charge, and were available to Catholic girls and young women from all over the world.

And it was to this residency, the Jeanne D'Arc, that Maddy went in October of 1977.

Within a week of her arrival at West Twenty-fourth Street, she had settled in and was beginning to get her bearings.

The sisters were warm and helpful, the girls friendly, and the residency itself was pleasant, convenient, and well run. It had five floors of rooms, with showers and bathrooms on each floor. There was a small but rather beautiful chapel, where the young residents and the sisters could pray or meditate, and close by were the common rooms—a library and a television parlor. Other facilities included a kitchen and a canteen in the basement, for the cooking and serving of meals, plus a laundry room, and lockers for the storage of personal belongings.

One of the first things Maddy had done was to put her nest egg of forty-thousand dollars in the bank, opening both checking and saving accounts. After this she had had her own phone installed in her room on the fourth floor. Patsy Smith, who lived across the corridor from her, had recommended that she do so, explaining that it would simplify her life.

She had then gone looking for a job.

Ever since she had decided to make a career for herself in retailing, Maddy's role model had been the late Emma Harte, one of the greatest merchant princes of all time. In the past few years she had read everything about the renowned Emma that she could lay her hands on, and Harte's in New York was the only store where she wanted to work. But she quickly discovered there were no vacancies when she went for an interview. The personnel manager had been impressed with her, however, and had promised to be in touch if something suitable came up. Her résumé and application had been duly filed for future reference.

By the end of her third week in the city, Maddy had managed to find employment in the business offices of Saks Fifth Avenue.

Exactly one year later there was finally an opening at Harte's and she had grabbed it immediately, filled with enthusiasm at the opportunity to work there, and within six months she had made her mark.

And she had come to the attention of Paula O'Neill.

Paula had spotted her in the marketing department, had been struck by her personal style, pleasant demeanor, efficiency, and vivid intelligence. Thereafter, Paula had constantly singled her out, given her a variety of special assignments, and had ultimately moved her to work in the executive offices. A year after this, in July of 1980, Paula had promoted Maddy to be her personal assistant, actually creating this job for her.

With this big promotion and a sizable increase in salary, Madelana had at last felt secure enough to look for her own apartment. She had found one she liked in the East Eighties, and had had her possessions shipped up from the storage warehouse in Kentucky. And she had finally left the residency, feeling a little pang as she had said good-bye to Sister Bronagh and Sister Mairéad.

The first meal she had cooked at the new apartment had been for Jack and Patsy one Sunday night, just before Patsy had gone back to Boston to live.

It had been a lovely evening, very celebratory, and Jack had kept them amused and laughing. But she and Patsy had grown a bit sad toward the end, knowing they would be living in different cities soon. They had promised faithfully not to grow apart, and they had corresponded on a fairly regular basis ever since.

With her new promotion, Madelana's life had changed in other ways, and a whole new world had been opened up to her. Paula had brought her over to London so that she would understand the inner workings of the famed Knightsbridge store, and she had visited the Harte stores in Yorkshire and Paris. And twice Paula had taken her to Texas, although this had been on Sitex business rather than Harte's. She had discovered how much she enjoyed traveling, going to new places, and meeting new people.

Her first year as Paula's assistant had fled by, filled with excitement, challenges, and continuing successes, and very quickly Maddy had begun to recognize that she had found her niche in life. It was at Harte's of New York, where she was a star.

11

Playing some of her favorite old folk songs had soothed Madelana. She was feeling at ease with herself at last.

Earlier in the evening, she had half expected Jack Miller to call her back, had been dreading that he would. But he had not. Now, at last, she was filled with a peacefulness, and she was completely calm. She got up, put the guitar to one side, and went over to the desk near the window.

The files she had brought home with her from the store were stacked and waiting for her attention. She sat down, glanced at the clock, saw that it was almost midnight. But that did not matter to her. She was wide awake and full of energy. Stamina had always been one of her strong suits, and she knew she could complete the work quite easily within two or three hours.

Picking up her pen, she sat back in the chair, staring at the wall, thinking for a moment.

The needlepoint sampler which hung there, and which her mother had made for her when she had been a little girl, suddenly held her attention. It had hung above her bed in her room in Lexington, and it was one of the things she had brought with her when she had first moved to New York.

If your day is hemmed with prayer it is less likely to unravel, her mother had stitched in royal blue wool against the beige background, and she had bordered the sampler with tiny flowers in brilliant primary colors.

Madelana smiled inwardly, seeing Fiona's lovely image in her mind's eye. I think she'd be proud of me, proud of what I've made of my life, and of where I am today. I know she wouldn't approve of Jack, of course. I don't believe I do, either. Not for me. Not anymore. I'll call him in the morning, ask him to have lunch, and I'll end it face to face, she added to herself, reiterating her earlier decision in her mind. That's the only decent thing to do. I can't tell him over the phone.

She put down the pen and began to shuffle

through her files, looking for the one which held her notes and the material for the fashion exhibit.

Each of these folders pertained to the forthcoming celebrations for Harte's sixtieth anniversary. Paula's theme was simple, but clever in its simplicity: sixty years of stylish retailing from the jazz age to the space age.

Paula had put her in charge of the anniversary program at the New York store, and she was responsible for the overall planning of different events and shows, and telexes had been flying back and forth across the Atlantic for many, many months. Ideas had been approved, or knocked down, by Paula, and merchandise ordered, campaigns put in work, advertising art completed, brochures and invitations printed. The files represented endless hours of work and thought and dedication, and she must complete the last few memorandums about each event and campaign tonight.

Maddy's own special projects included Fragrance Month; a stylish art show in the gallery of the store, highlighting decorative objects from the Art Deco period; an exhibit of real and costume jewelry from the Art Deco period to the present, featuring some of the world's greatest jewelry designers. These included Verdura, Jeanne Toussaint of Cartier, and Renée Puissant of Van Cleef and Arpels, and their work from decades past; Alain Boucheron and David Webb were two of the designers of the present who would be showcased. At the other end of the price scale, she had decided to highlight the unique costume jewelry and fabulous fakes designed by Kenneth Jay Lane, along with a collection of paste pieces from the nineteen thirties.

Her hands came to rest on the fashion folder at last. This held information and details of the fashion exhibition which Paula planned to hold at the London store next spring. Maddy had convinced her to bring it over to New York in the late summer of 1982. Having agreed, Paula had then suggested she try to expand the exhibit, by adding clothes borrowed from American women who had either been on the best dressed list at some time or other, or who owned a garment by a top couturier, whether living or dead. And this she had done—with great success.

The nucleus of the couture exhibition were clothes which had once belonged to Emma Harte, and which Emma had kept in good condition for years before her death. Paula had also preserved these clothes after they had been in the Fashion Fantasia exhibit at the London store some ten or eleven years ago.

Emma's clothing in the show dated as far

back as the early twenties, and included a Paquin evening coat of brown velvet trimmed with a huge fox collar, a short evening dress with a big bow on the back, designed in 1926 by Poiret, and a blue-and-green beaded evening gown by Vionnet. This was apparently in extraordinary condition, and looked stunning in the photograph the London marketing department had sent over. It seemed hardly dated at all to Madelana.

Sifting through the other drawings and photographs, she poured over Emma's Chanel suits from the twenties, a huge collection of her hats by French and English couturiers, outfits by Lanvin, Balmain, and Balenciaga, two Fortuny pleated silk evening gowns, evening pajamas by Molyneux, and an exquisitely cut coat by Pauline Trigère, designed in the fifties but as chic now as it had been then. There were other modern outfits by Dior, Givenchy, Yves Saint Laurent, Bill Blass, and Hardy Amies.

Maddy began to make her notes, creating the exact order in which she wanted the drawings and photographs to appear in the catalog. She had already put this into work with the art department, and they were pressuring her for these illustrations.

One of Maddy's favorites was a charmeuse evening dress by Mainbocher, which according to Paula, her grandfather Paul McGill had bought for Emma in New York in 1935. It was trimmed with clustered silk flowers stitched as epaulets on the shoulders, and worn with a matching muff made of the same clustered silk flowers.

Picking up a photograph of Emma wearing the dress, Madelana studied it for a moment. God, what a beautiful woman she was, she murmured to herself, and decided to lead off with this particular picture.

After she had finished with the fashion exhibit file, she dealt with the information required for the Fragrance Month, and then tackled the Art Deco show, leaving the final details of the jewelry exhibit until last. She worked relentlessly for another hour and a half, making sure there could be no mistakes whatsoever while she was in Australia.

At two in the morning she stood in her little kitchen waiting for the kettle to boil for a cup of instant coffee. And as she carried this back into the living room a moment later, she braced herself for at least another hour of work.

Well, Maddy thought, seating herself at the desk, if Emma Harte could work around the clock, then so can I. After all, she has been my inspiration and my idol for years, and I want to emulate her in every way I possibly can.

12

"How did you manage to complete everything?" Paula asked, eyeing the files she had just read, then glancing across at Madelana.

"I stayed up until three-thirty this morning."

"Oh Maddy, you didn't have to do that. We could have finished the files together on the plane, and telexed our final instructions from Australia." As Paula spoke, she could not help feeling slightly relieved that they would not have to do this.

"But it's better this way, isn't it, Paula?" Madelana asked. "We'll have free minds, and we'll be able to concentrate that much more keenly on the boutiques with this stuff out of the way."

"That's perfectly true," Paula agreed. "And I must say, your hard work, what you've accomplished, is very commendable." Paula's violet eyes narrowed and she studied the other woman closely, then began to laugh. "And what's even more remarkable is that burning the midnight oil doesn't show on your face."

"Doesn't it?" Madelana laughed with her boss, whom she not only admired and respected, but genuinely cared for. "Thank you, it's nice of you to say so."

Paula tapped the folders. "I like the way you've managed to tie in so many different products and merchandise. By pulling everything together in the way you have, you've also strengthened my theme considerably. To be truthful, when I came up with the idea of calling our sixtieth celebration *From the Jazz Age to the Space Age,* I wondered if I was making it far too broad to be effective. But you've helped to prove yet again that I wasn't, and frankly, you've even gone a step further than Marketing has in London. That's what has been so exciting for me this last hour as I've read your memos."

Paula was a firm believer in giving credit where it was due, and now she added, "Congratulations. Some of the things you've thought of are brilliant, and I'm delighted with your efforts."

Madelana filled with satisfaction and her face was wreathed in smiles. "Thanks, Paula, but don't let's forget that your theme *was* clever, and very challenging. And everything was already there really, just waiting to be pulled out of the reference books and the research files."

"Not to mention your clever little head!" Paula exclaimed. She picked up the folder marked FRAGRANCE PROMOTION and opened it, took out the top sheet.

After glancing at the paper again, she said, "Some of this stuff's really fascinating. For instance, *I* never knew that Chanel actually considered the number five to be her lucky number, and that that was the reason she called her first perfume *Chanel No. 5.* Nor was I aware that Jean Patou created *Joy* in 1931, and that Jeanne Lanvin brought out *Arpège* in 1927. Here we have three of the world's greatest perfumes, which are still enormously popular today, and they are actually fifty years old."

"Quality always lasts, doesn't it," Madelana said. "And I thought some of those odd little items were kind of interesting, too. Perhaps we can use them somewhere in our promotional material, or in our advertisements."

"Absolutely. That's a terrific idea. And you

might tell the art department to make up display cards featuring a few of the items, for the counters in Perfumery."

"Okay. Talking about displays, could you spare me a minute, please? I'd like you to see a piece of artwork I had created, I hope for use here in the store. If you approve."

"Let's go and look at it then." Paula jumped up, followed Madelana into the adjoining office.

An easel had been placed in one corner, near the window which looked out onto Fifth Avenue. Madelana picked up a large display card and put it on the easel. She said, "I'd like to use this on silk banners throughout the store, and if I could get a yea or a nay from you now, I'd appreciate it. The banners have to be ordered today, at the *latest* on Monday, if they're going to be ready for the commencement of the celebrations in December."

"I understand. So come on, let's see it."

Madelana flipped the tracing paper that protected the hardboard card, and then stepped aside.

Paula stood staring at the bold lettering, which read: FROM THE JAZZ AGE TO THE SPACE AGE: 1921 TO 1981.

Underneath the giant-sized slogan was a smaller subheading: *Sixty years of style and elegance at Harte's.*

Paula continued to study it.

This was her slogan, the words she had written down over a year ago, when she had first started to plan the anniversary celebrations and special events. The only thing which made this suggested banner different to the ones created by the marketing department in London was a portrait of Emma Harte etched in shadowy form behind the lettering.

Paula said nothing. Her eyes grew thoughtful.

Watching her intently, and anxiously, waiting for her reaction, Madelana held her breath. When Paula remained silent, she said worriedly, "You don't like it, do you?"

"I'm not sure, to be honest," Paula murmured, then hesitated. She moved around the office, looking at the board from different angles. "Yes . . . yes . . . I think I do," she finally said, her voice more positive. "But I wouldn't want to use my grandmother's image on *every* banner in the store. I think that would be in poor taste, and overkill, really. And I certainly don't want to go over the top. But the more I look at this, I think we *could* use it, in a *limited* way . . . in some of the big halls in the London and Paris stores, and on the first floor here. Oh, and in the Leeds store, too! That's a *must,* I suppose, since that's where it all began."

"Are you really sure? You still sound a bit uncertain."

"No, I'm positive. You can order the banners, and why don't you get enough for the other stores. We might as well have them made in New York. They can be shipped out air express to London and Paris when they're ready."

"Good idea. And I'm glad you approve of the things we've done. Everyone's going to be thrilled that you're so pleased, and that we can now go forward with these plans."

Paula half smiled. "Well, I suppose that's about it, as far as the special events are concerned. Come back to my office for a moment, though, would you, Madelana, there's something I wish to discuss with you."

"Yes," Maddy said, hurrying after her, wondering what this was all about. All of a sudden there had been an anxious note in Paula's voice, which was unusual for her, and therefore disconcerting.

Paula walked around her desk and sat down. Madelana took the chair facing her, perched on the edge, and looked across at her boss, asking herself if trouble was brewing.

Paula sat back, steepled her fingers, and contemplated the tips of them for a moment. Then she said, "I want to take you into my confidence about something, Madelana, but I must stress that it *is* confidential. I haven't mentioned it to Shane or Emily yet, although actually that's really because I haven't had the right opportunity. However, since you work so closely with me, I thought you should know immediately."

"You have my confidentiality, Paula. I'd never discuss your business with anyone. That's not my way."

"I'm aware of that, Madelana."

Paula sat back, her eyes serious. She said carefully, "I've had several phone calls from a Harvey Rawson during the past few days, which I'm sure you know, since you put a couple of those calls through to me."

Madelana nodded.

"He's a lawyer with a Wall Street firm, and a friend of Michael Kallinski's. He's been doing some work for me. Private work."

"You don't have a legal problem, do you?"

"No, no, Maddy. For a long time I've wanted to go into an expansion program in the United States . . . I've wanted to take Harte stores right across the country, and I've been looking for an existing chain to buy, with that purpose in mind. Michael's known about this, and he put the word out some time ago, without mentioning my name, of course. Last week he heard about a small suburban chain through Harvey

Rawson. Before I left for New York, I spoke to Michael, and told him he could tell Harvey I was the one interested in the chain and to get in touch with me directly."

"So Harvey Rawson's actually representing you in the buy out," Madelana asserted, sitting up straighter in the chair, pinning her eyes on her boss.

"It's not a buy out yet. But yes, he is representing me, inasmuch as he's approaching the chain, but without saying I'm the interested party."

"Yes, I understand. That would jack up the price, and then some, if they knew it was you. But I think this is a wonderful move you're making, Paula, and very visionary." Madelana's excitement was reflected on her face and she leaned forward with eagerness. "What's the name of the chain? Where are the stores located?"

"The chain is called Peale and Doone, and there are seven stores altogether, in Illinois and Ohio," Paula explained. "This is not the type of chain I was originally looking for—I'd prefer my stores to be in big cities. Still, Peale and Doone would be a beginning."

"Are they a public company?"

"No, private. And next week Harvey will ascertain whether or not the stockholders are interested in selling, and then we'll take it from there. He'll be in touch with me, and with Michael, and they both have the Australian itinerary, at least the part of it that's planned," she finished, sitting back in her chair.

Standing up, recognizing that Paula had just brought this conversation to a close, Madelana said, "Thanks for telling me about your plans, Paula, for sharing with me. I'm flattered, and I'm looking forward to working with you on the expansion program."

"Good. I hoped you would be. I want you to be very involved with me in this, Maddy." Paula also stood. Lifting the stack of files off her desk, she brought them to Madelana.

Together the two women walked across the room, paused at the door to Madelana's office, turned to face each other.

Paula remarked, "You seem to be finished, so there's no reason for you to come back after lunch, if you don't want to. I don't need you for the rest of the day, and I'm sure you've plenty to do between now and tomorrow morning."

"Oh thank you, that's nice of you, Paula, but I'm sure I'll be back, and anyway, I want to pick up a couple of track suits in Active Sportswear. Didn't you say that was the only way to fly? To Australia, I mean."

Paula laughed. "It is, and I'm afraid the suit

is not very elegant, but it *is* very practical. And don't forget your Reeboks or a pair of tennis shoes. Los Angeles to Sydney is around thirteen to fourteen hours flying time, depending on the winds, and every part of the body seems to swell up. Not only that, I find that I sleep much more comfortably when I'm dressed in a track suit."

"Then I'll be sure to get myself properly outfitted after I've had lunch with Jack—" Madelana broke off, and her face instantly changed, grew taut with anxiety.

Paula did not miss this. She frowned, asked softly, in concern. "Is something wrong?"

Maddy shook her head. "Not really," she began and again stopped abruptly. There was a closeness between Paula and herself, and they had always been open and forthright with each other. "I shouldn't say that, Paula, because it's not true. Things are pretty lousy between Jack and me, and I'm going to break off with him. I want to get it out of the way before I leave. That's why I'm having lunch with him."

"I am sorry," Paula murmured, giving her a small, sympathetic smile, touching her arm lightly. "I thought everything was working well between the two of you. At least that's the impression you gave the last time we spoke about him when you were in London."

"It was then, and he's a nice guy in many

ways. But there's such a lot of conflict between us. I think he resents me these days, and resents my career." Madelana shook her head. "There's no future in it as far as I can see."

Paula was silent, remembering words of Emma's, words uttered at a time when she had been where Madelana was today. She said quietly, "Many years ago, when I was having great difficulties in my first marriage, my grandmother gave me a bit of advice that I've never forgotten. She said, 'If something's not working, then don't be afraid to end it whilst you're still young enough to start again, to find happiness with someone else.' Grandy was a very wise woman. And I can only reiterate those words of hers to you, Maddy, and add that you must trust your own instincts. From what I know of you, they've never let you down yet."

Paula paused, gave her a quick, penetrating look, and went on, "Personally, I think you're about to do the right thing. The best thing for you."

"I know I am. And thanks for caring, Paula. I'll break up with Jack today, make it clean and swift. And then I want to concentrate on my career."

13

It rose up against the azure sky like some great monolith, an immense, unyielding structure of black glass and steel. It was a statement of wealth and privilege, prestige and power, and a glittering monument to the founding fathers of a gargantuan business empire.

The McGill Tower was its name, and it dominated the skyline of Sydney.

The man who had conceived this extraordinary and beautiful edifice, and caused it to be built, occupied the tower in the manner of a magnate from a time long past, completely in control, overseeing and operating all that he owned from this stylish, modern command post, and doing so with a shrewdness, wisdom, and fairness that went far beyond his years.

The black glass tower was his true domain.

He worked there from early morning until late at night, and during the business week he frequently lived there. His executive offices and his penthouse flat were situated one above the other, and occupied the entire two top floors of the building.

Late on this Monday afternoon, the man stood with his back to the immense sweep of plate glass which formed the window-wall at one end of his private office, and which offered a panoramic view of Sydney Harbour and the city. With his head tilted to one side, his eyes narrowed in concentration, he was listening attentively to his visitor, a young American businessman.

Always the most handsome of Emma Harte's grandsons, at thirty-five Philip McGill Amory was in his prime and at his full power. He had magnetism, and a mystique in international business circles and with the press, and to many people he was an enigma. Like his mother and his sister, he had inherited Paul McGill's coloring. His hair was the same glossy black and his eyes were that uncanny blue which was almost violet, and he possessed the vitality and virile looks and height which had made his grandfather such an arresting man.

Today he was wearing a stone-colored light gabardine suit that was fashionably cut, and he was perfectly groomed from the collar of his deep-blue shirt to the tip of his dark brown loafers that gleamed like highly polished glass.

"And so," his visitor was saying, "that's the story. And before I put up a couple of million dollars—U.S. dollars that is—I thought I'd better high-tail it over here and get your advice. Shane told me, before I left London, that if I felt the need, I *should* come and talk things over with you, because you know more about opal mining than anybody else."

Philip let out a deep chuckle.

"Not quite, Mr. Carlson. I'm afraid my brother-in-law tends to exaggerate, but I'm fairly knowledgeable, yes. We've been mining opals for years—among other things. One of our subsidiaries, McGill Mining, was founded by my great-grandfather in 1906, a few years after the famous black opal field at Lightning Ridge was discovered around 1903. But to get back to your situation, from what you've told me so far, I don't believe you've been getting the best guidance. If I were you, I'd move with some caution, think twice before putting your money into this syndicate you've been telling me about."

Steve Carlson sat up straighter, gave Philip a questioning look. "You don't think it's some sort of scam, do you?" he asked, his voice rising nervously, sudden anxiety filling his eyes.

Philip shook his head. "No, no, not at all," he answered swiftly and emphatically. "But we've heard of Jarvis Lanner, and whilst he's honest enough, as far as we've been able to ascertain, he's hardly the right man to be advising you about opal mining in the outback."

"That's not the way he presents himself."

"Maybe not. But he's a pommy jackeroo, for God's sake!"

Carlson looked baffled. *"Pommy jackeroo. What's that?"*

Philip tried, unsuccessfully, to smother a laugh. "Sorry, I shouldn't be confusing you by using Australian slang. It means an English immigrant who's a greenhorn."

"Oh, I see." Carlson nodded, then continued, "It did strike me, a few days ago, that Jarvis Lanner didn't know as much as he professed, that's why I came running to you, I guess."

Philip made no comment. He strolled over to his desk, stood behind it, regarding the young man for a moment, feeling sorry for him. Now here was a jackeroo, if ever he'd seen one. Wanting to help him, and also to bring the meeting to a close, Philip now said, "I think the best thing I can do for you, Mr. Carlson, is to put you in touch with a couple of reputable mining experts and some leading geologists. They'll be able to steer you in the right direction. Would you like me to do that?"

"Well, gee, yes, I guess so, and I really appreciate that you've taken the time and trouble to see me. But just as a matter of interest, what's *your* opinion of Queensland, as far as opals are concerned? Don't you think it offers as much as I've been led to believe?"

"I wouldn't say that, no."

Philip sat down, pulled a pad toward him, reached for his gold pen. "A lot of prospectors and miners will tell you that the Queensland fields still have a lot to offer, and I suppose that's true, in certain ways. But I doubt you'll find much precious opal there. That's very rare. Plenty of common opal, of course, in the Queensland fields. Jarvis Lanner was not lying to you when he told you that. But I do stress *common* opal. You indicated to me that you want to mine *quality* stones."

"Yes." Carlson got up off the sofa, meandered over to the desk, took the chair facing it. "Where do *you* think I should do my mining, Mr. Amory?"

"There are any number of places," Philip responded with a light shrug of his shoulders, not wanting to be drawn on this one, or held responsible for making a recommendation that might turn out to be the wrong one for young Carlson. But he had no wish to appear discourteous either, and so he said, "Our company's still mining at Lightning Ridge in New South Wales, and also at Coober Pedy. That's actually Australia's largest opal center where we get our exquisite light opal from. Then there's Mintabie, in South Australia. Prospectors have been mining there very successfully since about 1976."

"So it's a new field."

"No, it was discovered in 1931, but lack of water, very harsh conditions, and bloody awful equipment made it hard to coax the opal out of the ground, prevented proper mining for many, many years. Today's modern machinery has opened it up pretty good. In any case, let me give you the names and phone numbers of the experts I mentioned. Go and talk to them. I'm confident they'll put you on the right track. They'll also be able to tell you whether or not you should invest in the syndicate Lanner recommended to you."

"Do you think that group might be A-okay then?"

"I never said there was anything wrong with the syndicate, merely that you should think twice about investing your money with it,"

226

Philip was swift to remind the other man. "And I pointed out that you'd not received the best advice from Lanner." Philip smiled faintly, and not giving Carlson a chance to say anything, he murmured, "Excuse me," picked up the gold pen for the second time, and began to write in his neat, rapid hand.

"Sure, go ahead," Steve Carlson said, somewhat after the fact, and sat back in the chair, his scrutiny keen. He was impressed with this man who had agreed to see him so quickly and without fuss. Admittedly, he'd had the best introduction. On the other hand, tycoons of Amory's caliber and power were hard to get to personally, even when members of the family opened the door. They were usually too busy, up to their eyeballs in high finance and balance sheets, to be bothered with strangers wanting advice. Invariably they had assistants stand in for them. But not this cowboy, who seemed like a decent enough guy, unaffected, with no bullshit about him. He'd been struck dumb when he'd first met him an hour ago. Philip McGill Amory was so goddamned good looking he ought to be in front of a movie camera in Hollywood, for God's sake, not behind a desk. That handsome face, those mesmerizing blue eyes, the gleaming teeth, and the very deep tan had to be seen to be believed. And what about the fabulous suit he was wearing and the custom-made voile shirt, not to mention the sapphire cuff links? Why, this guy was larger than life, more like a superstar than a businessman. He hadn't expected Amory to have a mustache though. He decided it was dashing, gave the tycoon the look of a riverboat gambler . . . no, a buccaneer.

Steve Carlson suppressed the laughter rising in his throat, thinking that there were surely plenty of pirates around these days—all plowing the waters of Big Business. But Amory didn't have the reputation for being a predator, one of those modern-day corporate raiders who swooped down on other companies and commandeered them for their own ends. Amory didn't need to raid anybody, did he? Not with a conglomerate the size of the McGill Corporation to play with, and keep him busy. It was worth millions, no, billions.

Carlson shifted in his chair, gave Philip a glance that was full of speculation. I bet this cowboy has one helluva private life, a real ball, the young American thought with a stab of envy tinged with admiration. With his physique and looks, all that power, all that dough, women probably drool all over him. Boy, oh boy, what I wouldn't give to be in that pair of handmade Italian loafers just for one night.

Philip flipped the intercom. "Maggie?"

"Yes?"

"Mr. Carlson is about to leave. I'm giving him a list of names. Please affix the appropriate telephone numbers, will you?"

"Certainly."

Philip strode around the desk.

Carlson jumped up, took the sheet of paper being offered, walked with him to the door.

Philip shook the young man's hand firmly. "Lots of luck, Mr. Carlson. I'm certain it'll all pan out."

"Gee, thanks, Mr. Amory. I sure am grateful for your time, and the advice you've given me."

"My pleasure," Philip answered, and motioned to his secretary, who was standing waiting near her desk. "Look after Mr. Carlson, would you please, Maggie?" he added before stepping back into his inner sanctum and closing the door firmly behind him.

Alone at last, and glad to be, Philip ambled over to the plate glass window-wall and looked out toward the harbor. It was the beginning of spring and the weather had been glorious all day. Any number of sailboats were out there on the bright water, racing in front of the wind, their multicolored spinnakers billowing straight out, the mainsails set out wide over the sides, catching every bit of the wind following behind them.

What a beautiful sight it was . . . Sydney Harbour Bridge so majestic in the distance, the white racing yachts and their colorful spinnakers, the glittering, sunlit sea, and off to the side, the Opera House with its unique roof of curved white demidomes that from this angle looked like the giant sails of a galleon set against the edge of the sea and the powder-blue sky.

A smile touched Philip's eyes. He had loved this city since he was a boy, and to him there was no sight in the world quite like the Sydney harbor. It never failed to give him pleasure, especially when he surveyed it from this vantage point.

As he turned away from the window, he made a mental note to have the spinnaker on his own racing yacht checked. The big parachute was made of gossamer-thin nylon and attention had to be paid to it and to the other sails. He smiled wryly to himself. Yacht racing was an expensive hobby these days. A full suit of sails, ranging from the light-weather spinnaker to heavy-weight Kevlar for a storm mainsail, cost just under a million Australian dollars.

There was a knock on the door. It opened, and Barry Graves, his personal assistant, poked his head around it, grinning. "Can I come in?"

"Sure," Philip said, walking over to his desk.

"Got kangeroos in his top paddock then, has he?" Barry asked, a brow lifting eloquently.

The two men exchanged knowing looks and then they both started to laugh.

"No," Philip said, "he's not crazy. Carlson's just young and inexperienced. He's been bitten by the adventure bug, I guess. Apparently he heard somewhere that Australia supplies ninety-five percent of the world's opals, and he decided to come over here, try his luck, and invest his inheritance in opal mining."

"Another jackeroo." Barry sighed. "Poor sod. Oh, well, I guess there's one born every minute. What's he to Shane?"

"Nothing really. Carlson's brother-in-law is one of Shane's top executives at O'Neill International in New York, and Shane was just trying to do the guy a favor. The kid went to see him in London and Shane told him to check with me before he did anything wild."

"Good thing he did, too." Barry hovered at the side of the desk, went on rapidly. "I just came in to say goodnight, Philip. If you don't need me for anything else, I'd like to push off. Committee meeting at the tennis club tonight."

"Go ahead, Barry."

"Thanks. Oh, there's just one thing—do you want me to send a car to pick Paula up at the airport tomorrow morning?"

"No, thanks anyway, but it's not necessary. My mother's taking care of that."

"Good-o." Barry headed for the door. He paused as he went out, swung to face Philip. "Don't stay too late tonight."

"I won't. I'm driving out to Rose Bay in a little while, to have dinner with my mother."

"Give Daisy my best."

"I will."

"See you tomorrow, Philip."

Philip nodded, turned to the papers on his desk, and began to work. Just before six o'clock he buzzed Maggie on the intercom and told her to go home.

"Thanks, Philip."

"Oh and Maggie, please call down to the garage and tell Ken to have the car outside at seven."

"I will. Good night."

"Good night, Maggie." He flipped off the intercom, and went on working on his papers with the diligence and dedication that had been instilled in him by his grandmother years before.

From the moment he had taken his first breath, in June of 1946, it had been understood by his mother and father, and everyone else in the family, that Philip McGill Amory would be raised and groomed to run the McGill Corporation in Australia.

Before he had shot himself to death in 1939, after being partially paralysed in a near-fatal car crash, Paul McGill had drawn a new will. In it he had bequeathed everything he owned to Emma Harte, his common-law wife of sixteen years.

His immense personal fortune, personal real estate, and other personal possessions in Australia, England, and America he left directly to Emma, to do with as she wished. But the business empire in Australia and his big block of shares in Sitex Oil of America, the company he had founded in Texas, were to be held in trust by Emma for Daisy, the only child they had had together, and any offspring Daisy herself might one day have.

From 1939 until 1969, Emma herself had run the McGill Corporation, both at close range in Sydney, and long distance from London. She had managed to do this successfully with the help of trusted appointees, some of whom had worked for Paul McGill until his death. These men, the managing directors of the various companies within the conglomerate, carried out her instructions and were responsible for the day-to-day running of their divisions. These were diverse, ranged from the mining of opals and minerals to coal fields, land development, and commercial real estate, and included the family sheep station at Coonamble.

The McGill family's vast business enterprises, which were now the responsibility of Philip, had begun with that sheep station, one of the largest in New South Wales. Called Dunoon, it had been founded in 1852 by Philip's great-great-grandfather, Andrew McGill, a Scottish sea captain, who was a free settler in the Antipodes. The McGill Corporation, as such, had been created by his great-grandfather, Bruce McGill, and later expanded to become one of the most important companies in the world by his grandfather, Paul.

When he was still only a very little boy, Emma had begun to talk to Philip about Australia, telling him of the wonders and beauty and riches of that extraordinary land. And she had filled his head with adventurous yarns about his grandfather, speaking to him about Paul so beautifully, so vividly, and with such an enduring love she had brought the man to life for the small child. Certainly Philip sometimes felt as though he had actually known his grandfather.

As he grew older, Emma had explained that one day Paul's mighty empire, which took *her* so frequently to Australia, would belong to him and Paula, but that he would run it, as she herself was doing on behalf of their mother and them.

Philip had been six years old when Emma had first taken him out to Sydney with his parents, Daisy and David Amory, and his sister, and he had fallen in love with it from the first moment he had set foot on Australian ground. That love had never waned.

Philip had been educated in England, attending Wellington, his grandfather's old school, but at seventeen he had rebelled, had told Emma and his parents that he wanted to leave school, that he had no intention of going to a university. He had explained, and in no uncertain terms, that the time had come for him to start learning about the business he was supposed to run when he was old enough.

Eventually his father had given in, had shrugged philosophically, knowing he was not going to win the day.

Emma's attitude had been somewhat similar. She had brought Philip to work with her, hiding a smile on that first day, knowing that her grandson had not the slightest idea of what was in store for him. And so it had begun—Emma's relentless training program which demanded complete dedication. She was stern, exacting, and the hardest taskmaster he had ever met. She insisted on excellence in all things, and diligence and concentration, and his life was hers until the time came when he had absorbed the precepts of her business ethos.

But Emma was eminently fair, and Philip had eventually come to understand that his grandmother's unremitting pounding on himself, his sister, and his cousins was merely her way of ensuring they would be able to hold their own when they were out on their own, and when she was no longer there to guide or protect them.

During the years of his training, Philip traveled constantly to Australia with Emma, and whenever possible he spent his holidays there, invariably going up to Dunoon at Coonamble, wanting to learn as much as he could about their sheep station. Sometimes Emma went with him, and he enjoyed it even more when she did, because she would reminisce about the old days, the times she had spent there with Paul, and he was always captivated by her stories.

In 1966, when he was twenty, Emma sent Philip to live permanently in Australia.

She wanted him to learn firsthand about the business empire he would operate and control as chief executive officer and chairman of the board.

At the end of three years, Philip had proved himself to be worthy of Emma's belief in him.

She had not been unduly surprised, since she knew that he had inherited her astuteness, her canny Yorkshire ways, and her instinct for making money, and that he had the ability to turn situations to his own advantage, as she had done all her life. Also, Emma was aware that quite aside from being the spitting image of his grandfather, Philip was blessed with Paul's acumen and financial genius.

Philip was soon entrenched professionally and socially in Sydney, and he made a good life for himself in Australia. The country of his McGill forefathers, which had so fascinated and intrigued him since those childhood visits, became his true home. He had not the slightest desire to live anywhere else in the world.

Two of Emma's appointees, Neal Clarke and Tom Patterson, had been instrumental in Philip's training in Australia, and they had earned his genuine respect and affection. However, it was usually Emma to whom Philip turned for guidance and counsel when he was uncertain, or when he faced a crisis. After his grandmother's death in 1970, his father took her place, inasmuch as he became his confidante and sounding board whenever Philip deemed it necessary to seek advice outside his own organization. David Amory's untimely death in the avalanche at Chamonix in January of 1971 had robbed Philip not only of his beloved father, but of a wise counselor and guiding hand.

When Philip had returned to Sydney in March of that year, fully recovered from the minor injuries he had suffered on the mountain that fateful day, he had been an extremely troubled young man of twenty-five. He was not only grieving for his father, but filled with anxiety and concern about the future. He had a mighty business to run, enormous responsibilities to shoulder, and he was entirely alone with Emma and his father now dead.

Paula, never anything but devoted and loyal, had her own problems to contend with, and he could not inflict his terrible worries on her.

His mother, Daisy, who had returned to Australia with him at Paula's urging, was crushed by sorrow at the loss of her husband. And although the McGill Corporation was hers, technically speaking, she had never been involved in business, and he knew she could be no help whatsoever. In fact, he was aware that she was looking to him for strength and support.

But quite apart from these problems, Philip was grappling with another emotion at this particular point in his life: *survivor guilt.*

Few people would be left unaffected after surviving an avalanche in which other members of the family had been killed, and Philip was no exception. He had floundered, been unable to come to grips with himself. Why had *he* been singled out to live when the others had died? This question had dominated his thoughts, jostled for prominence in his mind.

He had no ready answer.

However, gradually, he had recognized that he must get over the traumatic experience, put it behind him, and if at all possible, somehow turn it positive. His mother and sister needed him, and he had the conglomerate to run, he repeatedly reminded himself in the ensuing months. And so he focused on the future, and hoped that perhaps the reason for his survival, the purpose of it, would one day be revealed to him.

With the blood of Emma Harte and Paul McGill coursing through his veins, Philip was nothing if not a hard and dedicated worker, and as he began to marshall his turbulent emotions, he directed his full energies into the McGill Corporation. Work blocked out problems and worries, and as far as he was concerned, it was also the most satisfying way to lead his life, to fill his days and nights.

And so by 1981 Philip McGill Amory had become one of Australia's leading industrialists, an important man in his own right, and one to be reckoned with.

The conglomerate had had its ups and downs in the eleven years since Emma's death. But he had held the helm firmly, kept it steady, and steered the company ahead. He had divested himself of losing divisions, diversified his holdings, purchased other companies which mined iron ore and harnessed natural resources, and he had branched out into communications with the acquisition of newspapers and magazines, radio and television stations.

Under Philip's aegis, the company founded and brought to prominence by his forefathers, and immeasurably strengthened by Emma during the years of her trusteeship, had moved forward into the 1980s with greater power and financial growth than it had ever known in the past.

The phone on Philip's desk buzzed several times. He picked it up.

"Yes?" he asked, glancing at his watch.

"It's Ken, Mr. Amory, I have the car waiting."

"Thanks, Ken, I'll be right down." Philip replaced the receiver, put a pile of financial statements, other documents, and *The Asian Wall Street Journal* in his briefcase, snapped it shut, and left his private office.

His wine-colored Rolls Royce stood outside

the McGill Tower on Bridge Street, and Ken, his driver of the last five years, leaned against the hood.

"Evening, Mr. Amory," Ken said, straightening up, opening the back door for him.

"Hello, Ken," Philip replied and stepped into the car. A second later they were pulling away from the curb, and he instructed, "Rose Bay, please, Ken. Mrs. Rickards' house."

"Right you are, sir."

Philip settled back into the soft, beige-leather upholstery, endeavoring to shed the general preoccupations of the business day.

He closed his eyes, relaxing, letting the tension ease out of him. He thought of Paula and experienced a small rush of happiness, knowing she would be arriving in Sydney in the morning. He missed her. So did their mother. Philip's mind swung instantly to Daisy. He had not seen her for the past week, since she had been in Perth with her husband, Jason Rickards, and had only returned to the city late last night. But he had no doubt she was hardly able to contain herself, impatiently waiting for Paula's arrival.

He was aware that the only thing casting a faint shadow across their mother's happiness these days was being so far away from her daughter and grandchildren. But she did have Jason, and for that he was extremely thankful.

241

What a vital role timing plays in life, Philip suddenly reflected. He had introduced his mother to the Perth industrialist in 1975, when Jason had finally recovered from his messy divorce of three years earlier, and when his mother was at last ready to enter into a relationship with another man. Despite their busy lives and their many commitments, both Daisy and Jason had been lonely, and they had welcomed the introduction. And then, lo and behold, much to everyone's surprise but his, these two had fallen in love and had married a year later.

Seemingly it was a good marriage. Jason had a permanent smile on his rugged face and his mother never looked anything less than radiant these days, and she had put her sorrow truly behind her. But then his mother was a wise woman.

In the years immediately following his father's death, she had done her best to make the most of her new life in Australia. She had acted as Philip's hostess, had then gone on to create her own social circle, and she had eventually thrown herself into charity work with a great deal of zeal and dedication to her chosen causes, mostly to do with the welfare of children. This had given her tremendous satisfaction, added purpose to her existence.

As the only child of Paul McGill, who had

been one of the richest men in Australia, heiress to his great fortune, and half Australian herself, Daisy believed that doing good works was her duty, the responsibility of wealth and privilege such as hers. She had created the McGill Foundation, had endowed millions to medical research, children's hospitals, and education. Yes, living in Sydney had been good for his mother, just as she, in her way, had been good for Sydney.

Jason Rickards was an added bonus in her life, in all of their lives, really. He was well liked by everyone, was very much a part of the family. Childless, Jason had thrown himself heart and soul into being an adopted grandfather, and Paula's children adored him.

Yes, timing *was* on their side, Philip thought. *And luck . . . lots of it.*

He opened his eyes, pulled himself upright on the seat, smiled ruefully. *His* timing was invariably wrong and *he* never had any luck when it came to women. Just the opposite. But he didn't really care. He had no desire to get married, much preferred the life of a bachelor. There were, after all, worse fates.

14

The balmy night air drifting in through the open French doors was fragrant with a variety of mingled scents . . . honeysuckle, wisteria, rambling roses, and eucalyptus, and inside the room there was a faint hint of *Joy,* Daisy's favorite perfume, the one she invariably wore.

A Chopin *étude* played softly on the stereo in the background, and silk-shaded lamps added their mellow glow to the gracious drawing room, where peach, white, and pale green predominated, and where a certain gentle calm prevailed.

Philip sat facing his mother across the antique Chinese coffee table made of hand-carved ebony, enjoying a snifter of cognac after the delicious dinner they had just shared. Fernando, the Filipino chef, had prepared Barramundi, his favorite fish, and Daisy had made an English trifle, which had always been a special treat when he was a child. Now he was feeling well satisfied, replete with good food and vintage wine, and completely spoiled as he relaxed on the comfortable sofa.

He brought the brandy balloon up to his nose and sniffed, appreciating the strong, almost harsh bouquet of the alcohol. He took a mouthful, savored it, then sat back, nursed the balloon in his hands, nodding from time to time as he listened to her softly modulated voice, giving her his entire attention.

"And since Jason will be back from Perth on Thursday, I thought it would be nice to take Paula up to Dunoon for the weekend. Don't you, darling? And you will come with us, won't you?"

Philip put the balloon down on the end table and frowned.

"Do you honestly think she'll want to start traveling the minute she gets here, after she's flown halfway across the world?" He shook his head. "I doubt it, Mother." Instantly a grin surfaced, replaced his frown. "Besides, if I know *my* sister, *your* daughter, she'll have her nose to the grindstone on Saturday, trying to bring order to the boutique at the Sydney-O'Neill. That's why she's flying out here, remember."

"Oh but she's coming to see us as well!" Daisy asserted, giving him a sharp look. She wondered if either of her children ever thought about anything else except business. She doubted it. They took after her mother.

Daisy's face changed, became reflective, and after a moment, she said, "But perhaps you're right, Philip. It is *rushing* her a bit, I suppose. Maybe we can go up to the sheep station the following weekend."

"Yes, why not, Mother," he agreed, humoring her.

The smile flicked into Daisy's vivid blue eyes again, and she leaned forward, her face full of enthusiasm and eagerness. "Jason and I have decided to spend an extra month in England, Philip. We're leaving at the beginning of November instead of December, and we won't be back until January. Three months . . . and I'm *so* looking forward to them, to being in London and at Pennistone Royal. Christmas in Yorkshire with Paula, Shane, and the grandchildren, and the rest of the family as well, is my idea of sheer bliss. It's going to be like old times . . . when Mummy was alive."

"Yes," Philip said. A brow lifted as he next

asked, "Can Jason afford to be away so long though?"

"Of course. And it's one of the reasons he's been spending so much time in Perth these last few weeks, making sure everything will run smoothly during his absence. And in any case, he has every confidence in his staff, just as you do." She smiled at him. "You're coming too, aren't you? To England for Christmas, I mean."

"Well, I'm not sure," he began, and stopped abruptly when he saw his mother's expression. Her face had dropped.

"I hope I can get away, darling," he said noncommitally, having no desire to make a decision about Christmas so far in advance, or to promise her anything. She would hold him to it.

"Oh Philip, you must! You *promised* Paula! Have you forgotten about the sixtieth anniversary of Harte's? You *have* to be at the dinner dance she's giving on New Year's Eve. Everyone's going to be there, and it will look simply awful if you're not."

"I'll do my damnedest, Mother, okay?"

"Yes, all right," she responded quietly, leaning back against the big pillows on the sofa, smoothing the skirt of her silk dress, sighing under her breath. After a moment, Daisy raised her eyes, studied Philip, trying to gauge his mood, wondering if she dare mention his current girlfriend. He could be touchy at times, especially when it came to his private life.

Deciding to take a chance, she said in her low, even tone, "If you do come to England, I think it might be rather nice if you bring Veronica with you. She's such a lovely young woman."

Philip started to laugh, gave his mother an odd look.

Daisy stared back at him in surprise, perplexity flitting across his face. "What is it?"

Still chuckling and catching his breath, Philip finally managed to say, "Honestly, Mother, you *are* behind the times. I broke up with Veronica Marsden weeks and weeks ago. It's over . . . finished . . . caput."

"You didn't tell me," Daisy replied, sounding reproachful. She filled with dismay. "Oh darling, I *am* sorry. As I said, she is a lovely person, and frankly, I thought the two of you were quite serious about each other. But never mind, I expect you know best, Pip," she murmured, using the diminutive of his childhood.

Her look became quizzical when she ventured, "Perhaps you'd like to bring the current favorite?"

"There isn't a current favorite, Mother. And please stop trying to get me married off!" he exclaimed crossly. At once conscious of the hurt invading her eyes, he softened his harsh tone, added, with a light laugh, "You just want to get me hitched so that you can have lots of grandchildren to fuss over here in Australia."

"Yes, there's some truth in that," Daisy admitted.

She lifted her cup, took a sip of the lemon tea, and fell silent, slipping down into her thoughts. And she asked herself why her son continually broke off with suitable young women at the most crucial time in his relationship with them. She remembered Selena, his girlfriend before Veronica, who had come to see her after she and Philip had parted company last year. Selena had confided that Philip had the need to end a relationship the moment it became serious, or rather, became *threatening* was the way Selena had put it. Daisy wondered if the girl had been correct. She stifled another sigh. Her son was as baffling to *her* as he was to many other people. There were those who said he was an enigma, and wasn't that the absolute truth?

Philip, watching her closely, said, "Hey, Ma, what are you cooking up in that head of yours? I can almost see your mind working."

"Nothing, nothing at all, darling." Then Daisy gave a little laugh, and went on confidingly, "Actually, I was asking myself if you would ever marry."

"I have the reputation of being the biggest

playboy in the Western world. I aim to keep the title." Lifting the brandy balloon to his mouth, he winked at her over its rim, his expression mischievous.

"Hardly a playboy, not the way you work, Philip. That's an exaggeration, and merely the press pinning a label on you, because you're so eligible."

Now Daisy shifted on the sofa, crossed her long legs, and a new seriousness entered her voice as she continued, "But I can't bear to think of you being alone later in your life, Philip. That's a terrible prospect for you, and not a very comforting one for me to envisage either. And I certainly don't want you to become a crusty old bachelor."

Daisy paused, gave him a penetrating stare, hoping her words would sink in. "Not like poor John Crawford," she finished, thinking of her solicitor in London. He had once had a crush on her, had wanted to marry her after David's death. But she had harbored only friendship for John, nothing deeper than that.

"Yes, poor John indeed," Philip agreed. "He is a bit of a sorry case these days. Yearning after you, Ma, I do suspect. But me *crusty?* Never. The ladies will keep *me* young and merry into my old age." He gave her a cheeky grin. "You know what they say . . . variety's the spice of life, and so I shall always make sure I have a pretty girl on my arm, even in my dotage."

"I don't doubt it," Daisy conceded, laughing with him. But privately she wondered if these fleeting liaisons with countless women were ever going to be enough for her son in the final analysis. If that was what he wanted, then she supposed they would be. On the other hand, he was missing so much, not being married. She longed to continue the conversation in this vein, to speak to him seriously about his personal life, his future, and the future of the McGill Corporation if he did not produce heirs. But instinct, and her better judgment, told her to keep quiet. After all, Philip was thirty-five and answerable to no one but himself, and he might easily resent her probing.

The phone trilled in the adjoining library, and a second later Daisy's Filipino houseman, Rao, appeared in the arched doorway to the living room. "Excuse me, madam, it's Mr. Rickards."

"Thank you, Rao," Daisy said, and glanced across at her son. "I won't be a moment, darling."

There was a faint swish of silk, a whiff of *Joy,* as Daisy rose and hurried out.

Philip's eyes followed her.

He could not help thinking how young his mother looked tonight. She had celebrated her

fifty-sixth birthday in May, but she appeared to
be years younger. She had a slim, almost girlish
figure, and her lovely face was quite unlined,
and because she had stayed out of the sun most
of her life, she had preserved her flawless English complexion. There was a freshness, a
youthfulness about her still, and even the few
strands of gray streaking her black hair did
nothing to age her. She was remarkable, but
then Emma had been well preserved too.

Philip was finishing the last of his cognac
when Daisy returned to the living room.

She said, "Jason sends his love, Pip. I told
him what you said about dragging Paula to
Coonamble, and he tends to agree with you that
it wouldn't be fair. Perhaps we'll have a little
dinner party for her on Saturday. Is that all
right with you? You will come, won't you?"

"Of course! I wouldn't miss being with old
Beanstalk for anything. Listen, Mother, I'd really like you to take a look at the financial statements and balance sheets I brought with me. I
want to go over them—"

"You know very well that's not necessary,
Philip," Daisy interrupted. "I don't know a
blessed thing about business, yet you constantly
force these papers on me."

"But the McGill Corporation is *your* company, Mother."

"Oh fiddlesticks, Philip, it's yours and Paula's, except in name, and you know that. And obviously I trust you implicitly. Good Lord, darling, my mother trained you all those years ago to do the job properly. *She* had immense faith in your judgment and business acumen, and so do I."

"Thanks for that lovely vote of confidence, Ma, but I insist you look at the papers. Let me go and get them." As he was speaking he hurried out to the foyer and returned at once with his briefcase.

Reluctantly, Daisy took the papers he offered, and settling back on the sofa, she began to read them slowly, although she did so only to please her son.

For his part, Philip sat observing her quietly, thinking that she looked stunning in the silk dress she was wearing. It was a peculiar bluish-purple, like the wisteria growing in her garden, and it underscored the blueness of her eyes. So did the sapphires on her ears and at her throat, a recent gift from Jason, she had told him over dinner. Jason Rickards is a lucky man, Philip thought, and then as his mother lifted her dark head, looked across at him, he smiled and handed her a second sheaf of papers.

"Oh God, not more of them," Daisy groaned,

making a face. "This is a pointless exercise, you know, they're double Dutch to me."

Philip merely grinned. This was now an old story between them.

"Here, let me explain," he said, and went to join her on the sofa. For the next half hour he patiently walked her through the balance sheets, striving hard to explain everything in the simplest of terms, as he had been doing for years.

He did not return to the city that night.

He went instead to his house at Point Piper. Earlier, he had phoned, and had told his housekeeper he would be arriving later, but not to wait up for him. She and the rest of the staff were in their own quarters when the car dropped him off at eleven.

He went straight to his den, laid his briefcase on the sofa, and strode over to the bar, where he poured himself a brandy. Carrying it out to the terrace, he stood leaning against the balustrade, sipping the drink and staring out at the ocean, dark as pitch now under a moonless sky.

His mother's words reverberated in his head.

She wanted him to get married because she did not want him to end up a lonely man. That was a belly laugh. Being married didn't necessarily prevent loneliness. Sometimes it even underscored one's very aloneness. He'd never been married, but he had lived with a woman at one point in his life, and he was well aware that the company of another person did not change a damn thing. Certainly it did not chase the devils away.

He had had an unconventional private life for years now. It worried Daisy, and he understood why. But there was nothing he could do about changing it. He sighed. Too many women over too short a period lately, and too damn many even for me, he thought, filling with sudden distaste.

As he examined his life with a new objectivity, he saw that it was as arid as the Great Sandy Desert. A meaningful relationship with a woman *had* eluded him. It would *always* elude him. But did that really matter? Long ago he had decided it was simpler to settle for sex. A physical relationship was reasonably uncomplicated. Anyway, he was a loner by nature. At least he could live comfortably with himself.

As he swallowed the last drop of brandy, swung around, and walked back into the house, Philip McGill Amory had no way of knowing that his life was about to change, for better and for worse. And forever.

15

"I want to sell the Sitex stock."

Paula's words fell like an exploding bomb into the quiescence of her mother's beautiful peach drawing room, and she realized she had startled herself as much as she had her mother and her brother.

Daisy and Philip were obviously flabbergasted, and neither of them spoke; they simply stared at her for the longest moment.

Paula glanced from one to the other. She had not meant to tell them tonight, nor had she meant to be so blunt about it, but since she could not take the words back, she might as well finish what she had started.

She took a deep breath, but before she could continue, her mother broke the short, uncomfortable silence.

Daisy said, "I don't understand, Paula. Why do you want to sell the stock all of a sudden?"

"Any number of reasons, Mummy, but mainly because oil prices have dropped considerably, and since there's currently a glut of oil on the world market, I feel they're going to drop even lower. And anyway, you know that Sitex has been a pain in the neck to me for years now, so I think we ought to get out, once and for all. Sell our entire forty percent and be done with it."

"I see," Daisy murmured, puckering her eyebrows. She swung her head, stared at Philip.

Philip returned his mother's questioning glance, but remained silent.

He rose, walked over to the French doors, stood gazing out across Rose Bay to the lights of Sydney glittering in the distance. The McGill Tower, soaring up into the starlit sky, dominated the cityscape even at night.

Paula's unexpected announcement puzzled him, and he wondered what was *really* behind it. He turned slowly, his eyes sweeping over her as he returned to his chair. Despite her tan, she looked drawn and tired, and he thought she ought to be in bed, not discussing business at this hour. However, her eyes told him she was waiting for some sort of comment from him.

"The situation's bound to change, Paula, it usually does," Philip said at last. "Oil prices have always fluctuated, sometimes even wildly, and in my opinion, if we're going to sell, it should be at a more auspicious time than now, when we can get the most for the stock, don't you think? When oil is at a premium and prices are high, for instance."

"And when will that be, Philip? I just told you, there's an overabundance of oil in the world today, but you know that as well as I do." Paula sighed, shook her head wearily. "Hundreds of thousands of barrels are being stored up, yet the world demand for oil has dropped by fifteen percent—ever since those artificially high prices were imposed by the cartels in 1979. I honestly believe the demand for oil will continue to fall. It'll go down, down, *down.* You'll see, this current trend will go on for several years . . . in my estimation until 1985."

Philip laughed. "Come on, darling, your outlook is awfully bleak."

Paula said nothing. She sat back on the sofa, rubbed her neck, feeling very tired, once more wishing she had not begun this.

Daisy, whose blue eyes were still troubled, turned to her daughter and said, "But I promised my mother I'd never sell our Sitex stock, Paula, just as she promised the same thing to Paul all those years ago. My father told her to hang on to it, insisted that she never let it go, no matter what, and—"

Cutting in, Paula muttered, "Times have changed, Mummy."

"Yes, they have, and I'm the first to acknowledge that. On the other hand, I would feel very funny about selling our interest in Sitex. Uncomfortable really."

Paula gave Daisy a pointed look. "I bet if Grandy were alive today, she'd agree with *me,*" she asserted, and stifled a yawn. She felt dizzy, woozy actually, and the room seemed suddenly to swim before her eyes, and she thought that if she didn't lie down soon she would collapse right there on the peach sofa. But Philip had started to say something else, so she endeavored to focus on him, to listen to his words.

He was saying, "What does it matter if the shares bring in lower dividends for a year or two, or even three or four. Mother doesn't need the additional income."

"That's absolutely true, I don't," Daisy concurred. "In any case, Paula darling, I really don't think we should be discussing this matter right now. You look exhausted and seem about ready to keel over. I'm not a bit surprised either

—as usual, you've done far too much since you arrived yesterday," she chastised gently.

Paula blinked again. "Too true, Mother, and the jet lag generally hits me hard on the second night, doesn't it?" She was struggling to keep her eyes open as waves of exhaustion almost engulfed her. "I think I do have to go to bed. Right now. I'm so sorry, I shouldn't have brought this up . . . we'll have to finish our chat about Sitex another day."

Pushing herself to her feet, Paula went and kissed her mother goodnight.

Philip, who had risen at the same time, put his arm around her and walked her across the drawing room and out into the entrance foyer.

They stood together at the bottom of the staircase.

"Shall I help you upstairs, Beanstalk?" he asked, his eyes kind, full of brotherly affection.

Paula shook her head. "Don't be daft, Pip, I'm not *so* decrepit that I can't make it to my bedroom." She covered her mouth with her hand and yawned several times, then grasped the bannister, put a foot on the first step. "Oh dear, I *think* I can make it . . . I shouldn't have had the wine with dinner."

"It'll make you sleep like a top."

"Gosh, I don't need anything to do that," she

murmured, then leaned forward and kissed his cheek. "Good night, love."

"Night, Paula darling, and let's have lunch tomorrow. I'll meet you in the Orchid Room at twelve-thirty. Okay?"

"You're on, brother o' mine."

When she got to her room, Paula was so bone tired she hardly had the strength to undress and take off her makeup. But she managed somehow, and within minutes she was pulling a silk nightgown over her head and gratefully sliding into bed.

As her head touched the pillow, she admitted to herself that she had made a tactical error, *had* picked the wrong time to discuss Sitex. With a sudden flash of insight, she knew her mother would never agree to sell the stock, no matter what *she* said, and that this would drastically interfere with her plans.

Or would it? Her last thought, before she fell asleep, was of her grandmother. "There's more than one way to skin a cat," Emma had been fond of saying. Remembering this, Paula smiled to herself in the dark before her eyelids fluttered and closed.

Silence reigned in the back office of the Harte Boutique in the Sydney-O'Neill Hotel the following morning.

Paula and Madelana sat facing each other across the large desk, their heads bent and close together as they poured over two ledgers.

It was Madelana who looked up first.

"I can't imagine how Callie Rivers managed to make such a mess," she said to Paula, shaking her head, her face a picture of disbelief. "It took some sort of perverse genius to create a muddle of these proportions."

Paula raised her eyes, looked at Madelana, and grimaced. "Either she's totally dense and my judgment was haywire when I hired her, or her illness debilitated her to such an extent, she just hasn't known what she was doing these past few months."

"It had to be her illness, not you, Paula. You're far too smart not to spot a dud the minute you see one," Madelana said confidently, and closed the ledger in front of her with a degree of finality. "I've checked these figures three times now . . . twice with the calculator and once by hand. You're right, I'm afraid. We are in the red here . . . and the red is *very* red."

Paula took a deep breath, expelled it, stood up, and began to pace for a few seconds, her face reflective. Returning to the desk, she took the ledgers, put them in the filing cabinet and locked it, then dropped the key in the pocket of her gray linen jacket.

"Come on, Maddy, let's go back to the stock room and try to make some sense there."

"Good idea," Madelana answered, rising immediately, following Paula out of the office and into the main area of the three-level boutique.

"We'll be downstairs, Mavis," Paula informed the assistant manager, and swept on across the floor without pausing, making for the heavy glass doors which opened into the hotel lobby.

"Yes, Mrs. O'Neill," Mavis answered quietly, staring after Paula, her gloomy face reflecting her worry.

Madelana merely nodded to the young woman.

But once she and Paula were crossing the dark-green marble lobby, she confided, "I think Mavis is all right basically, Paula. Just out of her depth. Callie Rivers should never have made her the assistant manager. She doesn't have what it takes to run a boutique of this size, and she's not very imaginative either. Still, she *is* honest, and that counts for a lot, I guess."

"Everything you say is quite true," Paula agreed, walking briskly into the empty elevator as the door opened, pushing the button for the floor below. "Callie left her a mess to cope with, and she didn't know what to do to correct it, I realize that now." Paula glanced at Madelana through the corner of her eye. "I don't hold Mavis responsible, you know. I just wish she'd had the sense to tell me everything. She knew she could phone me, or telex me, any time she wished."

The two women stepped out of the elevator, and Paula went on, "Let's face it, if the hotel manager hadn't mentioned it to Shane on the phone a few weeks ago, I still wouldn't be any the wiser."

"Yes, it was a good thing he found out there were problems, and that Mavis was in a panic and floundering. I think we just got here in time to avert a real disaster."

"You can say that again," Paula muttered.

The stock room which belonged to the Harte Boutique was located on the mezzanine floor of the hotel, and was actually a series of rooms. These included an office with filing cabinets, a desk, chairs, and telephones in the entrance, and several large storage rooms behind this. Racks of clothes were kept there, along with chests of accessories ranging from costume jewelry, scarves, hats, and belts to handbags and shoes.

Madelana grimaced as she and Paula paced along the lines of bulging racks, looking at the stock for the second time since their arrival, but only now doing their first proper assessment. Groaning, she eyed her boss. "We're going to have one hell of a job making inroads into this lot. It's worse than I realized yesterday."

"Don't I know it," Paula responded grimly. "And I dread to think what awful secrets those chests over there hold." She shook her head, and her annoyance and dismay rose to the surface yet again. "This is partially my fault. I shouldn't have let Callie persuade me to carry several less expensive lines, as well as the Lady Hamilton Clothes. But she convinced me she knew this market better than I did, and fool that I was I gave her a good deal of leeway. And so here we are today, looking at clothes she bought from other manufacturers and which haven't moved."

"I think we do have to have a sale, like you suggested yesterday," Madelana volunteered.

"Yes. We must get rid of the old merchandise, including the remainder of the Lady Hamilton line from last season. A clean sweep, that's the only thing to do—and then we can start again from scratch. I'll telex Amanda this afternoon, instructing her to send as much Lady Hamilton stock as she has available. She can air freight it out to us. We need spring and summer merchandise, of course, since Australia's heading into those seasons now." She broke off, staring at the clothes hanging there, a look of anxiety settling on her face.

"What's wrong?" Madelana asked, as always quick to sense any change in Paula's demeanor.

"I hope we *can* move these clothes in a sale, and make *something* on them, however little that is."

Madelana exclaimed, "Oh I'm sure we will, Paula, and I've got an idea . . . why not make it a Grand Sale. Capital *G,* capital *S,* and advertise it as being comparable only to the one at Harte's of Knightsbridge. That's the world's most famous sale—so let's cash in on it. Surely the agency here in Sydney can come up with some clever copy for the newspaper advertisements." Maddy thought for a moment, and when she continued, it was with a rush of enthusiasm. "I think the message we want to convey to the public goes something like this . . . *You don't have to fly to London to go to the Harte's sale of the year. It's right here on your own doorstep.* Well, what do you think?"

For the first time that morning, a genuine smile flickered on Paula's mouth. "Brilliant, Maddy, I'll put a call into Janet Shiff at the ad agency this afternoon, and have her start working up some of her snappy copy. Now come on, let's sort through these clothes, and pick out as much as we can for the sale."

Madelana needed no further encouragement. She dashed over to one of the other racks, and began her own ruthless process of selection and elimination.

The Orchid Room of the Sydney-O'Neill Hotel was considered to be one of the most beautiful places to lunch or dine in the city. It was also a very *in* spot where people went to be seen and to see, and so it had acquired a certain cachet in local society.

Situated on the top floor of the hotel, two of its walls were made entirely of plate glass running floor to ceiling, and thus it appeared to float, as though suspended between the blue sky and the sea far below, and offered a sweeping view for miles around.

Breathtaking giant-sized murals of hand-painted white, yellow, pink, and cerise orchids covered the other two walls, and there were real orchids everywhere . . . arranged in tall cylindrical glass vases, planted in Chinese porcelain pots, and clustered in bowls on every table.

Paula was particularly proud of the room, since Shane had conceived it and had taken an active part in its planning with the architects, at the time the hotel was being designed and constructed. He liked to use animals, birds, or flowers endemic to a country as the motif for a lobby, a dining room, or a bar in his foreign hotels, and since orchids grew in such profusion in the forests, heaths, and woodlands of Australia, this species had seemed appropriate to him. Also, because of the orchid's various shapes and sizes, and lovely, vibrant colors, the flower lent itself to any number of artistic effects and decorative themes.

Paula sat in the elegant, sun-filled restaurant, sipping a mineral water before lunch, and she glanced around admiringly, realizing she had forgotten how truly magnificent the real orchids were, and how brilliantly the hotel florist arranged them in the room, so that they were shown off to their best advantage. Talented gardener that she was, she could not help wishing she could grow these exotic blooms in England.

"Penny for your thoughts," Philip said, peering at her across the table.

"Oh sorry, I didn't mean to drift off like that . . . I was just thinking about the possibility of growing orchids at Pennistone Royal, but I don't think it's feasible."

"Of course it is. You could have a greenhouse built in which to cultivate them . . . you know, like growing tomatoes." He chuckled and there was mischief in his bright blue eyes, and he went on teasingly, "After all, *you* have so much free time on your hands these days."

Paula smiled at him. "If only I did . . . Gardening is very relaxing for me though. And why not a greenhouse? That's a very good thought of yours."

"Oh Lord, what have I done now?" her brother groaned in mock horror at himself. "Shane'll kill me."

"No, he won't, he loves me to garden, to grow things, and he's always giving me new seed catalogs, and packets of seeds and bulbs, and similar stuff. I shall tell him I want an orchid greenhouse for Christmas. How about that?" she finished, laughing, her eyes as merry as her brother's.

"If *he* doesn't give it to you, *I* will." Philip sat back in his chair and went on, "By the way, Mother phoned me just before I left the office. She's thrilled you're spending the weekend at Dunoon. But you proved *me* wrong, you know."

"What do you mean?"

"When Ma told me she wanted you to go up there, I said you wouldn't be interested, not after stepping off a fourteen-hour flight from L.A." He studied Paula for a moment. "And I must admit, I was a bit surprised that you agreed to go. And so readily, she said. I thought you'd be hard at it in the boutique on Saturday. Don't tell me that you've already sorted out the mess there?" This came out sounding like a question and he raised his brows.

"Not completely, Philip, but I'm on my way to doing so."

"Good for you! So come on, tell me the real story, Beanstalk."

Paula quickly filled him in, then explained, "And after I've had the sale next week, I'll do new window displays with the Lady Hamilton stock I'm bringing in from London in a hurry, and I'll back the merchandise with a fresh advertising campaign. With the spring-summer season ahead of me here, I think I can turn the boutique around again in a relatively short period of time."

Philip nodded. "You're one terrific retailer. If you can't do it, no one can, darling. And what about your manager? You're not having her back, are you?"

"I can't, Pip, even though I do believe that some of the mistakes she made were because she wasn't in good health. Obviously I've lost my faith in her, and I know I'd be worried to death if I put her in charge again."

"I can't say I blame you. What's happening at the boutiques in the hotels in Melbourne and Adelaide? They're not affected, are they?"

"Fortunately not. They seem to be all right, from what the managers told me yesterday. Callie was no longer involved with them, thank God. If you remember, I set up a new system some time ago, made each manager autonomous, answerable only to me. However, since I am here in Australia, I'm going to fly down there later next week, just to make sure all is well."

"Good idea. And you shouldn't have too many problems finding a new manager for the Sydney boutique. There are plenty of excellent people around."

"Yes, so I understand. I hope to start interviewing on Monday, and if I haven't found anybody suitable before I leave in a couple of weeks, Madelana O'Shea will follow through for me. In any case, she's staying on for a while, to work with the advertising agency, and get the Sydney boutique organized and running properly. I trust her judgment, and I've every confidence in her."

"So you've said before. I'm looking forward to meeting her sometime."

"It'll be this weekend, Pip. I've invited her to Coonamble. Are you flying up with us tomorrow night?"

"No, I can't. You'll be going with Mother in Jason's plane, and I'll come in on Saturday morning. I'm glad we're going to have the weekend together, and it'll do you good. You can have two days complete rest, and lots of fresh air."

Paula smiled faintly, and leaned across the table, pinning her gaze on her brother. There was a slightly different nuance in her voice when she asked, "Do you think Mummy will change her mind about the Sitex stock?"

"No, I don't," Philip was swift to reply. "Ma's attitude about the stock is all tied up with her emotions about her father. You know as well as I do that she worshipped him, and she just can't bring herself to go against his wishes. And she believes that is what she *would* be doing if she sold the stock. It may sound farfetched, but it happens to be the truth."

"But those were Paul's wishes over forty years ago, for God's sake!" Paula cried vehemently. "His view of the situation would be quite different today, just as Grandy's would be."

"Maybe so, but I know Mother won't budge." Philip gave Paula a searching look. "Anyway, why *do* you want her to sell the stock? *Why* are you so anxious about it?"

Paula hesitated fractionally, wondering whether to tell her brother the truth, but decided against it. "I gave you the reasons last night," she said, keeping her voice neutral. "Although I do have to admit I'm also rather fed up with Marriott Watson and his cronies on the board. They do everything they can to obstruct me, to make my life as difficult as possible."

Philip gave her a curious look. "But Paula, they always have—that's nothing new, is it? Furthermore, they were always at loggerheads with Grandy." He paused, scowling, and rubbed his hand over his chin, reflecting for a moment. "Still, if their behavior is beginning to get to you, perhaps I should explain this to Ma, and—"

"No, no, don't do that," Paula cut in rapidly. "Look, let's forget about selling the Sitex stock. I'll cope with Marriott Watson and the board."

"Yes, I know you will," Philip said. "You always have. You're very much like me. It's impossible for you not to do your duty—it goes against the grain." He flashed her a loving smile. "Now come on, let's order lunch."

16

Sunlight filtering through the shaded windows awakened Madelana.

Blinking, she sat up abruptly in the antique four-poster bed, feeling at once both startled and disoriented, wondering where she was. And then she adjusted her eyes to the gentle, hazy light and looked around, took in the details of the lovely room, and remembered that she was at Dunoon, the McGill sheep station near Coonamble.

She turned her head, glanced at the little carriage clock on the taffeta-skirted bedside table, saw that it was early, only six o'clock. But that did not matter; she was accustomed to rising at the crack of dawn. Anyway, last night Daisy had told her she could get up whenever she wished, that she should make herself at home, explaining that she would find the housekeeper in the kitchen after six-fifteen. From that time on, such things as freshly squeezed juices, coffee, tea, toast, and fruit were always set out in the breakfast room; after seven, when one of the two cooks arrived, she could order a hot breakfast if she wanted, Daisy had added.

Throwing back the sheets, Madelana leapt out of bed, and hurried into the adjoining bathroom to shower.

Ten minutes later she emerged, wrapped in her white toweling bathrobe, and went over to the windows. She pushed up the shades on both of them, stood for a moment looking down into the gardens below. They were brilliantly green, filled with an abundance of vivid flowers planted in spectacular herbaceous borders, and in huge central flower beds cut into the rolling lawns. It was a radiant day, very sunny, with a bright blue sky scattered with billowing white clouds that looked like handfuls of cotton candy.

The excitement and anticipation she had experienced on arriving the night before flowed through her again, and she could hardly wait to go outside and investigate her immediate surroundings. Most especially she wanted to walk through those inviting gardens, which she knew Paula had had a hand in creating some years earlier.

Seating herself at the kidney-shaped dressing table positioned between the two soaring windows, Madelana began to brush her thick chestnut hair before applying her makeup, and as she wielded her brush, her thoughts centered on this unique place where she had come with Paula, and Daisy and Jason Rickards, to spend the weekend.

Dunoon was unlike anything Madelana had expected, or had imagined it to be.

It was approximately five hundred and seventy kilometers from Sydney, situated in the North West plains region of New South Wales, and the flight in Jason Rickards' corporate jet had been short and fast. They had left Sydney at five yesterday afternoon and had landed on the private airfield at Dunoon just after six o'clock.

Tim Willen, the station manager, had met them, greeting them jovially, and laughing and joking with them as he had helped the pilot and the steward load their luggage into the vintage station wagon.

Ten minutes later, when they were driving off the airfield, Madelana had been startled to see several different types of planes resting in the huge hangars they passed, as well as two helicopters parked on the nearby helipad.

She had voiced her surprise to Daisy, who had explained that it was easier to use air power to get around Dunoon, especially if there was some kind of sudden emergency. On the flight up, Daisy had told her that their fully operating sheep station covered thousands upon thousands of acres, and from the air it had looked like a small kingdom. Seeing the planes and the helicopters had only confirmed this sense of vastness to Madelana.

The main house was five miles away from the airfield, and on the way there Madelana had sat with her nose pressed to the window, frequently feeling awestruck by the things she was seeing. Daisy had been her guide last evening, had pointed out a variety of interesting sights as the station wagon rolled along the wide tarmac road, which cut through the huge property and also encircled it.

At one point they had passed a cluster of buildings which resembled a small village, and Madelana had learned from her hostess that these included sheep-shearing sheds, barns for storing the raw wool shorn from the Merino sheep bred and raised on Dunoon, sheep pens, a smithy, a small abattoir for slaughtering the livestock used for consumption on the station, a small freezer plant for preserving the sides of lamb, mutton, and beef, and a series of other large barns where feed, hay, and grain were stored. There was also a water tower off to one side, and a generator which provided the sheep station with its own electrical power.

A short distance beyond these buildings were several fenced-in paddocks shaded in parts by beautiful golden elm trees and willows. Here cattle and horses grazed contentedly in the luxuriant grass, and overlooking the bucolic paddocks was a compound of attractive houses built on a slight rise against a backdrop of golden elms and thick old oaks.

Tim had slowed down so that she could see everything better, and he had told her that he and his wife lived there, as did the station hands and some of the indoor staff from the main house; adjoining the compound were tennis courts and a swimming pool for the sole use of the staff and their families.

A quarter of a mile farther along the main road, they drove past indoor and outdoor riding rings, where the horses were trained, and close by were large stables.

These buildings had captivated Madelana. Low, rambling and very rustic in appearance, they were made of dark gray and black stone, and were partially covered in creeper. They seemed very old to her, and she had mentioned this to Daisy, who had explained that the stables dated back to the 1920s and had been built by her father, Paul McGill.

The landscape had made a deep impression on Madelana during the drive from the airfield to the house. Somehow, she had not expected the countryside to be so beautiful, had not anticipated such green lushness in Australia. Until she had arrived here, she had always pictured the continent as being arid and dry, and composed almost entirely of scrub-laden outback once the great coastal cities had been left behind.

But Dunoon was glorious, set amidst lovely, undulating hill country, where gentle slopes fell down into verdant valleys, wide paddocks, and wooded areas. It was truly a pastoral landscape, with the Castlereagh River running through its dark rich earth, and where everything seemed to flourish.

The driveway leading up to the main residence, known simply as the manor, was half a mile long, and the minute they had pulled into it, Daisy had rolled down one of the windows. Instantly the station wagon had filled with the all-pervasive scent of lemon. "It's the *Eucalyptus citriodora,*" Daisy had explained, gesturing

to the trees towering up above them and border-
ing the drive on both sides. "They stretch all the
way to the house, and they're very aromatic."
And Paula had added, "When I smell lemons,
no matter where I am in the world, I immediately think of Dunoon." Madelana had nodded.
"I can understand why," she had murmured,
breathing in the lovely sharp fragrance of citrus.

The manor had blazed with lights to welcome
them in the dimming light of gloaming, and
when Madelana had alighted from the station
wagon and had looked up at the house, she had
been momentarily dazzled, and transported
back to her beloved bluegrass country. Instanta-
neously filling with nostalgia and a flock of
memories, she had choked up, had had to blink
back incipient tears. The manor at Dunoon was
built in a classical style reminiscent of the great
plantation houses of the American South, somewhat antebellum in feeling, and it was magnificent.

Its front facade was mainly of white-painted
wood, with sections of very dark red brick. Wide
verandas swept around its four sides, shading
the walls in summer but allowing the sun to
reach them during the winter months. Standing
at the edge of the front veranda were eight elegant white columns, four on each side of the

front door made of polished mahogany. These columns were tall, stately, and soared up past the first two stories to support a terrace that encircled the entire third floor.

The green foliage of wisteria growing against the manor's white paintwork contributed greatly to the feeling of cool serenity, as did the many leafy trees shading the graceful house in the back. Lawns bordered with huge pink and white azalea bushes sloped away from the gravel driveway, and the flower gardens were situated beyond these smooth and spacious greens.

Once inside the manor, Madelana had discovered that the interiors did justice to the exterior architecture. The rooms were furnished with choice antiques, crystal chandeliers, fine old carpets, and marvelous paintings, many of them French Impressionists. Later she learned that the collection had been Emma Harte's and included works by Monet, van Gogh, Gauguin, Cézanne, and Degas.

Paula had brought her upstairs to this charming bedroom located next door to hers. Decorated in delicate shades of apricot, lime, and pale blue, it was large and airy, with a high ceiling, a white marble fireplace, and watercolors of Dunoon hanging on the walls. The antique four-poster took pride of place, and there was a loveseat and two chairs arranged in a grouping in front of the fireplace.

Fresh flowers in vases had been placed everywhere and they permeated the room with the mingled scents of the gardens outside. The flowers were potent this morning, but Madelana did not mind.

She peered at herself in the dressing-table mirror, smoothed the brush over her hair again, and then went over to the armoire, took out tailored, gray flannel slacks, a white silk shirt, and a hand-knit jacket of a bluish-gray mohair.

After she had dressed in these clothes, she slipped her feet into a pair of brown leather moccasins, put on her gold watch and a pair of gold Tiffany shrimp earrings, and left the bedroom.

It was just after six-thirty when she pushed open the door of the breakfast room and looked inside.

The housekeeper, Mrs. Carr, whom she had met last night, was nowhere in sight, but Madelana's nose twitched from the tantalizing aromas of coffee and warm bread and ripe fruit. She noticed that these were set out on the table placed against the far wall underneath a painting of a circus clown. The round table in the middle of the octagonal-shaped room was covered with a fresh white organdy cloth and had been set with pretty floral china for four people.

Madelana went over and poured herself a cup of black coffee. She stared at the painting of the clown. Oh, it's a Picasso, she thought, as she turned away, not at all surprised. Nothing about Dunoon could surprise her anymore. It was a magical place.

She carried her cup of coffee outside, sat down on the steps of the back veranda, and drank it slowly, enjoying the smell of the grass and green-growing things, the lemony tang of the eucalyptus trees pervading the air, listening to the stillness of nature. The silence was broken only by the twittering of the small birds and the faint rustling of the leaves under the soft breeze.

How peaceful it was here. It was the kind of peace which was only ever found in the country, and she had forgotten it existed. It's such a luxury, she thought, and closed her eyes, allowing the peace to penetrate her bones, to settle deep inside her. And she realized, quite suddenly, that she had not known a peace like this since her childhood.

A little later, Madelana went back into the house, deposited the cup and saucer in the breakfast room, and then wandered out to the main entrance hall. Earlier, when she had been doing her makeup, she had intended to take a stroll through the gardens in front of the house, but now she hesitated.

Opening off the other end of the foyer was the gallery. Paula had pointed it out last night on their way upstairs; they had not had time to go in then, since they were in a hurry to change for dinner. As they had mounted the grand, curving staircase together, Paula had said, "The gallery is hung with portraits of our McGill ancestors, but there's also an extraordinary painting of Emma in there. You must see it, Maddy, before you leave Dunoon."

Her curiosity of last night was aroused again, and Madelana decided to take a peak at Emma's portrait. She would go for her walk afterward.

The gallery was much longer than she had envisioned, with a high ceiling and a huge window at one end. The polished wood floor was bare, the walls were painted white, and a dark oak refectory table stood in the middle. A Chinese porcelain horse, quite large in size, had been placed on the table, and this appeared to be yet another priceless antique to Madelana.

She hurried down the length of the gallery, barely glancing at the portraits of the McGills, mainly interested in finding the one of Emma Harte.

When finally she stood in front of it, she caught her breath. It was extraordinary, just as

Paula had said, so very lifelike, and so much better than any of those she had seen in the Harte stores, and even superior to the one at Pennistone Royal in Yorkshire.

She gazed at it for the longest time, marveling at the vividness of the painting, and the exceptional brushwork. It had obviously been painted in the 1930s, and the evening gown Emma wore was of the period and made of white satin, and Madelana felt that if she reached out, touched the painting, her fingers would rest against the real fabric. Emeralds blazed around Emma's throat, at her ears and wrists, and there was a square-cut emerald on her left hand, and the stones echoed the color of her radiant eyes.

What small hands she had, Madelana thought, stepping closer, peering at the picture. Why, they're so tiny, they're almost a child's hands.

The portrait which hung next to Emma's was of a darkly handsome man, elegant in a white tie and tails. He had the most piercing blue eyes she had ever seen, a strong, arresting face, a black mustache, and a deep cleft in his chin. Clark Gable, Maddy thought, and then smiled to herself, knowing it could not possibly be the late movie star. It was undoubtedly Paul McGill.

Tilting her head to one side, she studied the painting carefully, thoughtfully, wondering what kind of man he had been. A match for Emma Harte, she had no doubt.

Philip came running downstairs as the grandfather clock in the entrance foyer was striking seven.

He crossed the vast hall, heading in the direction of the breakfast room, when he noticed that the double mahogany doors leading into the gallery were slightly ajar. He walked over, intending to close them, and immediately saw the young woman inside. She stood at the far end, and she was leaning toward the painting of his grandfather, studying it, and he realized she must be Paula's American assistant.

As if she sensed his presence, she swung around swiftly. When she saw him in the doorway, her eyes opened very wide and a look of astonishment crossed her face. She stared at him intently. He found himself staring back.

And in that instant his life changed.

It seemed to Philip that all about her was the light. Not simply the bright sunlight pouring in through the big window, but the light which emanated from within her. She was an incandescent being.

He knew at once that he wanted her, and that he would have her. Philip could not comprehend how he knew this, but it flashed through his brain like a bolt of lightning, and he accepted it as the undeniable truth.

Slowly he began to walk forward, his riding boots clattering loudly against the wood, and the noise was overwhelming to him, a dreadful intrusion on the perfect stillness enveloping her. She stood there waiting for him, not moving, appearing hardly to breath, still watching him intently. And his eyes did not leave her face.

She was a stranger, yet entirely familiar to him, and he experienced a deep sense of predestination—of fate—as he finally drew to a standstill in front of her.

Looking up into his face, she smiled a slow, tentative smile, and he was aware that something stupendous was happening to him, and what startled him the most was that it was happening here, in his own home, in the one place he truly loved on this planet. She continued to smile up at him, and he felt as though a burden was lifting from his shoulders, and there was the total cessation of pain, and a sense of peace flowed through him.

Dimly, as though from far away, he heard his own voice. "I'm Philip, Paula's brother," he was saying, and he was surprised he sounded so normal.

"I'm Madelana O'Shea."

"So I'd guessed."

She put her hand in his, and he clasped it firmly, knowing he had been waiting for her all his life.

17

It was a great effort for Philip to let go of Madelana's hand, but finally he did so.

Immediately, Madelana slipped it into her pocket quickly. The feel of his strong fingers lingered, as though their imprint had been permanently burned onto hers. She shifted on her feet, and glanced away. Philip McGill Amory unnerved her.

Philip, watching her closely, said, "You looked surprised when I appeared in the doorway. I'm sorry, I didn't mean to startle you."

"I thought for a minute that Paul McGill had suddenly sprung to life—"

His vibrant laughter cut into her sentence,

echoed around the quiet gallery, and he glanced at the painting through the corner of his eye, but made no comment.

"Also," she went on, "Paula said you wouldn't be arriving from Sydney until around noon today."

"I changed my mind, decided to fly up last night. I got in at eleven-thirty, but everyone was already in bed."

She nodded, said nothing, stared up at him.

"You were studying my grandfather's portrait very closely." He gave her a lopsided grin and his bright blue eyes were full of laughter, danced teasingly. "Did it reveal anything to you? Secrets of his character, perhaps?"

"I was thinking that he must have been very special, a true man, to have won Emma Harte and to have married her."

"From what my grandmother told me about him, Paul McGill was everything you or I could ever imagine him to have been. And *more,* I suspect," Philip said. There was a slight pause, before he went on in a softer tone, "But they were never married, actually . . . his wife wouldn't divorce him. So they took matters into their own hands, flouted convention, and lived together for about sixteen or seventeen years. Until his death in 1939, in fact. I suppose what they did was considered quite scandalous in those days, but they didn't care." Philip shrugged. "They were madly in love, wildly happy, and apparently they never regretted a thing. And naturally they adored their only child, my mother." There was another pause, then Philip said, "She's illegitimate, of course."

Madelana was taken aback. "I didn't know that, or any of the things you've just told me. Paula has never said anything about your grandmother's personal life. And what I've heard or read has been to do with her business achievements."

"Yes, she had quite a success story, didn't she? She was so far ahead of her time. A brilliant and truly emancipated woman who showed a lot of other women the way . . . into big business and the corporate world. And I'm glad she did. I for one don't know what I'd do without the women executives in our company."

Philip chuckled, suddenly looked amused again. "But I'm sure everybody's forgotten about Emma's private life by now. After all, it happened so long ago. Anyway, she has become something of a mythical figure. A legend. And there are any number of keepers of the flame around, both in the family and out . . . who don't want her image tarnished in any way." He pursed his lips, shook his head. "Of course, as far as I'm concerned, nothing could tarnish Emma's image, least of all living out of wedlock with a man she truly loved—and with all her heart."

"I agree with you. But *why* wouldn't she divorce him? His wife, I mean."

"Her religion got in the way, and rather conveniently, *I* think. Constance McGill was a Roman Catholic, and *I* feel she simply hid behind the church and its teachings in order to frustrate Paul. She didn't want him, but she didn't want anyone else to have him. And she didn't want him to be happy, that's an *absolute* certainty. So, she put a bunch of priests and a lot of ridiculous religious mumbo-jumbo in the middle of their marital affairs, merely to confuse the issue, in my opinion."

"Oh—"

Philip was acutely aware of Madelana, and he immediately saw the oddest look entering her eyes. Sensitive, possessing real insight, he knew instinctively that he had blundered. "I've offended you . . . you're a Roman Catholic, aren't you?"

"Yes, I am, but you haven't offended me. Honestly."

"I'm so sorry."

"It's all right, really, Philip . . ." Her voice trailed off. She glanced up at him.

Their eyes met and held. Neither of them

could look away. The silence between them deepened.

As he stared into her luminous eyes, silvery, curiously transparent, Philip understood that it *was* all right. She meant exactly what she said, and would always mean it. For there was no guile in her. She was open and honest, and this pleased him. Once more, he had that peculiar feeling of familiarity. It was as if he had known her long ago, had been separated from her, and had found her again. He felt natural with her, comfortable as he had never been with any other woman, and completely at ease. *I want her,* he thought for the second time that morning. *And I aim to have her.* But go slowly, go very slowly, a voice inside him cautioned.

Madelana, held by his mesmeric blue gaze, was also filled with strange feelings, ones she had hitherto never experienced. Her throat was constricted and dry, she had a tight pain in her chest, and she was shaking inside. She was reacting strongly to Philip, physically and emotionally, and in a way she never had in her entire life, not even with Jack Miller. But then she had never met anyone like Philip McGill Amory before. He was so masculine, so potent, and there was all that charm. Fatal charm. He threw her off balance. And worse still, he frightened her.

Inexplicably, Madelana thought she was

293

about to burst into tears. She averted her head swiftly, broke the eye contact between them. She had begun to tremble, and afraid that he would notice, she walked to the other side of the gallery.

Clearing her throat, she said, without looking back at him, "And which ancestor is this?"

Philip followed her across the room.

He stood directly behind her, breathing in the fragrance of her hair, her perfume. It was something spicy, musky almost, and he found it provocative. He had the sudden urge to put his arms around her, and he had to exercise enormous constraint not to do so.

In a tightly controlled voice, he said, "Oh, that's Andrew, the Scottish sea captain, who came to Australia as a free settler in 1852, and that's his wife, Tessa, in the portrait next to his. Andrew was the founding father, settling here on this land, starting the sheep station, and putting down the original foundations of this house, which he called Dunoon, after the place he came from in Scotland."

"It's a very beautiful house," Madelana murmured in a husky voice, so conscious of Philip's proximity she could barely speak.

"Thank you . . . I think so, too. But actually, it was Andrew's son, Bruce, my great-grandfather, who gave the manor its feeling of the American Old South in the early 1900s, after a trip to America. He built the new facade, added the pillars, and superimposed the look of the plantations of Georgia and Virginia."

"And Kentucky . . . it reminds me of home."

Philip walked around her so that he was able to see her face, and his dark brows lifted in surprise. "You come from bluegrass country?"

Madelana nodded.

"But you don't sound at all Southern."

"And you don't sound particularly Australian," she said, and then she laughed for the first time since meeting him, and this eased the tension which had been building inside her. "I was born and raised in Lexington."

"Then you must have grown up around horses. You *did,* didn't you? And you *do* ride, don't you?"

"Yes."

His eyes lit up, and his voice was buoyant as he exclaimed spontaneously, "Come riding with me! *Now.* I want to show you the land, take you over the station . . . you can't have seen very much last night, especially in the dusk." He glanced at her clothes. "I'm sure we have breeches and boots to fit you."

"I brought my own riding things," Madelana said, then explained, "Before we left New York,

Paula told me we'd probably be coming here for a weekend, and to be prepared. In fact, she told me exactly which clothes to bring."

"Smart girl, my sister," he said, the lopsided grin sliding onto his mouth again. "Come on then, what are we waiting for!"

Philip grabbed hold of her hand, hurried her out of the gallery and into the hall, adding, "I'll have a quick cup of coffee in the breakfast room while you're changing. I'll be waiting for you in there."

"I'll only be a few minutes," she said quietly, swept up by the power and magnetism of this man.

True to her word, she arrived in the breakfast room within the space of ten minutes.

When she appeared in the doorway so quickly, he was surprised, but pleasantly so. Women who fussed about their hair and their makeup, and dawdled and kept him waiting, had always been an irritant to him. He was accustomed to the Harte women, who rarely primped but always looked smart, and he was glad Madelana fit into this mold.

As he rose and went over to her, admiration flickered in his eyes. He liked the way she was dressed. She was obviously a genuine horsewoman, not an amateur who merely fancied herself in the getup and did not take riding seriously. Her clothes announced this to him. Her man-tailored, red-and-purple-plaid wool shirt and cream breeches were in good condition, but by no means new, and her black boots, as highly polished as his own, were well worn and obviously a few years old.

Smiling broadly, taking her elbow, he led her out of the house and across the back courtyard to the garage.

As they walked past the collection of vintage automobiles lined up against the wall of the roofed-in walkway, he asked, "Which way did you drive to the manor from the airfield last night?"

"Tim Willen brought us on the main road," Madelana answered. "I saw quite a lot of the station—the sheep pens, the shearing sheds, and that whole area of work buildings, as well as the compound."

"Good-o . . . then we can get out to the countryside immediately, go for a *real* ride, instead of just puttering around," he announced, helping her into his dark blue Maserati.

Philip had phoned through to the stables while she had been changing, and when they arrived at the old buildings which she had so admired the night before, their horses were already saddled.

The head groom was waiting for them, and after Philip had introduced her to Matt, he took her over to the stalls. "This is Gilda," he said, opening the stall gate, leading out the roan mare. Handing Madelana the reins, he went on, "She's all yours. You'll find she's gentle, but with enough spirit not to be too boring for you."

Philip stepped away from the horse, and resisted the temptation to help Madelana mount.

"Thanks, and she's beautiful," Madelana said, looking at the roan appreciatively. She began to stroke and fondle the young mare's nose and head, and nuzzle her, then she whispered in her ear, endeavoring to make friends, as the grooms in Kentucky years before had taught her always to do with a strange horse. After a couple of minutes of this play, Madelana felt that they knew each other well enough, and she put her left foot in the stirrup, swung herself up into the saddle.

Philip had watched her performance with Gilda, nodding to himself at her expertise, and smiling inwardly. Now he mounted Black Opal, his glossy ebony-colored stallion, and led the way out of the cobbled stable yard, across the main road, and down a dirt track that sloped toward a small copse.

They trotted single file along the narrow track overhung with golden elms and willows, and soon came out into a wide meadow where the green grass rippled under the light breeze. For a while they cantered side by side, and then unexpectedly Philip broke into a gallop, spurring Black Opal forward, leaving Madelana behind.

"Come on, Gilda girl, come on, mah honey," Madelana cooed, leaning forward on the mare's neck, rising slightly out of the saddle, standing as she broke into a gallop and streaked after Philip.

She caught up with him, and they galloped together through several adjoining meadows, jumping fences, racing neck and neck, until Philip finally slowed and reined in Black Opal.

Madelana instantly followed suit, knowing that she must take his lead, since she was on strange ground and in unfamiliar surroundings.

As they caught their breath, they looked at each other.

"That was great. You're terrific," Philip said. "But we've got to cool it now, we're coming to the sheep and cattle grazing fields."

"Yes, I understand," she said.

They wandered at a gentle pace through the beautiful pastoral countryside, passing herds of cattle and flocks of sheep roaming the meadows and the lower slopes. They skirted copses filled with the ever-present golden elms and eucalyptus, and traveled along a deep and lovely valley, following the winding, silver thread of the river Castlereagh for a short way, and finally they went slowly up into the green hills of Dunoon.

They spoke intermittently.

Madelana asked the odd question now and again, and occasionally Philip volunteered bits of information, but for the most part they were quiet.

This pleased Philip. He did not always wish to talk, was frequently introspective and preoccupied, and women who chattered nonstop got on his nerves. Her silence was like a balm. He was conscious of her in every respect, yet she was not an intrusion on him or his inbred sense of privacy, and there was no awkwardness between them, at least as far as he was concerned. In fact, just simply riding along with her like this made him feel lighter, happier than he had been in years.

Madelana was having similar feelings.

The anxiety and tension she had experienced in the portrait gallery had lessened when she was in her room changing her clothes, had dissipated almost entirely during the time she had been out here in the open air with him.

Although New South Wales was as far away from Kentucky as anyone could get, she felt closer to home than she had since leaving her beloved bluegrass country four years ago. The stillness of the gardens, which had struck her so forcibly earlier that morning, was even more pronounced in this vast landscape, and the over-whelming peacefulness was filling her with a sense of tranquility. And because she was re-laxed, she was unexpectedly at ease with herself and with Philip.

They rode together across his land for almost two hours.

At last they came to the place he had been heading for since they had left the stables. It was the highest point on Dunoon, and Philip led the way up the steep incline. When he reached the top of the hill, he jumped down off Black Opal, stood waiting by the side of the horse for Made-lana, who was only a short distance behind him.

She came up onto the crest, handling the roan beautifully and with the skill of a seasoned equestrian. Nevertheless, he wanted to help her dismount, but once again he refrained. He was afraid to touch her.

As she swung out of the saddle, dropped lightly to the grass, he strolled over to the huge oak that spread its ancient branches across the hilltop like a giant parasol of lacy green.

Madelana joined him, and he told her, "My great-great-grandfather planted this oak over a hundred years ago, and this is my favorite spot. It was Emma who first brought me up here when I was a little boy—she loved it, too. You can see for miles around. Just look!" he exclaimed, flinging his arm out in a sudden sweeping gesture. Then he shaded his eyes with his hand, gazed out across the undulating terrain, and there was pride and love in his voice when he said, "There's nowhere in the world like it, at least not for me."

"It is staggeringly beautiful," Madelana replied, meaning her words. Everything seemed more vivid to her at Dunoon . . . the sky looked infinitely bluer, the clouds whiter, the grass and trees greener, the flowers more colorful. It was a paradise, as he had said earlier when they were riding through the valley. She took several deep breaths. The air was crystal clear up here, and so pure and bracing.

Philip took off his wide-brimmed hat, threw it down, ran his hand through his thick black hair. "Let's take a rest before heading back," he suggested, then motioned to the ground and sat down.

Madelana nodded and also seated herself, enjoying the dark green coolness under the shady tree after their long ride in the sun.

They were both silent for a short while, and then Philip said, "It must have been wonderful to feel the way they did, don't you think?"

"Yes," Madelana said, understanding immediately that he was referring to Paul and Emma.

"Have you ever been in love like that?" Philip asked.

"No, have you?"

"No." He immediately fell silent, slipped down into his thoughts, and Madelana was quiet.

"Are you married?" he asked suddenly.

"No, I'm not . . . nor have I ever been."

Philip gave her a sidelong glance. He wanted to ask her if she was involved with anyone special, but he did not dare. Already the conversation had been more breathtakingly personal than he had intended.

As if aware that he was studying her surreptitiously, she turned her head, gave him a long look through those quiet, unwavering gray eyes.

He smiled at her.

She smiled back. Then she pulled her knees up to her chest, rested her chin on them, sat staring out into the blue-and-white haze of sky and cumulus clouds, drifting.

Philip leaned back, rested his head against the

gnarled tree trunk. Intuitively, he knew that she knew about his reputation as a playboy. He stifled a sigh. It had never bothered him in the past. Now it did.

18

The evening had turned suddenly cool, and a strong wind was blowing down from the hills above Dunoon, ruffling the curtains, making them billow about wildly, and chilling the air in her bedroom.

Paula shivered, rose from the dressing table, and went to close the window.

Once seated again, she picked up her pearl choker, fastened it around her neck, put on the *mabé* pearl-and-diamond earrings, and then sat back, staring at her reflection in the mirror. Not bad, she thought, for an overworked executive and harassed wife and mother of four who's knocking thirty-seven.

She turned her head, glanced at the color photograph on the dressing table. It was of Shane and herself with Lorne, Tessa, Patrick, and Linnet, taken by Emily on the terrace of Pennistone Royal in the spring. Her heart tightened imperceptibly when she thought of her two youngest children; in their different ways they were both so vulnerable, and they needed her.

They had been in bed and fast asleep when she had phoned Shane earlier that morning. With the difference in time between Australia and England she was actually one day ahead, and it had been almost midnight on Friday when she had reached him at Pennistone Royal. He had just returned from dinner with Winston at Beck House; Emily had already left for Hong Kong, on her buying trip for Genret, and apparently the two best friends had enjoyed a rare bachelor evening together.

It had been wonderful to hear his loving and reassuring voice, to know that all was well at home. Lorne and Tessa were now properly settled in at their respective boarding schools, and Nanny Pat, back from her week's holiday in the Lake District, was once again in command of the nursery and her young charges.

"No problems, darling," Shane had said, sounding so close he might have been in the next room. "I'll spend the weekend here with the kids, then push off to London on Sunday night. And listen, angel, I heard from Dad today. He phoned to tell me he and Mother are definitely coming for Christmas, and so young Laura will be with us too, and Merry and Elliot have also accepted. It looks as if we're going to have quite a mob with us up here in Yorkshire . . . It'll be like the old days when Blackie and Emma were alive. And we'll have a wonderful time."

His news had delighted her, and they had chatted for another half hour about the Christmas plans, the children, and other family matters, and Shane had promised to ring her in a couple of days. She had felt much better when she had hung up. She missed him and the children enormously when she was traveling, was never completely at ease when she was separated from her family. She tried not to worry, but invariably she did, and she suspected she would never change. Her nature, after all, was her nature.

Paula glanced at her watch, saw that she had ten minutes to spare before going downstairs for drinks. Rising, smoothing down the skirt of her silk cocktail dress, she walked across to the writing desk where she began to sort through the papers strewn there. Among them were the Christmas lists she had started in Sydney earlier in the week. Shane's family were marked down for major gifts, but not for stocking stuffers and tree presents. She must add their names, now that they were coming to Yorkshire, along with ideas for suitable little tokens, since she planned to do all of her Christmas shopping in Hong Kong when she met Emily there in ten days.

Paula's thoughts focused on Shane's parents as she leaned over the desk, rapidly making notes for herself. She was truly thrilled that Bryan and Geraldine were coming to England in December; they had been ambivalent about it for a number of weeks. Ever since Bryan's heart attack five years ago they had been living in Barbados. Bryan kept an eye on the other O'Neill hotels in the Caribbean, but for the most part he took it easy these days, and was semiretired at Shane's insistence.

She missed them, and there had been a void in all their lives since the O'Neills had lived abroad. She missed Miranda, too. She and Shane's sister had been close friends from childhood, and although they managed to see each other in New York, they were forever grumbling that they never had enough time together these days. As head of O'Neill Hotels International in the United States, Merry was a busy executive, and now that she was married to the noted American architect, Elliot James, she wanted to spend any free time she had with him at their homes in Manhattan and Connecticut. In consequence, Merry had not been to England much lately, and even her business trips were brief. "Hit and runs," Merry laughingly called them.

For once all the O'Neills would be under one roof at the same time, along with the Hartes. Sir Ronald and Michael Kallinski had already accepted to come for Christmas dinner, so the three clans would be represented, and for the first time in years. This thought made Paula smile with pleasure.

Clipping the sheaf of papers together, she slipped them into her briefcase for safekeeping. When she had another free moment, either later tonight or tomorrow morning, she would make a few more notes, allocate bedrooms at Pennistone Royal, do the menus for the holiday period, and start the guest lists for the parties she wanted to give. Christmas was three months away, but that was not really very long, not with the schedule she had, and all she had to accomplish. Planning ahead, being well organized, was the only way she knew how to cope with everything. That was how she had been brought up by her grandmother, and sometimes she wondered if this was indeed the secret of her success.

Paula believed herself to be the first one downstairs when she stood in the doorway of the living room a few minutes later. It was so hushed, so still.

But then Jason Rickards stepped into the room from the veranda, closed the French windows, locked them firmly, and swung around. His tanned, craggy face lit up when he saw her.

"Hi there, sweet'art," he said, striding across the floor toward her.

Lean and rangy, Jason had the gait of a man who had spent years on a horse, a weatherbeaten complexion from being constantly outdoors, and dark hair silvered at the sides. He was in his early sixties, but looked younger. Tonight he wore a navy blue cashmere jacket and dark gray pants, with a white shirt and a navy tie, and was as impeccable as he generally was, but to Paula he seemed to be uncomfortable when he was dressed up for the evening. It was as if more formal clothes constrained him, and she couldn't help thinking that Jason would much prefer to be in blue jeans, riding boots, and an open-necked shirt.

Coming to a standstill, he caught one of her hands in his, twirled her around. "My, you look pretty, Paula. And red suits you as much as it does your mother."

"Thank you, Jason." Paula smiled up into his face, tucked her arm through his, and walked with him to the fireplace. "Where is Mummy, anyway?"

"Upstairs, finishing dressing. She'll be down in a minute. Now, me darlin', let's have a drink together. What would you like?"

"If that's a bottle of champagne I spy over there in the silver bucket, then that's what I'll have, please."

"Good-o." He loped over to the console, where a tray of liquor, glasses, a bucket of ice, and the champagne stood, and proceeded to open the bottle of Louis Roederer Crystal.

Paula watched him, her eyes full of warmth. She thoroughly approved of Jason, had grown very fond of him, admired his down-to-earth attitude toward life. Her respect for him was immense, not only because of his brilliance as a businessman, but for his personal qualities as well. He was kind and thoughtful. Like Philip, she was overjoyed that her mother had become his wife. Despite the disparities in their backgrounds, they got along beautifully and he was a devoted husband. A self-made man, Jason had married late for the first time, and had lost his wife from cancer after only seven years; he had then had a brief, disastrous second marriage. "Third time lucky," was his favorite expression these days, and he was most adoring of Daisy, as she was of him. Sometimes they reminded Paula of a couple of young lovers, and this pleased her.

Pouring champagne into a Baccarat crystal flute, then mixing a scotch and soda for himself, Jason remarked, "It's damn windy out there tonight, Paula. I bet you there's one helluva damn storm down in Sydney."

"I hope it doesn't hit here," she said, accepting the glass from him when he brought it to her.

"I doubt it will, and if it does, it'll soon blow over. We always get a drop of rain in the spring, you know. And we'll have a nice sunny day tomorrow, never fear." He clinked his glass to hers. "Cheers, darlin'."

"Cheers, Jason."

They stood together in front of the fire, perfectly at ease, and full of affection for each other.

Suddenly Jason eyed her speculatively. "There you go again, Paula, smilin' quietly, and looking mighty damn pleased with yourself." He chuckled. "As your mother would say, you look like the cat that's swallowed the canary."

Paula could not help laughing. Jason had adopted many of her mother's expressions, almost all of which Daisy had learned from *her* mother, but they did not sound quite the same without Emma's pithy delivery.

She said, "I'm thrilled about the way Christmas is shaping up, Jason, that's all. It's going to be the biggest get-together we've had in years, now that Shane's parents and sisters are coming."

"Your mother's worried that—"

"What am I worried about?" Daisy asked from the doorway, and floated into the living room on a cloud of *Joy* perfume and a swirl of purple silk.

"Sweet'art, you look gorgeous!" Jason exclaimed, his dark brown eyes glowing with love and admiration. He hurried to Daisy, took her arm, ushered her over to the fireplace. "What can I get for you, sweet'art? Champagne, or a vodka tonic?"

"Champagne, please, Jason darling."

"Jason's right, you *do* look fabulous tonight, Mummy," Paula said. "I've not seen you in purple for years. It's a great color for you, and simply marvelous with those exquisite opals. Are they new?"

"Thank you, dear, and yes, they are. Jason gave them to me on Thursday night. They're from his mine in Coober Pedy."

"Lightning Ridge," Jason corrected, grinning, bringing her the drink. "They're very rare black opals, Paula."

"Thanks," Daisy said, taking the glass. She

repeated, "And what am I worried about, Jason?"

"Philip."

Daisy frowned, sat down on the sofa, raised her flute. "Cheers."

"Cheers," Paula and Jason said in unison.

Daisy took a sip of the champagne, peered quizzically at her husband over the rim. "And *why* am I worried about him?"

"Because he's so reluctant to commit himself . . . about coming to England with us for Christmas," Jason explained. "Paula was just remarking how thrilled she is about the big family reunion and I was on the verge of telling her that her brother was undecided about his plans."

"Oh I think he'll come now," Daisy murmured with a small, but knowing smile.

"You *do?*" Jason sounded surprised and he stared hard at Daisy. "What's happened to make you change your mind, sweet'art? You were pretty damn adamant about it when I got back from Perth on Thursday night, and that's only two days ago."

"At lunch today Paula invited Madelana to go to London for Harte's sixtieth anniversary dinner and dance at the Ritz, and she also invited her to spend Christmas with us in Yorkshire. And Madelana accepted, didn't she, Paula?"

"Well, yes, she did, Mummy." Paula seemed slightly baffled, and she frowned. "But what's that got to do with anything?"

Daisy sat back, beamed first at her daughter, and then at her husband, and said, "It has everything to do with Philip coming to England in December."

Both Jason and Paula gaped at her, but neither of them said a word.

"Haven't you noticed how Philip looks at Madelana?" Daisy asked softly. "When he thinks no one else is watching, of course. And haven't you also noticed how he was behaving around her today . . . at the pool, during lunch, and at teatime? *So very solicitous.* And they were out riding *all* morning, you know, Paula. For about four hours or so."

"Oh Mummy, honestly, you're such a romantic!" Paula exclaimed. "He was merely being a good host. After all, you brought him up to be well mannered. He's a gentleman." Paula laughed dismissively. "He's only known her for *one* day! Not even that, for heaven's sake!"

"So what?" Daisy said, and took another sip of champagne.

Paula frowned at her mother, then looked at Jason, raising a brow.

Jason let out an amused chortle. "I'd only known your mother for one hour when I realized I wanted to marry her, and I was hell-bent on getting her, I don't mind telling you, Paula. I think a man and a woman *know* immediately if they've clicked in a special way, *know* how they truly feel about each other. It's kind of . . . well, it's kind of an instinctive thing. And *time,* as such, doesn't make a helluva lot of difference. You can know a person for years, yet never really know them, feel nothing for them. Or you can suddenly meet someone, and *bang!* That's it!" He glanced across at Daisy. "What's that French expression, sweet'art?"

"Coup de foudre . . . a clap of thunder, an unexpected blow . . . meaning love at first sight," Daisy replied. "And you're absolutely right, Jason, I agree with everything you say." She smiled at him lovingly.

"Madelana and Philip," Paula muttered. "Oh no!" Her heart sank. She adored her brother, but the last thing she wanted was for him to become involved with Madelana. For Madelana's sake. She did not want her to get hurt. Also, she had her own important plans for her assistant in the future.

Paula said slowly, "He might be interested in her, Mother, but you know what he's like with women. He thinks they're a dime a dozen. Why, he's told me that so many times, and *you* also know better than *anyone* that he breaks off with them the minute the relationship starts developing into something more meaningful than a romp in the hay." She shook her head. "I hate to say this about him, but Philip is actually only interested in one-night stands."

"Really, Paula, how can you make a statement like that! He went out with Veronica Marsden for almost three months," Daisy exclaimed vehemently, although she kept her voice muted.

Paula groaned wearily. "Yes, that *is* about the duration of his affairs, isn't it? *Three months.* I sincerely hope he *doesn't* get involved with Maddy, because he'll only cause her heartache, and that I couldn't bear. She's had too much pain in her life already. Please don't encourage him, Ma. Promise me."

Daisy's face dropped. "Yes, I suppose you're right, as usual, Paula." She let out a heavy sigh. "Oh, dear, and I do like her so much. I was so happy today when I saw how keen he seemed to be . . ." Her voice tapered off lamely.

Paula insisted, "Mummy, please promise me you won't encourage Philip. I'm very *serious* about this."

Daisy nodded swiftly. "Oh, I do, dear, I do." She instantly noticed Paula's stern, almost forbidding expression, and added, *"I promise."*

Daisy recognized that her daughter was only re-iterating what she herself had been thinking ear-lier in the week, and dismay lodged in the pit of her stomach. She could not bear to think that her son was destined to be a playboy for the rest of his life. What an empty and shallow existence that would be for him.

Jason said, "I think we'd better get off this subject mighty damn sharpish, I'm sure they'll both be down any minute."

"Of course, Jason," Daisy was quick to agree. "And it really isn't very nice, talking about them in this way, is it?"

"No," Paula muttered, still feeling disturbed, and wondering why *she* hadn't noticed Philip's behavior around Madelana, the attention he had supposedly paid to her. Renowned in the family for being eagle-eyed, for never missing a trick, she suddenly asked herself if she was slipping.

Jason strolled over to the console, refilled his glass, and remarked, "By the way, Paula, when are you planning to go to Hong Kong?"

"Not for about ten days or so. It really de-pends on what I find in Melbourne and Ade-laide. Madelana and I are flying down there on Wednesday, once we've got the Sydney boutique organized for the sale. But why do you ask, Ja-son?"

"One of my executives, Don Metcalfe, has to

go over to the crown colony around that time. It occurred to me that you might like a lift on the corporate jet."

"Gosh, Jason, that would be wonderful," Paula exclaimed, smiling at him. "If our dates coincide, of course."

"Don can leave any time around the twenty-first, the twenty-second, or even the twenty-third of September, whichever suits you, darlin'."

"Thanks so much, I'll let you know."

"You never did say why you're going to Hong Kong, dear," Daisy murmured, giving Paula a questioning look.

"To meet Emily, Mummy. She's there now, on one of her buying trips for General Retail Trading, and we thought it would be fun to have a few days together, relaxing, doing our Christmas shopping. Then we'll continue on to New York, spend a day or two there, return to London on the Concorde."

Daisy smiled somewhat ruefully. "I don't know, Paula, here you are, the head of one of the greatest department stores in the world, and you have to do your shopping in Hong Kong." She shook her head, looking a trifle perplexed. "It doesn't make sense to me."

Paula grinned at her mother. "It's much more fun shopping in foreign places—" She cut her sentence off when Madelana appeared in the doorway. "There you are, Maddy! I was just beginning to wonder what happened to you. I was thinking of sending out a search party," Paula teased, her expression affectionate.

In view of the previous discussion, three pairs of alert and curious eyes automatically fastened on Madelana as she glided across the floor with her usual gracefulness, her elegant and beautifully cut dress moving with fluidity around her long legs.

"Forgive me for being so late," Madelana apologized. "I decided to have a rest earlier, and promptly fell asleep. It must be all the fresh air I've had today . . . and the riding. I haven't been on a horse in a coon's age."

"Then you'll feel it tomorrow," Jason warned. "You'll have damn sore muscles. Take a very hot bath filled with Epsom salts tonight, that'll help a bit. I know Mrs. Carr has plenty of salts in the kitchen. We'll get a box or two for you before you go to bed. Now, what can I get you to drink? A glass of champagne?"

"Thanks, Jason, but I'd prefer a mineral water for the moment," Madelana murmured, and joined Paula in front of the fireplace.

Paula eyed Madelana's cocktail dress. It was a superb piece of clothing, made of cut velvet on silk chiffon, and was a light gray color that emphasized the silvery lights in her eyes. Paula said, "That dress is perfection on you, Maddy. It's a Trigère, isn't it?"

"Yes, it is, and thank you very much." Madelana smiled at her boss. "You're pretty elegant yourself . . . that's a Christina Crowther."

"Yes, but an old one which I left here a couple of years ago. Still, it's not a bit dated is it? Like Pauline Trigère's clothes, Christina's have a wonderful timelessness."

Daisy was smiling approvingly at Madelana. "Paula just took the words right out of my mouth, Maddy, you *do* look particularly lovely tonight." Patting the sofa, she added, "Come, sit next to me, dear."

Madelana did so, and the two of them immediately fell into a conversation about clothes, and the merits of various fashion designers in New York, Paris, and London.

Paula continued to hover in front of the fire, only half listening to Daisy and Maddy. She had the distinct feeling that her mother *would* encourage Philip in his pursuit of Madelana, if indeed he was interested, despite Daisy's promise to her to the contrary. Her mother was desperate for him to get married, and it was patently obvious she thought Madelana was the perfect candidate for daughter-in-law.

Jason brought Madelana a Perrier water, carrying the champagne bottle in his other hand. He topped up Paula's glass, then Daisy's, and as he walked back to the console, he said over his shoulder, "Philip's late coming down, Paula. I hope everything's all right on the station. That wind is damn strong, more like a gale, if you ask me."

Paula said, "I'm sure there's nothing wrong, Jason. Oh, here he comes now."

Philip sauntered into the living room a split second later, looking nonchalant, without a care. He apologized for being late, adding, "Tim Willen kept me on the phone longer than I expected."

"Any problems with the weather?" Jason asked.

"None at all," Philip assured him. "How about fixing your old cobber a scotch on the rocks, since you're standing right next to the bottle, Jason?"

19

The cautionary voice inside his head had warned Philip to go slow with Madelana. But on this Wednesday night, ten days after meeting her at Dunoon, he was asking himself if he had perhaps gone *too* slowly.

He walked across the living room of his penthouse atop the McGill Tower and stood looking out the window absently, for once not seeing the magnificent view of the harbor which he so loved. He was thoroughly preoccupied with his interior meanderings.

Instinctively, he had known not to rush Madelana, had recognized that he had his reputation as a womanizer to overcome with her. If she had thought she was merely going to be another notch on his belt, she would have undoubtedly fled from him. But she was rarely if ever out of his thoughts. He was obsessed with her, and his longing to know her more intimately had created the most enormous tension within him, and there had been times lately when he had felt as though he was about to explode.

I *should* have made my moves before, he thought dismally, regretting the way he had delayed, acknowledging that time was running out on him. She would be leaving soon for the States. On the other hand, even if he had decided to go more quickly with her, it would have been difficult to do so with Paula around.

His sister had become Madelana's self-appointed chaperone during the weekend at Dunoon. She had not left them alone for one minute on the Sunday. Wherever they went, she went too, and then she had spirited Madelana off to Melbourne and Adelaide for most of the following week, and the two of them had not returned to Sydney until Friday evening.

In their absence, he had hit on the idea of showing Madelana the sights of Sydney, thinking that at least he would get to know her *better,* if not more intimately. But Paula had accompanied them on their jaunts around the city, and whilst it had been fun, it had not been what he had originally planned. Although seduction had not been his intent, he had thought a bit of mild flirting would enable him to test the waters. But once they were a threesome this was impossible.

A wry smile touched Philip's mouth as he re-flected on the past few days. Just as Paula had striven hard never to leave them alone together, so his mother had done everything in her power to push him toward Madelana. Without appearing to do so, of course. But he had seen through Daisy's discreet little ploys. Sadly, none of them had worked, because of Paula's vigilance.

Finally, his sister had left this morning for Hong Kong.

He had driven her to the airport himself, and on the way there he had told her that he intended to invite Madelana out for dinner that evening.

"Yes, I suspected you would," Paula had said. There had been a small silence between them, before he had exclaimed, "She's twenty-seven, Paula, and a grown woman. Not to mention extremely intelligent, and quite capable of making her own decisions. You shouldn't have done her thinking for her . . . you haven't been fair to me, or to her. And that's so unlike you, darling."

At once, his sister had apologized, had admitted that he was absolutely right, and she had endeavored to explain her protectiveness. "I care about Madelana," Paula had said. "She's one of the most special women I've ever met, and I couldn't bear it if you, of all people, did anything to cause her grief." She had then gone on to tell him something about Madelana's past, the tragedies that had befallen her family, her dreadful losses, and he had been profoundly touched. He had promised Paula he would do nothing to hurt her assistant, and he intended to keep his promise.

Philip glanced down at his watch. It was seven-forty and time to go. Turning away from the floor-to-ceiling window, he hurried across the huge, modern living room decorated entirely in shades of white and cream, and went on through the marble foyer at the same rapid pace. He was going to be alone with Madelana at last and he could not wait to get to her.

As he rode down in his private elevator, it suddenly struck him that he had no idea whether Madelana was interested in him or not. Her behavior had not revealed her thoughts or her feelings; her calm gray eyes had told him nothing. In fact, the only certain thing was the way he felt about her. And it was quite possible that she would consider his overtures repugnant and so reject him.

The same wry smile flickered in the cool blue eyes. He would soon find out exactly where he stood with her . . . if anywhere at all.

Madelana's suite at the Sydney-O'Neill was on the thirtieth floor of the hotel. It covered a corner of the building, and the L-shaped expanse of windows in the sitting room offered panoramic vistas.

She stood at one of the windows, looking out toward the Opera House on Bennelong Point and the Sydney Harbour Bridge beyond. It was almost eight o'clock, and the night sky was aglow with stars and the myriad lights of the city.

The spectacular view was familiar to her by now, and she was beginning to feel at home here, had become enamored of Sydney and its people. She had quickly discovered she liked the Australians, who were down to earth, open, and friendly, and she had come to understand, through Philip, that their sardonic humor was simply an insurance against pomposity and pretentiousness. "It goes way back, to the early settlers, the Cockneys in particular," he had explained.

Walking over to the sofa, Madelana sat down. Spread out on the coffee table were the photographs which had been taken last weekend on their sight-seeing tour of the city. She began to sort through them, selecting the best for the album she had bought that afternoon.

Memories of the weekend brought a smile to her face. Here was one of Paula and herself at Taronga Park Zoo. They were standing next to a kangaroo with a joey in its pouch, and again it struck her how much the roo reminded her of a deer with its narrow, sensitive face and soulful eyes. She had not realized they were such gentle animals until her visit to the zoo on Saturday morning. The photo was good and she put it on one side to include in the album later.

Picking up a shot of Philip and Paula, which she had taken in the rain forest aviary at Taronga, she marveled again at the jewel-colored parrots and other brilliant, exotic birds shown in the background. This was another must for the album. Next she reached for the small stack of pictures taken on Philip's boat, the *Saraband.* He owned two yachts. The one called *Dunoon,* after the sheep station, was used solely for racing; the *Saraband* was for cruising and entertaining. Magnificently decorated and appointed, it slept six and had a permanent crew.

To Madelana, Sunday had been the best day of the weekend. Certainly she had reveled in their jaunt up the coastline, past Philip's house at Point Piper, and Daisy's and Jason's at Rose Bay. Loving the sea as much as she did, the excursion on the water had been wonderful for her. Deciding that the yachting trip should take pride of place in the album, she selected a handful of snaps of the three of them on board the *Saraband,* and fanned them out in front of her.

A shot of Philip caught her eye, and she picked it up, studied it for a moment.

Paula had not told her very much about him before they had left New York, and what little she did know had been gleaned from various magazines, where she had also seen pictures of him from time to time. Now, staring at the snap in her hand, she realized that nothing could have prepared her for Philip McGill Amory. His presence overwhelmed her. There was something about him, something within him, that reached out to her, moved her in a way she had never been moved before by any other human being. Her reaction to him had been intense from the first moment she had set eyes on him at Dunoon. She felt unsteady when she was with him, and breathless, almost as if she had been punched in the stomach.

Peering closer at the picture, she could not help thinking how debonair and dashing he looked, standing there on the deck of the beautiful *Saraband.* His sailing whites emphasized his tan, his vivid coloring. It had been windy on Sunday, and his black hair was ruffled, his laughing blue eyes screwed up against the glare of brilliant sunlight and glittering sea. How irresistible he seemed.

She was most powerfully drawn to him, and this disturbed and worried her for a number of reasons. He was her boss's brother, but quite aside from this, he was hardly likely to be interested in her. He was immensely powerful, immensely rich, and devastatingly attractive, and therefore he could have any woman in the world he wanted. His reputation as a playboy only verified this as a fact. A career girl like herself, who was not a member of the international social circles he moved in, was hardly a candidate for one of his romantic interludes. Nor did she care to be. The last thing she wanted was a quick fling. She was not cut out for brief encounters. No, Philip McGill Amory was not the kind of man a woman like her should *ever* become involved with. He was too dangerous, guaranteed to wreak havoc and heartbreak.

I don't need any more problems with beautiful, difficult men, she thought, remembering her recent experiences with Jack Miller. Her career was her priority now. And in any case, she would be leaving Sydney in ten days, and that would be that. She and Paula had fortunately found a manager for the boutique yesterday. The young woman met all of Paula's requirements, and had already started working on a week's trial. Providing all went well, she would soon be winging her way back to New York . . . far, far away from Mr. Amory.

The telephone on the writing desk shrilled and she went to answer it. "Hello?"

"It's Philip," he said, "I'm in the lobby."

"I'll be right down," she said, and replaced the receiver. Picking up her bag, her silk shawl, and the doorkey, she left the suite.

Going down in the elevator, she wondered what the evening would be like. She had accepted his invitation against her better judgment, and only because he had been so gracious, and just a little bit insistent on the phone that morning. Also, being who he was, she had not wanted to offend him. But this was the first time she was going to be alone with him, since they had gone riding at the sheep station, and sudden nervousness invaded her.

She saw him the moment she stepped out of the elevator.

He wore a dark blue blazer, a pale blue shirt and tie, and gray slacks. He dominated the lobby with his height and his arresting looks, his inbred confidence, and his commanding air of authority.

When he saw her he raised a hand in greeting, and strode toward her.

She instantly tensed up in the way she had when she had met him in the portrait gallery, and she almost missed a step as she walked across the marble floor. Then she took hold of herself, and pushed a bright smile onto her face, and as they came together in the middle of the lobby, she extended her hand, still smiling.

Philip took it, gave it a small squeeze, instantly released it. Looking down at her, he returned her smile, and said, "It's nice to see you, Madelana, you look lovely, as usual." He glanced approvingly at her full, black wool skirt and the tailored, white silk shirt.

"Thank you. You did say to dress simply."

"Yes," he murmured, escorting her across the lobby, then explained "I've booked a table at Doyle's . . . it's a fish restaurant on the beach. Very casual, lots of fun, and they have the best fish and chips in Sydney, not to mention the most wonderful view of the city skyline from there."

"It sounds terrific."

They went out into the street. His wine colored Rolls-Royce was parked immediately in front of the hotel, and after helping her inside, Philip strode around to the driver's side, got in, turned on the ignition, and pulled away from the curb.

"Doyle's is out at Watson's Bay," he informed her. "It'll take us about half an hour. So sit back, relax, and enjoy the music." As he spoke he turned on the tape in the dashboard and the voice of Mel Torme singing "Moonlight in Vermont" filled the interior of the car.

Madelana tried to do as he suggested, not even attempting to make conversation. She could think of nothing to say to him. Unexpected panic choked her, made her throat dry. She did not know how she would manage to get through the evening. Sitting here next to him, in such close proximity, she was filled with some awful kind of terror, and she fervently wished she had not accepted his invitation.

"Relax," he said, as if reading her mind.

She looked at him through the corner of her eye, and laughed nervously.

"I am relaxed."

"No, I don't think so."

She was silent. She bit her inner lip.

Now it was his turn to laugh, and he sounded as nervous as she had.

Eventually, he murmured in a low voice, "We both work too hard, I suspect, and I suppose you've had as rough a day as I have. It takes a while to unwind . . . and I haven't been very

333

thoughtful. I should have taken you for a drink at the bar in the hotel first."

"No, I'm fine," she told him, and realized that this was partially true. The feeling of panic was easing somewhat. Anyway, she was being silly, wasn't she? He had no way of knowing how attracted she was to him. Thank God. She had cultivated a bland face for the past few days, worn an inscrutable expression especially for him. Anyway, he was obviously only being polite, taking care of her for Paula. Undoubtedly, it was her boss who had asked him to take her out. Paula was always so thoughtful, so solicitous of her welfare.

The exterior architecture of Doyle's had lovely Victorian mannerisms. Made of red brick and beige stone, the building was two stories high, and its upstairs balconies were decorated with fancy, pierced-wood valances painted white, and these were repeated around the edge of the front portico. The rooms inside were bright and cheerful, simply furnished, and there was a pub-like atmosphere.

It was busy when they arrived, but Philip was quickly shown to a table in a quiet, windowed corner overlooking the beach and the dark sea curling away to the edge of a dim horizon. He insisted Madelana take the chair facing toward the city, and just as he had said earlier, the view of Sydney from Watson's Bay was breathtaking, with the McGill Tower dominating the skyline.

He ordered a bottle of Pouilly Fuisse, dry and cold and refreshing, and as they sipped it he asked her about the new manager, and how the Grand Sale was going at the boutique. She felt on safe ground, talking about business, and as they chatted she began to relax further, and so did he. He answered her questions about their opal mines at Coober Pedy and Lightning Ridge, told her about opal mining in general, and he talked at length about the various divisions of the giant conglomerate he ran. The McGill Corporation fascinated her, and she gave him her entire attention, as always intrigued by big business. Before either of them realized it almost an hour had passed.

"I think we'd better order," Philip said, when the waitress appeared at their table for the third time.

"I'll have the same as you, please," Madelana murmured, after a quick glance at the menu.

He grinned. "Fried fish and chips . . . how does that sound?"

"Just great. Thanks."

Once he had ordered dinner, he asked her exactly what she did for Paula at Harte's in New York, and she told him a little about her work, how she had been planning and organizing the special events for the sixtieth anniversary of the stores.

When she finished, he laughed, shook his head. "And I thought Paula was a workaholic! My God, you're as bad as she is!"

"I guess I am," Madelana agreed, also laughing, enjoying being alone with him; her earlier apprehension had entirely dissipated.

"And tell me, how do you manage to have a private life, working the way you do? Doesn't your boyfriend object?"

"I don't have one."

"Oh." A black brow lifted. "A girl like you . . . so beautiful . . . so bright . . ." He did not finish, merely stared at her intently.

Ignoring his compliments, she said softly, "I just broke up with someone."

"I'm sorry."

"You don't have to be. It was for the best . . . I'd made an error in judgment."

Now the black brows drew together in a frown. "What do you mean?"

"I mistook personality for character."

"Ah, I *see,*" he said, liking the shrewdness of this observation. He was suddenly eaten up with curiosity about the man she had so recently been involved with, and he couldn't help probing. "What does he do? You know, for a living?"

"He's an actor. A rather brilliant one, too. On the Broadway stage."

"Famous? Would I know him?"

"Possibly . . . probably. Jack Miller."

"Oh sure, I saw him in something a couple of years ago when I was in New York. A Eugene O'Neill play, I think."

Madelana nodded.

"What went wrong between the two of you?"

Madelana bit her inner lip, glanced away.

But after a brief moment, she brought her eyes back to his, smiled faintly. "Mah daddy used to say there's nothing worse than the ole moonshine for killin' a romance and curin' a woman of fanciful ideas she might be havin' about a dude. Ah doan know that a truer word has ever been spoken."

Philip smiled, loving the sudden, Southern intonation in her voice. It was soft, beguiling, very feminine. "Now you really sound as though you come from Kentucky," he said. "And I must admit, I agree with your daddy . . . about a drinking man."

"It wasn't just the booze," she now said in her New York voice. "Jack was always a bit odd with me . . . about my work, I mean. He is a male chauvinist, by his own admission, and he resented my career. Anyway—"

At this moment the waitress arrived with

their food, and Madelana changed the subject by asking him about yacht racing. Since this was Philip's favorite sport and his only genuine hobby, he was happy to discuss it with her. And when he finally paused, she told him how much she loved the sea, and how she had first gone sailing with the Smiths at Nantucket.

"I met Patsy Smith the first day I arrived at the residence, and we became friends instantly. And we're still close, even though she's gone back to Boston."

"What's the residence?" Philip asked, between mouthfuls of fish.

She proceeded to tell him about Sister Bronagh, the other nuns, what life had been like at the residence, and her early days in New York.

Philip listened carefully, nodding from time to time, occasionally laughing at her anecdotes. But he did not interrupt her once. She was truly opening up to him tonight, revealing a great deal about herself for the first time, and he wanted to encourage this. He needed to know everything there was to know about this woman. She was under his skin.

It was later, over coffee, that Philip suddenly said, "I thought you might like to come up to Dunoon this weekend, Madelana. It'll do you good after all your running around with Paula, all your hard work. And it *is* your last chance, since you're leaving at the end of next week. Aren't you?"

"Yes, I am." She lifted her cup, took a sip of the coffee.

He waited a moment, then pressed her. "Say you'll come, Madelana. I want you to . . . so very much."

An odd nuance in his voice made her glance at him more closely, and she saw there was a curious expression in his eyes, one she could not quite fathom. And then intuitively she knew he was interested in her, and she felt a sudden tightening in her chest. She found it impossible to speak. Her throat went tight and dry again. She instantly understood that to go to Dunoon with him would be playing with fire. Therefore she must refuse his invitation. To protect herself. That was the only wise thing to do.

She said, "Yes, I'd love to come. Thank you very much, Philip." As these words left her mouth, she sat back in the chair, surprised at herself, and at her perversity. You fool, she thought. You're just asking for trouble.

Philip was beaming at her and saying, "We can fly up tomorrow afternoon."

"No, no, I can't go then," she exclaimed

quickly. "I've got to be at the boutique. I couldn't possibly come until Saturday."

"Friday," he insisted, holding her with his eyes. "You can come up Friday morning. Everything will be all right at the boutique. Don't worry so much."

She swallowed hard, wondering why she had ever accepted. "I must go into the boutique for a couple of hours at least," she compromised.

"Okay, if you say so," Philip agreed. "But Ken will collect you there at eleven, drive you out to the airport. My plane will be waiting, and if you leave Sydney at noon, you'll get to the station in time for lunch." Philip smiled deeply into her eyes, reached out, took her hand, held it in both of his.

Madelana nodded, not trusting herself to speak.

20

Philip took off his soaking wet sweater and shirt, and threw them to one side. Hooking his right foot into the boot jack, he pushed off one riding boot, and then the other, stripped down to his underpants, and hurried through into the bathroom, feeling chilled to the bone.

He took a very hot shower, letting the steaming water sluice down over his body for a few minutes, until his blood was tingling and he felt warmer. Stepping out of the shower stall, he dried himself, pulled on his toweling robe, and walked over to the sink. He stood in front of the mirror, combing his wet hair, slapping on cologne, and thinking of Madelana.

What a pity the thunderstorm had blown up when it had, so suddenly, about an hour ago. It had curtailed their ride. They had been up in the hills above Dunoon, and he had begun to sense a lessening of the tension in her out there in the peaceful countryside. Certainly she appeared to be more at ease with him today. When she had arrived yesterday at lunchtime, she had been very quiet, and so taut he thought at one moment that she might snap in half, and she had remained tense for the rest of the day. She had seemed a bit better in the evening though, had evidently enjoyed their dinner with Tim and Anne Willen.

By the time they had gone riding this afternoon she had been lighthearted, almost gay, and she was opening up to him once more, and he knew he was gaining her confidence. So much so, he had been on the verge of telling her how strongly he felt about her when the weather had changed abruptly. The sky had grown overcast and dark. Heavy torrential rain had started to fall, and they had mounted their horses and galloped back to the stables at top speed. Even so, it had taken them a good twenty minutes to get there. Matt had been waiting for them with one of the other grooms, and they had led Gilda and Black Opal off to the tack room; he had driven Madelana up to the manor in the Maserati, the two of them drenched to the skin and shivering. She had become very white, her teeth chattering uncontrollably as they had dashed into the house, and now, as he went through into his bedroom, Philip hoped that she had not caught a cold.

He stood warming himself in front of the fire for a few minutes before crossing to the black lacquer Chinese cabinet, which contained a small, fully stocked bar. He poured two cognacs into small brandy balloons, gulped one down, then went to dress, pulling on a thick Fair Isle sweater and socks, and heavy gray flannels. He slipped his feet into a pair of brown loafers, collected the other brandy balloon, and left the room with it.

A second later he stood in front of Madelana's door. He was about to knock, but hesitated fractionally, wondering if he had given her enough time to shed her wet riding clothes, shower, and change. Deciding that he had, he rapped softly.

"Come in," she called.

He did so, stood hovering on the threshold.

She was huddled in front of the fire, seated on the floor with her back to the sofa, dressed in a track suit and thick socks, sipping the tea he had asked Mrs. Carr to have sent up to her a short while before.

"I thought you might want to drink this," he said, holding out the brandy balloon. "It'll warm you through."

"Thank you." She put the cup she was holding back in its saucer on the end table. "Yes, I'd like it, Philip." There was a pause. "Thank you," she said again.

He pushed the door closed with his foot, walked over to her, handed her the glass. She took it from him, and as she did, their fingers grazed. She jumped slightly, as if surprised, drew back, pushed herself harder against the sofa. Then she lifted her eyes to his.

It was still raining outside, and somber, and she had not turned on the lamps, and in the shadows of the dim room she looked ethereal, illuminated as she was by the blazing fire. Her face shimmered with an incandescent, fragile beauty, and her eyes were huge, transparent, and shining.

He found it impossible to look away.

They continued to gaze at each other. For a split second Philip thought he was looking deep into her soul. Finally he dropped his eyes. He did not trust himself with her, and he swung around without a word, walked back to the door, intending to leave her alone until dinner. But he could not help turning to glance at her before he went out, his eyes irresistibly drawn to hers once more.

She returned his long, penetrating stare steadily, solemnly. Her face was infinitely quiet. She did not move, nor did she speak. The air was hushed, very still between them.

He took a step forward, then another. "I want to be with you," he said in a voice that was unexpectedly hoarse. "Please don't send me away."

"I'm not going to."

At first he thought he had not heard her correctly, and he looked at her swiftly, through narrowed eyes.

She put down the brandy glass, lifted her arm, held out her hand to him.

He hurried back to her, took the slender hand in his, brought it to his mouth, brushed his lips over her long fingers. Then he knelt down on the floor by her side.

"Oh Maddy," he said, using the diminutive of her name for the first time. "Oh Maddy."

"Philip," she whispered in a voice so low it was hardly audible.

He pulled her forward. She was in his arms, clinging to him, saying his name over and over, and he held her close to his body, tightening his grip. With one hand he stroked her hair. His mouth found hers, and he kissed her as he had wanted to kiss her from the very first day, deeply, fiercely, passionately, his tongue thrusting as if he was taking possession of her with his mouth. She returned his kisses, and her tongue grazed his, and he realized that her ardor for him matched his own for her. This knowledge sent a thrill searing through him.

There was no going back, he knew that. They must make love at once, now, here, on the rug in front of the fire. There was no time to waste . . . too much time had been wasted already. He pulled her down under him, slid his hand under her loose top. When his fingers closed around one of her breasts she let out a long sigh; he stroked her gently, smoothed the tips of his fingers across her nipple, caressed it lovingly. Almost instantly, he felt it harden under his fondling, and this inflamed him even more. He tugged at her top, wanting to lift it over her head.

She sat up, pulled it off. He tore at his own clothes, flung them to one side. Suddenly they were stretched out next to each other on the rug, completely naked. They began to kiss again, frantically, more urgently than ever, and they could not keep their hands off each other. They reached out hungrily, longingly, to touch, to explore, to caress, to excite. The urgency between them grew and intensified as they became more and more aroused.

There was a violence in his desire for her, and he sensed the same turbulent emotion in her. She wanted him as desperately as he wanted her, and she was making that quite clear. And so he fell across her, slid into her. As he did he felt her tense, gasp, and then relax.

He braced his hands on either side of her, rose up above her, looked down into her face. It was full of yearning and desire, and the wild expression that blazed in her eyes mirrored exactly what he was feeling, and his breath caught in his throat in surprise and pleasure.

Philip began to move against her, very slowly, expertly, and she thrust her body forward to meet his, cleaving to him.

Their rhythm grew faster and the urgency of their passion spiraled up into total abandonment, and they were on a dizzying climb, rising higher and higher together, out of control. He had fantasized about her for days. Now his fantasy had become his reality, and he was unable to hold back. He flowed into her, gave himself to her, and then his mouth was on hers, devouring hers. And she was flying with him on that dizzying flight, and she cried his name suddenly and stiffened, and they began a slow slide down over the edge, down into scorching white heat.

Her arms and legs were woven around him, binding him in their silken vise. He was welded to her, part of her, and she was part of him, and the miracle was that they had become one single being . . .

Entirely spent, they lay still, locked in each other's arms. There was no sound except for their labored breathing, the crackling of the logs on the fire, the faint ticking of a clock somewhere in the background.

Philip stirred first. He buried his face in the mass of her chestnut hair, murmured against her neck, "I've wanted you since I first saw you downstairs in the portrait gallery, Maddy."

When she made no comment, he asked, "Didn't you know that?"

"No, I didn't," she whispered. With a small smile, she confessed, "I wanted you too."

"You certainly hid it very well," he exclaimed quietly.

She said, "And so did you."

They both laughed, but fell silent immediately, caught in the webs of their own thoughts. After a short while, Philip released his hold on her, got up, took her hands in his, pulled her to her feet. He slipped an arm around her, and they stood together in front of the fire, gazing at each other as though mesmerized. He tilted her chin, bent down, kissed her on the mouth, lightly, gently, and then reached for the brandy balloon. He offered it to her. She shook her head. He took several swallows, placed the glass on the table, and as he led her over to the large four-poster bed, he said, "I do hope you don't think that I'm a drinking man, too . . . ."

Madelana laughed, said nothing, slid under the bedclothes. Philip joined her, wrapped his arms around her. She curved her body into his, relaxing her shoulders against his broad chest, filled with a rare joy. It had as much to do with the pleasure she had given Philip as the fulfillment and release he had brought to her. The tension which had been building in her for days had disappeared. She felt as though she were wrapped in a cocoon of peace and contentment and happiness. And she knew it was because of him, all the things he was.

Philip continued to hold her close to him, nuzzling his face into the nape of her neck, her hair, the space between her shoulder blades. To his surprise he was suddenly at full arousal again. He threw the bedclothes to one side, pushed himself up on one elbow, looked down at her.

Madelana smiled up at him. Her face was radiant.

He smiled back, lifted one hand, began to

stroke her cheek, his eyes spilling with emotion. The truth was, he loved her. He had fallen in love with her that very first day. He was glad it had happened at Dunoon, and that they had first made love here. It seemed very right to him that something as important as this had taken place in his home. He knew that he would always love her. This was not a passing thing. There could be no other women in his life now. Never, ever again.

"You look thoughtful," she said, her eyes quizzical.

He leaned over her, answered in a low voice, "It was too quick, Maddy. I'm sorry . . . anxiety on my part, I'm afraid." He laughed lightly, ruefully. "But I'd ached for you for days . . . fantasized about you."

"You were wonderful."

"Perhaps you're prejudiced, darling."

He brought his mouth down to her breasts, began to kiss them, whilst stroking her body, running his hands all over her. Her skin felt like satin to him, and in the firelight it had a lovely roseate cast to it. He marveled at the beauty of her lithe body, so slender, so delicately formed, her long legs, the heavy, voluptuous breasts, taut now under his touch.

Lifting his head, he brought his mouth to her mouth, kissed her deeply, traced a line down her stomach with one finger, until his hand came to rest between her thighs. He caressed her lightly, adeptly, and she reached out for him, began to stroke him. As he felt her tense and spasm, he pushed her hand away from him, entered her, and again they were instantly swept away by the intensity and urgency of their passion for each other.

They were together for a long time, and then he got up and left the bed. He strode over to the fireplace where he had discarded his clothes earlier, began to dress.

She watched him as he moved around in front of the fire, thinking what a beautiful man he was. He had a wonderful body. He was over six feet and broad shouldered with a barrel chest, and there was not an ounce of extra flesh on him, and he was tanned from being constantly in the sun.

Madelana had the sudden curious feeling that she had known him before . . . long ago. There was something so very familiar about him to her that it was startling. And yet they *were* strangers . . . albeit *intimate* strangers now.

He came back to her, sat down on the edge of the bed, moved a strand of hair away from her eyes. Bending over her, he kissed her lightly, said, "This is just the beginning, Maddy darling."

"It's the beginning of the end—" She stopped abruptly, stared up at him, her eyes wide with surprise at her words.

He scowled. "What an odd thing to say. What do you mean?"

"I don't know," she exclaimed. "It was a thought that flashed through my head, and I said it without thinking."

"I'm not going to talk about the *end* of anything." He laughed dismissively, and pulled her into his arms, hugged her tightly. Then he let her go, stood up. "I'll see you downstairs shortly. Dress casually, darling, it's just the two of us."

"Yes," she said.

She lay there for a while after he had gone. There was an indentation on the pillow next to her, where his head had been, and she reached out to touch the spot, slithered to his side of the bed, buried her face in the pillow. It smelled of him . . . of his hair and his cologne. She began to weep.

An enormous sense of loss overwhelmed her and she was afraid.

21

Hong Kong glittered. It was all color and light and movement and noise.

From the moment Jason Rickards' private jet had thundered down the runway at Kai Tak Airport five days ago, and Paula had alighted, she had been caught in the spell of the British Crown Colony.

She had not been there for fourteen years, and she had forgotten what it was really like. It overpowered in every sense.

Visually it reminded her of Manhattan, with its towering skyscrapers, air-conditioned shopping emporiums, boutiques, banks and businesses, stylish restaurants, and elegant hotels.

Yet withal, Hong Kong had a rhythm that was uniquely its own, a tempo that was rapid, pulsating, full of excitement and tumult.

Paula felt movement all around her. Wherever she looked she saw perpetual motion. Great jets soared up into the misty blue skies above Victoria Peak; sailing boats and sampans, yachts and junks, hydrofoils and ferries plowed the busy harbor waters around Central and Kowloon; automobiles, trams, buses, and rickshaws surged through the streets; and people jostled each other in swarming crowds as they rushed about their business. It was overpopulated. Space was at a premium, on land and sea, and there was so much teeming life and deafening noise that Paula had begun to feel slightly battered by it.

Yet in contrast, there were lovely little pockets of calm and tranquility that caught her by surprise . . . the quiet hills of the New Territories, that rural area between Kowloon and mainland China . . . the temples and shrines . . . and even a spot down near the Star Ferry Pier, where every morning a group of Chinese men performed the slow, meditative movement of t'ai chi.

To Paula, it was the many contrasts which so startled, and which made the deepest impression on her.

Nowhere on earth was there such limitless wealth and grinding poverty within the same few miles, such breathtaking beauty rubbing shoulders with sickening squalor. Ritzy high life was perilously juxtaposed against dangerous low life. Grand and ancient families lived in close proximity to desperate refugees. Hong Kong was a place of old money and taipans, over one hundred and forty years of British rule and colonial traditions, newly made fortunes, stunning success stories, and mind-boggling business bonanzas. It also had one of the highest suicide rates in the world.

It had captivated Paula, and she fully understood its extraordinary allure for residents and visitors alike.

Until Paula's arrival, Emily had been ensconced in the Peninsula in Tsimshatsui on Kowloon side. This was the hotel where she invariably stayed on her buying trips. It was convenient for her business dealings with mainland China, since she had ready access to the factories which manufactured the varied products she purchased for Genret.

The night before Paula had flown in with Don Metcalfe of Rickards International on the company plane, Emily had "moved Hong Kong side." She had checked into the vast and beautiful suite she had booked in the famous Mandarin Hotel in the heart of the Central District.

"I've finished all my business, and Central's much more convenient for us, and what we want to do," Emily had explained to Paula when she was settling in after her arrival. "It's the shopping mecca of Asia, and anyway, I think it's much more interesting for you to be on Hong Kong Island itself." Paula had nodded and agreed. "Whatever you say, Emily. You're in charge."

Emily had planned a program which hardly left them a moment to breathe. Nevertheless, Paula had been enthusiastic about doing everything, and tremendously energized by the sightseeing, the shopping, the visits to various restaurants and several of the other smart hotels, not to mention their tour of night clubs in Wanchai.

The first evening she was there, Emily had taken her to Gaddi's for dinner. It was considered to be the finest European restaurant in Hong Kong, and Rolf Heiniger, the renowned maître d'hôtel had lived up to his reputation for knowledge and attentiveness, had suggested the most delicious dishes and the finest wines.

The following morning they had gone browsing and shopping in Emily's favorite boutiques, shops, markets, and galleries. "Don't forget, I'm an old China hand," she had confided to Paula with a grin. "Trust me and you'll get the best bargains. Quality merchandise at the right prices."

Paula had laughed, had exclaimed, "Oh I trust you all right, Emily. You had a sharp eye even as a child. I think that's one of the reasons Grandy gave you Genret to run."

In the course of several hectic days they did all of their Christmas shopping, buying important gifts as well as stocking stuffers and tree presents. They purchased pearls, jade jewelry, cuff links for the men in the family, embroidered silks and brocades, Chinese evening jackets and cheongsams, beaded evening bags, unusual wooden toys, cloisonné, hand-embroidered linens, trinkets, and knickknacks.

Emily had suggested they pay a visit to Hollywood Road, just above Central, explaining that this was an imperative, and Paula quickly discovered that she was right. Many of the more important antique shops and art galleries were located here, and as they had gone on the rounds, Paula had been enchanted by the artifacts on display. She had bagged an ancient nefrite vase for Jason, who collected oriental art, and a beautiful antique jade necklace for her mother.

And in between the shopping expeditions and all manner of exotic meals in unique restaurants,

Emily had arranged a few other fascinating excursions. She had taken Paula to Aberdeen Harbour, where thousands of Boat People lived and worked on junks and sampans; they had made a trip to the New Territories on Kowloon side; had driven up to the top of misty Victoria Peak to see the spectacular view; and visited various temples and shrines.

On the flight from Sydney, Paula's traveling companion, Don Metcalfe, had said he would like to take her and Emily out to dinner before they left for New York. And this he had done the previous night. They had gone with him on the hydrofoil to Macau, the Portugese enclave at the entrance to the Pearl River, just fifty minutes away, where they had dined in an elaborate restaurant before visiting some of the famous gambling casinos. It had been a memorable evening. They had enjoyed themselves tremendously with Don, who had kept them laughing and entertained; Emily, in particular, had been excited by the trip to Macau, where she had never been and had always wanted to go.

In the early hours of the morning, when Paula had finally fallen into bed exhausted, it struck her that they had packed in more in a few days than she had imagined possible. Every minute of her stay in Hong Kong had been enjoyable, and being alone with Emily had been an added bonus. It reminded her of the trips they had taken together as girls, and she felt young again, lighthearted, almost carefree.

Today was their last day in Hong Kong; they were taking the night flight to New York. Emily had been determined that she see the beautiful Regent Hotel in Kowloon, and the unparalleled view of Hong Kong Island from this vantage point. And so they had gone there for lunch. She had had to get up very early to do her packing first, but it had been worth making the effort. The lunch and the view would linger in her mind and memory for a long time.

Immediately after lunch, they had caught the Star Ferry back to Central. Emily had made for the hotel to finish her suitcases; Paula had returned to the jewelry shop where she had seen a pair of exquisite earrings, which she wanted to buy as a Christmas gift for Emily.

Once inside the shop, Paula had bargained in the way she had seen Emily doing it for the last few days. Much to her surprise, and enormous delight, she had won the earrings at a far better price than she had expected. And now, as she walked the short distance to the hotel, she was filled with a great sense of satisfaction at this small success.

Hurrying across the lobby of the Mandarin,

Paula realized she was twenty minutes late to meet her cousin for tea. And so she headed straight for their point of rendezvous, the Clipper Lounge, which floated like a gallery above the lobby on the mezzanine floor, and ran lightly up the steps.

Emily saw her, raised her hand in greeting.

Paula waved back.

A moment later she was sitting down in one of the comfortable chairs facing Emily.

"Sorry I'm late. The last hour just flew by," Paula said with an apologetic smile.

"It's all right. I've not been here long, and you know I love this place. I feel as if I'm on a boat, what with the brass portholes and all this mahogany. Oh, and before I forget—" Emily opened her handbag, fished around, handed Paula two small envelopes, and finished, "These were in the suite waiting for you when I got back after lunch."

"Oh, telexes! Thanks, darling." Paula took them, opened the first, scanned it quickly, then read the second. She pursed her lips, filling with disappointment. One was from Michael Kallinski in London, the other from Harvey Rawson in New York, and both effectively said the same thing: Peale and Doone, the small chain of stores in the Midwest, had been sold right under their noses to another buyer. Too bad, she thought, the chain would have been a good beginning for my expansion program. On the other hand, she had never been quite as enthused as Michael about the locations of the shops. This thought consoled her a little.

Emily was watching Paula closely. She said, "Is something wrong at home?"

"No, no, nothing like that," Paula responded quickly, reassuringly. "These are business telexes."

"Oh. Who from?" Emily probed, as usual inquisitive.

"One's from Michael, the other from a Wall Street lawyer who was doing some work for me." Paula smiled faintly. "A deal we wanted didn't come off. Now, let's order. I think I'm going to have the mulberry tea again. I've grown rather partial to it."

"Yes, I'll have the same." Emily swung her blond head, caught the attention of the waiter, motioned to him.

Once she had given the order, she leaned across the table, leveled her shrewd green eyes at her cousin. "What kind of deal didn't come off?" When Paula did not immediately answer, Emily remarked, "It must have been something important to you. I noticed how put out you looked."

Paula nodded. "Actually, I *was* disappointed,

Emily. I was hoping to buy a small chain of stores in the States. Unfortunately, we missed getting them by a hair's breadth."

"Why do you want to buy more stores?" Emily was perplexed, and she frowned.

"I've been wanting to expand Harte's in America. Buying an existing chain seems to be the best way to go about it to me, Emily."

"One store in America was enough for Gran. Why would *you* want more?"

"Times have changed radically. You know that as well as I do. I must expand, darling, it's the only way to survive as a retailer today."

Emily said, in her blunt way, "I think you're biting off more than you can chew, if you ask me."

Paula laughed. "Now how many times did our grandmother tell us that everyone said *that* to her, and throughout her life, too, and *she* never paid a blind bit of notice."

Ignoring this comment, Emily said strongly, "I bet Shane agrees with me. What does *he* think about this expansion idea of yours?"

"Well, very frankly, Emily, I haven't had a chance to tell him yet. This summer, the south of France was so hectic, and there seemed no point in bringing it up until there was a chain available. And the week we were together, before I left for Australia, was so rushed, you know."

"I don't think he'll like it, Paula. You've enough to keep you pretty busy, what with Harte's in London, Paris and Yorkshire, Sitex Oil, and the boutiques in the hotels."

"Grandy used to tell us that organization was the key to everything, and that an organized woman had the world by the balls."

"That's true, she did say that. Nevertheless, Shane *won't* be happy. And there's something else, Paula. I don't think Gran would approve of this idea of yours if she were alive."

"Nonsense! Of course she would! She'd see the wisdom behind everything I plan to do," Paula cried spiritedly, sounding confident. She drew closer to Emily, and began to outline her plans for the future of the Harte stores in the United States.

Emily listened attentively, nodding from time to time.

They were so absorbed in their conversation that neither of them saw the man who was regarding them intently from the stairs leading up to the Clipper Lounge.

He was stunned at the sight of the two women, and was momentarily rooted to the spot. Recovering himself rapidly, he pivoted, ran down the steps, sped across the lobby, and went out through the front door.

The blood rushed to the man's head, and he filled with a fulminating rage as he raced back to Pedder Street, dodging in and out, pushing past people almost violently in his haste and anxiousness to put distance between himself and the Mandarin.

Exactly two minutes after leaving the hotel, he was standing in an elevator, riding up to the top floor of the skyscraper where his company, Janus and Janus Holdings Ltd., was housed. Avoiding the front entrance, and in so doing bypassing the large outer offices where his staff worked, he hurried down the long corridor, let himself in through the private door.

This opened into a foyer, handsomely furnished with Chinese antiques, which in turn led through double mahogany doors to his inner sanctum, luxuriously appointed, with a stunning view of Victoria Harbour visible through a wall of plate glass.

Going straight to the small mirrored bar, he poured himself a straight vodka. To his annoyance his hand shook as he lifted the glass to his mouth. He downed the drink, strode over to his desk, flipped on the intercom.

"Yes, sir?" his English secretary said.

364

"Please have Lin Wu bring the Daimler around to the front, Peggy. I'm leaving early today. And I'll sign my letters now."

"Yes, sir, I'll be right in with them."

He arranged a suitably inscrutable expression on his face, and sat down, willing his anger to subside.

22

His rage lingered.

He carried it with him in the Daimler on the drive up the Peak to his home. It was still with him now as he sat in the library of his elegant duplex apartment, going through his personal mail. The rage was of a kind he had not experienced for the longest time, and the fact that he had reacted so strongly when he had seen the two women had unnerved him. He seethed inside, and with good reason. However, he knew he must bring the anger under control. He dare not allow emotion to cloud his vision or flaw his judgment.

Exhaling, he put the half-dozen or so social

invitations, various thank-you notes, and personal letters to one side, pushed the carved rosewood chair away from the antique rosewood desk, went out into the gallery.

It was from this long and spacious hallway that the other rooms in the apartment flowed; a staircase at one end led up to the second floor. He crossed the flowing space, walking in the direction of the drawing room, thinking how restful the gallery was after the busy activity of his offices. It never failed to give him pleasure. The floor was stained ebony and highly polished, the walls white and hung with his collection of very fine Chinese paintings by past masters, dating from the fifteenth century to the present.

Drawing to a standstill in front of an ink-on-paper painting by Sun Kehong, dated 1582, he straightened it, then stood back, regarded it for a prolonged moment, smiling, nodding to himself in appreciation of its refinement, elegance, and simple beauty.

Moving slowly, he continued along the gallery, admiring the art he had so lovingly assembled. The gallery was sparse, the only piece of furniture a console table made of ebony upon which rested a carved celadon vase with a cover from the Qianlong period, balanced by two white nefrite rams carved in the Song spirit. At the far end, against a short wall, glass shelves suspended on brass chains from the ceiling appeared to float, held his prized collection of rare Ming bronzes.

Recessed ceiling spots, discreet, strategically placed, illuminated the art; these were the only lights, and this area of the apartment was dim, shadowy, tranquil. He lingered, allowed the peacefulness to penetrate his bones, calm his turbulent spirit, in the way he had learned to do over these many years.

After a short while, he entered the drawing room, and his face changed, lit up, and so lost some of its tightness. He hovered in the doorway.

It was early evening, and the mist was rolling down the Peak. Outside the long wall of window, the sweeping view of Hong Kong, Victoria Harbour, and Kowloon across the water was slightly obscured. Familiar images were smudged, indistinct, wrapped in a haze of grayed blues and whites, the color combination reminding him of the faded glaze on a piece of ancient Chinese porcelain. Ah Qom, the Chinese amah who had looked after him and his home since the beginning, had turned on the silk-shaded carved jade lamps and lighted the fire, and this airy graceful room of perfect proportions was bathed in warm and mellow light. It welcomed him.

Huge overstuffed sofas and chairs, covered in pale blue and lavender and gray Thai silks by Jim Thompson, were balanced by Chinese cabinets, chests, and tables of varying sizes and shapes made of black or dark red lacquered wood. Wherever he looked, his eyes rested on an object of rare beauty. His possessions were meaningful to him. They nourished him, helped to restore his mood when he was feeling out of sorts.

He felt this lightening now, and a return to normal, and he moved forward across the antique Chinese silk carpet, sat down on the sofa. He knew that in a moment, Ah Qom's niece, Mee-Seen, would bring his jasmine tea, as she usually did half an hour after he had been home, no matter what time he returned from the office. It was a ritual, as so many things were a ritual here.

This thought had no sooner passed through his head than the pretty, delicately formed Chinese girl in her black silk cheongsam came hurrying in with the tray.

Smiling and bowing, she placed it on the low table in front of him.

He thanked her graciously, inclining his head.

Smiling and bowing, she departed.

He poured the fragrant tea into the small, paper-thin porcelain bowl, drank it quickly, poured another, sipped this more slowly, let his mind relax and empty itself of all thoughts. After savoring a third bowl, he placed it on the dark red lacquer tray, leaned his head against the sofa, and closed his eyes.

Gradually the last shreds of his anger drifted away.

He had been half dozing, and awakened with a start when the antique chiming clock on the mantelpiece struck the hour of six.

Sitting up, stretching his long frame, he realized he must go upstairs to shower and change for Lady Susan Sorrell's dinner party at her house in Recluse Bay.

Immediately pushing himself to his feet, he walked swiftly across the drawing room, but stopped suddenly in front of the long console next to the coromandel screen. The silver-framed photographs arranged there glittered brilliantly in the light from the adjacent lamp. He stared at the photograph of his father, then let his glance wander to the smaller picture of the woman.

His hatred for her had never dimmed. It rose up in him again. Impatiently, he shoved it away. Nothing must impinge on his newfound calmness, or ruin the evening ahead, which he had been anticipating for several days.

He had never intended to keep a photograph of *her* in his home, where every single object was perfect, chosen by him, the perfectionist, for its very perfection. But his better judgment had triumphed over emotion when he had unexpectedly found the picture amongst a trunk full of old possessions years ago. He had been on the verge of throwing it away when he had recognized its great usefulness.

Hong Kong was a place of status, of keeping face. Both were of paramount importance. And so it did him no harm whatsoever to be known as the grandson of that late great international tycoon, Emma Harte. However, tonight he could not bear to see that diabolical old woman's face, and he pushed her picture behind the larger one of his father standing outside the Commons. Being the son of Robin Ainsley, respected Labour politician, Member of Parliament, and former Cabinet Minister, had done him no harm either. His family ties had made him eminently acceptable, had propelled him into the highest echelons of local society.

Returning to the library, Jonathan Ainsley seated himself at the desk, took a ring of keys from his jacket pocket, opened the bottom drawer. He lifted out the folder marked HARTE'S and opened it, let his eyes scan the top sheet covered with several columns of meticulous figures in his own neat handwriting.

A smile of triumph brought a lift to his mouth, and he chuckled quietly. He generally laughed when he reviewed this list, reminded himself exactly how much stock in the stores he now owned. Harte's shares were traded on the London Stock Exchange, and for years he had been buying shares through nominees: his Swiss bank and other financial institutions. Today he was a major shareholder in the Harte department store chain, although only he knew this.

Closing the folder, he set it down on the desk, leaned back in the chair, and steepled his fingers, gloating to himself. Paula O'Neill would make a mistake one day. No one was infallible. Not even she. And then he would strike.

Jonathan reached down into the drawer for another folder, this one unidentified, and slipped out a sheaf of papers. They were detailed reports from the London detective agency he had been employing for a number of years.

Since 1971, Jonathan had had his cousin Paula O'Neill watched on a regular basis. Nothing scurrilous about her had ever been turned up, and he had not expected it to be. On the other hand, it suited his purpose to know as much as possible about her and her life, her family, her friends, and any business moves she made.

From time to time, he had had Alexander Barkstone and Emily Harte watched and reported on as well. Like Paula, they were pristine. In any case, he was not particularly interested in them. As long as his cousins continued to run Harte Enterprises on a profitable basis, and he continued to get his large dividend check every quarter, that was all that mattered to him. After all, it was Paula O'Neill who was his target.

He glanced at the last report which had come in from the agency in London. It placed her at the Villa Faviola in late August. He supposed that was why he had been so startled to see her in the Clipper Lounge of the Mandarin Hotel earlier. Obviously she was either on her way to Australia, or going back to England from there.

Damn her, he thought. He returned the folders to the drawer, locked it, and hurried out, climbed the stairs to his bedroom, having no wish to become enraged again. Thinking about that bitch made his blood boil.

He paused on the landing, breathing deeply, exhaling, cleansing his mind of her infuriating image.

As he went into his room, Jonathan expected to see his valet, and was surprised to find the room empty. Tai Ling was nowhere in sight, although his pleated dress shirt, black tie, and black silk socks had been laid out on the bed. Undoubtedly Tai Ling was downstairs in the laundry, steaming his dinner jacket, and would reappear at any moment. Humming to himself, he strolled over to a Ming chest, emptied his pockets of keys, credit card wallet, and money, and began to undress.

Like the other rooms in his home, the bedroom was furnished in excellent taste, with the emphasis on all things Chinese and unique oriental objects of art. It was understated, masculine in feeling, a trifle cold and austere, and the women who were brought by him to his bed soon discovered that the ambience reflected something in Jonathan's nature.

Taking a dark blue Chinese silk robe from the armoire and slipping it on, he went into the adjoining bathroom, wondering who it was that Susan had invited to the dinner party especially to meet him. She had sounded mysterious on the phone the other day, but it was bound to be an interesting woman. Susan knew his taste very well.

He sighed, thinking yet again how much he missed the arrangement they had had for almost a year. It had been purely sexual, a relationship convenient for them both. Although they had also enjoyed each other on an intellectual level, there had been no emotional involvement to spoil things. Just sex and intelligent talk. Perfect, to his way of thinking.

Three months ago, when she had told him her husband was suspicious of her, that they must end their affair, he had believed her, had immediately agreed to do as she wished. He had not realized at the time that there would be such a void in his life when she was no longer available to him. It was not particularly the sex he missed, even though she was very good in bed, since sex was an easy commodity to find anywhere in the world these days. Rather, he missed their conversations, their repartee, their shared English upbringings and backgrounds.

But he had not tried to pursue Susan, or reinstitute the affair. The last thing he wanted was to be cited as co-respondent in a messy divorce, or spotlighted as one of the chief players in a nasty little scandal in the crown colony. After all, he was a man of great standing here, and it was his home.

He stared at himself in the mirror over the washbasin, ran his hand over his chin. He had risen very early to play squash before a business breakfast at seven, and there was a hint of blond stubble on his chin. The electric razor was handy, and he plugged it in, ran it over his jawline. As he did, he thought of his cousins Paula O'Neill and Emily Harte, but ever so fleetingly. And with a sudden rush of pride he congratulated himself on all that he had accomplished in eleven years. He had come a long way.

When Jonathan Ainsley had alighted in Hong Kong in 1970, he knew at once that he had found his natural habitat and his spiritual home.

The air was full of excitement, mystery, adventure, and intrigue. Anything—and everything—seemed possible. Furthermore, he smelled money. Vast amounts of it.

He had come to the Far East licking his wounds, after being ignominiously kicked out of Harte Enterprises, where he had been head of the real estate division. Alexander had fired him; Paula had banished him from the family. And forever after he had blamed her for everything, believing that Alexander did not have the guts to stand up to him without her encouragement and support.

Before he had left England, Jonathan had done three things. He had dissolved his partnership with Sebastian Cross; sold his interest in Stonewall Properties to Sebastian for an excellent price; put his real estate holdings in London and Yorkshire on the block, and had made a tidy profit in the process.

When he had set out on his travels he had had two overriding goals—to amass a great fortune and to wreak revenge on his cousin Paula, whom he loathed.

Jonathan had been attracted to the Eastern world ever since his youth. Its religions, philosophies, and customs fascinated him; he drew aesthetic pleasure from its art, decorative objects, and furniture. And so he decided to do a tour of this part of the world before settling in Hong Kong, which he had concluded was the most logical place to set up in business. For the first six weeks of his self-imposed exile he had wandered around, sight-seeing and enjoying being a tourist. He had stopped off in Nepal and Kashmir, gone hunting in Afghanistan, made a leisurely trip through Thailand, before proceeding to the crown colony.

Prior to leaving London, he had taken the precaution of collecting letters of introduction from friends in the city and in real estate. Within a few days of arriving at the Mandarin Hotel, he had begun to call on those to whom the letters were addressed. At the end of his second week he had met a dozen or more bankers, businessmen, owners of land and construction companies, as well as a number of wheeler-dealers whom he considered to be dubious and not worth pursuing.

Two of the men he was particularly drawn to were a fellow Englishman and a Chinese. Separately, they had decided to help Jonathan get started, for their own reasons and to suit their own ends, and they were to prove invaluable to him. The Englishman, Martin Easton, was a real estate developer; the Chinese was a highly respected banker by the name of Wan Chin Chiu. Both were highly influential in their own circles, professionally and socially, but it was Jonathan who brought them together.

Exactly four weeks after he had landed at Kai Tak Airport, he had set himself up in business. With the help of his new associates he had found small but attractive offices in Central, had hired a small staff consisting of an English secretary, a Chinese expert in land and construction, and a Chinese bookkeeper, and had formed his own company, Janus and Janus Holdings Ltd. In Greek mythology Janus was the god of portals and the patron of beginnings and endings, and Jonathan had selected the name with relish— tongue in cheek—deeming it highly appropriate under the circumstances.

Luck was on his side when he started out in Hong Kong. It was to hold for over a decade.

This extraordinary luck, and the guidance and patronage of his two very powerful friends and backers, were the keys to his immense success. And timing played an important role.

It just so happened that when Jonathan arrived in the crown colony in 1970, land and construction were on the upswing. Since his expertise was in real estate, he knew he had accidentally landed on his feet. Shrewd enough to recognize a grand opportunity when he saw it, he plunged into local business with a gambler's instinct for the main chance, and a certain amount of courage, in that he was risking almost everything he had, plus the money invested in Janus and Janus by Martin Easton and Wan Chin Chiu.

Afterward he was to realize that he had been unable to throw the dice wrong once, figuratively speaking. His number always came up.

He made a considerable profit in the first six months, and in 1971, when the really big boom in property and land hit Hong Kong, he was well positioned. Suddenly there was a great deal of activity on the Hang Seng Index, the major index for the Hong Kong Stock Market. Like many others, Jonathan took advantage of the market activity. He cashed in quickly by taking his company public.

His two advisors, who had been guiding him all along, but independently of each other, warned him to start easing off a few months later. He continued to do a considerable amount of wheeling and dealing through the end of 1971 and 1972, but he had reduced his investments in the Hong Kong Stock Market by the beginning of 1973. Wan Chin Chiu, who had his ear to the ground and seemed to know everything, had been more cautionary than Easton, and wisely Jonathan had followed his advice scrupulously.

In any case, he had already made a killing, and was on his way to parlaying those profits into a huge personal fortune. He never looked back from that moment on.

By 1981 he had become a force to be reckoned with in Hong Kong and the world of Far East Asian business. He was a millionaire many times over, owned the skyscraper where his offices were located, the duplex on the Peak, several expensive cars, and a string of Thoroughbreds which he raced at the Happy Valley racetrack in Hong Kong.

Some years earlier, he had bought out Martin Easton, who had decided to retire to Switzerland, but he had remained closely associated with Wan Chin Chiu until his death two months ago. Tony Chiu, the American-educated son of the banker, had taken his father's place, and Jonathan's association with the bank continued to flourish. His personal outside investments were secure, and Janus and Janus Holdings was rock solid.

Business aside, he was socially prominent, one of the most eligible European bachelors in the community, and considered to be something of a catch. Except that no woman had managed to get anywhere near catching him.

Jonathan sometimes wondered about his own elusiveness, asked himself if he was far too fastidious, too much of a perfectionist when it came to the kind of woman he wanted to marry. Maybe no such woman existed. Yet he had discovered he was unable to alter his disposition.

Perfect, Jonathan suddenly thought, remembering the word Susan Sorrell had used to describe the young woman who was to be his dinner partner tonight.

"She's just the girl for you, Jonny darling," Susan had said, sounding sincere. "She's divine. Simply *perfect.*" He had laughed, had pressed for more information, but Susan had merely murmured, "No, no, I won't tell you anything at all. Not even her name. You must wait and see for yourself." Well, he *would* see very shortly.

Now he stepped back from the full-length mirror on the door of the armoire, took a last look at himself. He adjusted his bow tie, straightened the black silk handkerchief in the breast pocket of his white dinner jacket, and shot down his cuffs.

At thirty-five, Jonathan bore a strong resemblance to his grandfather, Arthur Ainsley, who had been Emma's second husband. He had inherited Arthur's blond hair and coloring, his light eyes, his polished, rather refined good looks, and like Arthur, he was tall, slender, and extremely English in his appearance. If anything, he looked better than he ever had. He had aged well and knew it.

But fair and handsome though he was, Jonathan's character had changed little in the decade that had passed. He was as devious and as manipulative as ever, and despite his unquestioned success, he was profoundly bitter about his ousting from Harte Enterprises. Nevertheless, he was able to camouflage his innermost feelings behind a facade that was a combination of his own natural blandness, an inscrutability learned from his Chinese friends, and a manner that was insouciant and charming.

He glanced at the paper-thin Patek Philippe watch on his wrist. It was not quite seven. He had to leave in a few minutes. But within half an hour he would be arriving at Susan's house in Recluse Bay. And finally, meeting the mysterious lady she had found for him.

As he hurried out of the bedroom and ran down the stairs, he grinned. He hoped she lived up to Susan's description, hoped she was indeed perfect. But if she was not, no matter. He would date her a couple of times anyway, and see what happened. Besides, she was obviously a newcomer to Hong Kong. *A stranger.* And strangers were always fascinating, weren't they?

23

He spotted her at once.

She stood at the far end of the living room, just near the French doors leading out to the terrace, talking to Elwin Sorrell, Susan's American banker husband.

He hesitated on the threshold for a moment, before going in, scrutinizing her intently. Her face was in profile and in the shadows, and it was difficult to ascertain whether she was beautiful or not.

And then suddenly Susan spotted him and glided over to greet him, and he thought again, as he had so often in the past, how beautiful *she* was. Her red hair was like an aureole of bright amber light around her lovely tranquil face, and her eyes were vividly blue tonight and full of her irrepressible laughter.

"Jonny darling," she exclaimed as she closed in on him, "I was just beginning to wonder where you were."

She lifted her face to be kissed. He pecked her cheek quickly, perfunctorily, but squeezed her arm in a more intimate fashion. "I'm only a few minutes late," he said. Dropping his voice, he whispered, "Can't you find a way to meet me one afternoon at the flat? Or at my office? We can be just as private there. I've missed you."

She shook her head rapidly, looked around the room, smiling brightly. "I daren't," she muttered as she brought her gaze back to him. Tucking her arm through his, she laughed gaily, said in her normal voice, "By the way, Jonathan, I forgot to mention that Elwin and I are going to San Francisco the day after tomorrow. For a couple of months. That's the real reason for tonight's dinner party. A sort of farewell get-together with a few of our favorite people."

"We'll all miss you," Jonathan said, following her cue, aware that several of the other guests were looking across at them.

One of the Chinese houseboys came up to him with a tray of champagne, and he took a glass, murmured his thanks, turned to Susan.

"Cheers," he said as he took a sip. "Now, tell me about the mystery lady. That's her, isn't it, talking to Elwin in the doorway?"

"Yes, but I can't tell you much, because I don't know her well. I've only met her once, at Betsy Androtti's house last week. I was instantly struck by her. She's extremely attractive, charming, well turned out, and intelligent. Naturally I thought of you immediately."

"You used the word 'perfect' on the phone."

"I think she *is* perfect. For you at any rate. There's something about her that will appeal to you tremendously." Susan paused, gave him an appraising stare. "I *do* know you very well, you know, Jonny."

His mouth twitched with sudden hidden laughter, and he asked, "Didn't Betsy give you *any* information about her?"

"Betsy doesn't know her either. She came to the dinner with some visiting banker. German, I think. And seemingly *he* met her last summer in the South of France. Or was it Sardinia? Oh dear, I'm not sure."

"So she's truly the mystery lady, eh?"

Susan laughed. "I suppose she is. On the other hand, that makes it more fun, doesn't it? And anyway, a stranger in our tight little group always elicits a great deal of curiosity, wouldn't you say?" She eyed him knowingly and, not giving him a chance to respond, rushed on, "Some of the single men are bound to be interested in her. That's why I wanted to nab her at once for this dinner. And for my darling Jonny."

"How very thoughtful of you." He stared at her speculatively for a split second, then murmured *sotto voce,* "I'd much rather have you though."

"But I'm married, Jonny," she shot back softly, her tone as low as his had been. "To Elwin. And I always shall be married to him."

"I wasn't proposing to you. Merely propositioning you, my love."

Looking highly amused at his retort, she made a moue, but did not comment.

Jonathan went on, "Anyway, what's the mystery lady doing in Hong Kong? Seeing the sights?"

"She's living here now. She told me she's opened a small antique shop and gallery on Hollywood Road."

"Oh really!" he exclaimed, pricking up his ears, looking at Susan alertly. "What kind of antiques?"

"Jade, I think. I got the impression she's an expert. That's another reason I thought the two of you would hit it off. So come along, my darling, don't let's loiter here in the doorway. Let me take you over to meet her. After all, that's why I invited her to this dinner in the first place. For you. Before any of the other young blades could scoop her up and carry her off."

"Lead the way," he said, following his hostess —and former lover—across the room.

Elwin Sorrell's face lit up at the sight of Jonathan. They were good friends and Jonathan was convinced that the American had never once suspected him of a dalliance with his wife.

The two men greeted each other warmly, and then Susan said, "Arabella, I'd like to introduce Jonathan Ainsley. Jonathan, this is Arabella Sutton."

"Hello," she said, stretching out her hand. "I'm so pleased to meet you."

He took her hand, shook it, half smiled. "I'm delighted to meet you, too, Arabella." He paused, then added, "You're English."

"Yes."

They stared at each other, sizing each other up.

She had silver-gilt hair, parted in the center, that was absolutely straight and fell in smooth fluid folds around her face and down her back to the top of her shoulder blades. Her face was extremely pale, without a spot of color in the cheeks. It looked carved from alabaster, the features cleanly defined. She had a narrow nose, high cheekbones, a rounded chin with a cleft, and her mouth, wide, sensual, was painted brilliant red. At first glance this was startling in the very white face, yet somehow it was right on her. A young woman of medium height, and slender, she was dressed in an elegant white silk dress that shouted Paris and *haute couture* to his discerning eye.

Thirty, thirty-two, or thereabouts, Jonathan thought, and decided that her looks were more interesting than beautiful. It was her eyes that held him. They were large, curiously elongated, almost but not quite almond-shaped. Dark as pitch, they seemed bottomless.

Arabella was studying Jonathan as intently as he was her.

She had heard a lot about him, knew he was from a famous family, and the grandson of the legendary Emma Harte. She had not expected him to be so prepossessing, though. His blond good looks were arresting. He was well groomed, expensively dressed, and he had an air about him—something indefinable. And then she realized that it *was* definable. He had the air of a man who was accustomed to authority and power and money, and the things money bought.

She liked what she saw.

So did Jonathan.

Susan said, "Why don't you two get better

acquainted? Come along, Elwin, let's mingle with our other guests."

Suddenly Arabella and Jonathan found themselves standing alone. He put one hand under her elbow and guided her out to the empty terrace. He said, "That's the most extraordinary piece you're wearing, Arabella."

She looked down at the large carved jade pendant hanging on a string of carved jade beads. "It's of the Daoguang period," she told him. "Very, very old."

"I realize that. Susan told me you have an antique shop, that you're a dealer in jade."

"Yes, jadite jewelry and nefrite carved pieces."

He smiled inwardly, immediately noting the way she had made the distinction between the two types of jade, something only a real expert would do. He said, "Where do you find your jade? Do you buy it here in Hong Kong from other dealers? Or on the mainland?"

"Both. I've been finding some wonderful things in Shanghai, especially jade jewelry like this piece"—she paused briefly, fingered the pendant—"and snuff bottles and vases. I came across some old nefrite belt buckles from the Qing period last week, and I've started to collect the multicolored Beijing glass. Mostly the deep yellow."

"Very clever of you, buying the glass, I mean. It's become highly prized because it's so difficult to craft. I'm interested in those nefrite belt buckles, by the way. I'd like to come over to your shop to look at them. Tomorrow perhaps?"

"Oh, but I haven't actually opened yet! I've been busy buying, collecting stock. My official opening is a week from this coming Monday." Noticing the disappointment registering on his face, she added, "Do come tomorrow. It's still a bit of a mess, but I'd love to show you some of the truly rare objects of art I've managed to find in the last couple of months."

"I'd enjoy that, Arabella. Would you care to dine with me afterwards?"

There was only the merest hesitation on her part before she said, "Why yes, Jonathan. Thank you very much."

He nodded. "Give me the address later, and I'll be there about six." He shifted his weight slightly, looked down at her. "I understand from Susan that you're an expert in Chinese jades and antiques. Where did you actually study?"

"Oh, I didn't—I mean everything I know I sort of taught myself, and I've read a great deal. I also took several courses at Sotheby's in London, at different times during the past three years." She shook her head, laughing. "But I'm hardly an expert. Just knowledgeable. And I hope I learn more here in Hong Kong."

"Oh, you will. Indeed you will," he murmured and averted his face, not wanting her to see the predatory gleam entering his eyes.

"Susan told me you have quite a collection of Chinese antiques yourself, Jonathan, including some marvelous bronzes."

"Yes, I do. Would you like to see them? We could go to my flat for drinks before dinner tomorrow. Would you enjoy that?"

"It would be nice. Thanks."

"Where do you come from, Arabella?" he asked suddenly, changing the subject.

"Hampshire. My father's a doctor. And you're from Yorkshire, aren't you?"

"Among other places." Jonathan smiled thinly, put his hand under her elbow, and ushered her into the living room. "I think we'd better join the others now, don't you? I've not said hello to any of my friends yet. Besides, I mustn't monopolize you."

Arabella smiled up at him, thinking how easy this had been, much easier than she had anticipated. She felt a rush of success, allowed her eyes to linger on him for a brief moment. And then she drifted off to talk to Vance and Marion Campbell, whom she vaguely knew and who had given her a lift to the dinner party. She was determined to leave with them at the end of the evening.

Susan had placed Arabella opposite Jonathan at the table, and he was able to study her surreptitiously throughout the dinner.

He was seated between Susan, who was at the head of the table to his left, and Marion Campbell, on his right. He paid enough attention to them both so as not to appear rude.

Mostly though, he watched Arabella Sutton and listened to her, and he was impressed in a variety of ways. He was captivated by her voice. It was husky, very beguiling. And her presence was hypnotic. Elwin seemed entranced, and so did Andy Jones, seated on her other side.

Jonathan noted how poised she was, and she was articulate, well informed on many subjects, not just Chinese art. He liked her intelligence, her sophistication. She had obviously traveled extensively, had done a good bit of living, and this pleased him. He did not care for women who were gauche or inexperienced, whether in bed or out of it. He preferred women to be his equals. To match him.

The more Jonathan studied her, the more he realized that she *was* beautiful. It was an unusual kind of beauty, different, intriguing. In the candlelight her face had become oddly mysterious and highly sexual.

It was the perfect curve of the rounded cheek, the depth of the sloe eyes, the lusciousness of the full mouth, the silken sheen of the silver-gold hair that made her such a sensual-looking woman. To him there was something exceedingly erotic about her, and the sexuality was not only visible in her face and in the seemingly perfect body under the white gown, but was even apparent in her hands.

Jonathan had never seen hands like hers before. They were extraordinary. Slender, very white, with tapering fingers, and the long, perfect nails were painted brilliant red to match her inviting mouth.

He wanted those hands on him, wanted her. But thinking about seducing her was too tantalizing, anticipation too dangerous a game at this particular moment. And then, before he could switch gears in his head, he was aroused and fully so, much to his amazement. Getting an erection at a dinner table had not happened to him since he had been a schoolboy. How remarkable, he thought, feeling hot under the collar.

Shifting his gaze from the fascinating—and potent—Arabella, he brought his attention to

Andy Jones and began to talk to him about sports.

"Why do you do it?" Jonathan whispered in Susan's ear as they strolled across the living room after dinner. They came to a stop near the fireplace, stood waiting for the Filipino butler to serve the coffee.

"Do what?" she asked, swiveling her eyes around the room, making sure Elwin was fully occupied elsewhere.

"Procure for me," Jonathan replied and surreptitiously ran his hand down her back, let it rest in the hollow above her buttocks.

"Don't do that, Jonny, someone might see you," she whispered.

"Come on, confess. It turns you on, doesn't it?"

"Of course not!" she hissed. Sudden anger made her swing to face him. Then, catching herself swiftly, she adopted a bland expression, took a deep breath, said in a steady voice, "Perhaps it's because I still feel guilty about ending our affair the way I did. I want to make it up to you, Jonny. You've always been very special to me, and you were such a wonderful lover. The best I've ever had. Besides, this is the first time I've procured for you, as you so crudely put it. *I* prefer the word 'introduce.' "

He grinned, said nothing, wondering what it would be like to take the two of them to bed together. Arabella and Susan would be quite an interesting and exciting combination. But he knew neither of them would go for it. English women were not a bit adventurous when it came to sex. And especially these two—the daughters of an earl and a doctor. No way.

Susan was saying, "I was right though, wasn't I, Jonny? Arabella is perfect, isn't she?"

"Outwardly, on the surface, yes." He waited for a second, eyed her carefully, and continued softly, suggestively, "However, I can't really give you an assessment, a truthful answer until I've stripped off those elegant clothes and bedded her."

His gaze had not left Susan's face and he saw the sudden flicker, the expression at the back of her eyes. Jealousy? Anger? Or a mixture of both perhaps? The idea that he might have hurt her, if only ever so slightly, pleased him. He had not wished to become involved in a marital scandal, but deep down it rankled that she had dumped him the way she had.

There was a painful silence.

Eventually she said in an amused voice, "What a pity I won't be in Hong Kong to hear your report."

"You probably will be."

"Oh." Now her eyes were surprised.

"I'm going to see Arabella's antique shop tomorrow. In the late afternoon. And then I'm taking her to my flat for drinks. Before dinner, an intimate little dinner at home. And perhaps we'll get down to something even *more* intimate later in the evening. I have high hopes. I really do."

"Bastard," she muttered under her breath, but loud enough for him to hear.

"But my love, you started all this," he retorted, grinning, now understanding that he was glad she had. Arabella Sutton was a challenge. He had not had a challenge in the longest time.

Much later that evening, Jonathan sat near the window in his bedroom, brooding and still, his eyes focused on the cloudless night sky sprinkled with countless stars. The room was in total darkness, the only illumination coming from the very bright full moon that cast a silvery sheen over everything.

He held a pebble of mutton-fat jade in his hands, turning it over and over, rubbing it between his fingers occasionally. It was his talisman, his lucky piece, and he had owned it since he had first come to the British Crown Colony.

He was contemplative for a long while, considering the two women he had encountered to-day.

His cousin, Paula O'Neill.

The stranger, Arabella Sutton.

In their different ways they haunted him now. He separated the images in his head, and as he did he made two promises to himself.

The first woman he would destroy.

The second he would conquer and own.

The vows made, he sighed deeply, filled with a curious sense of satisfaction. Rising, he slipped off his blue silk Chinese robe and walked slowly over to the bed. He could not resist smiling smugly to himself. There was not the slightest doubt in his mind that he would succeed.

It was only a question of time.

SAINTS
&
SINNERS

A lure more strong, a wish more faint,
Makes one a monster, one a saint.
Walter Learned

'Tis the eye of childhood that fears a painted devil.
William Shakespeare

Riches and power are but gifts of blind fate,
whereas goodness is the result of one's own merits.
Héloise

24

Success was in the air.

From the moment the dance had begun, Paula had known the evening was going to be magical.

Everything was exactly right.

The grand ballroom at Claridge's had been decorated by the design staff of Harte's to her specific instructions, and it was stunning. Extraordinary, really. Forsaking the staid, the traditional, she had had them create a color scheme of silver and white and crystal, developed with silver lamé tablecloths, white candles in silver sticks, crystal bowls filled with mixed white flowers. More white flowers—lilies, orchids, chrysanthemums, and carnations— were banked around the room in great masses and spilled out of huge urns standing in various corners.

To Paula the ballroom looked like a winter ice palace, all silvery and glittering, yet it had a neutrality that made a splendid backdrop for the guests in their finery—the women in their colorful, stylish evening gowns and fabulous jewels, the men in their impeccable, well-cut black dinner jackets.

She was delighted that everyone she had invited had come to this very special party. In attendance was a mixture of family and close friends, executives from the Harte stores and Harte Enterprises, honored guests, and celebrities.

Glancing about yet again, she could not help thinking that in particular the women in the family looked especially beautiful tonight.

Her cousin Sally, the Countess of Dunvale, lovely in delphinium-blue taffeta and the famous Dunvale sapphires that exactly matched her eyes . . . Emily, a vision in dark ruby silk and a superb ruby-and-diamond necklace and earrings Winston had given her for Christmas . . . Emily's half sisters, the twins Amanda and Francesca, pert and pretty in magenta chiffon and scarlet brocade respectively . . . her vivacious red-haired sister-in-law, Miranda, a law unto herself when it came to fashion, striking in a russet-satin column, stark, simple, strapless, worn with a long matching stole and an antique topaz-and-diamond necklace that fell down from her neck in a lacy cobweb of a bib.

Paula's gaze shifted over to the three sisters.

They were sitting at a nearby table, talking amongst themselves. Her mother, Daisy, dramatic in dark green chiffon and the magnificent McGill emeralds that Paul had bought for Emma almost half a century ago . . . Aunt Edwina, the Dowager Countess of Dunvale, in her seventies, white-haired, frail, yet regally elegant in black lace and the Fairley diamond necklace, presented to her by Emma the last Christmas she had been alive.

These two were the youngest and the eldest daughters of Emma Harte, both born on the wrong side of the blanket, bonded together, more than likely, by similar circumstances of birth and by her mother's deep compassion for the older woman. And seated between them was the legitimate daughter, the middle one . . . Aunt Elizabeth. Still a raven-haired beauty and looking half her age, she was positively stunning in silver lamé and a king's ransom of rubies, diamonds, and emeralds.

The three sisters were the only children of

Emma Harte who were present tonight. Paula had not invited Emma's two sons, Kit Lowther and Robin Ainsley, and their wives. They had been *persona non grata* for years because of their treachery to Emma and the treachery of their children, Sarah and Jonathan.

A nest of vipers, she thought, remembering something her grandmother had said to her once. How horribly true that statement had turned out to be. Paula pulled her thoughts away from those despicable family members, whom she had no time for, and lifted her glass, took a sip of champagne.

The evening was drawing to a close, and it suddenly struck her that this dinner dance, the first of the celebrations she had planned to mark the sixtieth anniversary of the opening of the Knightsbridge store, was going to be the talk of the town tomorrow. The newspapers would be full of it. The stunning backdrop, the delicious food, the fine wines, the designer clothes and fabulous jewels, the celebrity guests, Lester Lannin and his orchestra . . . all added up to glamour with a capital G, something the press and the public could not resist.

Paula was pleased. Good publicity was a tremendous boost for the store. She smiled inwardly. It was New Year's Eve. The end of 1981. The beginning of a New Year. And she hoped the beginning of a new and brilliant era of retailing for the chain stores founded by her grandmother.

Leaning back in the chair, she silently made a New Year's resolution: *The stores were going to be greater than ever in the coming decade.* She owed that to her grandmother, who had had such faith in her, and to her own daughters, who would one day inherit the chain from her.

Shane, who had been chatting to Jason Rickards and Sir Ronald Kallinski, cut into her thoughts when he suddenly turned to her, murmured, "You look as though you're miles away, darling." He took hold of her hand, leaned closer. "You can relax. The evening's an assured success, and everyone's having a wonderful time. It's a smashing party, Paula."

She gave her husband a radiant smile. "Yes, it is, isn't it! And I'm so glad I decided on the ballroom at Claridge's, rather than a series of private rooms at the Ritz. This has worked so much better."

Shane nodded. Then he half groaned, half laughed, and exclaimed, "Oho! Here comes Michael! Obviously I'm about to lose you again, and you only just sat down a few minutes ago."

"They are keeping me busy tonight, aren't they? Actually, it's a bit exhausting, but I *am* the hostess, Shane, and I have my duty to do."

Her mouth curved up with laughter. "I'm doing enough dancing to last me for the whole of 1982. I hope this is it, that we won't be going to any more dances for a long time. Remind *me* not to plan any, darling." Despite these words, her face was still covered with smiles and her eyes were sparkling.

Shane gazed at her, loving her. Admiration flooded his face. He thought she had never looked more ravishing than she did tonight in all the years he had known her. She wore an elegant evening gown of midnight blue velvet, beautifully cut, but understated with long sleeves, a round neckline, and a straight skirt. It had been designed by Christina Crowther especially for her, and it emphasized her height and her slenderness. Pinned to one shoulder was the large pansy brooch he had commissioned Alain Boucheron, the Paris jeweler, to make for her. Composed entirely of sapphires, it echoed the bright blue of her eyes, as did the matching sapphire earrings. He had given the set to her on Christmas Eve, had known from the look on her face how much she liked them, how thrilled she was, even though she protested he had been overly extravagant. "After all, you had the orchid greenhouse built for me. That is enough," she had said. He had grinned, had told her the greenhouse was a present from the kids

406

as well. "They all chipped in, darling," he had explained.

Michael drew to a standstill next to Paula's chair. "Come on, shake a leg, Paula . . . you promised me the first slow number, and I have a feeling this one's it. Possibly for the rest of the evening." He grabbed Shane's shoulder. "You don't mind, do you?"

"Not half I don't," Shane shot back swiftly, but in a jocular tone. "However, since it's you, okay."

"Philip's wife is a beautiful woman," Michael said as he steered Paula around the ballroom floor. "He's a lucky chap."

"Yes, he is," Paula agreed.

"But his gain is your loss."

Paula laughed. "Too true, Michael, in some ways." She looked over his shoulder, focusing on Philip and his new bride gliding ahead of them to the strains of "Strangers in the Night." "But I've never seen him so happy. He adores her. As she does him. And I may have lost the best personal assistant I've ever had, but I've gained a lovely, and very loving, sister-in-law."

"Mmmm," Michael murmured, moving nearer to Paula. Instantly he checked himself, pulled back, realizing that he was taking chances, holding her in such an intimate way.

Her presence continued to inflame him, and being entwined on the dance floor was dangerous. Physically dangerous, for him at least. Their proximity was far too close. Also, it might cause tongues to wag. And besides, joke though Shane might, his eyes seemed to have been on *him* all evening. If Shane suspected him of being enamored of Paula, *she* certainly did not. She was blithely unaware of his romantic interest in her, continued to treat him like an old shoe, the childhood friend, familiar, dependable, trustworthy. And that was the way he wanted it.

Paula was saying, "Anyway, Maddy's going to continue working when they return to Sydney. I've made her the managing director of the Australian division of Harte's. She'll be supervising the running of the boutiques in Shane's hotels out there. But I *will* miss her in New York, no two ways about that, Michael. On the other hand, their happiness is so important to me . . . it must come first." Leaning away from him, she smiled into his face, finished, "Those two are madly in love, you know."

"That's patently obvious."

They danced in silence for a few minutes.

Michael grimaced to himself. He wished he had the same kind of private life and personal happiness as Philip Amory. But he had not been so fortunate. Valentine had been a strikeout as a wife, and he had never found anyone else who had the necessary attributes. He wondered then if he was in love with Paula or merely turned on by her. There was no doubt in his mind that he was sexually attracted to her and would like to take her to bed. But love? He wasn't sure.

Immediately squashing this thought, he said, "Daisy seems to be over the moon about Philip and Madelana."

"She is. Of course, she was disappointed they got married in New York at the beginning of December and only told the family after the fact. We all were, actually. But Mummy's relief at knowing her wayward, playboy son is finally hitched has canceled out the disappointment, I'm absolutely sure of that."

"I wanted to give a dinner party for them, but Philip was telling me earlier that they're leaving in a couple of days. Off on their honeymoon."

"Yes. To Vienna, West Berlin, and then down to the South of France and the Villa Faviola."

"Pretty coolish in those places right now. I would have thought they'd have chosen somewhere warm. Like Shane's hotel in Barbados, for instance."

"Philip's always loved the Imperial in Vienna, ever since Grandy took us there when we were children. He and Emily think it's one of the greatest hotels in the world, in fact, and he wanted Madelana to see it. They're going to be staying in the Royal Suite, which is quite magnificent. It was Maddy who suggested that they then go on to Berlin, ending up at Faviola. She's heard a lot about it from me and Emily. Anyway, Maddy seems to have an obsession about Grandy, is wildly curious about every blessed home she owned. So naturally Faviola is a *must.*"

Michael laughed, fully understanding why Madelana was obsessed with Emma Harte. So many people had been, throughout her life and after her death, which was why she was a legendary lady. Unexpectedly, he felt an easing of the tension within himself. "I haven't had a chance to tell you, Paula, but I think you've done Aunt Emma proud tonight," he said. "This is a fabulous party, one of the best I've been to in the longest time, and—"

"Mind if I take over, old chap?" Anthony said with a huge grin.

"Every time I dance with you, one of your male relatives cuts in," Michael grumbled, relinquishing her to the Earl of Dunvale. "No doubt about it, Paula, you're the belle of the ball tonight."

Paula laughed, winked at him mischievously.

Michael stepped to one side, ambled off, went in search of young Amanda.

Anthony took Paula in his arms and whirled her into the middle of the floor. After a couple of seconds, he said against her hair, "Any chance of talking you and Shane into coming over to Ireland for a long weekend soon? It's been ages since you've visited Clonloughlin, and Sally and I would love to have you. You could bring Patrick and Linnet with you."

"What a lovely idea, Anthony, and thanks for asking us. Perhaps we *can* make it . . . at the end of January. I'll talk to Shane. As far as I know, neither one of us is planning any foreign trips."

"What a change that is!" Anthony answered in an amused voice. "You two are worse than a couple of gypsies these days, forever trotting off around the world, wheeling and dealing. I can hardly keep track of you both."

Before she had an opportunity to answer, Alexander was tapping Anthony on the shoulder, exclaiming, "You're monopolizing the lady. It's my turn, Cousin."

So saying, Sandy maneuvered her into his arms and they swept away from Anthony. The latter stood gaping at them, a surprised look settling on his face.

They danced without speaking at first, enjoying being together on the floor. As children they had favored each other as dancing partners. They had been in step then, as they were now.

Eventually, Alexander murmured quietly, "Thanks so much, Paula."

She looked up at him in puzzlement. "What for, Sandy?"

"Christmas at Pennistone Royal, and this evening. For a short while you've turned the clock back for me, brought back so many lovely memories . . . of the past . . . of people whom I truly loved. Gran . . . my darling Maggie . . . your father . . ."

"Oh Sandy, you sound so sad!" Paula exclaimed. "And I wanted the Christmas holidays and tonight to be happy occasions for each one of us. I didn't—"

"And you succeeded admirably, Paula! They have been wonderful. And I'm not a bit sad. Quite the contrary, in fact."

"Are you sure?" she asked in concern.

"Positive," he lied smoothly, smiling at her.

Paula offered him a warm and loving smile in return, moved closer into his arms, gave his shoulder a squeeze. Her cousin Sandy had always been very special to her, and she was determined not to neglect him in the future. He needed her as much as he needed his sister, Emily. He was quite lonely, really. She realized that more than ever.

Sandy stared ahead, glad that they were on the floor, which was dim and crowded, since he was no longer able to keep the bleak look out of his eyes, the grim expression from his mouth. But Paula could not see his face, and everyone else was too preoccupied to notice, and for these small mercies he was thankful. They finished the dance to the end, and, to his relief, not once did his step falter.

Sandy was a devastated man, and it was only a matter of weeks before the others knew this. They would have to know. He had no alternative but to tell them. He dreaded the day.

"Well, Paula, what do *you* think? Can the modern woman have it all?" Sir Ronald asked, looking at her quizzically, his eyes twinkling. "You know—career, marriage, and children."

"Only if she's one of Emma Harte's granddaughters," Paula quipped with a wicked grin.

Sir Ronald and the others seated at the table chuckled, and then Paula went on, "But seriously, Grandy did teach us to be well organized, and that's my secret and Emily's too. So my answer is *yes*, the modern woman can have it all, provided she plans her life properly and is a past master of organization."

"There are many who would differ with you, Paula," Sir Ronald countered, "who would say you can have *two* of those things, but not all three. However, don't get me wrong, my dear, I applaud the way you and Emily run your lives. You're both quite remarkable, quite remarkable indeed."

Paula said, "Let's ask Maddy what she thinks . . . here she comes now . . . and if anyone personifies the modern woman of the eighties, then she certainly does."

Several pairs of eyes focused on Madelana and Philip, who were approaching the table. She was glowing and radiant in a Pauline Trigère evening gown of deep purple chiffon overpatterned with swirls of purple cut velvet. With it she wore a magnificent diamond-and-pearl choker and matching chandelier earrings, which had been wedding presents from Philip. Her hair was upswept, and, if anything, she was more striking than ever. Added to her natural gracefulness and poise was a new and lovely serenity.

She clung to her husband's arm as if never to let him go, and Philip looked equally possessive and proud of her as they drew to a standstill at the table.

"Join us," Paula said, beaming at them.

They did so, and Philip said, "Congratulations, darling. This has been a smashing evening, truly remarkable, and it was an inspiration on your part to fly Lester Lannin in from the States."

"Thanks, Pip." Turning to Madelana, Paula went on, "Listen, Maddy dear, Uncle Ronnie just asked me if the modern woman can have it all . . . marriage, career, babies. And I said who better to answer that than you . . . the career girl newly married."

"I *hope* I can have it *all,*" Madelana laughed, glancing at Philip out of the corner of her eye. "Philip wants me to continue working, to have a career, and I think I'd like to do so even after I have a child."

"Anything that makes my wife happy is perfectly all right by me," Philip announced, endorsing her words. He reached for her left hand, on which she wore a platinum wedding band and a flawless thirty-carat diamond that blazed in the candlelight.

Madelana returned Philip's squeeze, looked from Paula to Sir Ronald, said quietly, "I think it's a terrible waste for an educated woman with a career to stop working when she has a baby. I believe one can do both . . . it's all a question of juggling. And of course it depends on the woman, to a certain extent."

Shane exclaimed, "This is it! The last waltz!"

He sprang up, walked around the table, took hold of Paula's arm. Leading her off, he said, "I wasn't going to let anyone else grab you for this one, my love."

"I would have refused anyone who asked."

They moved into each other's arms, and Shane held her tightly as they waltzed. Paula relaxed against his body, feeling safe and content with him, as she had since childhood. They were lucky, she and Shane. They had so much together. Their deep and abiding love. Their children. Shared interests. A common background. And he understood her so well, understood her immense need to fulfill her destiny as Emma Harte's heir. She wished she had pointed out to Sir Ronald a few seconds ago that a woman could only *really* have it all if she were married to the right man. She was.

She thought of Jim then, but in the most fleeting way. He had become a dim figure in her mind, and her memories of him were fragmented, blurred by events that had taken place since his death, by those whom she loved, those who now peopled her life, by time passing. It seemed to her that she could not remember when she had not been Shane's wife. But the years *had* flown by since their marriage. This sudden thought made her draw away, look up at him.

He stared down at her, his black brows knitting together.

"What's the matter?"

"Nothing, darling. I was just thinking that very soon a new year will begin, and I expect that it, too, will disappear in a flash, as all the others have."

"Too true, my love. On the other hand, look at it this way—1982 is only the *first* of the next fifty years we're going to spend together."

"Oh, Shane, what a lovely thing to say, and it's a beautiful thought with which to start the new year."

He brushed her cheek with his mouth, tightened his arm around her, swirled her around several times, and moved her out into the middle of the ballroom. Paula smiled inside, loving him so very much. Then she peered around the ballroom, seeking members of the family, her closest friends. It truly was a gathering of the clans . . . the Hartes, the O'Neills, and the Kallinskis were all represented tonight.

She spotted her mother dancing with Jason, looking as much in love as Madelana, who dreamily floated by in Philip's arms. Her father-in-law, Bryan, was leading Shane's mother in a sweeping, old-fashioned waltz, and Geraldine winked at her as they went sailing grandly past. Emily and Winston were coming onto the floor, followed closely by Michael and Amanda. She saw her Aunt Elizabeth gazing into the face of her French husband, Marc Deboyne, who was obviously enjoying himself tremendously tonight; even her old Aunt Edwina was on her feet making an effort, being solicitously shepherded around by a gallant Sir Ronald.

The music stopped abruptly, and Lester Lannin was saying into the microphone, "Ladies and gentlemen . . . it's almost midnight. We have BBC radio on the hotel's relay system. Here it comes . . . here's Big Ben . . . the countdown to midnight commences."

Everyone had stopped dancing to listen to the orchestra leader, and the ballroom was quiet, perfectly still. The chimes of the great clock in Westminster boomed out again and again. When the last stroke finally reverberated, there was a resounding drumroll, and Shane was hugging Paula, kissing her, wishing her a happy new year, to be followed by Philip, then Madelana, doing the same thing.

Paula returned Madelana's affectionate embrace.

"Let me say it again, Maddy . . . welcome to the family. And may this be the first of many happy years for you and Philip."

Maddy was touched by Paula's lovely words, but before she had a chance to respond the orchestra struck up "Auld Lang Syne."

Paula and Philip grabbed hold of her hands, pulled her forward as they began to sing.

Encircled by her new family, Maddy felt their love flowing out to her, and she wondered how *she* had ever been so lucky to become one of *them*. But she had, and she would be forever grateful. For years she had had nothing but sadness and loss. Now at last everything had changed.

25

Madelana lay with her head resting on Philip's shoulder.

The bedroom was shadow-filled, quiet except for the sound of his even breathing as he dozed, the faint rustling of the silk curtains, the ticking of the ormolu clock on the antique French Provincial chest.

The weather was somewhat mild for January, springlike almost, and earlier Philip had opened the tall window. Now the night air blowing in was fresh and cool, laden with the tangy salt smell of the Mediterranean, the freshness of green-growing things in the sprawling gardens of Faviola.

She slipped out of bed, glided over to the window, leaned against the sill, looked out at the grounds, enjoying the gentle silence that pervaded the landscape at this late hour. She lifted her eyes. The sky was a deep pavonian blue that was nearly black and resembled a canopy of velvet, high flung like a great arc above the earth, and it was filled with brilliant stars. Earlier, clouds had obscured the moon, but they had drifted away, and she saw that it was full tonight, a perfect sphere, and clear.

A long sigh of contentment trickled through her. They had been at the villa for ten days, relaxing, taking it easy after their trips to Vienna and Berlin. They had done very little since they had been here except love each other, sleep late, go for walks in the gardens and on the beach, and take leisurely drives along the coast. They had spent most of their time at the villa, where Solange fussed over them like a mother hen, and Marcel cooked imaginative and delicious meals, and was forever thinking up some new dish with which to tempt them.

And they read and listened to music. Sometimes she played her guitar for Philip and sang her favorite Southern folk songs. He listened as if enraptured, and Madelana was pleased and flattered that he found her music entertaining. "It's been ten days of absolute bliss, doing nothing in particular, having you all to myself," Philip had said to her that morning, and she had told him she felt exactly the same way as he did.

A special tranquility abounded here at Faviola, just as it did at Dunoon, and she drew enormous strength, as well as pleasure, from the quietness and the natural beauty of both places. *Dunoon.* It was her home now, just as the penthouse atop the McGill Tower in Sydney was her home. But it was the house on the sheep station at Coonamble that she loved the most. She had fallen in love with it at first sight. As she had with Philip. And he with her.

Madelana shivered and goose bumps spreckled her arms, as she remembered the first time they had made love. She had lain in bed, weeping into his pillow after he had left the room, because when she had tried to envision the future with him she had seen no future. How foolish she had been that day . . . and how wrong. She *did* have a future with Philip McGill Amory. She was his wife. And, as Paula had said, 1982 was only the first of many happy years to come. They had a lifetime together stretching out before them.

She loved him . . . loved him so much it seemed almost unbearable at times. When he was absent from her, she felt an enormous sense of loss and experienced genuine physical pain, a tightness across her chest that only went away when he returned. Fortunately they had not been apart much since he had followed her to New York last October. He had suddenly arrived without warning, two weeks after she had left Sydney, had breezily walked into her office at Harte's on Fifth Avenue, unannounced, grinning from ear to ear. But his eyes had been anxious—she had noticed that immediately.

He had swept her off to lunch at "21," then taken her to dinner at Le Cirque, and it had been wonderful to be with him again. The minute she had left him at the airport in Sydney, she had suddenly known how much she cared. And on the long flight home there was a yearning for him in her heart that she knew would never go away. Never, not as long as she lived. The love she felt for Philip superceded everything in her life, even her career, if she had been asked to choose.

Later that same night, as they lay enfolded in each other's arms, after making love in the privacy of her apartment, he had asked her to marry him. She had not hesitated, had accepted his proposal at once.

They had talked well into the night, making their plans for the future. He had insisted they keep their engagement a secret. "But only because I don't want a big fuss," he had carefully explained. Equally as strong-willed as he in certain ways, she had endeavored to persuade him to tell Paula. "Because she will have to find a replacement for me. I can't—I won't—leave her in the lurch, Philip. She's been far too good to me. Besides, that's not my way of doing things. I have a responsibility to her, and to myself."

Philip had understood her sentiments. Nevertheless he had pointed out that she could find a replacement without informing Paula, and he had been so tough with her about it she had had no option but to agree. And, oddly enough, she had not had to look far in the end. Cynthia Adamson, who worked in Marketing, had been a protégé of hers and a favorite of Paula's for some time. The young woman showed extraordinary promise, was quick, intelligent, diligent, and devoted to Paula and Harte's.

Maddy had realized that Cynthia could handle most of her work when she left, had the necessary potential to become Paula's personal assistant eventually. This had put her mind at ease to some extent, and she had made a point of bringing Cynthia into her orbit for the remainder of her time at the store.

Philip had stayed on until the end of the month, had then gone back to Australia for two weeks to attend to certain business matters, and had finally returned to New York at the end of November.

The minute he had arrived, he had announced that they were going to get married immediately. To have a big wedding, with his family in attendance, would have meant too much of a delay for him, he had explained. And far too much excitement. "But we ought to give them a chance to come over. And we ought at least to inform your mother. And Paula," Maddy had pointed out, filled with discomfort about excluding them.

He had been adamant. "No, I won't wait for them to make their endless plans, to take over. It's got to be now." He had laughed then, had said lightly, "I'm afraid of losing you, don't you see? I must marry you at once." Despite that laughing face, the carefree tone of voice, she had noticed the anxiety dwelling there once more, clouding his clear blue eyes. She had agreed to do anything he wished . . . just to make that panic-stricken look go away. She could not bear to see him troubled or upset.

And so they were married quietly at the beginning of December, in a Roman Catholic ceremony at St. Patrick's Cathedral on Fifth Avenue, with only her Boston friend, Patsy Smith, and Miranda O'Neill and her husband Elliot James present. She had worn an elegant winter-white wool dress with a matching coat by Trigère, and had carried a trailing spray of pink and yellow orchids; afterward Philip had taken them all to lunch at Le Grenouille.

"I think we'd better consummate this marriage at once," he had said teasingly later in the day, when they had returned to their vast suite at the Pierre Hotel. And only after they had made love did he finally agree that they could telephone his family in England.

They had spoken first to Daisy, who was staying at Pennistone Royal in Yorkshire, and then to Paula, who was at the house in Belgrave Square. His mother and his sister had not sounded particularly surprised, and they had been overjoyed at the news, if somewhat disappointed to have missed the actual wedding. And both of them had welcomed her warmly into the family. She had felt their sincerity and love coming across the transatlantic wire as they had reached out to her.

And then it had begun . . . a whole new life for her.

Philip loved her as deeply, as desperately, as she loved him. This not only manifested itself in his physical passion for her, his tenderness and kindness, but in the manner in which he showered gifts on her, spoiled her outrageously, and in countless ways. The flawless diamond engagement ring, the pearl-and-diamond choker and chandelier earrings had been only the first of many valuable jewels he presented to her. There had been other gifts as well . . . furs, Hermès bags, and couture clothes. But he was just as likely to show up with a pair of gloves, a silk scarf, a favorite book or tape he wished to share with her, a bottle of perfume, a bunch of violets, or some other such small yet meaningful token.

But the most important aspect of her new life was her husband. Philip filled the empty spaces of her heart, and he gave her such a sense of security and of belonging that she no longer felt so alone.

There were times when she had to pinch herself to make sure this was not all a dream. That it was real, that he was real . . .

She did not hear Philip get out of bed, and she started in surprise when he wrapped his arms around her. She swiveled her eyes to look up at him.

He kissed the top of her head. "What are you doing, standing here at the window? You'll catch cold, darling."

Madelana turned around within the circle of his arms so that she was facing him. She reached up to touch his cheek. "I couldn't sleep, so I got up to look at the gardens. They're so beautiful in the moonlight. And then I started thinking—"

"What about?" he interrupted, gazing down at her.

"Everything that's happened in the last few months. It's like a dream, Philip. And sometimes I have the awful feeling I'm going to wake up and discover none of it is true, and that you're not real."

"Oh but I am very real, my darling, and this is not a dream. It's reality. *Our reality.*" He drew her closer to him, held her tightly against his bare chest, stroked her hair. There was a long moment of silence between them, before he said, "I've never known peace like this. Or such love. I cherish you, my lovely Maddy. And I want you to know I will always be constant. There will never be another woman in my life, not ever again."

"I know that, Philip. Oh darling . . . I do love you so . . ."

"Thank God for that! And I love you, too."

He bent down, kissed her gently on the lips.

She clung to him.

He found himself involuntarily sliding his hands down her back, over her lovely, small, rounded buttocks. The satin of her nightdress was smooth and cool and curiously erotic to him. He pressed his body closer to his wife's, and in an instant he was aroused.

Madelana began to tremble, wanting him again, as she knew he suddenly wanted her, even though they had made love only a short while before. They were always like this, reaching out to each other, unable to keep their hands off each other. She had never known this kind of aching, all-consuming physical desire, this overwhelming passion, this constant need to possess and be possessed. The depth and strength of her feelings for him were unlike anything she had ever experienced in her life.

The heat was flowing through her, rising from her thighs, from the very core of her, spreading through her body up into her neck and face. Her cheeks were flaming. She kissed his chest, then put her arms around him tightly. Her fingers pressed against his shoulder blades, smoothed down over his broad back.

Philip was conscious of the heat from her body, and it seemed to scorch him. He reached for one of her breasts, began to caress it, and as he did he kissed her neck, then brought his mouth to hers once more. Their kisses were deep, sensual, and they stood in front of the window, locked in a fierce embrace, welded together as if never to be separated. And then finally, unable to contain himself any longer, he lifted her in his arms and carried her over to the bed.

They slipped out of their nightclothes, and he ran his strong but gentle hands over her slender body, marveling at its beauty. Moonlight was flooding the room, and in its soft and muted light her skin was taking on a silvery sheen and she looked ethereal, of another world.

He bent over her, kissed the cleft between her breasts, trailed his mouth down her stomach, and she shivered and reached for him. And quickly, with little preamble, he took her to him, joined himself to her, and they loved each other for a long time.

She told him two days later.

It was a radiant day, bright and hard as a diamond. The sky was a sharp azure blue and cloudless, the glittering Mediterranean Sea the color of lapis, the sun a golden orb, but without any warmth. And despite the beauty of the day there was a nip in the air, a hint of snow coming down from the Alps.

They were sitting on the terrace overlooking the vast sun-filled gardens of Faviola, bundled up in thick sweaters and warm coats. Earlier they had gone for a walk, and now they were sipping an aperitif before lunch. Philip had been talking about their travel plans for the next few weeks. Maddy had listened, said little, even though he had given her the opening she'd been looking for, and a small silence had fallen between them.

She broke it when she said, "I don't think we should go on to Rome, Philip. I think it would be better if we returned to London."

He looked at her swiftly, struck by the odd note of tension in her voice, a nuance that had been absent for weeks. A black brow arched. "Why, darling?"

Madelana cleared her throat, said softly, "There's something I've been wanting to say for a few days . . . I have a strange feeling . . ." She stopped, cleared her throat, and after a slight hesitation, finished quietly, "I think I'm pregnant."

He looked startled for a moment, taken aback, and then a smile broke through and his vivid blue eyes sparkled with joy. His excited voice echoed the expression on his face, when he exclaimed, "Maddy, this is the most wonderful news! The best I've had since you said you'd marry me."

Reaching for her, he brought her into his arms, kissed her tenderly, then pressed her head close to his chest, stroked her hair.

After a moment, he murmured, "But you said *think*. Aren't you sure, darling?"

Drawing away from him, she looked up into

his face and nodded. "Pretty sure. All the signs are there, and when I see a doctor I know he'll confirm it. That's the reason I'd like to go back to London instead of continuing on to Italy."

"Absolutely, darling. You're right. That's what we must do. Oh Maddy, this is just marvelous."

"Then you're happy about it?" Her voice was low.

"Thrilled." He gave her a puzzled glance, frowned. "Aren't you?"

"Of course . . . I just thought you might think it's a bit too soon."

"To have a son and heir! You must be kidding. I'm elated, angel."

"It might be a girl . . ."

"Then she'll be a daughter and heir. Let's not forget, I'm the grandson of Emma Harte, and she never drew distinctions between men and women when it came to heirs. And neither did my grandfather Paul. He made my mother his heir, you know."

Madelana nodded, half smiled.

But there was a quietness about her that gave Philip reason to pause for a moment. He studied her, then asked, "What's wrong, darling?"

"Nothing. Truly, Philip."

He was not so sure about this. He said, "Are

you worried about your career? About running Harte's in Australia?"

"No, I'm not."

Still unconvinced, he went on quickly, "Because if you are, you mustn't be. You'll have no problems with me about working. My grandmother went to business when she was pregnant. So did Paula and Emily, and neither Shane nor Winston objected. That's the way the men are in this family, since we were raised and trained by the famous matriarch."

"I know all that, darling."

"So what's wrong? You seem so quiet, almost deflated."

Reaching out, she took hold of his hand, held it very tightly. "I've been worrying about telling you for days, worrying that you would think the timing was wrong, that it was too soon in our marriage, that we needed more time alone together, to get to know each other better before a child came along. I suppose I thought you might be annoyed, think I'd been careless."

"It takes two to tango," he murmured.

"Yes." She paused, smiled at him tremulously. "I love you so much, Philip . . . you're everything in the world to me. And I want you to be happy with me . . . I want to please you . . . always."

He saw the sudden glitter of tears in her lovely gray eyes, and his heart twisted inside. He brought his hand to her cheek, stroked it lovingly. "You *do* please me. In every way. And you make me very happy. You're my life, Maddy. And the baby will be my life."

Unexpectedly, he threw back his head and began to laugh, entirely changing the mood between them.

Baffled, she looked at him curiously. "What is it?"

"To think that the dyed-in-the-wool international playboy is now very much a married man and an expectant father! Who would have believed it?" he asked, eyeing her merrily, chuckling again.

Maddy laughed with him. He always managed to assuage her worries, to lift her spirits.

He jumped up, took her hand in his, pulled her to her feet. "Come on, love. Let's go inside. I want to make some phone calls."

"To whom, darling?"

"The family, of course."

"All right."

They walked along the terrace toward the French doors, their arms wrapped around each other.

Abruptly, Madelana stopped, turned to Philip.

"Once I've seen the gynecologist in London, and we've spent a few days in Yorkshire with your mother, as we promised, I'd like to go home, Philip . . . home to Australia. Home to Dunoon."

He hugged her to him, loving her more than ever for saying this. "Yes, my darling, we'll go home," he said, "and make ready for our first child . . ."

Half an hour later he was still on the phone in the library.

He had spoken first to Daisy and Jason in Yorkshire, then to Paula at the store in London, passing along the news about her pregnancy. And each time he had brought her to the phone to have a word.

There had been many congratulations and lots of love sent, and Daisy, in particular, had been ecstatic, knowing she was to become a grandmother again.

Now Philip was talking to his cousin Anthony at Clonloughlin in Ireland.

She had not anticipated this, had not expected him to shout their news to the world in this way. Philip was such a private man when it came to his personal life, and, after all, he had insisted on a secret engagement and marriage. Maddy knew then, with a sudden flash of insight, why he had excluded his family from their wedding. It had been for her to save her from undue heartache, to balance the situation. He had a vast family; every member of hers was dead.

How painful her wedding day might have been . . . Philip would have been surrounded by his loved ones; she would have been alone, with no one from her side to witness that very special and important day in her life. And she would have longed for her parents and little Kerry Anne, for Young Joe and Lonnie.

Philip had understood all this. Of course he had. Everything was suddenly clear to her.

Madelana curled up on the big, comfortable sofa, listening to him speaking, watching him, thinking what an extraordinary man he was. Shrewd, brilliant, tough in business, yet so sensitive and loving when it came to his feelings for her.

She blinked, sat back, held her head to one side, trying to visualize him objectively for a split second. What a handsome man he was. It was his vivid coloring that so startled her at times—the dark glossy hair, the black mustache, the tanned face, the eyes so supernaturally blue. He seemed larger than life. And he was so wonderfully alive and vital, and he positively glowed with well-being at this moment.

He must always be like this, the way he is today, she thought. Full of laughter and life and joyousness. And I must never be the one to cause him pain.

26

There was no question in Arabella's mind that Sarah considered her to be a usurper of sorts.

No, that's too strong a word, she thought, impatiently throwing down the magazine she had been reading, unable to concentrate. I'm the . . . *interloper.* Yes, that's the right word. Until I strolled into his life, Sarah had him all to herself whenever he came to Europe. The woman enjoys being the center of attraction. That was only too apparent at lunch today.

Arabella rose, glided across the sitting room of the guest suite of the farmhouse in Mougins, stood looking out of the window for a moment.

It had been a glorious day, but now dusk was

falling, and the gardens below were bosky, mysterious, almost eerie in the dimming light. A faint, vaporous mist shrouded everything in a mantle of gray and opal tints, and the trees in the apple orchard beyond the white fence were inchoate, illusory.

She shivered, filling with melancholy, feeling unexpectedly sad. She shrugged these feelings away before they took hold. She had no reasons to be sad. She had everything. Arabella smiled a small, secret smile. Well, not *everything*. But she was getting there.

Swinging around, she returned to the fireside, settled herself on the sofa once more, enjoying the warmth and cheerfulness of the blazing logs. She liked a fire. There was something comforting about it . . . perhaps because it reminded her of her childhood in Hampshire, the big old house where she had grown up.

After a few moments reflection and several adjustments to her plans for the next few weeks, she glanced around for the umpteenth time since they had arrived that morning, admiring the room again.

Here and in the adjoining bedroom, ancient, dark wood ceiling beams, white, half-timbered walls, and old brick fireplaces had been left intact. In combination with the slightly slanting ceiling, they gave this top floor under the eaves a coziness and character. Thick wool carpet stretched wall to wall, and its *café-au-lait* beige was the perfect backdrop for the lovely English chintzes on the huge sofa and the chairs, the French Provençal country furniture made of ripe woods polished to a mellow gleam. The same coffee-colored carpet flowed through into the bedroom, where Porthault linens dressed the bed, upholstered the antique headboard, and hung as curtains at the mullioned windows.

The suite was as fresh as a flower garden, overflowing with diverse floral patterns that somehow blended well together, and it was infinitely comfortable. A fortune had been spent on the entire farmhouse, and all of the rooms had been put together with taste, discernment, and an eye to color and design.

Whatever else Sarah Lowther Pascal might be, she is certainly a clever homemaker, Arabella decided. She had done wonders with the sprawling old farm perched on a hillside high above Cannes, had decorated it with flair, given it undeniable cachet and charm. And in the grounds outside she had turned a series of decrepit barns into one huge, superb studio for Yves, had covered the central section with a roof of glass to let in the maximum amount of light.

Yves Pascal's paintings hung everywhere in the farmhouse. They were bold, modern, not to

Arabella's taste, which ran to Old Masters and the traditional. But the artist was a powerhouse in the international art world, and his paintings were in great demand; apparently others liked his works, even if she did not. These days they were commanding huge prices.

On the other hand, she had really taken to the small, wiry Frenchman from the moment she had met him. He was a bit of a peacock, a strutter, and obviously rather hyper. But nonetheless, he was the possessor of an inordinate amount of Gallic charm. She did not quite understand his relationship with Sarah. They seemed to be poles apart. Yet he adored his wife and their child, Chloe—she had noticed that immediately.

Jonathan had told her that the little girl had his grandmother's looks and coloring. He had not volunteered much about the legendary Emma Harte in the four months she had known him, but from a remark Sarah had made at lunch, she had gathered that the two of them were at loggerheads with their cousin, Paula O'Neill. After lunch, later that afternoon, she had asked Jonathan why there was a feud in the family, and he had muttered something about Paula turning their grandmother against them, persuading her to make certain changes in her will. He had seemed suddenly upset, even angry,

441

and after murmuring a few sympathetic words, she had wisely let the matter drop. She had not wanted to underscore his unprecedented agitation. She had never seen him like that before.

Her thoughts centered on Jonathan.

She had been led to believe he would be difficult to ensnare. But this had not proved to be the case. He had immediately and heavily fallen for her, had courted her assiduously in Hong Kong. She had withheld herself in every way in the beginning. Then slowly she had opened up, both mentally and physically. She had let him see her intelligence, her knowledge about art and antiques, her sophistication; and she had tempted him with her body. Their fraternal good night kisses had led to deeper kissing, then petting and increasingly intimate touching, until she had finally succumbed to his potent sexuality, had allowed him to take her to bed.

All along she had never pretended to be a virgin, had let him know there had been other men before him. But she had carefully pointed out that she was discriminating, not promiscuous, and wanted to be certain of her feelings, his feelings, before they embarked on an affair. He had applauded her candor and had confided he was only interested in women who were as experienced and worldly-wise as he. And he had shown patience with her.

442

A knowing look slid into Arabella's pitch-black eyes. She had expertise. She knew how to give him pleasure in countless ways . . . ways he had no comprehension of as yet. She did not want him to know just how experienced she was in the art of sex. She wanted him to become totally besotted with her, to fall truly in love with her first. Only then would she take him to heights he had never dreamed of, as only she knew how.

And so she continued to lead him along gently, and little by little it was all happening . . . every day he became more committed to her. There was a new warmth in him, and he could not get enough of her. In bed and out of it. He wanted her with him all the time.

Arabella looked down at the plain gold wedding band on the third finger of her left hand. It was gleaming brightly in the firelight. Jonathan had wanted to give her a circle of diamonds. She had asked for this plain, old-fashioned gold ring, telling him that it was more symbolic. He had been surprised, yet obviously touched, by her sentiments.

How thunderstruck Tony had been when Jonathan had married her so quickly in Hong Kong just before Christmas, then swept her off to Europe on their honeymoon. He had been startled to discover she was suddenly going to be out of reach for several months. Very put out, in actuality. And she had taken great satisfaction in being able to ruffle Tony's infuriating equanimity for once.

Her new husband had wanted to take her to Paris. But there was so much of her past in that city, so much sadness to be recalled, she was not excited about honeymooning there. Nor did she particularly want to take the chance of running into someone who had known her in the old days. She did not need to deal with friends long since departed from her life, nor confront memories gone stale and cold. And so she convinced Jonathan they would enjoy Rome more, had suggested that they then go on to Mougins in the South of France, to visit his cousin Sarah, whom he had spoken about so warmly. This had delighted him, and he had readily agreed to her travel plans.

Rome had been fun. Since she knew the city like a native, she had been able to take him sightseeing, and to the chicest restaurants and clubs, which were well off the usual tourist track, patronized by local society and the international jet set.

And she had been very loving, sexually pliable, catering to his desires, more than ready to please him, and this had made him extremely happy.

It was in Rome that he had bought her yet another wedding gift, an extraordinary necklace he had presented to her as a surprise on their last night in the Eternal City, before they had left for France. Composed of a single strand of large black pearls, it had a cream-colored, teardrop pearl hanging from a ten-carat diamond in the center of the strand.

Although she had some good jewelry of her own, the black pearl necklace was not only rare but surpassed everything in her possession. Except, of course, for the huge Burmese ruby-and-diamond ring Jonathan had given her when they had become engaged.

The chimes of the little carriage clock brought Arabella out of her reverie. She glanced at it, surprised to see it was seven. Jonathan, who had gone to Cannes with Yves, had said he would be back by seven-thirty. She must be ready for him.

Rising, she hurried into the bedroom, took a sheer, black-chiffon nightgown trimmed with coffee-colored lace out of the armoire, then went into the bathroom to undress and freshen up.

A few minutes later, wearing the glamorous nightgown and a matching black chiffon peignoir that floated around her in a cloud, Arabella seated herself at the dressing table. She had worn her silver-gilt hair in a severe chignon all day; now she pulled out the pins and let it fall around her face and down her back. She brushed it until it gleamed.

Leaning forward, she peered at herself in the glass. Sometimes she was startled by her own beauty, by the lack of lines around her eyes and other telltale signs of aging, by the suppleness of her skin, the flawlessness of her complexion. Life had left hardly any marks on her face, and nothing seemed to mar its youth and beauty. Even when she was ill with a cold, or some other minor complaint, she appeared to be in blooming health. How lucky she was. She looked much younger than her thirty-four years.

After scrubbing off her bright red lipstick with a tissue, she toned down her flushed face with creamy foundation and transparent powder until she was very pale, almost wan-looking. She added extra eyeliner to her lids, emphasizing their natural, almond shape. Smoothing on black shadow, she then highlighted the bones under the brows with touches of purple and silver, and instantly her eyes stood out like huge, dark coals in her face. Once she had blotted her lips, she smeared on colorless salve, and sprayed herself generously with the musky perfume Jonathan preferred. She then lifted the black pearl necklace out of its leather case and clasped it around her neck. Jonathan liked her to wear jewelry in bed. It was a fetish of his.

Hurrying now, she stepped over to the armoire, opened it, stared at herself in the full-length mirror, approving of her reflection. She looked so young, like a girl of sixteen, her face full of innocence—and promise. Yet in contrast her body was the body of an alluring woman, shapely, sensual, and provocative in the revealing nightgown.

The black chiffon was taut across her breasts. Her nipples and their dark aureoles were faintly visible through the filmy chiffon and lace. She had had the nightgown made in Hong Kong, and the seamstress had cut it to fit her body perfectly, and so it clung to her in all the right places. And in the most tantalizing way.

Stepping into a pair of high-heeled, black-satin mules, she went through into the sitting room where she stood for a moment warming herself in front of the fire. And then she stretched out on the Chesterfield sofa to wait for her husband.

As the minutes ticked by, Arabella began to realize she was anxious for Jonathan to return, looked forward to seeing him, even though he had only been gone for a couple of hours. She hoped he would want to make love before they went down to dinner.

Startled by these thoughts, she sat upon the

sofa with a jolt, frowned, reached for a cigarette, lighted it.

As she smoked, her mind turned over at a rapid pace, and it dawned on her how much she liked Jonathan's blond good looks, his lovely manners, the finesse with which he did things, his very Englishness. It was such a change, such a relief, to be with an Englishman after the foreigners she had known. She also enjoyed the avid attention he paid to her, his passion for her, his sexual prowess. Jonathan Ainsley, her husband, was as good a lover as she had ever had, if not, indeed, the very best.

She suddenly suspected she was falling in love with him, and she was further surprised at herself.

Fifteen minutes later Jonathan hurried into the sitting room. It was dimly lit, but the logs blazing in the hearth cast a roseate glow throughout.

Arabella was standing in front of the fireplace, and he thought she looked quite extraordinary tonight. This brought him to a standstill.

He paused in the center of the floor, staring at her, appreciating her beauty, her sensuality. How inviting she was in the black-chiffon negligée. He could faintly make out parts of her body through the delicate fabric . . . the high, full breasts, the slender waist, the blond mound of Venus below. Black was a color that suited her well. It brought out the creaminess of her incomparable skin, the silver lights in the cascade of glorious, shimmering blond hair.

She held out her arms to him, half smiling.

Her black eyes seemed to burn right through him, and they held an expression he had never seen reflected there before. But curiously enough, whatever the expression meant, it excited him. As he moved forward he felt his desire for her stirring.

"I've missed you, darling," she murmured in her low, husky voice as he came to a stop next to her.

"I've not been all *that* long," he replied. Nevertheless he was pleased. He reached for her, took her in his arms, kissed her on the mouth. When they finally drew apart, he held her away from him, gripping her shoulders firmly with both hands, gazing deeply into her face.

"What is it?" She asked at last.

"You are so very, *very* beautiful tonight, Arabella. More beautiful than I have ever seen you, I do believe."

"Oh Jonathan . . ."

He leaned into her, kissed the hollow in her throat, and as he did he slipped the peignoir off her shoulders. It slid to the floor. Next he pulled at the narrow nightgown straps tied in bows, and as they came undone this garment, too, fell in a swirl of chiffon at her feet.

She stood before him naked except for the black pearls encircling her slender throat.

Jonathan stepped back. Of all the women he had ever had, she was the most experienced sexually, and therefore the most exciting, the most desirable . . . Of all the objects of art in his collection, she was the most beautiful thing, the biggest prize of all . . . his greatest possession. She was perfection itself. And he owned her. Owned every part of her. No, that was not quite true. She was still withholding. This continued to surprise him. But soon she would give herself up to him completely, abandon herself fully. He was confident of his powers . . . and his power over her.

Arabella said slowly, "Jonathan, is something wrong? You're looking at me oddly."

"No, of course there's nothing wrong," he replied. "I'm just admiring you, thinking how lovely you look . . . wearing only my black pearls. How white your body is in contrast." As he spoke, he reached out, ran a finger down one of her breasts.

Suddenly he thought he would explode. He was terribly excited. The blood rushed to his face, and he trembled as he moved closer to her, put his hands around her neck, unclasped the necklace.

"There, that's much better," he said, slipping it into his pocket. "You need no adornment, Arabella. You are perfect as you are . . . like a Grecian statue exquisitely chiseled out of the finest alabaster."

He removed his sports jacket, threw it on a chair. Then, taking hold of her hand, he led her toward the sofa. "Come, let us lie here together for a while. Let us love each other, enjoy each other," he said. "I want to know you more intimately than I already do, possess even more of you. And then more . . . and more. Will you let me, Arabella?"

"Yes," she whispered huskily. "If you will do the same."

"Ah, Arabella, we are so alike, you and I, and in every conceivable way." He chuckled softly. "A couple of sinners, I do believe."

Jonathan held her with his eyes. A knowing look crossed his face. He pressed her down onto the cushions with one hand. With the other he began to unbutton his shirt.

451

27

"I'm not quite sure how to tell you this," Alexander began, looking from his sister, Emily, to his cousins, Paula O'Neill and Anthony Standish, the Earl of Dunvale.

The three of them were seated on the two sofas in front of the fire, sipping the drinks he had poured for them a short while before.

"In fact," Alexander went on, "I've wracked my brains for weeks now, seeking the right words, the best way of explaining—"

Breaking off, he rose from his chair, walked across the drawing room, stood at the huge, bow-shaped window that soared to the ceiling, overlooked the small garden behind his Mayfair house.

He suddenly wished that he hadn't asked them to come over, that he didn't have to tell them . . . *fervently* wished that he could simply . . . let it happen. But that would be unthinkable. Unfair of him. And besides, there were too many things to be decided, too many legalities involved.

Alexander was tense, held himself stiffly, his shoulders hunched underneath his jacket. He took a deep breath, summoning his courage. This was perhaps the most difficult thing he had ever had to do in his entire life.

Emily, watching him intently, had detected the strained note in his voice when she had first arrived at the house. And now she noticed how taut he was. They had been unusually close throughout their lives, and she knew him as well as she knew herself. Intuitively she felt that something was radically wrong.

Pressing back her alarm, she said, "You sound awfully serious, Sandy."

"Yes," he responded, continuing to stare out of the window, wondering how to begin. In the gathering dusk of this January evening, the patch of garden looked sad and bereft with its blackened skeletal trees, empty flower beds frosted with old snow turned gray by London soot. It seemed to him that this bit of earth echoed his bleak mood.

The three cousins were waiting for Alexander to continue, to explain why he had invited them here, had actually *insisted* they come tonight. And they exchanged concerned glances behind his back.

Paula swung her head, focused on Anthony, lifted a brow questioningly.

The Earl shrugged, half raised his hands in a helpless gesture, indicating his own considerable bafflement.

Next Paula peered at Emily on the sofa opposite. Emily tightened her lips, shook her head rapidly, expressing her own puzzlement. "I don't know what this is all about either," Emily mouthed silently to Paula. After a moment, she cleared her throat, ventured aloud, "Sandy dear . . . Gran always said that if a person had something difficult to explain, or unpleasant to say, the best thing to do was simply to blurt it out. Why don't you do that?"

"That's not as easy as it sounds," her brother answered quietly.

"Whatever problems you have, you know you have our full support," Anthony volunteered in his most reassuring voice.

Alexander pivoted on his heels, stood with his back to the great window, regarding the three of them thoughtfully, "Yes, I do know that, Anthony, and thanks," he said at last. A faint wavering smile touched his mouth, then faded instantly.

Paula, studying him alertly, saw something strange in the back of his light blue eyes, the emptiest of expressions, and it made her heart tighten. "There's something awfully wrong . . . it's . . . it's bad, isn't it, Sandy?"

He nodded. "I've always prided myself on being able to handle anything, Paula. But this . . ." He discovered he was unable to finish his sentence.

Paula remembered then, remembered the telephone conversation she had had with him at the end of August last year. She had sensed he had a problem that particular morning, had then dismissed it as being merely her vivid imagination at work. But she had been right after all, she was sure of that. She clasped her hands together tightly, feeling unaccountably nervous and filling, unexpectedly, with apprehension.

Alexander said slowly, "I asked the three of you to come round this evening . . . because of our closeness over the years, the special relationship I have with each one of you." He waited, took a breath. "I do have certain problems. I thought we could discuss them rationally and that perhaps you would help me to come to a few decisions."

"Of course we will," Anthony said. His cousin was behaving out of character and he was desperately worried. He fixed his clear, steady gaze on the other man, wanting to convey his affection and devotion. They had helped each other over some rough terrain in the past and would no doubt do so again.

Leaning forward with a degree of urgency, Anthony asked, "Is it to do with business? Or is it a family matter?"

"Personal really," Alexander answered.

He moved away from the window, walked slowly across the elegant, period drawing room, lowered himself into the chair he had vacated a short while before. He knew there was no point in putting it off any longer. They simply had to be told.

Alexander let out a deeply weary sigh. He said, in a controlled voice, "I'm very ill . . . I'm dying, actually."

Emily, Paula, and Anthony gaped at him. None of them had expected to hear anything as devastating as this. They were stunned.

Alexander went on hurriedly, "I'm sorry to have told you in such a blunt manner, but I took Emily's advice. And Gran *was* right, you know.

It *is* the only way . . . best to blurt it out, get it said without too much preamble.''

Paula was so shaken she was unable to respond. Blindly, she groped for Anthony's hand.

He took it, enfolded it in his comfortingly. He was as stupefied as she, at a complete loss. There were no words. A great sadness flowed through him. What an appalling thing to happen to poor Sandy, who was in his prime. He would notice it most acutely when his cousin was gone. Sandy had been such a source of strength during his own travails over the years. And most especially at the time Min had been found drowned in the lake at Clonloughlin. Anthony reached for his glass of scotch-and-soda on the end table. He suddenly needed a drink.

Emily was ashen with shock.

She sat perfectly still, staring at her brother in disbelief, her eyes dark with sudden pain. She felt as though all blood had drained out of her. Then taking hold of herself, she got to her feet a bit shakily, and went to him. Kneeling down next to his chair, she took his hand in hers, clung to it.

"Sandy, it's not true! It can't be!" she cried in a low but vehement tone. "Oh please say it isn't . . ." Emily's voice quavered, came to a stop, and her green eyes brimmed. "Not you, Sandy, oh please, not *you.*"

"I'm afraid so," he said in the steadiest voice imaginable, "and there's not much I can do to change this one, Dumpling. It's out of my hands."

His use of her old nickname made her choke up, and long-forgotten memories came rushing back unbidden, evoking their childhood years together, and she remembered how he had protected her, looked after her, and her throat suddenly ached and her heart felt as if it was being squeezed in a vise. She closed her eyes for a split second, striving to come to grips with her brother's tragic and frightening news.

"You say you're d-d-dying." She stumbled on this last word, had to take several deep breaths before continuing, "But of what? What's wrong with you, Sandy? You seem perfectly well to me. What are you suffering from?"

"I have acute myelogenous leukemia . . . it's also known as acute granulocytic leukemia."

"Surely that can be treated!" Anthony exclaimed, sudden hope leaping onto his worried face. "Tremendous strides have been made in medicine today, especially in the treatment of cancer, and perhaps—"

"There is no cure," Alexander interrupted.

"But what actually is it?" Emily demanded, anxiety making her voice rise, giving it a shrill-ness abnormal for her. "What on earth *causes* it?"

"A malignant change in cells that produce granulocytes, one of the types of white blood cells made in the bone marrow," he explained, so well educated about his disease that the details were now readily on the tip of his tongue. "They multiply and survive longer than normal cells. Very simply put, they destroy. As their numbers increase, they invade the bone marrow, enter the bloodstream, and eventually attack the organs and tissue."

"Oh God, Sandy—" Paula began and came to a halt. Her feelings got the better of her. The words she had been about to say strangled in her throat. She steadied herself; somehow she managed to hang onto her self-possession. After a few moments, she went on, "I'm so sorry, so very sorry, darling. I'm here for you, we're all here for you, whenever you need us, day or night."

"Yes," he said, "I know you are. I'm counting on it, actually, Paula."

"Isn't there any chance of at least *arresting* the leukemia?" Paula probed, her manner gentle, her sympathy and compassion reflected in her eyes.

"There really isn't," Alexander replied.

With sudden fierceness, Emily said, "I realize

you must have been to the best doctors in London, but we must go farther afield. We really must. What about the States? Sloan-Kettering in New York, for instance? We can't just stand by and *allow* this to happen, Sandy. We must do *something.*"

"I agree with you, Emily," Anthony said. "There has to be some sort of advanced treatment in this day and age. *Somewhere.* I can't accept this either, Sandy. I won't." He averted his face, struggling with his feelings.

Alexander shook his head, and it was with a finality that was unmistakable. "I understand how the three of you feel. I was exactly the same as you in the beginning. Looking for a cure, full of hope, but the hope rapidly changed to frustration, then anger, and finally to *acceptance.* You see . . ." He stopped, took several deep breaths, continued slowly, "There is absolutely nothing that can be done for me. And believe me, I *have* been to the very best specialists in London, New York, and Zurich. What I'm suffering from *is* fatal. I'm having treatment, of course, but there has been hardly any remission."

A grim silence settled in the drawing room.

Alexander sat back in his chair, relieved at last to have finally told them. He had resigned himself to his fate some time ago, but he had worried greatly about the family and how they would take it, most especially Emily.

For their parts, his sister and his cousins were trying to come to grips with the heartbreaking news he had just imparted, striving to absorb it and to get a hold of their emotions as well. They each, in their different ways, loved Alexander, and although they did not know it, they were sharing the same thought at this precise moment. All were asking themselves why it had to be Alexander who had been stricken in this manner. He was the finest, the kindest, the most loving of men. The very best. He had always been there for them, whenever they had needed him, no matter what the problem, and that was how he had been since childhood. The three cousins believed him to be the one truly *good* man they knew. If anyone was a saint, it was Alexander.

Paula eventually spoke. "You've known for some months, haven't you?"

Alexander nodded, then picked up his glass of white wine, took a sip.

"Was it the end of August last year when you found out you were ill?" she asked.

"No, it was October. But you're close enough, Paula." He gave her an odd look. "How did you know?"

Paula's grave face was infinitely still. "I

didn't. Not really. But I did have a queer feeling things were not right with you, when you phoned me from Leeds—the day we missed each other at Fairley. There was such a peculiar nuance in your voice, it prompted me to ask you if there was a problem, and, if you recall, you said no. So I dismissed it. I thought it was my imagination getting the better of me."

"You were very perceptive that morning," Alexander murmured. "I felt uneasy, wanted to talk to you. I was already starting to have symptoms. I was becoming fatigued quickly, and it worried me, and I discovered I bruised and bled very easily . . . if I merely knocked myself against something."

Alexander got up, went to fetch the bottle of wine, refilled Paula's and Emily's glasses and his own, took the bottle back to the silver ice bucket on the console.

The others waited in silence, dreading what else he had to say to them.

He went on as he sat down, "I was doing a lot of work on the estate at Nutton Priory in late September, and I was baffled. I wondered if I'd become a hemophiliac overnight—if that was possible. Then early in October I developed the most frightful ulcers in my mouth. I was growing more alarmed than ever, and that's why I canceled our lunch date, Paula. I finally went to see my doctor. He immediately sent me to a specialist in Harley Street. The tests and the bone marrow biopsy were quite conclusive."

"You say you're having treatment," Anthony said. "It must be doing you some good, Sandy, having some effect. You don't look as though you're dreadfully ill. You're a trifle pale perhaps, thinner, but—"

"All it's doing is keeping me going for the moment," Alexander interjected.

Emily looked at her brother closely. "What sort of treatment is it?"

"Transfusions of red blood cells, and platelets when I need them. I also take antibiotics from time to time, to help reduce the chances of my getting infections."

"I see." Emily bit her inner lip nervously. "You just said the treatment is keeping you going . . . for . . . for . . . how long?" she asked in a voice that shook. She was filled with fear for her brother.

"Four to five months at the outside, I think. Not many people last much longer than a year after this type of leukemia has been diagnosed."

Emily's mouth trembled. "I can't bear it. Not *you*. It's just not fair. Oh Sandy, you can't be dying!" She endeavored to push back the tears, knowing he wanted her to be strong, to face this with the same kind of courage he was displaying. She was unable to do so.

She jumped up, hurried out of the drawing room, suddenly aware that she was about to break down completely.

28

Emily stood at the bottom of the staircase in the entrance hall, holding the bannister, filled with an internal shaking. And slowly the tears slid down her cheeks unchecked as she quietly wept for her brother. He was only thirty-seven. Her mind balked at the thought of his imminent death. It was unacceptable to her.

After only a matter of seconds, the drawing room door opened and closed softly. Emily felt Alexander's arms encircling her. He turned her around to face him, took a handkerchief out of his pocket, wiped the tears from her face.

"Come on, Dumpling, try to hang in there. For me," he said. "I can't stand to see you so upset. It doesn't help me. I realize this has been a ghastly shock for you; on the other hand, there is no *easy* way to break this kind of news. How *do* you tell those you love that you're dying?"

Emily was incapable of responding. Her eyes welled again, and she buried her face against his chest, held on to him tightly.

He said, very softly, "I'm glad you reminded me of Gran's attitude . . . you know, about just blurting it out. It *did* help me to screw up my courage and get it said. I'd been putting it off for weeks."

Alexander smoothed his hand over her hair, and there was a pause before he remarked, "I've hidden my illness from you for a very long time, old thing. However, it is going to start showing very soon. So you *had* to be told. And there are a lot of things which must be properly dealt with. *Now.* They can't be put off any longer . . . time does go so *quickly,* especially when one is trying to hold on to it."

Emily swallowed hard, wanting to be strong, but finding it difficult. She stood very still, snapping her eyes shut.

After a moment, when she had regained a little of her self-possession, she said, "Nothing will ever be the same again, Sandy, not when you're . . . gone. Whatever will we all do? Whatever will *I* do?" As the words left her mouth, she realized how selfish she was being, but she could not take them back. They had been said, and to apologize to him would only make matters worse.

He said softly, in a confident tone, "You'll be all right, Emily. You'll keep going, and with the strength and courage you've always had . . . Gran's kind of fortitude. She taught you how to soldier on when you were a little girl. And you have Winston and your family." A long sigh trickled through Alexander, and as if thinking aloud, he murmured against her hair, "Francesca's all right, too, now that she's married to Oliver, but I do worry about Amanda. She's such a vulnerable young woman, so impressionable, really. You will keep an eye on her, won't you?" For the first time Alexander's voice held a slight tremor. He glanced away, hid his face from her, then coughed behind his hand.

Emily said, "You know I will, darling."

They stood together for a few minutes longer.

Alexander held her closer, gathering as much of his diminished strength as possible, aware that he had a great deal to say in the next half hour. He was not looking forward to it. But it had to be done, and the best way, he had decided earlier, was to be very businesslike about everything.

Emily could feel Sandy's bones through his

clothes, and she realized how thin he had grown. She drew away, stole a quick glance at him, took note of his pallor, the faint purplish smudges under his eyes, and her heart sank. She could not understand why she had not noticed signs that he was ill before now, and she cursed herself angrily for not having paid more attention in the last few months.

Alexander finally released her, and taking out his handkerchief once more, he blotted her damp cheeks. A fleeting smile touched his eyes. How blond and small and dainty she was. She had always reminded him of a fragile piece of Dresden china. Yet she had a backbone of steel, and there was an indomitability about her that reminded him of their grandmother. And he knew that as distressed as she was now, in the long run she would be strong for everyone. He could count on his sister. Like Emma Harte before her, she had grit.

Emily was acutely aware of Alexander's intense scrutiny. She returned it, said, "I'll be fine, Sandy," as though she had read his mind.

Alexander smiled at her, nodded.

There was a brief silence before Emily went on slowly, in a low voice, "You've not only been a wonderful brother to me, but mother, father, best friend as well. You've been . . . everything to me, Sandy. I've never *really* told you before how I feel, but I do want you to know that I—"

"I'm very aware of how you feel," he interrupted swiftly, unable to deal with any more emotion at this time. "And I love you too, Emily. Now we'd better go back to the drawing room, join the others, don't you think? There are arrangements to be made. For the future."

"I'd like to talk about business first. About Harte Enterprises to be specific," Alexander said once they were all gathered around the fire again.

"Yes, of course, anything you wish," Paula answered. Her eyes were red and watery, and betrayed her, despite her air of calmness. It was obvious that she had wept whilst her cousins had been out of the room, but she now appeared to be in total control of herself.

"I've had time to think things out," Alexander began, "and I'd like to share some of my thoughts with you before I come to my final decisions. I suppose I'm looking for your input before I put my plans into motion."

"But I'm not involved in any of the family businesses," Anthony immediately reminded him. "Are you sure I'm not in the way?" His expression turned quizzical.

"No, you're not. And anyway, you're the eldest of Emma Harte's grandchildren, and you ought to—"

"Paula's the head of the family, though," Anthony countered. "And thank God she is, too. It's not a job I'd relish, I don't mind telling you."

Alexander smiled with a certain wryness. "I know what you mean. But to continue, you're my closest male friend, and very simply put I want you here. Let's just say for moral support, shall we, old chap?"

The Earl nodded, got up, strode over to the console where he refreshed his scotch-and-soda. He glanced across at Paula and Emily. "Do either of you want another drink?"

Both women shook their heads.

"How about you, Sandy?"

"I'm fine right now, thanks."

Alexander waited until Anthony had returned to the sofa before he turned to Emily, and went on, "I'm sorry I called this meeting when Winston is in Canada, but I had to have it this week because I'm going into the hospital tomorrow for treatment. He ought to have been here, of course, as head of the Yorkshire Consolidated Newspaper Company and our Canadian papers. On the other hand, the divisions he runs are not actually relevant to this discussion."

"He'll understand, Sandy." Emily leaned forward, pinned her brother with her green eyes. "How long are you going to be in the hospital?" she asked, her worry instantly showing.

"Only a few days, and don't be concerned about it. The treatment does help me. Now, I would like to move along. Look, I know what I'm going to talk about is somewhat unsettling. But please, *don't be upset.* It must all be said, and I want my affairs to be in order . . . a Harte family trait, I believe."

Alexander's gaze swept over the three of them, and he went on to explain in a thoughtful tone, "I've analyzed Harte Enterprises in every conceivable way over the past couple of weeks, trying to decide what to do with the company. I considered selling it, knowing it would fetch hundreds of millions of pounds, which we could reinvest in the market. Then I thought of selling off only certain divisions, keeping others. And then it struck me how unfair I was being to you, Emily."

Before she had a chance to say anything, he rushed on, "After all, you run Genret, which is one of our biggest money-making divisions, and you're the only other shareholder—"

"Except for Jonathan and Sarah," Emily cut in. "And I don't suppose they're of any consequence."

"No, they're not," Alexander agreed. "In any

event, Emily, I realized it was rather imperious of me to make decisions without consulting you. And it was certainly wrong of me to assume, as I did initially, that you might not want to run Harte Enterprises yourself. A few days ago, yet another thought occurred to me . . . what would Grandy have wanted us to do with Harte Enterprises in view of my illness? I instantly concluded that she would not want us to sell it. The company is too solid, too rich, too important to the family as a whole for us to relinquish it. Don't you agree?"

"Yes," Emily managed, more aware than ever of what the future without her brother would actually mean.

"Paula, what is your opinion?" Alexander asked.

"You're absolutely right about everything," Paula said, striving to sound normal. "Grandy did have very strong feelings about Harte Enterprises. She would want Emily to continue in your stead. That *is* what you have in mind, isn't it?"

"Yes, I think Emily should become chairman of the board and chief executive officer within the next few weeks. That way we can make a smooth transfer of power in the company and I can step down. Fairly soon, too, I hope."

"I suppose you'll want Amanda to run Genret," Emily ventured.

"With your agreement. And the one division I think we should sell is Lady Hamilton Clothes."

"To the Kallinskis presumably," Paula interjected.

"Yes." Alexander cleared his throat, reached for his glass, took a sip of wine. "If anyone is entitled to buy Lady Hamilton Clothes, it's Uncle Ronnie. For sentimental reasons, and because of our long involvement with the family for over seventy years. I say let's keep everything in the three clans. As you both know—" He looked from Emily to Paula, continued, "Uncle Ronnie is prepared to meet our price. I'm not worried about that aspect. My only real concern is that you're comfortable with the deal, Paula. Whilst you're not involved with the running of Harte Enterprises, Lady Hamilton does supply the Harte stores and the boutiques."

"Uncle Ronnie assured me they would continue to do so, and on an exclusive basis, when we discussed the idea of Kallinski Industries buying the fashion division last August," Paula told him.

"Well, Emily?" Alexander peered across at her, lifted a brow.

"Yes, it's all right with me. But what about Amanda? She loves her division, Sandy."

"I know she does. But under these unexpected circumstances I'm sure she'll understand the necessity for making certain changes, for streamlining the company to an extent. Grandy's philosophy was that we must be loyal to the company as a whole, not just to our own divisions. I believe that, too, as you and Amanda are aware. Anyway, Genret will be a challenge to Amanda, just as it was to you when you took over from Len Harvey twelve years ago."

"That's true . . . yes . . ."

"What's the matter, Emily?" Alexander asked, frowning at her. "You look and sound rather hesitant."

"I'm not really. It's just that I'm not terribly well informed about the real estate division of Harte Enterprises. And that worries me."

"There's not *really* a problem, darling. Thomas Lorring is my right hand in that division, and he's been virtually running it for several years. And you *know* that he has, Emily." He leveled a long, very direct look at her. "He'll do the same for you, when you take over from me . . . and you *will*, won't you?"

"Of course I will." Emily sat back on the sofa jerkily, wishing she did not have to step into her brother's shoes. If only things could suddenly be the way they were yesterday. She longed suddenly for Winston, regretted her husband was not here, that he would not be returning to England for another week. The thought plunged her into deeper dismay.

Paula said, "You've made some very sound judgments, Sandy."

He rose, paced to the window, glanced out at the garden almost absently. He said, without turning around, "I think they're the most logical moves, given the situation." He remained motionless in front of the flaring bay for a few seconds longer.

No one said a word.

Finally Alexander returned to the fireplace, where he stood with his back to the blazing logs, warming himself.

And then without any preamble, he announced in a brisk and businesslike voice, "About my will. I intend to leave this house to Francesca and Nutton Priory to Amanda. Naturally, the Villa Faviola is yours, Emily."

"Oh Sandy—" She stopped abruptly. She could not speak. Her throat closed on her. She blinked back sudden tears.

He hurried on relentlessly, "Fifty percent of my personal wealth will be divided by the three of you, Emily, and the other fifty percent will go to the children in the family. And not just my nephews and nieces, but to your children, Paula, and yours, Anthony."

They both nodded their understanding.

Anthony looked away, not wanting Alexander to see the anguish suffusing his face. He stared fiercely at the painting on the opposite wall.

Paula twisted her wedding ring nervously, gazed down at her hands, thinking how uncertain life was. Only that afternoon she had been congratulating herself on so many things accomplished lately, and she had been happy. Now, without warning, she was miserable, filled with worry and concern, and facing the untimely death of a beloved cousin, who was also a dear friend and important business associate. The implications of Sandy's fatal illness were manifold and on a variety of levels.

"Now, Emily," Alexander proceeded, determined to be done with everything tonight, so that there would be no need for this kind of discussion again. "Next we come to my holdings in Harte Enterprises. To be precise, the fifty-two percent of the shares Grandy left me. I am going to give thirty-two percent to you and twenty percent to Amanda. I am not leaving any of my shares to Francesca since she does not work for the company."

"Yes, I see . . . thank you," Emily said in

the steadiest voice she could muster. "But I'm just wondering . . . is that quite fair to Amanda, darling?" She asked this softly, not wishing to argue with him, but at the same time wanting her half-sister to be fully involved and totally committed to Harte Enterprises. After all, it would be just the two of them running it eventually.

"I believe it is *eminently* fair," Alexander was quick to respond. "Grandmother insisted that one person had control of this particular company, to prevent any dissension among us, and that is how I want it, why I have divided my shares in the way I have. You will be the majority shareholder and head of Harte Enterprises, as I am now." His tone was unusually firm and uncompromising and it left no room for doubt about his feelings or for further conversation on the matter.

Emily made no comment, directed her gaze to the fire, grappling with her overwhelming sadness, still finding it difficult to comprehend that her brother would not be with them for much longer, that next year at this time he would be dead. Her heart was heavy, and once more she longed for her husband and his comforting presence, the emotional security Winston gave her.

Anthony now spoke up at last. He said, "When you've finished your treatment, I want you to come and stay with us at Clonloughlin, Sandy. And for as long as you can."

"Yes, I *would* like that. It'll do me good to be with you all. And then afterward, Emily, I'll work with you for a few weeks, take you through every aspect of the job. Mind you, I do believe you'll be capable of doing it blind-folded."

Emily bit her lip, nodded rapidly, glanced at Paula, her eyes full of mute appeal.

Paula quickly bridged this tense moment, when she said in a warm and cheerful voice, "Is there anything I can do, Sandy? Anything that will make things easier for you?"

"Not really, Paula, thanks anyway. Oh wait! Yes, there is one thing you can *all* do for me!" His intelligent, light blue eyes roamed over them, and he shifted on his feet, slightly changed his stance in front of the fire. "I'd like you to keep the news of my illness quiet, if you don't mind. I really don't wish it to become a topic for discussion in the family. And I certainly don't want to have to cope with sadness and sympathy, or be surrounded by a lot of long, gloomy faces."

A stricken expression settled in Emily's eyes. "I appreciate your feelings," she said and paused. Her voice wavered as she went on, "I'll try not to tell Winston, but I think it'll be ever so hard for me . . ."

"Oh, but of course, you must tell him!" her brother exclaimed. He looked at Paula and Anthony. "And naturally you must tell Shane and Sally. I didn't mean you to exclude them, only your children. And yours, Emily, and our half-sisters, I don't want Amanda and Francesca to know—at least not just yet."

"What about Mummy?" Emily asked, worry flaring. "Has she got to be kept in the dark, too?"

Alexander inclined his head. "Oh yes, very much so. It's better Mother doesn't know anything at all. She has a tendency to become hysterical about the slightest thing. She would only upset me."

Striding over to the Georgian console table, Alexander picked up the bottle of white wine, brought it to Paula and Emily. "Well, that's about it," he said as he refilled their crystal goblets. "I've covered everything I think. Incidentally, Emily, John Crawford knows about the situation. Obviously, as my solicitor, he had to be told, and he'll help you with any and all legalities after I'm . . . er . . . when I'm no longer around."

"Yes," she said in the smallest of voices, and she clenched her hands together in her lap, wishing he would not keep alluding to his impending death.

"This has been a terrible burden for you to carry alone, Sandy," Anthony said a short while later.

Emily and Paula had left together, and the two men were finishing their drinks in the drawing room before going out to dinner.

Looking across at his cousin intently, the Earl added, "You ought to have told me before, you know."

"Perhaps I should have," Alexander admitted. "But to be honest, *I* had to come to grips with my illness first. As I explained earlier, I went through any number of different emotions —disbelief, anger, frustration, and acceptance. Then the fury came back, and the frustration, and the sense of total *helplessness.* I was on an emotional seesaw for the longest time, and naturally it was impossible for me to confide in anyone until I could handle myself properly. And, of course, I did want to pursue every avenue, look for a cure, if there was one to be found. I soon discovered there was absolutely nothing I could do except take the treatment and seize a bit of borrowed time."

Alexander smiled faintly, shrugged. "I am resigned to it now, Anthony, and completely in control. That is why I was finally able to tell you tonight. And now that that ordeal is over, I can relax, get on with my life for the next few months. I aim to make the most of it . . ."

"Yes," Anthony said, then discovered he could not go on. He took a quick sip of his scotch. What a bloody waste, he thought, and asked himself if he would have been able to handle himself with the same kind of courage and grace his cousin was displaying if he had been in similar circumstances. He was not sure. It took an awful lot of character to cope with one's own imminent death with such extraordinary stoicism.

Alexander said, "Come on, Anthony, don't look so morose. And please don't start getting maudlin on me. I couldn't cope . . . I had a difficult time dealing with Emily's emotion this evening. I realize how rough it is on all of you . . . but it's not quite as rough as it is on me."

"So sorry. Do forgive me, old chap."

"Nothing to forgive . . . I want everything to be as normal as possible. That makes it so much easier for me. I must now endeavor to ignore my illness, go about my business as best I can, and in the most controlled manner. Otherwise it'll be pure hell."

"You will come to Clonloughlin, won't you?"

"Yes, in about two weeks' time."

"Marvelous. Sally and I will enjoy having you. How long do you think you can stay?"

"Ten days, two weeks perhaps." Alexander swallowed the last of his wine, put the glass down on the end table near the fireplace. "I've booked a table at Mark's Club for nine o'clock. Perhaps we should stroll down there shortly, have a drink in the bar—"

Alexander rose at the sound of the phone ringing in the library which adjoined the drawing room. "Excuse me," he said as he hurried to answer it. He returned a second later. "It's for you, Anthony . . . Sally calling from Ireland."

"Oh yes, I expected to hear from her. Thanks."

"Don't tell her anything now. Not over the phone," Sandy instructed.

"I wouldn't dream of it," Anthony reassured him as he strode across the floor, went through the double mahogany doors and into the library.

Left alone, Alexander sat down on one of the sofas and closed his eyes.

The last couple of hours had been trying, had vitiated his energy. Even though the others had striven hard not to display their feelings, to be brave, they *had* been terribly upset. As he had known they would be. That was why he had so dreaded telling them. He had only managed to get through the ordeal of breaking his bad news by being utterly detached and matter of fact.

He accepted his death with equanimity now, had come to terms with his fate. And in so doing he had been able to confide in those closest to him, because he could help *them* to do exactly the same thing. It was going to be hardest on Emily, of course. They had been as close as two peas in a pod when they were growing up. They had relied on each other in a certain sense. Their mother had been so flighty in those days, running from man to man and marrying all sorts of disreputable characters. And their sweet but weak-willed father, crushed by the burden of his broken heart, had scarcely seemed aware of their existence. Alexander sighed under his breath. What a catastrophe his father's life had been. And his mother's, too. But wasn't life itself a catastrophe?

Alexander instantly let go of this thought, not wanting to sink into deep philosophical ruminations this evening, as he had been so wont to do of late. Grandy wouldn't approve, he said to himself and smiled, remembering Emma Harte. How invincible *she* had been, and right up to the end. Life for her had been a triumph. So much for *his* theories . . . but then perhaps life *was* rooted in doom and tragedy for some.

Opening his eyes, Alexander glanced around

the room, blinking. It looked beautiful tonight in the glow of the lamps and the warming firelight. Maggie had decorated this room just after their marriage, and he always thought of it as a bit of English spring, whatever the time of year, with its primrose and daffodil yellows, pale blues and greens. Whenever it needed redoing, he simply had the scheme repeated. He had been doing so since her death . . .

His cousin interrupted his musings when he said, "I say, Sandy, are you all right?" Anthony hovered over him, looking concerned.

Alexander pushed himself upright on the sofa. "Yes, I'm fine. I was recouping . . . the last few hours have been a little wearing."

"Of course they have. Come on, let's go to Mark's."

Within the space of ten minutes the two cousins were leaving Alexander's house in Chesterfield Hill and heading for Charles Street where the club was located.

It was a chilly night and windy, and Alexander hunched further into his overcoat, shoved his hands in his pockets, shivering slightly. "Anyway, how was Sally?" he asked, falling into step with Anthony.

"Wonderful, as usual. She sends her love. I told her you were coming to stay . . . but that's all I said."

"Quite."

They walked on in silence. Suddenly Anthony remarked, as if to himself, "There was something odd though . . ."

"Oh, in what sense?" Alexander asked, looking at him curiously.

"Sally told me that Bridget has been pestering her . . . wanting to know when I'm returning to Clonloughlin. According to Sally she seems rather anxious to talk to me. In fact, Sally said she seemed a trifle agitated today."

"That *is* odd. On the other hand, I have always found your housekeeper to be somewhat eccentric, if you don't mind me saying so."

"Have you really? Mmmm. Perhaps she is . . . and a bit fey too, like most of the Irish. Well, it can't be anything important," Anthony finished as they crossed Charles Street in the direction of the club.

But he was wrong. Events that had happened a decade ago were about to come back to haunt him.

29

It was raining at Clonloughlin the first morning Anthony was back, and there was a faint mist that softened the dark skeletal trees and the tall chimneys of the house etched so starkly against the leaden sky.

As he walked up the central path carved out between wide lawns he thought how lovely it looked even on this bleak winter's day, with its symmetrical, harmonic proportions, soaring windows, and the four white Palladian pillars supporting the front portico. Georgian in origin, it was a stately looking mansion situated on a small rise in the middle of a splendid park, with excellent views from its many windows. There

were three hundred and sixty-five of them altogether, one for each day of the year, a fine madness on the part of his ancestor, who had built
the house in the eighteenth century. But it was a
madness that Anthony had always secretly applauded. The many windows were unique, gave
the exteriors a certain gracefulness, opened up
the interiors to the pastoral landscape, filled
those beautiful rooms with light and air the
whole year round and hazy sunshine in the summer months.

Anthony loved Clonloughlin with a fierce and
abiding passion. It was his ancestral home and
the only place he had ever wanted to live. He
had been born here forty-five years ago and he
would die here when his time came. And his son
Jeremy would continue in his place, the Standish line unbroken as it had been for centuries.

His mind swung to Alexander and a rush of
sadness engulfed him as it had last night when
he had been talking to Sally. Although she had
met him at Cork Airport, he had resisted giving
her the grave news about Sandy on their drive
home. He had not even told her when they finally reached Clonloughlin, had waited instead
until they were in the privacy of their bedroom
suite.

Sally had been dreadfully upset once she had
heard the stark facts about Sandy's illness. She

had wept and he had comforted her. And then, to cheer themselves up and trying to be as positive as possible, they had made extensive plans for Sandy's stay with them after he left the hospital. But later, when Sally had fallen asleep in his arms, her cheeks had been tear-stained once again. She and her brother Winston had grown up in Yorkshire with Sandy and Emily. They had been unusually close, and Sandy was one of the godfathers to Giles, their nine-year-old son.

Anthony now veered to the left as he drew nearer to the house, and went around to the other side, entered through the back door. Inside the small indoor porch he shed his barbour and tweed cap, which were both drenched with rain, hanging the oilskin and the hat on the coat stand to drip. Seating himself on the wooden chair, he pulled off his green Wellington boots, slipped into a pair of brown loafers, then hurried down the back passageway to the library.

The house was very quiet.

It was early, only seven, and Sally was still asleep, as were the younger children on the nursery floor. Settling himself at the desk near the window, he pulled a pile of correspondence toward him, began to sort through the mail that had accumulated in the week he had been in London on business.

He did not hear the housekeeper come into the room until she spoke.

"Good morning, your lordship," said Bridget O'Donnell. "I didn't expect you to be up so early after your late arrival last night. Excuse me for not having the fire going in here."

"Ah, good morning, Bridget," Anthony said with a quick smile as he looked up. "It's not a problem. I'm not cold."

"The kettle's boiling. I'll just be putting a match to the fire, and then I'll be back with your pot of tea and toast."

"Thank you," he murmured, glanced down at the papers, wondering whether to ask her what it was she wished to discuss with him, then decided against it. Far better to wait until he had been fortified by his light breakfast. Bridget had a tendency to be garrulous at times, which required an enormous amount of patience on his part. He was not in the mood for her this morning.

He heard matches being struck, a faint *whoosh* as the paper and wood chips ignited and flames flew up the wide chimney back. Then there was the sound of bellows being pumped, the scraping of metal against stone as she placed the guard around the fire and finally departed to the kitchen.

Anthony reached for the letter addressed to

him in his son's handwriting. Jeremy had only just returned to boarding school after the Christmas holidays, and as he slit open the envelope he wondered what his eldest son and heir had to say to him. There would be a request for cash, no doubt. Eleven-year-old schoolboys were forever hard up. He smiled. Jeremy was exactly as he had been at the same age. But the boy worried him at times. Jem was not strong physically, did not have the robust health of his brother, Giles, and his sister, India, and Anthony had to constantly resist the temptation to mollycoddle him, as did Sally.

Anthony scanned the letter quickly. It was, as usual, a sketchy, imprecise report of Jeremy's activities over the last few days since he had been back at school, with a postscript, underscored, to *please send money urgently, please, Daddy, please.*

Bridget came sailing in with the breakfast tray sooner than he had expected, and Anthony put the letter down as she approached.

"Where would you like this, your lordship?"

"You can put it here on the desk," he answered her, pushing aside the papers he had been perusing a moment before.

She did so, then went around to the other side of the large partners' desk, stood looking at him.

Lifting the teapot, he poured tea into the

oversized breakfast cup, added milk, then glanced at her. "Yes, what is it, Bridget?"

"I've got to talk to you, Lord Dunvale. About something important."

"Now?"

"Yes, sir, I think so . . . I'd like to get it out of the way . . . this morning."

Anthony smothered a sigh. "All right." He spread his favorite thick-cut Frank Cooper marmalade onto the buttered toast, crunched on it, took a sip of tea. When the housekeeper was silent, he said, "Go on, Bridget, get it off your chest. And don't hover there, you know I detest people who do that. Please, do sit down."

She lowered herself into the chair, sat facing him, twisted her hands together nervously in her lap, focused her dark blue eyes on him.

The Earl finished his slice of toast as he waited for her to begin. Finally he raised a brow.

Bridget said slowly, "I'm not quite sure how to tell you this," and stopped abruptly midsentence.

Anthony, who had his cup halfway to his mouth, put it down with a clatter, stared at her in alarm. This was the second time in the space of several days that someone had begun a sentence with those words. First Sandy, and now Bridget, and it seemed like a bad omen. "You really ought to be able to tell me anything,

Bridget. After all, we've known each other since we were children."

The housekeeper nodded. "Well, your lordship . . . what I have to say . . . Well, it is about Lady Dunvale."

"Oh." He sounded surprised and his eyes narrowed.

"Not this Lady Dunvale. The first one."

"My mother?"

"No, no, not the Dowager Countess. Your first wife . . . that's who I mean . . . the Lady Minerva, sir."

Startled, Anthony sat back in his chair and gave Bridget a long, probing look. "What *about* the late Lady Dunvale?" he asked at last.

"It's . . . er . . . er . . . about her death."

For a moment he could not speak or move. Instinctively, he knew that something awful was about to be said, and he braced himself before muttering, "Is it important to discuss her death now . . . so long after the event?"

"Yes," Bridget said tersely.

"Why?" he probed, unable to resist the question, yet conversely not wanting to hear a word she had to say.

"Because I don't want it on my conscience anymore," Bridget replied. "I have to tell you what really happened . . . it's been a burden for me to carry, a nightmare still, even after all these years."

His mouth had gone very dry.

"It wasn't suicide like they said it was at the inquest."

He frowned, at first uncomprehending, not fully understanding her meaning. "Are you trying to tell me that Lady Dunvale fell into the lake, that she had an *accident,* as I've always maintained? That she didn't take her own life?"

"No, she didn't, she—" Bridget cut herself off, pursed her lips, then muttered, "She was *put there.*"

"By whom?" His voice was barely audible.

"Michael Lamont. They had a quarrel that fateful Saturday night, those two did, and he struck her. She fell, hit her face on the brass fender in his living room. If you remember, she did have a bruise on her face. The pathologist and Doctor Brennan mentioned it at the inquest. Well anyway, Lamont couldn't revive her. She appeared to be unconscious. Within seconds he realized she was actually dead. He said she'd had a heart attack or something. All that liquor she had drunk continually through the afternoon and evening, the tranquilizers she was forever swallowing . . . the combination killed her, he said. So Lamont took her and put her in the lake to cover everything up, and the next morning he drove past, pretended to have found her body . . . then he came up to the mansion to tell you there had been an accident, and he sent for the police and no one ever suspected *him* of being involved in any way. But they did suspect you, though. At least, Sergeant McNamara did.''

Events that had happened over a decade ago came rushing back to hit Anthony between the eyes, and he remembered every tiny detail with great vividness and clarity. He felt as if he had been kicked several times in the stomach, and he began to tremble all over, clasped his hands together to stop them from shaking, took several deep steadying breaths. He said at last, "And how do you know all this, Bridget?"

"I had seen her ladyship that afternoon, when she had driven over to Clonloughlin from Waterford. You know she came to the estate quite a lot, even though you had forbidden her to do so and were in the middle of the divorce. But Lady Min couldn't stay away, she loved Clonloughlin so much. She often came to see me. And *him.* We had tea together that afternoon, and she drove off around five, told me she was going down to the lake . . . she'd always been drawn to the lough, even when she was a small girl. Don't you remember the picnics the three of us used to have there when we were children? In any case, sir, you saw her little red car at the edge of the lake, after your Land-Rover had stalled, and you'd decided to walk home, taking the long way round in order to avoid her. And her ladyship also took a walk . . . over to Michael Lamont's house. She'd told me she was going to have dinner with him, but explained that she wouldn't be staying the night. You see, your lordship, they were—"

Bridget took a gulp of air, rushed on in breathless haste, the words pouring out of her, "They were having an affair. Lady Min had told me she would come by the kitchen at ten-thirty to say goodnight to me. She never *ever* left Clonloughlin without doing that. When she hadn't arrived by eleven-thirty, I got worried, so I went down to Lamont's house looking for her."

Bridget paused and her face crumpled and she almost broke down. She was suddenly thinking of their childhood, remembering how close they had been . . . she and Lady Minerva Glendenning, daughter of the Earl of Rothmerrion and the young Lord Anthony Standish, now the Earl of Dunvale. So long ago. And yet those days were as clear to her as yesterday, and they had been the best part of her life.

Watching her, Anthony saw the distress on Bridget's face, the anguish in her eyes, and he was about to make a sympathetic gesture toward her, but inexplicably changed his mind. He said, a trifle harshly, "Continue, Bridget, tell me everything. *I must know.*"

She nodded, swallowed. "When I got to Lamont's door, it was locked and the curtains were drawn, but I could hear them. Screaming at each other like banshees they were, saying horrible things, vile they were, and her ladyship . . . well, she sounded very drunk. Out of control. And then suddenly everything was quiet. There was absolute silence. I was frightened. I banged hard on the door, called out that it was me, and Michael let me in. He had no option, did he. Besides, he knew how close I was to Lady Min. When I saw her lying on the floor, my heart stopped. I ran to her, tried to revive her. But she was gone. It was then that Lamont dreamed up the idea of putting her in the lake, so as to make it look as if she had drowned herself. You see, he didn't want you to know that he'd been sleeping with Lady Min for all those years. He was afraid you'd sack him if you found out. He couldn't afford to lose his job. And even though he hadn't had a hand in Lady Min's death, it might have *looked* as if he had. That's what he said to me, your lordship. And he kept repeating it, over and over again, and he told me that circumstantial evidence can be very damning."

Anthony was appalled and outraged. "Why in God's name didn't you come up to the mansion to get me?" he demanded furiously, his voice rising in anger and disgust. "Why did you go along with Lamont?"

Bridget compressed her lips, said nothing.

He saw the stubborn set of her jaw, the defiance in the ice-blue eyes and he knew he was wasting his breath. She had been independent and difficult as a child; she had changed little over the years. If she did not want to confide her reasons for her silence at the time of Min's death, and for so many years after, then nothing could drag it out of her.

Sitting back in the chair, he studied her thoughtfully, trying to still his rage, the urge to shake her violently. And then suddenly a terrible thought occurred to him, one so unacceptable he tried to squash it, was barely able to face it. But he found himself saying carefully and with great deliberation, "Why were you so sure Lady Min was actually dead?" He leaned forward, fixed his probing, steely eyes on her. "Lady Min may only have been *unconscious*, Bridget. In which case, Michael Lamont did murder her if he put her in the lough whilst she was still alive."

"No, no, she was dead, I know she was dead!" Bridget cried excitedly, her eyes wide and flaring. "I know she was dead!" she insisted, verging on hysteria.

"Do you not recall the pathologist's report? Doctor Stephen Kenmarr said that when he did the autopsy he discovered an excessive amount of alcohol and barbiturates in her bloodstream and a quantity of water in her lungs. This led him to conclude that her death had been by drowning. And since her lungs were full of water, she could not have been dead when she was placed in the lake. I don't believe a dead body can take in water."

As the implications of his words sank in, Bridget paled. She had loved Minerva like a sister, had mothered her from the first moment she had set eyes on her as a child.

"No!" Bridget shouted. "She wasn't alive. She was dead. I would never have harmed *her*. I loved her. I loved her. You know I did. The water must have somehow seeped into her lungs afterward."

Anthony wondered if this was actually possible. He decided it might be, depending on the length of time Min had been dead before she had been submerged in the lake. He rubbed his forehead wearily, looked across at the housekeeper, asked in a quiet, very controlled voice, "Was her body still warm when Lamont took her out to the lake?"

Bridget nodded, not able to speak, shaken by the Earl's horrifying suggestion.

"Rigor mortis doesn't set in for about two to four hours after death. I suppose she might have been able to take water into her lungs for a short time after she died. Maybe for half an hour. But no longer, I'm absolutely sure of that. Still, only a pathologist could give me a truly accurate answer," Anthony said softly, almost to himself, as if thinking aloud.

Bridget stared at him, twisted her hands in her lap.

There was a long and deadly silence. The strain between them was a most palpable thing; it hung heavy in the air.

Eventually the Earl spoke. Pinning his eyes on the housekeeper, he said, "Why did you suddenly decide to speak up, to confide in me now, after so many years? Tell me that, Bridget O'Donnell?"

Bridget cried, "But I already told you . . . I couldn't have it on my conscience any longer . . . I mean about you not knowing the truth, not knowing the real circumstances of Lady Min's death. I realized how much it troubled you . . . the idea that she had committed suicide while the balance of her mind was disturbed. You'd blamed yourself for years, blamed her death on your decision to leave her and get a divorce. And I was sure you believed your relationship with your cousin Miss Sally Harte had been a contributing factor in your wife's death."

Anthony flinched. There was a certain truth in all this.

Bridget gave Anthony a hard stare. "I wanted to put your mind at rest, your lordship," she finished.

Like hell you did, Anthony thought, not for one moment believing her. And then, in a flash of sudden insight, he understood. There was no question in his mind that Bridget had been having an affair with Michael Lamont. But Lamont was leaving Clonloughlin in a few days and he was never coming back. He was going to America to work for Mrs. Alma Berringer, the young American widow who had recently returned to her horse farm in Virginia after renting Rothermerrion Lodge for the past year. Lamont and Mrs. Berringer had been friendly, but Anthony had not realized just how intimate they had become until Lamont had given his notice a month ago, announcing that he was moving to the States.

Anthony rose, walked over to the huge stone fireplace, picked up the poker, and stirred the logs. His expression was ruminative. He was convinced he was right. Slowly he spun around, stood facing Bridget, studying her with infinite care. Never really pretty, she had, however, been arresting when she was younger, with her blazing red hair and milk white skin and corn-flower blue eyes. Her striking coloring and long legs and lissome figure had always caught men's attention. But sadly she had not aged well. The red hair was a faded salt-and-pepper auburn rapidly turning gray, her figure had lost its willowy appeal. Only those bright blue eyes remained unchanged, vivid, and youthful. And very calculating, he decided. Yes, Bridget O'Donnell was always manipulative and devious even when she was a child. And oh, how she had dominated poor Min. Odd that he had never realized this until now.

"There's an old saying, Bridget," Anthony remarked in an icy, contained voice. "Hell hath no fury like a woman scorned."

"I'm sorry, sir, but I'm not following you."

"You're in love with him. You've always loved him since the first day he came to run the estate for me. That's why you helped him, protected him since my wife's death. And after she was dead, *you* became involved with him. And now, because he's leaving you, going off, chasing after another woman, you want your revenge. You're sticking the knife between Michael Lamont's shoulder blades with a real vengeance, aren't you? That's what all this is about, isn't it?"

She stared him down. "No," she said flatly. "It isn't. I simply wanted to put your mind at rest. I didn't want you to blame yourself for Lady Min's death."

"But I don't," Anthony said coldly, in all truthfulness, "and I haven't for years. You're pointing a finger at Lamont because he's found somebody younger and prettier than you. Let's face it, Bridget, your lover has passed you over."

At these words she flushed deeply, looked down at her hands.

Anthony knew his words had struck home.

After a moment, she asked in a low, subdued voice, "What are you going to do about Michael Lamont? Are you going to have it out with him?"

Anthony looked at her with steadiness for several seconds, then slowly walked across the floor, resumed his position behind his desk. He leaned over it, looked deeply into those blue eyes so warily returning his penetrating gaze.

"Obviously I shall confront Lamont. The facts you have given me cannot be ignored. As you know they cannot. That's why you told me in the first place." There was a small pause before he said, "However, I may also go to the police and open up the investigation into my wife's death again. And I wonder, Bridget, if it's ever occurred to you that you helped to tamper with evidence in a sudden and questionable death. And that you perjured yourself under oath. Also, if my first wife *was* alive when Michael Lamont put her in the lake, then you are also an accessory after the fact. *An accessory to murder.*"

Once Bridget had returned to the kitchen, Anthony made a telephone call to Cork. It lasted for ten minutes and mostly he listened. When he quietly put the receiver back in the cradle, his face was white and his expression was grim.

Glancing at the clock on the mantle, he rose to his feet, left the library, and went down the passageway to the indoor porch. After putting on his Wellingtons and his barbour, he took his tweed cap off the coat stand and went outside.

He looked up. It had stopped raining, but the sky was still overcast and a light mist persisted. Walking at a brisk pace, he took the path which led to Michael Lamont's house. It was just a few yards away from the lake, set back against a copse of trees next to a field. When he reached the front door, he barged inside without knocking, strode through the hall, across the living room, and into the adjoining office.

Lamont, a dark-haired, heavy-set, but good-looking man, was seated behind the desk, entering figures in a large estate ledger. He looked up in surprise as the door was flung open unceremoniously and a gust of air caused the papers on his desk to flutter and lift.

"Good morning, Lord Dunvale," he said pleasantly, his weatherbeaten face breaking into a smile. And then the smile vanished as he became aware of Anthony's dire expression, his angry stance.

"Is something wrong?" Lamont asked, rising.

Anthony did not at first reply. He stepped into the room, closed the heavy oak door behind him firmly, leaned against it. He studied the estate manager through icy eyes. Lamont had worked for him for almost twenty years, and he suddenly wondered what in God's name made him tick. Anthony had always believed he knew Lamont inside out; apparently he had not known him at all. He had considered him to be a trustworthy and devoted employee and a good friend. Now he was filled with loathing for him.

At last Anthony said, "Bridget had rather a strange tale to tell earlier this morning. About the late Lady Dunvale's death."

Taken by surprise and off guard, Lamont gaped at him, opened his mouth to speak, then closed it. He walked away from the desk swiftly, moved to the far end of the room, hovered near the fireplace, wanting to put distance between himself and Anthony. Reaching for a cigarette, he lit it, then pivoted to look at the Earl.

Lamont's expression was one of uncertainty and his dark brown eyes flickered with apprehension. "What exactly are you getting at?" he asked finally.

"Bridget told me everything, confided every little detail about what happened here in this house that tragic evening." Anthony stepped forward, drew closer to the estate manager, let his eyes rest on him for the longest moment.

Lamont flinched under this intense and unwavering scrutiny. Blinking, he eventually glanced away, took a long drag on his cigarette, inhaling deeply.

"How could you be so certain Min was dead after she collapsed?" Anthony demanded in a hard voice. "You're not a doctor, Lamont."

Lamont's face turned brilliant red, and he cried out angrily, "She *was* dead! I'm telling you, she was dead!" Unexpectedly he began to cough, excessively so, and it took him a few minutes to recover. When he finally caught his breath, he added, "I might not be a doctor, but I do know when somebody has stopped breathing." He puffed on the cigarette again and then, with nervous intensity, exclaimed in a shaky voice, "I tried to revive her, to breathe life into her with mouth-to-mouth resuscitation, but she was gone. I loved Min. Which is more than you ever did."

Anthony took another step forward. His hands were clenched tightly at his sides, his knuckles shining white in the pale morning light. He wanted to ram his fist into Lamont's red, boozy face, smash it to a pulp until it was unrecognizable. But he resisted the impulse, hung on to his self-possession with a masterful control.

"You don't know the meaning of the word 'love,' Lamont. You're a philandering, double-dealing bastard and a menace to any decent woman."

"*You* talk to *me* about philandering. What about you!" Lamont snorted. "Certainly you drove Minerva into my arms with your constant womanizing and years of neglect."

Anthony held himself taut. He was once more afraid that he might do Lamont bodily harm. He said slowly, "Why didn't you come for me when my wife collapsed? Or at least call a doctor? Why did you take matters into your own hands? Your behavior was unconscionable and nothing short of reckless."

Michael Lamont was not the most brilliant of men, but he had sufficient native shrewdness to recognize that Bridget O'Donnell had done her work well. He decided there was no point in lying, and so he spoke the absolute truth when he mumbled, "I was afraid. Afraid that once you knew what had been going on between us you'd get rid of me. I couldn't lose my job. It also occurred to me that you might blame me for her death. Circumstantial evidence has condemned more than one innocent man. Don't you see," he finished in a whining tone, "I had no choice, I *had* to cover everything up."

Disgust and revulsion swamped Anthony as he continued to observe the estate manager with a steely gaze. "I wonder how you've been able to look me in the eye all these years, knowing the terrible things you did, knowing how you lied to everyone to protect your own skin. You're despicable, Lamont. Monstrous."

Lamont did not respond. How stupid he had been not to leave Clonloughlin years ago. He had stayed because of Bridget O'Donnell, the terrible hold she had over him. He had never really trusted her. Apparently he had been right not to do so. When their long relationship had ended by mutual consent, he had believed himself to be finally free of her. There had been no rancorous feelings on her part, or so he had thought. He had been wrong. The minute he had taken up with another woman, she had struck out at him like a viper, wanting to destroy him. She had succeeded.

"I ache to give you the biggest thrashing of your life," Anthony was saying. "But I'm not going to lay a finger on you. I shall let the law do my work for me."

Lamont started, drawn out of his thoughts. He peered at Anthony. "*What?* What are you saying?"

"I fully intend to reopen the investigation into my wife's death. I believe you killed Lady Dunvale. And I aim to see that you pay for it," Anthony said with cold deliberation.

"You're mad, stark raving mad!" Lamont shouted, his dark eyes popping out of his face, his expression one of sudden fear. "You don't know what you're talking about, Dunvale. Min poisoned her system with all that muck she was forever swallowing. She died within a few minutes of collapsing."

"That's where you're quite wrong," Anthony said in a voice that was murderously soft. "She was in a deeply unconscious state, which was indeed induced by excessive amounts of alcohol and barbiturates. But when you placed her in the lake, she was very much alive, and—"

"I don't believe you! You're lying! Inventing all this!"

"*I am not!*" Anthony shot back with ferocity.

508

"When Bridget confided in me this morning, I was not absolutely sure about certain medical facts! So I telephoned Forensic at the hospital in Cork, where I located Doctor Stephen Kenmarr. The pathologist who did the autopsy on Min's body, who discovered her lungs were full of water and testified at the inquest that she had died of drowning."

Anthony paused, finished emphatically and very slowly, as if to give added weight to his words, "Doctor Kenmarr confirmed to me what I already suspected . . . *that water cannot be inhaled by a person who is dead.* Therefore, Min was alive when you placed her in the lake. You drowned her."

Michael Lamont felt his hackles rising, and he was so shocked, so stunned by Anthony's dreadful accusation he could barely stand. He swayed slightly on his feet, reached out, supported himself against the mantelpiece. The idea that he might have actually caused Min's death struck horror in him, and he was reeling. Over the years he had suffered greatly, had been haunted by his deceit, the lies he had told, the cover-up he had wrought, and he had never stopped wrestling with his guilt and his conscience.

Now he cried out in protest, "No, Dunvale, no! She had no pulse, no heartbeat!" He choked on his words and tears came into his eyes and he broke down completely. "I could not have done anything to hurt her," he sobbed. "I loved her. Talk to Bridget again. *Please. Please.* She'll verify that I'm telling the truth. Min was dead . . . and Bridget O'Donnell knows that she was."

"She was alive, Lamont!"

"No! No!" Demented, Lamont rushed at Anthony, his arms flailing in the air, his face apoplectic. He felt a sudden and excruciating pain shoot across his temple and along the side of his face, but he did not let it slow him down. He lunged at Anthony. As he did, another searing pain blinded him. The blood rushed to his head and everything went black. He fell sprawling to the floor and then was still.

Startled, Anthony stood looking down at him, momentarily rooted to the spot, unable to move. He had noticed the sudden and dreadful change when Lamont had rushed toward him, had instantly realized that the other man was having some sort of seizure.

Pulling himself together, Anthony bent down, felt Lamont's pulse. It was erratic, faint, but it *was* there.

Hurrying to the telephone, Anthony dialed the cottage hospital in the village of Clonloughlin.

"Dunvale here," he said to the duty nurse when she answered. "Could you please send an ambulance immediately. To the estate manager's house. Michael Lamont has just had a stroke, I think. But he's still alive. If you hurry, we can probably save him."

To see justice done, Anthony thought as he hung up.

30

"I've really got to take it over!" Paula exclaimed, tightening her grip on Michael Kallinski's arm. "It would be nothing short of criminal if I let it slip through my fingers."

"Yes, I know it would." Michael looked at her through the corner of his eye. "Six hundred and fifty million dollars is a hell of a lot of money, though."

"That's true, it is. On the other hand, it isn't *really,* not if you consider what I'm actually buying. A chain of department stores that has a fine reputation, great prestige, with invaluable real estate assets and a balance sheet that's in the black. And it's a perfect chain for me, Michael. Thanks so much for bringing it to my attention." She leaned closer, added in an emphatic tone tinged with excitement, "Larson's locations couldn't be better for me if I'd hand-picked them myself. Westchester, Philadelphia, and Boston cover the Eastern Seaboard. Chicago and Detroit the Midwest. Los Angeles and San Francisco the West Coast. It's a deal made in heaven, as far as I'm concerned."

"If you make a deal."

Paula gave him a hard stare. "Is there a chance I might not?" she asked, her voice instantly changing, rising slightly in sudden concern.

"I suppose there's always that chance, Paula.

"But I don't think you have too much to worry about in this particular situation. As far as I know, there's no one else after the company, and I understand from Harvey in New York that the chairman of the board is willing to start talking, to open negotiations whenever you're ready. And what Millard Larson says goes, since he's the majority stockholder as well as C.E.O. If I were you, I'd make plans to fly to New York as soon as possible."

"I agree with you, and I want to go. But I can't . . . at least not for two weeks. Lorne and Tessa are both coming home from their schools tomorrow. It's the Easter break. I just can't be away right now."

"Oh God, I had forgotten about Easter! I have the same problem as you, I'm afraid, so I'll have to stay put, too."

"Oh." Puzzled, she frowned, asked, "Are you planning a trip to the States, Michael?"

"I thought I should be there in case you need me," he explained, his voice vibrant with enthusiasm, his face lighting up. "After all, I'm the one who introduced you to Harvey Rawson, found the Larson chain for you, set everything in motion." He gave her a small, confiding smile. "Besides, I have to be in New York on business sometime this month, and if I go when you're going I can kill two birds with one stone, so to speak." When she did not initially respond, he asked, "What do you think?"

"Well . . . yes . . . I suppose so." She realized how hesitant she sounded and rapidly nodded her head. "Yes, yes, why not," she added in a more positive tone.

"Good, it's settled then," he exclaimed, looking delighted, congratulating himself on his adroit little maneuver. The thought of being alone with her in New York excited him. But he said in the most neutral voice, "Now we'd better concentrate on Dad's exhibition. He's been giving us peculiar looks for the last ten minutes. I have a feeling he's a bit miffed."

Paula laughed. "I'm sure he is. We have been rather rude, standing here in the middle of the floor deep in conversation. Not only ignoring him and everyone else, but all these priceless art treasures as well. Come on, we must go and join him at once. He wants to show me around the exhibition himself, tell me about each piece of Fabergé he owns. And I must admit, I am rather staggered by all this. His collection is much larger than I ever imagined it to be."

"Not every piece on display belongs to him," Michael was quick to point out. "The Queen and the Queen Mum have loaned some of their Fabergé objects, as have Kenneth Snowman, the great British expert on Peter Carl Fabergé, and Malcolm Forbes, who's another avid collector like Dad."

"I know. Your father explained. Still, he does have a superb collection."

"I'll say. And it's given him a truly consuming interest other than business these last few years."

They moved together down the long salon, one of two in the Royal Academy of Art at Burlington House where the reception for the opening of the Fabergé exhibition was in full swing on this April evening. The event had been organized by Sir Ronald Kallinski to benefit one of his favorite charities, and the gallery was packed.

A waiter drew to a standstill in front of them.

Michael took two glasses of champagne from the silver tray being proffered, murmured his thanks, and handed a flute of Dom Pérignon to Paula.

When Sir Ronald spotted them coming toward him, he extracted himself from a small group of people and hurried to meet them.

"I know you two are committed to business and rarely think of anything else, but do you really have to have a confab during my reception?" he asked, obviously quite put out. But then his eyes became warm with affection and twinkled brightly as he took Paula's arm and led her along the gallery, his irritation instantly forgotten.

"Now, my dear," he said, "let me take you around. I have many new acquisitions, none of which you have seen. Neither have you, Michael," he added, glancing over his shoulder at his son.

"I've been looking forward to this for weeks," Michael replied in all sincerity. "And I'm sorry we got caught up with our business discussion the way we did. My apologies, Dad."

"Accepted, accepted, my boy," Sir Ronald

answered briskly, striding down the salon with Paula, Michael dutifully in tow. Suddenly he came to a stop in front of a display case.

Turning to Paula, he said, "This is not one of my pieces. Sadly, I might add. It was graciously lent for the exhibition by Her Majesty the Queen. And it happens to be a particular favorite of mine. It's called the Mosaic Egg, and I think it's perhaps the most poignant of all the Imperial Easter Eggs. It was presented to Czarina Alexandra Feodorovna by Nicholas II on Easter morning of 1914. As you can see, it's a gossamer platinum shell which has been 'embroidered' with flowers made of precious stones . . . rubies, sapphires, diamonds, and emeralds, the whole encircled with bands of pearls. And look, there on the little gold stand are the miniature sepia profiles of the Imperial children."

"It's exquisite," Paula said admiringly, leaning forward, peering at the egg. "And the stand is concealed inside the egg, isn't it, when not on display?"

"Correct." Sir Ronald took her arm, and the three of them progressed down the gallery slowly, pausing to admire other treasures in the show. "That's the beauty and genius of the Fabergé objects of art," he went on, "those extraordinary and very often magical surprises contained within the egg itself. Like that dazzling little golden chanticleer which emerges from the translucent blue-enameled Imperial Easter Egg your grandmother once owned," Sir Ronald reminded her, smiling.

Paula smiled back at him. "Oh yes, that egg is the most beautiful—at least that's what I think, Uncle Ronnie. And I'm glad it's in your collection, that you won it at the auction. At least it's still in the clans."

He chuckled. "I don't think I'll ever forget that day at Sotheby's. There was such competitive bidding for the egg. But it was exciting. And gratifying when I suddenly realized *I* owned it. Naturally it's on display tonight. Let's go and have a look at it, and then we can go through into the other salon. There are more breathtaking examples of Fabergé masterpieces, which were made for the Imperial family before the Romanov dynasty came to its tragic end."

"I didn't know Amanda was coming to the exhibition!" Michael exclaimed in surprise a short while later, when he spotted her standing in the doorway, glancing around, obviously looking for them.

"Oh, I forgot to tell you," Paula murmured. "I sent her a ticket and she said she would do her best to make it."

"I'll go and get her, bring her over to join us," Michael said, hurrying across the room.

Paula's eyes followed him and she smiled to herself, then looked at his father and winked.

Sir Ronald regarded her closely for a moment, then said slowly, "I'm not wrong in thinking you're playing *shadchan,* am I, Paula? *Matchmaking?*"

"And why not?" she answered, laughing. "Anyway, she has such a crush on him . . . wouldn't it be lovely if Michael reciprocated her feelings, Uncle Ronnie?"

Sir Ronald seemed initially startled, then suddenly pleased, and he nodded. "It would indeed. Amanda's a lovely young woman. Clever, too. Emily and Alexander have trained her well. She's certainly made our takeover of Lady Hamilton Clothes very smooth. But of course you know that, my dear. As I was telling Emily the other day, my people are terribly impressed with her. We're all sorry she won't be staying on to run the company for us. Emily explained she's needed at Harte Enterprises and I do understand that. Still—" He cut himself short, and a look of infinite sadness crossed his face fleetingly.

Paula was aware that he was thinking of Alexander, who had taken Uncle Ronnie into his confidence. She experienced a rush of sadness

519

herself. Sandy had retired at the beginning of March, and now Emily was chairman of the board and chief executive officer. Amanda had moved over to become head of Genret, whilst Winston continued to run his own division, the Yorkshire Consolidated Newspaper Company and its subsidiaries, of which he was a part owner. They had become a close-knit triumvirate, and Harte Enterprises was running as efficiently as it always had, but Paula knew that they missed Alexander terribly. She missed him herself now that he was living quietly at Nutton Priory, although they did speak quite a lot on the telephone.

"Hello, darling," Paula said, greeting Amanda warmly as she and Michael joined them. "You look stunning."

"Thank you, Paula," Amanda said, smiling at her cousin, pecking her on the cheek. "Hello, Uncle Ronnie. Sorry I'm late, but the traffic was ghastly tonight."

"That's all right, my dear," Sir Ronald said, taking her hand in his, giving her a quick kiss. "Now, Michael, do the honors, my boy, and get a glass of champagne for Amanda, would you please?"

"I certainly will. Be back in a jiffy."

Amanda turned to Paula, and it gave Sir Ronald a chance to study her surreptitiously, appraisingly, for a brief moment. Tall, slender, and blond, Amanda was a lovely looking young woman who bore a strong resemblance to her half-sister, Emily. Tonight she was wearing a smartly tailored red silk suit with a diamond Victorian bow broach pinned onto one lapel and antique diamond earrings. Chic but discreet, Sir Ronald thought, and very well bred. Suddenly he saw her through new eyes. As a potential daughter-in-law. The idea strongly appealed to him. Amanda was ideal for Michael, an intelligent, charming, and outgoing girl with perfect manners, like all of Emma's granddaughters. Just the sort of wife his son needed. The possibility that the Kallinski and Harte clans might finally be united in marriage thrilled him. He would encourage this friendship, as apparently Paula was intending to do. Yes, Amanda and Michael must become husband and wife. He would have a long chat with Paula later; together they would map out a plan of action. Michael needed to be gently guided into this relationship. His son tended to vacillate when it came to women. And he had been single far too long since his divorce.

31

The garden was still her most magical place.

Ever since childhood Paula had found satisfaction and reward in planting and weeding, pruning and hoeing. Working outdoors was soothing to her—it never failed to put her in the best of moods.

Also, she had discovered long ago that she often did her best thinking in her gardens at Pennistone Royal, and today was no exception. It was a bright April afternoon, just after Easter, sunny and brisk with a light breeze and a powder-blue sky that was cool and cloudless.

As she worked on the new rockery she was creating, she focused her thoughts on business, in particular the Larson chain in the United States. The deal was already in the first stage of negotiation, and Millard Larson was expecting her in New York next week, when they would sit down at the conference table and hammer out the terms and conditions of the sale.

When she had first had the idea of expanding her operations in the States, long before the possibility of Larson's had come up, she had made the decision to purchase any new retailing company that caught her eye with her own money.

Six hundred and fifty million dollars, she thought now, mulling the figure over in her mind whilst concentrating on the alpine plants she was sorting through. It *was* a lot of money, no doubt about that, and she had been wondering for several days which financial combination would work best for her.

Paula sighed under her breath. If her mother had agreed to sell the Sitex stock last year, her problem would have been solved. Under the terms and conditions of her grandfather's will, she and her brother Philip would automatically have received one third of the proceeds of that sale—hundreds of millions of dollars each. But her mother had refused to sell the oil stock and continued to be adamant about not doing so. Paula had acknowledged months ago that she would have to raise the necessary cash another way, once she found the right department store chain to buy.

She ran several possibilities through her mind, then dismissed each one as convoluted and complex, went back to her original idea. To her way of thinking, the best solution was to sell ten percent of her Harte shares which Emma had left her. They would realize between two hundred and three hundred million dollars on the market, but without making much of a dent in her holdings. She would still be the majority stockholder with forty-one percent, as well as chairman and chief executive officer of the Harte chain. The remainder of the money she could easily raise from the banks, by borrowing against the retail chain she was acquiring, pledging its assets, in particular its real estate holdings which were valuable.

Suddenly, after days of indecision, she made up her mind. She *would* do that. And she would put everything in motion at once. First thing on Monday morning when she got to her office in the Leeds store, she would speak to her stockbroker.

A bright smile broke through, expunging the worried and preoccupied expression she had worn all day, and she continued to smile to herself as she finished planting the small alpine species in the narrow crevices of the rocks.

"Mummy! Mummy!"

Paula lifted her head alertly at the sound of Patrick's voice. He and his sister, Linnet, were running as fast as their legs would carry them along the gravel path that sloped down from the long terrace at the back of Pennistone Royal.

They both wore sweaters and jeans under their duffel coats and mufflers, and she could not help thinking how healthy and fit they both looked today. Especially Patrick. That vacant expression which so often dulled his eyes was absent, as it had been for some weeks. This pleased her, raised her hopes that he was improving mentally, if only ever so slightly. She loved her sensitive, damaged, and beautiful child so very much.

"Patrick! Do be careful! You're going to fall!" she called out. "And you too, Linnet! Do slow down, both of you! I'm not going anywhere, you know." She rose as she spoke, picked up the basket full of her gardening tools, and carefully climbed down from the top of the clustered rocks.

Patrick hurled himself against her body, clinging to her, panting hard and trying to catch his breath.

She pushed his dark hair away from his temple and clucked quietly. "Dear, dear, you are a one, aren't you? Running so hard, I—"

"Puffed, Mummy," he interrupted her, raising his solemn little face to hers. "Linnet puffed too."

"I'm *not!*" Linnet protested fiercely, glaring.

Ignoring her, Patrick went on, "Horsey, Mummy. Patrick wants horsey."

Puzzled, Paula swung her eyes to her six-year-old daughter, as she so often did when Patrick spoke in riddles and she wanted edification. She gave Linnet a questioning stare.

Linnet explained, "The horse in the attic, Mummy. That's what Patrick wants. I said he couldn't take it, not without asking Daddy. And Daddy said to ask you."

"Horse in the attic. What on earth are you talking about, darling?"

"The cresel horse . . . the one that goes round and round and around and round. To the music, Mummy."

"The carousel, the horse on the carousel. Now I understand." Paula smiled at them both. "But I don't remember there being a carousel in the attic. I suppose it must be, since you've apparently seen it."

"It's in a trunk," Linnet rushed on excitedly. "We saw it just now. Daddy let us play in the attic after our walk this afternoon."

"Did he now." Paula pulled off her gardening gloves, threw them on top of the basket, and, taking a small hand in each of hers, she led her children back to the house.

A short while later the three of them were rummaging in the old trunks which had been stored in the attics of Pennistone Royal for many years. Patrick had already taken possession of the carousel, which Paula had immediately given to him, and he was turning the small key, making it work in the way she had shown him.

The horses on the merry-go-round were moving up and down to the strains of the "Carousel Waltz," and the little boy was fascinated, his happy, eager face a pleasure for Paula to witness.

Linnet and Paula left him to play with the carousel on his own, and they soon had their heads and their hands in another trunk which Paula had pulled out and opened.

Busily they sorted through the toys that brimmed to the top, taking out a large, painted wooden soldier, a box of bricks, a scruffy teddy bear with one arm and no eyes, several stuffed animals, various jigsaw puzzles, a box of tin soldiers, and various rag toys.

Paula's hands finally came to rest on a beautiful china baby doll at the bottom of the trunk, and lifting it out she caught her breath in surprise and pleasure. She remembered it very well.

Her grandmother had given it to her, and she had taken great care of it, had loved this doll more than any of her other possessions. Years ago she had packed it carefully away when she had moved from Long Meadow to Pennistone Royal after Jim's death. She had meant to give the doll to Tessa but had somehow forgotten all about it during the troubled year after the avalanche.

Sitting back on her haunches, she held the doll up, smoothed its golden curls, straightened its dainty ecru-colored lace dress. She was amazed that the doll was in such good condition and looked almost new.

Linnet was watching her closely, her eyes lingering with longing on the doll. "Was it yours, Mummy?" she asked at last.

"Yes, darling, it was. My grandmother gave it to me when I was your age."

"You mean Grandy Emma?"

Paula nodded.

"So you wouldn't want to give that doll to anybody then, would you? Not if *Grandy Emma* gave it to you," Linnet said gravely, her eyes still fastened on the doll.

Paula laughed. "Well, perhaps I would give it to a girl whom I knew would look after it, would take good care of it as I did."

"Tessa," Linnet said a trifle sadly in a small and quiet voice.

"No. I think her name's Linnet."

"Oh, Mummy! Mummy!"

"Here you are, my darling, it's for you." Paula held out the doll. "I used to call her Florabelle."

"Then I shall, too." Linnet struggled to her feet, took the doll, her eyes shining, her smile brilliant.

"Thank you, Mummy, oh thank you." Hugging the doll tightly in her arms, she leaned into Paula, nuzzled her nose against her cheek. "I love you, Mummy," she whispered. "Oh you do smell nice. Like a bunch of flowers." Linnet put her head on one side and observed Paula thoughtfully. Then she reached out, touched Paula's cheek gently with her small hand. "You won't get lost, will you, Mummy?" she asked, her voice unexpectedly wistful, almost fretful.

Paula's brows puckered together into a jagged line. "What do you mean, lovey?"

"Sometimes when we're waiting for you to come home, Daddy says, 'I think your mother must have got lost. I don't know *where* she can be.' And then he goes to the window and looks out. And I worry till you get home and so does Patrick. Well, I think he does."

"Oh darling, it's merely a *saying*. It doesn't

mean that I'm really lost," Paula said and smiled at her daughter reassuringly.

"Are you sure, Mummy?"

"Of course I am."

"Oh. That's all right then."

Paula smoothed a hand over her daughter's red-gold hair and sat back on the floor, watching her as she played with the doll. How easy it is to please children, she thought at one moment. As long as they receive love and care and kindness and discipline, that's all that really counts. Their needs are really very simple. If only adults could be the same . . .

"So this is where you're all hiding!" Shane exclaimed from the doorway, making the three of them start in surprise.

Paula pushed herself to her feet. "We've been finding all sorts of lovely treasures in the trunks," she explained, hurrying over to him. "A carousel for Patrick, and my old doll Florabelle for Linnet."

Shane nodded, put his arm around his wife. "But now I think you have to come downstairs . . . Nanny has tea waiting in the nursery . . . for all of us."

"That was such fun, and the kids enjoyed it too," Shane said to Paula that evening as they were dressing for dinner. "It's ages since we've had a nursery tea with them. We must do it more often."

"You're absolutely right, darling," Paula agreed, leaning forward, looking into the mirror of her dressing table, smoothing the silver brush over her sleek black hair. Putting the brush down, she outlined her mouth with bright red lipstick, then sprayed on Christina Crowther's *Blue Gardenia* perfume, one of her favorites. "And I'm really thrilled with Patrick, the progress he's making, aren't you?" She half-turned to look at Shane.

"I am indeed. He's so much better in every way, and there's been a vast improvement in his understanding of things. It's the new tutor. Mark is doing wonders for the boy."

"Yes, he is," Paula said.

Shane slipped into a dark blue blazer, adjusted his tie, walked across the floor. He stood behind Paula with his hands resting lightly on her shoulders, smiling at her in the mirror.

"You look beautiful, Beanstalk," he said, his lopsided grin surfacing briefly. "So stop titivating yourself. Come on, let's go into the upstairs parlor. I put a couple of bottles of champagne on ice earlier, and we can have a quiet drink together before Emily and Winston arrive for dinner."

"That's a lovely idea," Paula exclaimed,

pushing back the dressing table stool, rising to her feet, reaching up, kissing him on the cheek. "But then *you* usually *do* have the best ideas."

She tucked her arm through his, and together they walked across the floor into the adjoining room.

The upstairs parlor at Pennistone Royal had been Emma Harte's favorite room in the great old house in Yorkshire, and Paula loved it as much as her grandmother had. Its impressive architectural details and splendid furnishings belied the name 'parlor,' but for some reason it had never been called anything else. The soaring dimensions gave it a singular grandeur, and its high ceiling was Jacobean in style, decorated with elaborate plasterwork. Tall, leaded windows flanked an unusual oriel window, and there was a carved fireplace of bleached oak and the floor was of parquet. Emma had years ago balanced its imposing detail and size with a mellow charm, intimacy, and comfort, as well as her own brand of understated elegance.

Paula had never felt the need to change the room, even though it would be sacrilege to do so, and the decor was the same as it had been for nigh on fifty years. Since the day Emma had bought it in the 1930s, in fact. The primrose colored walls were repainted every year to the same shade, and new slipcovers and draperies were made when they were required; otherwise it was exactly the way it had been throughout Emma's lifetime.

The priceless Turner landscape filled with misty blues and greens hung above the mantelpiece, and the only other paintings in the parlor were excellent portraits of a young nobleman and his wife by Sir Joshua Reynolds. The three oils were in perfect harmony with the Georgian antiques, the Savonnerie carpet, and the rare Rose Medallion china in the Chippendale cabinet. Brightly patterned yellow chintz fabric covered the two huge sofas in the center of the room, which faced each other across a mahogany butler's tray table, and the antique porcelain lamps were shaded in cream silk, and everywhere there was the gleam of silver and crystal.

The lamps had been turned on and a huge fire blazed in the hearth. The warmth had opened up the narcissi, daffodils, and hyacinths planted in bowls, and the air was fragrant with their mingled scents.

As she moved toward one of the sofas and sat down, Paula thought the parlor had never looked more beautiful than it did this evening. It was dusk and the light was changing. Outside the great soaring windows, the sky was turning to navy blue tinged with lilac bleeding into amethyst and deeper purple. A strong wind had blown up, was rustling the trees, and distant thunder heralded a storm.

But here in the gracious room there was a sense of peacefulness and tranquility. To Paula, the parlor had a timeless quality, never changing. It was full of her past, her entire life really, and so many cherished memories . . . memories of her childhood, her youth, the days of her growing into womanhood. And there were memories of the most special people in her life . . . those dead and living . . . her father and Grandy . . . her mother . . . Philip . . . the special friends of her youth . . . and her cousins Emily, Winston, and Alexander. And Shane, too, was caught up in the memories which were held captive in this room. *Home,* she thought. The parlor represents home to me, and my roots, just as it did to my grandmother. And that's why I could never be happy living anywhere else . . .

"Penny for your thoughts," Shane said, looming over her, making her jump. He handed her the crystal glass brimming with icy, sparkling champagne.

"Oh darling, thank you," she said, taking the glass from him. "I was just thinking how lovely this room is, and it's truly filled with the past, isn't it?"

"All the days of our lives actually," he said,

touching his champagne flute to hers. "Since we were very little."

They smiled into each other's eyes, loving each other, and then Shane moved across to the other sofa, where he sat down, settled into the plump chintz cushions, relaxing.

Paula leaned forward, focused her violet eyes on him. "Talking of the past—I've been thinking of the *future* in the last few days, Shane, and I'm definitely going to go ahead and buy the Larson chain in the States."

Shane looked at her sharply. The expression in his black Irish eyes changed slightly, became anxious, but he said in the same even, well-controlled voice, "If that's what you want, then I'm glad you've made the decision to go ahead, darling." Privately he believed she might well be taking on too much responsibility, but he never interfered in her business, remained neutral and uninvolved. It was one of the reasons their marriage was so solid.

She said slowly, "Six hundred and fifty million dollars is a fair price for the chain, I think." She raised a shapely brow. "No?"

He nodded. "Yes, I agree with you. It is."

"Well, anyway . . . I've decided to buy it myself, with my own money," she added, giving him a direct look.

For the fraction of a second he was quite

floored and gaped at her in astonishment, but once again his tone was even, steady, as he said, "Have you now. And what are you going to sell to raise the necessary cash to pay for it?"

"I'll borrow from the banks, take out a mortgage on the Larson real estate, pledge some of the chain's other assets. I'll probably be able to borrow about three hundred million dollars or so. And to raise the other half of the money I need, I intend to sell ten percent of my Harte shares."

"Paula!" he cried, askance. "Do you really think you should?" Holding her with his eyes, he asked swiftly, "Isn't that rather *risky?* Far be it from me to interfere in your business, darling, but those Harte shares are a great weapon—and your security—in as much as they give you absolute power in the company. If you sell ten percent of your fifty-one percent, you're reducing your holdings in the company. You're leaving yourself wide open to challenge."

"Gosh, don't be silly, Shane. Whoever's going to challenge me!" she laughed. "I have the full support of my board and my shareholders. They're behind me. Good Lord, the store is *mine.* Nobody would ever dream of going against me, neither the board members nor stockholders. I *am* Harte's, just as Emma was."

"Well . . . I don't know . . ." Shane began

and stopped. He had finally broken the rule he had made the day he had married her. He had promised himself he would never give her any business advice, and he never had. She was far too much like Emma Harte to take it anyway. Paula was stubborn and independent. And usually infallible in her judgments, as her grandmother had been before her. He took a deep breath, resisted arguing against this planned move on her part.

"I can see from your face that you've made up your mind to do things your way," he said carefully. "You're confident, determined, and your attitude is admirable, the only one you *should* have when you embark on a venture like this." Shane smiled at her, and he meant every word when he added, "I'm behind you all the way, Paula."

"Oh Shane, darling, thank you . . . thank you for believing in me. That means such a lot. I was only saying so to Michael the other day."

"Were you?"

She nodded. "I told him I hoped you'd approve of what I'm doing. By the way, he'll be in New York next week when I'm there."

"That's a coincidence . . . or is it?" He gazed at her intently, his dark eyes narrowing.

"No, darling, it's not. Michael does have to be in New York some time this month, but he has made his plans to dovetail with mine. He thinks he should be there to give me any help I might need with the Larson takeover."

Stiffening, Shane held himself rigid on the sofa, and for a moment he did not respond. Then he cleared his throat. "You've never needed help with deals in the past. Not from anyone. Why *now* all of a sudden?"

She shrugged, laughed. "I don't need any help, but Michael introduced me to Harvey Rawson, found me the Larson chain, as you know. *He* thinks he ought to be there, and I don't want to hurt his feelings by telling him not to come over specially for me."

"I see."

Shane sprang to his feet, strode over to the console, not wanting her to see his sudden anger. He poured himself another glass of Dom Pérignon, pushed back the jealousy he was feeling, endeavored to arrange a suitably unconcerned expression on his face. Michael was irritating him of late. He had an instinctive, gut feeling that the other man was interested in his wife in a more personal way than she realized. He trusted Paula implicitly, knew that she loved him with all her heart. But he was no longer certain that he trusted Michael Kallinski. Certainly he did not want Paula to be placed in an awkward or embarrassing situation when she was in New York, and that might possibly happen. Or was he being unfair to Michael? After all, his old friend was a gentleman, wasn't he?

Shane made a snap decision and pivoted to face his wife, flashed her a brilliant smile. "I was keeping this as a little surprise, but I might as well tell you: I'm going to be in New York too next week, Paula darling," he improvised. "Miranda needs me to go over there. I know we try not to be away at the same time, for the sake of the children, but this trip is unavoidable. I do have some pressing problems to deal with."

"But how marvelous!" Paula cried, her face filling with happiness. "And Patrick and Linnet will be perfectly all right with Nanny and Mark . . ." Paula stopped, chuckled quietly. "It just so happens that Amanda is going to be in the States as well, on a buying trip for Genret. I plan to give a few dinner parties for her . . . and Michael. You see, Shane, Amanda's quite potty about him, and Uncle Ronnie and I think they would make a perfect couple."

"I'm not so sure that Michael is interested in matrimony at the moment," Shane remarked as he strolled back to the sofa and sat down. "Not after that debacle with Valentine. Still, I'm rather inclined to agree with you and Uncle Ronnie about Amanda being ideal for him." Shane leaned back on the sofa, feeling a curious sense of relief. He added, as an afterthought, "I think we'd better fly separately though, as we usually do."

"Yes, of course, that is wisest. Anyway, Shane —" Paula stopped midsentence as the door opened and her daughter, Tessa, came into the room.

"Goodnight, Mummy, Daddy." She hovered in the doorway, blew them kisses. "I'm off to Melanie's party now. Her brother's just arrived to drive me over there."

"You're not going looking like that!" Paula exclaimed and stood up.

Tessa frowned. "What do you mean, Mummy?"

"You know very well what I mean." Paula beckoned with one finger. "Come over here, Tessa, I want to look at you."

"It's only a bit of blush-on," Tessa muttered, throwing her mother a hostile look, not budging from the door. "Everybody wears it these days."

"I'd hardly say that. Please come over to the fire, Tessa."

Reluctantly the girl did as her mother asked. Paula took hold of her shoulders and gently turned her into the light emanating from the lamps on the tables on either side of the fireplace. She shook her head, grimaced. "Just a little blush-on, you said. But you're wearing mascara and lipstick as well."

"It's a very *pale* pink lipstick," Tessa protested.

"You're only *thirteen!*" Paula shook her head in dismay. "I can't allow you to wear cosmetics. Now run up to your room and wash your face, please."

"No! I won't! I'm not going to take it off! You're just old-fashioned! That's what's wrong with you!" Tessa cried angrily, and she glared at Paula, then tossed her head.

"Steady on, Tessa!" Shane warned, sitting up straighter on the sofa, throwing the girl a cautionary glance. "Don't speak to your mother in that way. You're being extremely rude. I will not have it."

"She *is* old-fashioned, Daddy. Out of date. All the girls in my class wear makeup after school."

"I sincerely doubt that." Paula took a step backward, regarded her daughter through freshly objective eyes. My God, she thought, Tessa could easily pass for seventeen. She's grown up all of a sudden. Whatever's happened to the years? It seems like only yesterday that she was a baby in her pram.

Adopting a conciliatory manner, softening her voice, Paula now murmured, "Please do as I say, darling."

Tessa compressed her lips in a stubborn line and her silver-gray eyes became defiant. "I won't go to the party if you make me take my makeup off. I'll look childish, ridiculous. The other girls will be made up, and they'll laugh at me."

Mother and daughter stared at each other.

Paula shook her head slowly. "No, they won't."

"Mother, please . . . you're being stupid!" Tessa wailed.

"No, I'm not. And as long as you live in this house and are supported by us, you will live by our rules," Paula said quietly, but with great firmness.

Tessa looked down at her feet, thinking hard. She admitted to herself that her mother had the upper hand; nevertheless, she was quite determined to get her own way. She took another approach when she said, "I'll make a deal with you. I'll—"

"No negotiating," Paula shot back.

"But the ability to negotiate is often the secret of business success," Tessa pointed out, quoting Paula to Paula.

Her mother swallowed a smile and glanced away to hide the merriment unexpectedly brimming in her eyes. Shane was less successful at concealing his amusement, and he burst out laughing.

Paula looked over at him and shook her head; then she turned to Tessa. "All right, you can wear the blush-on. But that's all. And for this concession on my part you must promise to spend an extra hour practicing the piano. You've been neglecting it lately."

"Okay, I promise. But please let me keep the mascara on. My eyelashes are so pale. I look awful. Bleached out. I'll double my piano practice, and . . . and . . . I'll take Linnet off your hands on Nanny's day off."

"That's tomorrow, you know," Paula pointed out, and relenting, she added, "All right, it's a deal. But no lipstick. *Understood?*"

"Yes. Thanks, Mums." Laughter touched Tessa's face and she danced lightly across the room, pirouetting until she reached the door.

"And don't be late," Paula instructed.

"I won't. Bye."

The door slammed behind her with such a crash that Paula grimaced, then winced as the Rose Medallion china trembled in the Chippendale cabinet. She murmured, "Tess looks older than thirteen, doesn't she, Shane?"

"Yes, she's suddenly becoming quite the young lady, and she's growing up a little too fast for my liking. I think it's time we considered taking her out of Harrogate College, Paula, sending her to Heathfield, as we've always intended."

"I'll get in touch with the headmistress next week. I agree that the sooner Tess goes there the better."

"I told you years ago that she was a maverick, Paula. She and Lorne are very different, even though they're twins. She's going to need a strong hand in the next few years."

Paula nodded, recognizing the truth in everything Shane said. She fell into her thoughts. Her daughter was headstrong, willful, reckless, and even defiant at times. She was a loving girl, warm, outgoing, and she was clever at school. And yet she could be temperamental, and to Paula this was a negative. Her daughter was very much a Fairley, had inherited many of their characteristics, not the least of which were the personal vanity, preoccupation with self that had always been Fairley flaws. There's not a great deal of Harte in her, Paula thought with a little stab of dismay. She even looks like her great-great-grandmother Adele Fairley, with her pale blond hair and those silvery, enigmatic eyes. Paula shivered unexpectedly and gazed into the fire.

"You've got the oddest look on your face,

Paula," Shane said. "Is something wrong, darling?"

"No, no, of course not," she exclaimed, rousing herself from her ruminations. "Can I have another glass of champagne, please?"

"I *was* right, wasn't I?" Emily said, glancing from Paula to Winston. "Now come on, the two of you, have the good grace to admit it."

"You were right about *everything,*" Paula acknowledged. "And I'm sorry I pooh-poohed your theories all those years ago." She lifted her wine glass, took a swallow of the claret. "Is that good enough for you, Dumpling?"

Emily grinned.

Winston said, "I apologize for ever thinking you were slightly bonkers when you kept on insisting that Min had not committed suicide."

"Apologies accepted." Emily smiled at her husband and then at her cousin, picked up her knife and fork, cut into the slice of spring lamb on her dinner plate, and ate a mouthful.

Shane, sipping his wine thoughtfully, said, "You always suspected it was murder, didn't you, Emily?"

"Yes."

"Why?" Shane probed curiously.

"It was the missing five hours that troubled me, Shane." Emily put down her cutlery, sat back in the chair. "I simply couldn't understand where Min had been from about six o'clock, when Anthony first saw her at the lake, until the time she died around eleven. Her car had remained at the lake, so I was sure she had been visiting someone . . . either in the village of Clonloughlin or on the estate. I even thought of a lover . . . but I was unable to figure it all out . . . it was a great mystery to me."

"One that has been solved at long last," Winston added. "And my sister, for one, is vastly relieved. For years poor Sally has believed that she and Anthony somehow drove Min to her death. Thank God that's finally been cleared up. A cloud has been lifted from the Dunvale family."

"Did Anthony explain why Michael Lamont suddenly confessed to accidentally killing Min?" Shane asked, leveling his eyes at Winston.

"Anthony told us that Lamont couldn't go on, that his conscience was troubling him so much it was making him ill," Winston said. "Apparently he went to Anthony, told him the truth about that night. When Anthony pointed out that a dead person couldn't take water into the lungs, and therefore Min had to have been alive when he put her in the lake, Lamont went berserk, was so shocked, so devastated, he had the stroke."

"At least Lamont's subsequent death enabled Anthony to bury the whole matter with him," Paula murmured. "It would have been ghastly for the family if Anthony had been obliged to reopen the case. Not to mention for Lamont, who would have been standing trial for murder, I've no doubt."

"I always felt that Bridget O'Donnell knew more than she was admitting," Emily remarked. "But when Anthony was here last week, I asked him about her, and he looked at me in the most peculiar way. He told me Bridget had known nothing about Min's death, that she had been suffering from a migraine in her room that night, just as she had said at the inquest, when she also gave Anthony his alibi. Still—"

"Excuse me, Mrs. O'Neill," the housekeeper said, coming into the dining room, "I'm sorry to interrupt you during dinner, but there's an important telephone call for you."

"Thank you, Mary," Paula said, pushing back her chair, rising. "Excuse me, chaps, I won't be a moment."

Paula hurried out to the Stone Hall and the nearest telephone, wondering who could be calling her at this hour on a Saturday night. Lifting the receiver, she said, "Hello?"

"Mrs. O'Neill, it's Ursula Hood here."

Paula tightened her grip on the receiver at the

sound of Mrs. Hood's voice. She was Alexander's housekeeper at Nutton Priory, and all of Paula's senses were instantly alerted to trouble. Her throat was slightly dry when she said, "Good evening, Mrs. Hood. How can I help you?"

"Mrs. O'Neill . . . I'm calling because . . . well, something dreadful has happened." The woman's voice cracked. She was unable to go on, and there was a small silence before she continued quietly, "Mr. Barkstone went out hunting in the woods early this evening. He . . . he . . . accidentally shot himself."

The short hairs rose on the back of Paula's neck and she began to tremble. She asked shakily, "Is he badly injured, Mrs. Hood?"

Mrs. Hood cleared her throat. "Oh, Mrs. O'Neill . . . he's . . . he's . . . Mr. Barkstone's dead. I'm so sorry. So very sorry."

"Oh God, no!" Paula cried and steadied herself against the oak table, trying to absorb the shock, blinking back the tears that had sprung into her eyes.

Mrs. Hood said softly, "I can't believe he's gone . . . Such a lovely man." The housekeeper broke down again, but managed to get a grip on herself, to explain: "I'm ringing *you* because I don't have the heart to get in touch with his sisters . . . I just wouldn't know how to tell

Mrs. Harte or Miss Amanda and Miss Francesca . . . I wouldn't . . ."

Paula said slowly, "It's all right, Mrs. Hood, I understand. And Mrs. Harte is here for dinner this evening. I'll break the news to her and to her sisters. But please . . . can you tell me . . . a little more about . . . what happened?"

"Not really I can't, Mrs. O'Neill. When Mr. Barkstone didn't come down for dinner this evening, I sent the butler up to his bedroom. Mr. Barkstone wasn't there. It seemed that no one in the house had seen him return from the woods. The butler, the houseman, and the chauffeur then went out to look for him . . ." Mrs. Hood blew her nose, finished, "They found him lying under one of the big oaks, the gun by his side. He was already dead."

"Thank you, Mrs. Hood," Paula managed to say, striving hard to control her feelings, to contain them as best she could. "I'll handle things here, and my husband and I will drive up to Nutton Priory within the hour. I'm sure Mr. and Mrs. Harte will come with us."

"I'll be waiting for you, Mrs. O'Neill, and thank you."

Paula put the receiver back in the cradle and stood for a moment longer in the Stone Hall thinking of her cousin. Oh Sandy, Sandy, why did you have to die like that? All alone in the woods. Her heart clenched. And then a most terrible and unacceptable thought flashed through her mind, stunning her. *Had he taken his own life?* No. Never. He wouldn't do that, she told herself. Sandy wanted so much to live. He fought so hard to keep going. Every minute was precious to him. He told me that so many times lately. She dismissed the idea of suicide, blocked it out of her mind.

Taking several deep breaths, Paula walked slowly back to the dining room, bracing herself to break the shocking news to Emily.

32

It was a bleak day for April.

Great clouds, curdled and gray, rolled with gathering speed across the lowering sky which merged into the grim and blackened Yorkshire moors. Lonely and implacable, their daunting aspects appalled the eye, cast dark shadows over Fairley this morning. There was not a drop of sunlight to soften those savage windswept reaches, the cold bracing air held a strong hint of rain and a thunderstorm seemed imminent.

Along the moorland road that cut through this great Pennine Chain of hills, a line of cars moved slowly, following the funeral cortege. Soon the cortege left the moors, began its slow descent into the village, and within fifteen minutes it was coming to a stop in front of the lovely little Norman church. Here the new vicar, the Reverend Eric Clarke, was waiting to greet the family and friends of the deceased on the ancient porch.

There were six pallbearers to carry Alexander's coffin. Anthony Standish, the Earl of Dunvale, and Winston Harte, his cousins; Shane O'Neill and Michael Kallinski, and two of his friends from school. They had known him most of their lives, and so it was fitting that they were with him at the end, had brought him to his last resting place in this old churchyard.

The six men lifted Alexander's coffin, shouldered it lightly, carried it through the lych-gate into the cemetery, moving at a slow and dignified pace down the flagged path. Their hearts were heavy and their sorrow was etched on their grieving faces. In their different ways, they had cared deeply about this man they had come to bury.

The pallbearers brought the coffin to the graveside where the vicar was now standing with Alexander's sorrowing sisters, Emily, Amanda, and Francesca, and his distraught and weeping mother, Elizabeth, who was being physically supported by her French husband, Marc Deboyne. At the other side of the grave stood the rest of the family and many friends, all of them dressed in mourning.

Anthony looked burdened down, his face morose and stark, as he walked over to join his wife, Sally, and Paula, who was next to her. He hunched further into his black overcoat, shivering in the gusting wind blowing down from the moors. It was making the new leaves on the trees rustle and ruffling the flowers in the wreaths. Anthony stared at them. They were a reminder that it *was* spring . . . tender blossoms, so colorful against the dark earth . . . the vivid yellow and purple of jonquil and crocuses, the transparent white of pale narcissi . . . the dark blood red of tulips. He was barely listening as the vicar began the burial ceremony, his mind awash with troubling thoughts.

Sandy's funeral was evoking memories of the one he had attended only a few weeks ago in Ireland. He was still disturbed about the way Michael Lamont had keeled over on that dreadful morning in Clonloughlin, when he had confronted him about Min's death. Lamont had died in the cottage hospital several days later, the victim of a massive stroke. He would have been a vegetable if he had lived. In a curious way, Anthony felt somehow responsible for the death of the estate manager. On the other hand, as Sally kept pointing out, Lamont had been

saved the agony and disgrace of a trial, which,
she insisted, he would never have survived anyway. Perhaps she was right. He tried to erase
Lamont from his mind, partially succeeded.

A long sigh trickled through Anthony, and he
turned his head, looked at Sally, gave her a faint
smile as she slipped her arm through his, drew
nearer to him. It was as if she understood everything. She did, of course. They were very close,
as close as two people could ever be.

He stole a glance at his mother, Edwina, the
Dowager Countess, wishing she had not insisted
on coming over from Ireland with them for
Sandy's funeral. She had not been well lately,
and how frail she *did* look, a white-haired old
lady in her seventies. She was the first-born
child of Emma Harte, the daughter of Edwin
Fairley.

There is so much history in this graveyard,
it's awesome, Anthony thought all of a sudden,
his eyes roaming over the gravestones. The
ground was full of Hartes and Fairleys. Generations of them. He was both Harte and Fairley, as
well as part Standish. It struck him then that it
had all begun here in the quaint little church
looming up behind him . . . begun with Emma
Harte when she had been christened here in
April of 1889. Almost a hundred years ago.
Good Lord, his grandmother would have been

ninety-three at the end of this month, if she had lived. He continued to miss her even after all these years.

An image of Emma slipped into his mind. What a unique and brilliant woman she had been. She had loved each one of her grandchildren, but he was aware she had had a special sort of relationship with Alexander. But then they all had, hadn't they? And Sandy had managed to bring out the best in them. Yes, they *were* better people for having known him.

Now his thoughts swung back to his cousin. The letter was in the inside breast pocket of his jacket. He had kept it on him ever since he had received it the day after Sandy's death. He already knew that Sandy was dead before the letter came in the morning post, because Paula had telephoned him from Nutton Priory the night before to tell him and Sally. Nonetheless, the letter had been a shock at first. Until he had understood and had accepted the words.

He had reread it so many times by now, much of it was committed to memory. He felt as if it were engraved on his mind. It was not a long letter, and it was level-headed, matter-of-fact, really, so like Sandy, and Sandy had meant it only for his eyes. That was why he had not shared it with his wife, close as they were, or with Paula, who, after all, was head of the family. But there was no need for them to see it.

Closing his eyes, he saw Sandy's handwriting in his mind's eye . . . and that particular fragment of the letter which had so moved him.

"I wanted you to understand why I am doing this, Anthony," Sandy had written in his careful script. *"Mostly it is for myself, of course. A chance to go at last. But it will save everyone the agony of my protracted dying. I know none of you could bear to see me suffer. And so before I take my life, I say goodbye, dear cousin, and friend. Know that I am happy to shed my mortal coil . . . I escape . . . I am free . . ."*

And Sandy had scribbled a postscript: *"You have been such a good friend to me, Anthony. You have helped me through my private hells more than once, perhaps without even knowing it. I thank you. God bless you and yours."*

Anthony realized it would be unwise to keep the letter, yet he had been incapable of destroying it. But he *must* do so. Today. After the funeral, in fact, when he returned to Pennistone Royal. He would go to the bathroom in their suite of rooms and burn it, then flush the charred pieces down the toilet. Only he knew that Sandy had carefully planned his death, had gone out into the woods hunting, and after bagging several rabbits and hares, had shot himself but rigged it to look like an accident. He would never reveal Sandy's secret to anyone. There had been an inquest, of course, and the coroner had returned a verdict of accidental death, exactly as Alexander had intended. No one suspected the truth.

So be it, Anthony said under his breath, looking out toward the distant moors, continuing to dwell on Sandy, so many memories seizing him . . . carrying him backward in time for a few more moments longer.

Unexpectedly, brilliant sunshine burst through the dark clouds and the leaden, somber sky was filled with a most marvelous radiance that seemed to emanate from below the smudged horizon. Anthony caught his breath at the sudden beauty and raised his eyes to the heavens, and he smiled. And in the quietness of his gentle, loving heart he said farewell to Sandy. His pain is over, Anthony thought. He's at peace at last. Gone to his beloved Maggie.

The brief ceremony was coming to an end.

The coffin was being lowered into the rich Yorkshire earth where Sandy's ancestors lay, and Anthony turned away from the grave as the vicar closed his prayer book.

He took Sally's arm. "Let's go back to Pennistone Royal for a drink and lunch," he said.

Sally nodded. "Yes, we do need something to warm us up. It's freezing this morning."

Paula, walking with them, shivered, looked from Shane to Anthony, and muttered. "I detest these hearty meals after funerals. They're barbaric."

"No," Anthony said in a muted voice, "they're not." He linked arms with her as they fell in step, went down the flagged path to the lych-gate and the waiting cars. "The lunch today gives us a chance to be together for a while, to console each other . . . and to remember Sandy as he was. To take comfort from having known him and known his love. And to celebrate his life."

Paula was to remember those words.

They were still echoing in her ears a week later, on the morning she was being driven out to Heathrow to take the Concorde to New York.

Amanda sat next to her on the back seat of the Rolls Royce, sad and withdrawn, hardly speaking. A few minutes before they arrived at the airport, Paula reached out, took her cousin's hand in hers, squeezed it.

Swinging her head, Amanda frowned slightly, and then she returned the pressure of Paula's hand.

Paula said, "You're thinking of Sandy, aren't you?"

"Yes," Amanda whispered.

Patting her hand lovingly, Paula murmured, "Grieve for him, by all means, and get the grief out. That's so very necessary . . . part of the healing process. But also take comfort from your lovely memories of Sandy, the years you had with him when you were growing up. Be glad he was your brother, that he gave you so much love, so much of himself."

"You're very wise, Paula. I will try . . ." Amanda's lips trembled. "But I miss him so much."

"Of course you do, it's only natural. And you will—for the longest time. But I also think you should take solace from the fact that Sandy is out of his suffering now." Paula paused, then added softly, "Let him go, darling, let him rest."

It was difficult for Amanda to speak, and she simply nodded several times, swung her head, stared out of the car window. She felt too emotional to respond coherently, and she knew that Paula would understand and would respect her silence.

But a short while later, when they were sitting in the Concorde lounge, sipping coffee before the flight, Amanda suddenly leaned closer to Paula, said in a low voice, "Thanks for being such a good friend. I do appreciate it." She looked off into the distance, before murmuring softly, "How uncertain life is, isn't it, Paula? None of us know what might happen to us next . . . people's lives can change in the flicker of an eyelash . . ."

"Yes . . . life *is* tenuous. But it's also quite marvelous, you know. And life is for the living. We must get on with it."

"Grandy always said that!" Amanda brought her gaze to Paula's and a smile broke through. "I had the most amazing phone call from Francesca last night . . . she's pregnant."

"That *is* lovely news! We'll have to do some shopping for baby clothes in New York." Paula picked up her cup, took a swallow of coffee, and eyed Amanda thoughtfully over the rim. Placing the cup in its saucer, she said carefully, "Forgive me for prying, but you're rather keen on Michael Kallinski, aren't you?"

Amanda looked at her, surprise flashing in her light green eyes. A faint blush tinged her neck, swept up into her pale cheeks. "Is it *so* apparent?"

"Only to me. I'm very observant and intuitive, and don't forget, I've known you since the day you were born."

"He's not interested in *me,* though," Amanda asserted.

"We'll see about that."

"What do you mean?"

"Michael's spent a great deal of time with you lately, but always on business, dealing with their takeover of Lady Hamilton Clothes. Now he ought to see you in a different light, in social situations, with other men flocking around you . . . which they generally *do,* so don't shake your head in that way. Whilst you're both in New York, Shane and I are going to be giving a few dinners and cocktail parties . . . I want to make certain Michael gets to know you even better. And in a more personal way."

"Oh" was the only thing Amanda could think of to say.

"Trust me. Your future looks very bright you know, from my vantage point."

"And so does yours," Amanda was swift to say. "I feel certain you're going to get the Larson chain."

"I sincerely hope you're right," Paula said and crossed her fingers.

As the British Airways Concorde flight took off for New York, a Quantas flight from Hong Kong was simultaneously landing at Heathrow.

Within an hour the passengers had disembarked, the luggage had come down on the carousel, and Jonathan Ainsley, looking like the prosperous business tycoon he was, walked through customs and out into the arrival hall.

His eyes scanned those people waiting near the barrier, and he raised his hand in greeting when he saw the flaming red hair and beaming face of his smartly dressed cousin, Sarah Lowther Pascal.

Sarah waved back, and a moment later they were embracing affectionately.

"Welcome home, Jonny," Sarah said as they drew apart, looked each other over appraisingly and with mutual approval.

"It's nice to be back. It's been ages." He grinned at her, motioned to the porter to follow with his luggage, and grabbing Sarah's arm, led her out to the car park.

"I *am* glad your trip to London coincided with mine," Jonathan was saying some ten minutes later as they rolled comfortably toward London in the large chauffeur-driven limousine Sarah had hired to meet him.

"So am I," she said. "Yves wanted me to come to see the gallery that represents him here, and I had some business of my own to attend to this week. So it was perfect timing, Jonny."

"And how is Yves?" Jonathan asked.

"Extremely well," Sarah answered, her voice full of enthusiasm. "Painting with great brilliance at the moment."

"And selling very well too," Jonathan murmured and glanced across at her. "And not stinting you, I see, if the jewelry is anything to go by . . . and that *is* a Givenchy suit, isn't it?"

Sarah nodded, smiled with pleasure at his compliments. "He's very generous, but my own investments have been paying good dividends . . ." She gave Jonathan a sidelong glance. "And how is Arabella?"

"Wonderful!" Jonathan's face instantly lit up, and he began to talk about Arabella and their life in Hong Kong in great detail, hardly drawing breath.

Sarah wished she had never brought up the woman's name. She hated her cousin's wife.

Settling back against the butter-soft, wine-colored leather of the car, she appeared to give her attention to Jonathan, nodding from time to time, looking as if she was absorbing every word he uttered, but, in point of fact, she was not listening to one single thing he was saying.

She's innocence, all innocence, Sarah thought, her mind focused on Arabella. But I spotted her type the minute I met her. She's clever and crafty and out for the main chance. And she's got a past, that one. I'm sure of it. I just wish I could warn him about her, but I daren't. She found it hard to believe that Jonathan had been taken in by Arabella Sutton. Even Yves, usually uninterested in other women, had appeared to be bewitched by her when Jonathan had brought her to stay at Mougins earlier in the year. Of course, she *was* charming. And beautiful. All that silver hair, the sloe eyes, the sensational figure. A sex pot, I bet, Sarah thought disparagingly, loathing her irrationally. What did it matter to her whom her cousin married. Except that she cared about Jonny, cared about his well-being.

She had her own family now, an adoring husband, an angelic and gifted child. But Jonathan represented her past, her ties in England. Her parents were alive and so were Jonny's, her Aunt Valerie, and Uncle Robin. But somehow Jonathan was the one she loved the most, even though he was mostly responsible for her estrangement from their other cousins and aunts and uncles. The rift in the Harte family had so distressed her. Although she harbored dislike for some of them, she nonetheless felt the sting of banishment, minded that she was no longer a member of that distinguished clan.

Arabella fascinated Jonny—that was quite obvious. Sarah hated competing for his attention. She had had to do that when Sebastian Cross was alive. Bosom chums they had been, from their days at Eton. And they had stayed close. She used to wonder why. Sebastian had not been very nice. Sleazy, in her opinion. And he had had such a strange fixation about Jonny. If she had not known otherwise, she would have sworn Sebastian was gay. But his reputation as a womanizer had preceded him. Now she wondered if that had actually meant anything. Sebastian had been such an odd bird. He had died of an accidental overdose of cocaine. He had had nothing but bad luck after Jonathan left England, had made nothing but disastrous business deals. She had heard that he died flat broke.

Jonathan touched her arm, exclaimed crossly, "You seem far away, Sarah. Haven't you been listening to me?" He peered into her face, his pale eyes narrowing shrewdly.

"Yes, yes, of course I have," she protested, now truly giving him her fullest attention, not wishing to displease him. Jonny had quite a temper, was easily provoked.

"Is something bothering you?" Jonathan pressed, as usual attuned to her as if he could read her mind. He had always managed to unnerve Sarah because of this ability.

"Actually, I was just thinking about Sebastian Cross," Sarah admitted. "It was odd the way he died, wasn't it?"

Jonathan was quiet for a fraction of a second.

"Yes," he said at last. "Very odd indeed." There was another pause, before he volunteered quietly, "He was bisexual. I didn't know, of course." He looked Sarah fully in the face, confided, "He only admitted that to me when he flew out to Hong Kong to see me, the first year I was there . . . he confessed that I was . . . well, the object of his passion, shall we say?"

"Oh dear," Sarah said, not particularly surprised by this sudden revelation. "How frightful for you."

Jonathan smiled narrowly. "In all truth, it was, Sarah. But he took my rejection of him very well indeed. Or so I believed at the time."

Sarah said not a word, watched him acutely.

He asked, "Do you think that's why he died, Sarah? Do you think that the overdose was intentional . . . you know, an *accident on purpose?*"

"It has occurred to me from time to time."

"Sad really."

"Yes."

"How rude of me, darling, I forgot to ask after that adorable child of yours. How is little Chloe?" Jonathan abruptly changed the subject, not wishing to dwell on Sebastian Cross, to rake over the past. He was only interested in the future, which he had been looking at very closely of late.

"Chloe is simply wonderful," Sarah said, glowing as she launched into a recital about her daughter, one of her two favorite subjects, the other being her husband. "She fell in love with her Uncle Jonny . . . and before I left France earlier this week she made me promise I'd bring you back to Mougins for the weekend. You will come, won't you?"

"I'll certainly try."

"Good," Sarah half turned in her seat, gave him a long and searching look. "What did you mean when you phoned me from Hong Kong and said our day would come, that we'd soon get our own back on Paula?"

Jonathan leaned closer. A wicked and knowing smirk spread across his bland face. "I believe that no one is infallible, that even the smartest tycoons can make flawed judgment calls at times. And I have always known that Paula O'Neill would make a mistake one day. I've been waiting . . . and watching . . . and my gut instinct tells me she's about to do something foolish. The odds are there, you see. She's had too good and too long a run for her money. And when she makes her fatal error, I shall be there. Ready to pounce."

Sarah gave him a penetrating stare, her green eyes quickening. "What do you mean? How do you know? Tell me, Jonny, tell me more!"

"Later," he said, squeezing her arm in the very intimate way he had with her. "Let's wait until we're in the privacy of my suite at Claridge's . . . and then I shall explain how I aim to destroy Paula O'Neill."

Sarah shivered with pleasure and anticipation at the thought of Paula's downfall. "I can't wait to hear your plan. I'm sure it's brilliant . . . and how I've longed to get *my* revenge on that cold, frigid, thieving bitch. She stole Shane from me, quite aside from everything else."

"Of course she did," Jonathan concurred, fanning Sarah's festering hatred of Paula, as he had for years, needing an ally in his scheming, if only for moral support.

He put his hand in his jacket pocket, and his fingers curled around the pebble of mutton-fat jade. His talisman. It had brought him great good luck in the past. He had no reason to doubt that it would do so again.

WINNERS
&
LOSERS

Unnatural deeds do breed unnatural troubles.
William Shakespeare, *Macbeth*

One must therefore be a fox to recognize traps,
and a lion to frighten wolves.
Machiavelli, *The Prince*

All or nothing.
Henrik Ibsen, *Brand*

33

"You really are the best thing that ever happened to Philip," Daisy said, filled with love and respect for the young American woman who was her daughter-in-law.

Madelana's face lit up, and she laughed lightly and with gaiety, and settled herself more comfortably on the sofa. "Thank you. That's a lovely thing to know."

They were sitting in the drawing room of the house at Point Piper in Sydney, which Philip had owned for a number of years, and where he and Maddy now lived for most of the week when they were not at Dunoon. It was August and a lovely afternoon, even though it was still the winter season in Australia, and earlier Madelana had opened the French doors leading out to the terrace and the garden beyond. A soft breeze drifted in, made the silk draperies flutter and whisper, carried with it the mixed scents of honeysuckle and eucalyptus and the salt tang of the sea.

After a moment, Madelana smiled at her mother-in-law and added, "Anyway, I have to say the same thing about your son, Daisy. He's made me a whole person again, chased all my sorrow and gloom away, and given me so much love there are times when I think I might just burst with happiness."

Daisy nodded, understanding exactly what she meant. It had always pleased her that Maddy was so open, without guile, and so readily able to articulate her feelings, with considerable eloquence at times. Also, it was gratifying to know that her son was such a good husband, had adjusted to being a married man after years of playing around, and that he and Maddy were so blissfully happy.

"When a marriage truly works there's nothing else like it in the world, nothing that can take its place," Daisy said with great feeling. "And it's pure joy to have a relationship with a man who gives so much of himself . . . as both Philip and Jason do."

Daisy paused, glanced to her left, stared at the various photographs of her late husband taken with Philip, Paula, and her twins, Lorne and Tessa, and with herself. Happy, loving family pictures which Philip kept grouped on a small side table near the fireplace. She was thoughtful for a moment, remembering her life with David, and when she swung her head and smiled across at Maddy it was with a certain ruefulness.

"When David was killed in the avalanche, I thought the world had come to an end for me. And of course it had in so many ways," Daisy confided, speaking to Maddy about her first husband in a more intimate way than she ever had before.

"You see, Maddy, I'd shared a perfect marriage with my darling David . . . ever since I'd married him at eighteen. I believed it could never be repeated or recaptured with another man, and it couldn't. For the simple reason that no two men are the same, no two women are either, for that matter, and every relationship is different, has its own strengths and weaknesses. Leaving England, coming out here, helped me to start over again, and my charity work for sick and needy children especially helped to give me a purpose. But it was Jason who made me come alive again as a woman. *He* made *me* whole, Maddy."

"He's a wonderful person," Maddy acknowledged in all sincerity, thinking of the gruff Australian's many kindnesses and loving gestures to her over the past few months. "We both lucked out, finding ourselves a couple of genuine forty-carat dudes."

"I'll say we did!" Daisy exclaimed, laughing, as usual amused by Madelana's quaint expressions. She couldn't wait to tell Jason of Maddy's assessment of him, which, she decided, was absolutely spot on. Continuing to smile, Daisy leaned forward, picked up her cup of tea, took a sip of it.

A compatible silence fell between these two women, who sprang from such different echelons of society, from such different worlds, yet who had grown to care deeply for each other in the year they had known each other. Their great common bond was the love they both felt for Philip and Paula, and Maddy's obsessional admiration of Emma Harte. Daisy was devoted to the memory of her mother, and she enjoyed answering Maddy's never-ending questions, speaking about Emma, recounting anecdotes about the legendary tycoon, and she had a rapt and enthralled listener in her daughter-in-law. And finally there was the bond created by the child Madelana was carrying. Philip's child . . . and the heir to the McGill empire Daisy had longed for.

Daisy thought of the baby now as she sipped her tea and quietly studied Madelana. She wished the baby would arrive. It was nearly two weeks late, and everyone was growing more impatient by the day. Except for Maddy, who was tranquil and healthy . . . and somewhat amused by their constant fussing.

"I'm glad you didn't have the amniocentesis test after all," Daisy said, breaking the silence, "even though I can't wait to know whether I have a grandson or a granddaughter inside that tummy of yours."

Madelana grinned. "I don't think I've ever wanted to know . . . I prefer to be surprised." She placed her hands over her stomach, feeling the baby, the gesture protective, and then she started to laugh. "However, I have a peculiar feeling that she's a girl, Daisy."

"Do you really?"

Maddy nodded, leaned forward, announced, "And if it's a girl we're going to call her Fiona Daisy Harte McGill. Rather a long name, isn't it? But we did want to name her after my mother and you, and to include the surnames of her great-grandparents."

"I'm touched and honored—and terribly flattered," Daisy responded, pleasure lighting up her vividly blue McGill eyes, which were so like her father's had been.

Madelana shifted her weight on the sofa, pushed herself into the pile of cushions, seeking a more comfortable position. She felt awkward and ungainly, slightly cramped all of a sudden.

"Are you all right?" Daisy asked, noticing Maddy's grimacing, her pained expression.

"I'm fine, just a bit stiff today. But to tell you the truth, I, too, wish the baby would come now. I feel like a giant-sized, overripe watermelon that's about to go plop! And I'm lumbering around after Philip as if I'm a fish out of water . . . a huge beached whale, or something of the sort!"

Daisy burst out laughing. "And what if you have a boy? Have you chosen a name yet?"

"Paul McGill. After your father."

"Oh, Maddy, how lovely of you and Philip. I'm delighted, thrilled actually."

Daisy got to her feet, walked across to the console where she had left her handbag when she had arrived earlier in the afternoon. She opened it, took out a small leather box, brought it over to Madelana. Handing it to her, she said, "This is for you."

Madelana looked up at her mother-in-law in surprise, then brought her eyes down to the jewel box in her hands. The leather was worn and scratched, the gilt-embossed edge faded by time. She lifted the lid and caught her breath when she saw the emerald bow lying on the black velvet.

"Why, Daisy, it's simply beautiful. *Gorgeous.* Thank you, thank you so much. It's old, isn't it?"

Daisy, who had seated herself next to Madelana on the sofa, nodded. "It dates back to the 1920s. I've wanted to give you something very special for the longest time, and I finally—"

"But you have!" Madelana interrupted. "I've had so many extraordinary gifts from you and Jason, as well as from Philip. You all spoil me."

"We love you, Maddy. But as I was saying, I wanted to give you something that would be truly meaningful to you at this particular time . . . and so I picked the emerald bow from my collection. Not only because it's exquisite and will suit you admirably, but also because it belonged to my mother. I felt you'd appreciate that, that you'd appreciate the sentimental value attached to the brooch more than anything else."

"I do. But I can't take it after all, Daisy . . . why it's a family heirloom."

"And what are *you,* if not family? Darling, you're Philip's *wife,*" Daisy said softly but emphatically. She took the brooch out of the box, and together they looked at it, admiring the exquisite workmanship, the beauty of the design, the luster and depth of color of the emeralds.

Presently, Daisy said, "There's a lovely story about this piece of jewelry . . . would you like to hear it?"

"Oh yes, I would."

Daisy smiled to herself as she laid the brooch in the velvet-padded box and settled back on the sofa. She was thinking of her mother, envisioning her as a little girl at the turn of the century, as she had so frequently done in the past, forever marveling at her extraordinary character.

"The story actually began in 1904," Daisy explained. "As you know, Emma was a servant girl in service at Fairley Hall in Yorkshire, where she had worked since she was twelve. One Sunday afternoon in March of that year, her best friend Blackie O'Neill arrived to see her. He had bought her a green glass brooch shaped like a bow for her fifteenth birthday at the end of April. He was going away, you see, and he wanted her to have something from him before he left. Anyway, Blackie explained to Emma that when he had noticed the bow in the window of a shop in Leeds the stones had reminded him of her emerald eyes. Naturally, young Emma was enchanted with the brooch, cheap as it was, because she had never had anything like it. She thought it was the most beautiful thing in the world. And that afternoon, Blackie made a promise to her . . . he told her that one day, when he was rich, he would buy her a replica of the brooch, and that it would be made of emeralds. He was true to his word. Many years later he gave her this . . . *this* is Blackie's emerald bow," Daisy finished. She thought to add, "When my mother died, she left the brooch to me, along with her collection of emeralds which my father had given her over the years."

"What a lovely story, and the bow *is* beautiful, but I'm still not sure I should accept it, Daisy. Ought it not to go to Paula in view of its history?"

"No, no, she and I want you to have it!" Daisy insisted, reaching out, squeezing Madelana's hand affectionately. "I've spoken to Paula, and she thinks it's a most fitting gift for you. As I do. And I know that if my mother were alive she would want you to have it, too."

Madelana realized there was no point in protesting further, that it would even be ungracious to do so, and she murmured her thanks again, permitted her mother-in-law to pin the emerald bow to her maternity smock. Then pushing herself up, she went to the mirror over the fireplace, looked at herself. The bow was an extraordinary piece, and she was greatly moved because Daisy had given her something which had once belonged to Emma Harte.

Madelana went back to the sofa, and after a moment Daisy leaned back against the cushions. "Speaking of my daughter, do you think she's made a mistake buying the Larson chain in the States?"

"Of course not!" Madelana cried, sitting up straighter on the sofa, returning Daisy's penetrating gaze. "She's a brilliant businesswoman and I've never known her to make a wrong move yet."

"I just wish she'd told me *why* she wanted me to sell the Sitex stock when she suggested I do so last year. Or at least given me the chance to let her have the additional money she needed for the takeover of Larson's." Daisy sighed heavily. "Paula can be awfully stubborn and she's determined to do everything her own way. She's so like my mother. Oh dear, I don't know . . . business does baffle me most of the time."

Daisy rose, moved to the fireplace, stood with one hand resting on the mantel. "And I don't understand Shane, if the truth be known. I can't imagine why he didn't tell me or Philip about her plans long ago. And why on earth didn't he advise her? After what he said last night, I think he should have, don't you?"

"I'm not sure anyone can advise Paula. She's so confident and self-assured and so truly brilliant in business that she doesn't need advice from anyone. Besides, Shane would never interfere. He would remain aloof . . . that would be the wisest course for anyone to take, as I'm sure he realizes by now."

Daisy frowned. "I was surprised by some of the things I heard over dinner last night, weren't you?"

"Not really," Madelana answered truthfully. "Don't forget, I was Paula's assistant at the New York store, and she has been after an American chain for a long time. In any event, as I said before, I trust her judgment implicitly. And so should you. I know Philip does, and from what Shane said at dinner, he does too." Madelana gave Daisy a look she hoped was reassuring. "There's one more thing I'd like to add. Hasn't it ever occurred to you that Paula might want to own something of her own?"

"But she does, Maddy dear," Daisy exclaimed in a startled tone. "The Harte chain, not to mention—"

"But that was founded by Emma," Madelana was quick to point out. "In fact, everything Paula runs she inherited from her grandmother. Perhaps emotionally she has the need to . . .

to . . . well, to *create* and *build* something of her very own and with her own money.

"Is that what she indicated to you when you worked together in New York?"

"No, it's just a feeling I have, knowing her as well as I do."

Daisy looked further surprised and fell silent, ruminating on her daughter-in-law's words. Eventually, she said, "Perhaps you're right, Maddy dear. I hadn't looked at it quite like that. Nevertheless, apart from anything else, I do think she has taken on an enormous amount of responsibility in addition to everything else she has to do."

Maddy said in a loving voice, "Try not to worry about Paula and her expansion program in the States. She'll be fine; it'll be fine. Philip believes she's a chip off the old block, and you said only a few minutes ago that she's like your mother. Being another Emma Harte can't be all that bad, can it?" Maddy finished on a teasing note, raising a brow.

Daisy had the good grace to laugh. "No, it can't," she said.

34

Later, after her mother-in-law had left to return to her house in Rose Bay, Madelana put on a thick, white wool cape and went outside. She walked slowly through the gardens as she did twice a day, enjoying the exercise and the air.

Although the wind had dropped, it had turned cold and dusk was falling, and in that lovely half light, neither day nor night but hovering somewhere in between, everything appeared to be softer, gentler.

The pristine sky of earlier had lost its sharp, icy blue-and-white tints, was slowly darkening, and its rim at the edge of the horizon was streaked with flaring ribbons of amber and rose as the sun sank into the sea. And in those hushed and silent gardens, where not a single thing stirred, the only sound was the lapping of the waves against the rocks of the jutting headland on which the mansion was built.

When she reached the end of the wide path, Madelana stood for a moment gazing out across the endless stretch of inky water. It looked cold, forbidding, bottomless, and she shivered despite the warmth of her cape. Turning swiftly on her heels, she hurried back up to the house. She could see that lamps were being turned on in some of the rooms, and narrow corridors of light were streaming out from the windows, illuminating her way.

How warm and welcome her home looked in contrast to the daunting sea behind her. She increased her pace, wanting suddenly to be inside. Within minutes she was closing the French doors of the library, walking through the room and out into the foyer, still shivering slightly.

As she hung her cape in the hall cupboard, she heard the chatter of voices coming from the kitchen area of the house. It was the two maids, Alice and Peggy, and Mrs. Ordens, the housekeeper, twittering away together like a flock of chirpy sparrows. The three women took care of them exceptionally well, eased the burden of running two homes in Sydney—the house out here at Point Piper and the penthouse atop the McGill Tower. She took a step toward the door, then decided to change her clothes in readiness for the evening before going in to speak to them.

A little sigh of happiness trickled through Madelana as she climbed the staircase leading to the upper floors. She had been experiencing a lovely sense of contentment in the last few days. It was Philip's love and the baby she was carrying that filled her with such abundant joyousness. Soon they would be three instead of two. She could hardly wait . . . she longed to hold her child in her arms.

The rosy glow of the fire greeted her when she pushed open the door of their bedroom and went in. This was one of the two rooms in the house she had redecorated after her marriage, and she had used a mixture of soft greens and a striking white chintz splashed with pink peonies, scarlet roses, yellow lilies, and dark green leaves. The play of greens in the overall scheme and the airy chintz, lavishly used, served to endorse the spaciousness of the bedroom. There was a sweeping bay window overlooking the gardens and the sea, a curving, cushioned window seat underneath, and a huge four-poster bed.

A small antique writing desk was positioned in a corner near the fireplace, and Maddy went and sat down, picked up the letter she had been writing to Sister Bronagh in Rome when Daisy had arrived for tea earlier than expected.

She read it quickly, added a last sentence and her love, then signed it. After sealing it in an envelope and addressing it, she propped it up with the others going to Sister Mairéad in New York, Patsy Smith in Boston, and Paula in London. Maddy was a diligent correspondent, regularly penned entertaining epistles with her latest news to her four favorites. After lunch today she had decided to get the letters written before she went into the hospital to have the baby; she was positive their child would be born this week.

Leaning back in the chair, Maddy began to ruminate on the past year. How extraordinary it had been. *Wondrous.* That truly was the only word to describe it. But it's not even a year, she suddenly thought. I didn't meet Philip until September, and it's only August. What a lot has happened in that short span of time. She rested her hands on her lap, linked her fingers under her large tummy, thinking again of the baby, making endless plans for the future.

Eventually she lifted her eyes, let them rest on the little sampler she had owned since childhood. It had been shipped out to Australia with her other possessions and it hung on the wall above her desk.

"If your day is hemmed with prayer it is less

likely to unravel," her mother had stitched so meticulously in bright blue wool all those years ago.

Oh Mom, she thought, everything did turn out beautifully for me, just as you said it would when I was little. I *am* your Golden Girl after all. I *have* been blessed.

Maddy swiveled her eyes to the photographs framed in silver standing on her desk . . . her parents, Kerry Anne, Young Joe, and Lonnie. You've been gone from me for a long time now, but I carry each one of you in my heart and I always will, she whispered to herself.

As she continued to gaze at her family, she realized her memories were much sweeter, far less painful than they had ever been. This was surely because she was a fulfilled and happy woman who no longer felt lonely or alone. At last her keen sense of loss was muted if not totally eradicated.

Maddy left the bedroom half an hour later, freshly made up and immaculately groomed, dressed in a well-cut navy blue silk tunic over loose, pajama-style pants of the same dark silk. Emma's emerald bow was pinned to one shoulder. With it she wore a strand of perfectly matched pearls, large pearl earrings, and her wedding and engagement rings. On her arm was a navy blue shawl of heavy jacquard silk, thickly fringed, and she carried a navy silk evening purse into which she had just popped her letters. She would mail them later at the Sydney-O'Neill Hotel.

Before going downstairs, she paused at a door a little farther along the corridor, turned the handle, and went inside. Switching on the nearest lamp, she beamed with pleasure as she looked around the former guest room, now transformed into the nursery. Philip and she had decorated it together. It was done in a cheerful combination of yellow and white, with shocking pink as a lively accent color. They had decided on this particular scheme since it was neither feminine nor masculine, and therefore suitable for a girl or a boy.

Lovingly she smoothed one hand along the edge of the crib, went over to the window wall to straighten a slightly crooked nursery rhyme print, moving around the large and pleasant room slowly, checking everything for the umpteenth time. Then she turned off the lamp, closed the door behind her as she went out, smiling beatifically, satisfied that everything was perfect and in total readiness for their child.

Maddy ran into Mrs. Ordens in the entrance hall.

"Oh there you are, Mrs. Amory," the housekeeper said, giving her a warm smile. "I was just coming up to tell you Ken has arrived with the car to take you into Sydney."

"Thanks, Mrs. Ordens," Maddy said, smiling back, "but there's plenty of time. Let's go into the kitchen for a minute. I'd like to go over a few things with you before I leave."

Shane decided that he had never seen Madelana looking more beautiful than she did tonight. She was obviously more head over heels in love with Philip than ever, and he with her, and their happiness was reflected in everything they did and said.

The first thing he had noticed when he had arrived in Sydney several days ago was the way her face had filled out since he had last seen her in Yorkshire in January. It was no longer quite so bony, and the extra bit of weight suited her. Her cheeks were slightly flushed, her large gray eyes filled with sparkling lights, and there was a special radiance about her which he found utterly breathtaking. She seemed lit from within. No wonder some of the other people in the restaurant kept glancing in their direction. But then Philip was a handsome son of a gun, very distinguished-looking, and his face was well known in Australia. That might also explain the numerous surreptitious looks. These two made a striking couple; they had an aura of glamor about them.

It had been a merry evening from the outset.

The three of them had laughed a lot over dinner in the Orchid Room of the hotel. In fact, from the moment she had arrived at Shane's suite, where Philip was having an aperitif with him, hilarity had been in the air. Philip had fussed over Madelana, pressed her into a comfortable chair, poured cool Evian water for her, and generally behaved like the besotted man he was. And she had been warm and loving and somewhat placid in her general demeanor, the beatific smile intact. Shane was happy for them, knowing full well what a good marriage meant. They were as lucky as he and Paula.

Philip was saying, "Anyway, Shane, we're not going to Dunoon this weekend. The baby is *so* overdue now, Doctor Hardcastle wants us to stay in Sydney. He's positive the birth is imminent, and so is Maddy, for that matter, and he thinks it's best we stay put."

"He's absolutely right, too," Shane said. "And from a strictly selfish point of view, I'm glad you'll be in the city. Perhaps I'll come out to Point Piper on Sunday, spend the day with you both, if you'll have me, and if the little scalawag still hasn't budged, of course."

Philip grinned. "That's what we had in mind,

although we hoped you'd come for the whole weekend. You could drive out with me on Friday evening; it'll give you a chance to relax, get away from the hotel and its problems."

"That's a splendid idea—I'll do that. It'll be nice being with you, taking it easy, doing nothing much except read and listen to music. I don't seem to have had a minute's peace since I arrived."

Maddy exclaimed, "Oh, I am glad you're going to stay with us, Shane! And Mrs. Ordens is a wonderful cook. She'll make all your favorite dishes if you tell me what you'd like."

Shane laughed, shook his head. "No fancy meals, darling girl. Paula's put me on a strict diet. She seems to think I gained weight in the South of France this summer. Mind you, Beanstalk's always been so bone-thin I suppose anyone looks fat next to her." He eyed Madelana, his expression merry and teasing. "You're pretty skinny yourself—when you're not pregnant."

"Yes," she agreed, "I think Paula and I both burn off pounds when we're working. It's all that nervous energy being expended, I guess."

"Talking of work, are you still planning to run Harte's-Australia after the baby's born?" Shane asked curiously.

"Oh yes, I think so," Maddy told him. "I plan to have a month or two off with the baby, since I can do paperwork and phoning from the house or the penthouse until I start keeping regular business hours again . . . nine to five and all that."

"Actually, I'm having a suite decorated for Maddy, next to my office in the McGill Tower," Philip said. "That way, she's only one flight down from the nursery we've designed in the flat upstairs."

"Paula has often hauled one of ours into the office with her . . . and so has Emily," Shane laughed. "It's a trait of the Harte women, I do believe. You might as well join the club, Maddy!"

She gave him a huge smile, which turned into a languorous yawn. She endeavored to stifle it without much success, brought her hand to her mouth, yawned again several times.

Philip did not fail to miss this. "I'd better get my lady home to bed," he announced, instantly rising, helping Maddy to her feet. "I hope you don't mind having an early evening, Shane, but I do think we should be making tracks."

"Of course I don't mind." Shane also pushed back his chair, stood. "I'll come down with you, and anyway it won't do me any harm to get to bed at a reasonable hour for once."

Shane escorted them through the Orchid Room, down in the elevator, across the dark green marble lobby to the front doors. "There's Ken with the car," he said as they stepped out into the street. He kissed Maddy goodnight, embraced his brother-in-law, and slammed the back door firmly shut when they were inside, waved them off.

As the Rolls-Royce pulled away from the curb, Philip put his arm around Madelana, drew her close to him on the back seat. "Are you feeling all right, sweetheart?"

"Yes, I'm fine, Philip. Very tired, that's all." She rested her head against his body. "It just suddenly hit me . . . the feeling of total and absolute exhaustion, I mean."

"Do you think the baby's coming? Do you have any labor pains?"

"Not a one." She smiled against his chest, slipped her arm inside his jacket and around his back, wanting to be even closer to him. "I'll let you know, and in no uncertain terms, the minute I get the slightest twinge," she promised.

He stroked her chestnut hair, brought his face down, kissed the top of her head. "Oh God, I love you so much, Maddy. I don't believe I can ever convey to you exactly how much you mean to me."

"Mmmmm, that's lovely," she said, smiling again, then stifling another series of long yawns. "I love you, too . . . I'll be glad when we get home . . . I can't wait to put my head on the pillow." Her eyelids felt so heavy she could hardly keep them open. They drooped and finally closed, and she dozed intermittently all the way to the Point Piper house.

After breakfast the following morning, Philip went back upstairs to say good-bye to Maddy.

But she was still fast asleep in the great four-poster bed, her chestnut hair tumbled across the pillow. In repose her face was tranquil, relaxed, devoid of the quickness and mobility that gave it such vivacity when she was awake.

How beautiful my wife is, he thought, bending over her, kissing her lightly on the cheek. He did not have the heart to awaken her. She had been almost speechless with fatigue the night before, and she needed her rest this morning. He moved a strand of hair away from her face, kissed her again, quietly crept out of the bedroom.

Ken was waiting in the driveway with the Rolls when Philip walked out of the house just before seven o'clock, and within seconds they were en route for Sydney. Philip opened his briefcase, went over the most urgent documents he had collected from his desk last night, preparing himself for the day's business as he usually did during the half-hour drive into the city.

He made a number of quick notations on his pad; studied a detailed memorandum from Tom Patterson, head of their mining division and one of the world's great opal experts; perused other communications from various executives who worked for the McGill Corporation, eventually returned all the documents to his case. He sat back, mulling over everything he had read for the remainder of the drive.

When he strode into the executive offices of the McGill Corporation atop the McGill Tower, it was exactly seven-thirty. His personal assistant, Barry Graves, and his secretary, Maggie Bolton, were both waiting for him. After greeting each other affably, the three of them went into Philip's inner sanctum for their usual early morning confab.

Lowering himself into the chair behind his desk, Philip said, "The most important meeting on our agenda today is going to be the one with Tom Patterson. Presumably he got in all right from Lightning Ridge last night?"

"He did," Barry said. "He phoned about ten minutes ago, and I confirmed that we were expecting him around eleven-thirty this morning, and that lunch would be with you in your private dining room here."

"Good-o!" Philip said. "I'm looking forward to seeing my old cobber, talking to him. It's been months since Tom's been to Sydney. He had a lot of pertinent things to say in his memo. I went over it again in the car on the way in, and I want him to elaborate on a number of points he's raised. But better not go into that right now." Philip glanced over at Maggie, sitting at the other side of the desk, her pad in her hand, her pencil poised.

"Anything special in the post today?" he asked, dropping his eyes to the pile of papers in front of him, then looking at her again.

"Nothing of any great consequence—mostly personal letters, a few invitations, charity requests, the usual daily stuff. Oh, and a cheery note from Steve Carlson. He's still in Coober Pedy. And doing quite well," Maggie finished with a small grin.

Philip couldn't help grinning with her. "So much for *my* assessment of him! The jackeroo seems to have turned out to be quite smart."

The three of them exchanged knowing glances, chuckling, remembering the young American they had characterized as a greenhorn when he had come seeking Philip's advice about opal mining a year ago.

Barry said, with a touch of acerbity, "Beginner's luck, that's all it is. You mark my words, he'll come a cropper yet." He opened one of the folders he was holding, went on briskly, "I now have all the information you require on the newspaper chain in Queensland. The boss man over there seems to be interested in selling. I've prepared a fact sheet, Philip, with all the salient details. Also, Gregory Cordovian phoned just a few minutes after you left the office last night. He wants to set up a meeting with you."

"Does he now!" Philip exclaimed, surprise echoing in his voice. He eyed Barry quizzically. "Could it be that he finally wants to call a truce?"

"Hard to say. He's a cagey sod, that one is. But I kinda got the feeling he was receptive to having a friendly little natter with you. More so than he's ever been in the past. Could be that he even wants to sell the television stations in Victoria. And listen, Philip, *he* called *us,* didn't he? I take that as a good sign."

"It is. And you may well be right—about the television stations."

Barry nodded, tapped the other folder he was holding. "Reports here about our natural energy companies, our Sydney real estate, and our other mining interests. You'll have to go over most of them before next Thursday week, when we have that series of meetings with the executives of these companies."

"I will. Leave the folders with me, Barry. Anything else from you, Maggie."

His secretary flipped back to a previous page on her pad. "Ian MacDonald called late yesterday afternoon. He has a full suit of sails for you, including the spinnaker and the Kevlar for the storm mainsail. He wants to know when you can get out to see him? Wonders if you'd like to lunch with him at the yard?"

"Tomorrow or Friday . . . I am free, aren't I?"

"Tomorrow you are, yes. But not on Friday. You have a meeting with your mother and the board of trustees of the Daisy McGill Amory Foundation. A working lunch here at the Tower in the private dining room."

"Oh that's right, I'd totally forgotten." Philip pondered a moment. "Perhaps you'd better make a date with Ian for next week sometime. That'll be more convenient."

"All right." Maggie stood up. "That's it for me, I'll leave you two alone. Buzz me if you want a cup of coffee, Philip."

"Thanks, I will."

Barry strode over to the desk. "I don't have anything else either at the moment. I want to get back to my office, dig into the report I'm preparing for you on your mother's foreign holdings. I'm still behind on it."

"Okay, go ahead, Barry, do what you have to do. In any case, I have enough to keep me busy with that lot," he said, gesturing to the folders Barry had just placed on his desk. "I'll see you at the meeting with Tom. Let me know the minute he arrives."

"Sure thing, Philip."

Left alone, Philip turned his attention to the two reports on their iron-ore mining interests. Settling back in his chair, he began to read the first one, which consisted of fifteen typed pages. He was still reading the second and making copious notes an hour later when Maggie brought him a cup of coffee, and he did not start on the report about their Sydney real estate until ten o'clock. He was halfway through this when Maggie's voice came over the intercom.

"Philip . . ."

"Yes, Maggie?"

"Sorry to disturb you, but I have your housekeeper on the phone. She says it's urgent."

"Oh . . . okay, put her through." The phone on his left immediately began to ring. He picked it up. "Yes, Mrs. Ordens?"

"Something's the matter with Mrs. Amory," the housekeeper said, getting straight to the point, her anxiety and concern echoing down the wire.

"What do you mean?" Philip demanded sharply, instantly alarmed. He sat up straighter, gripped the phone hard.

"I can't wake her. I looked in on her at nine-thirty, as you told me to, but she was sleeping so soundly I decided to leave her be for a while. I just brought her breakfast tray up, and I've tried for the past ten minutes to rouse her, but it's no good, Mr. Amory. I think she must be unconscious."

"Oh my God!" Philip sprang to his feet, alarm signals going off in his head. "I'll be right there!" he exclaimed. "No, no, that won't help. We must get her into the hospital. The emergency room at St. Vincent's. I'll send an ambulance. You must go with her. I'll meet you there with Doctor Hardcastle, but I'll call you back in a few minutes. Are you in the bedroom now?"

"Yes."

"Then stay there until the ambulance comes. And don't leave my wife alone for one moment."

"No, I won't. But please hurry, Mr. Amory. I know there's something terribly wrong."

35

A private ambulance transported Madelana to St. Vincent's Hospital in Darlinghurst, about fifteen minutes away from the Point Piper house. It was the hospital closest to the eastern suburbs of Sydney, and the only one in the city with emergency facilities.

Mrs. Ordens rode with her in the ambulance, holding onto her limp hand, watching over her as she had promised Philip she would. Not an eyelash flickered against that wan face, but Madelana's breathing was even, and for this at least Mrs. Ordens was thankful.

The moment the ambulance arrived at the hospital, Madelana was rushed straight into

Emergency, and Mrs. Ordens was shown into a private office which had been made available at the request of the patient's doctor.

Rosita Ordens sat down to wait for Philip Amory. He was on his way from the McGill Tower with Malcolm Hardcastle, the noted Sydney gynecologist who had been a close friend of Philip's for several years.

Clasping her hands together, Rosita Ordens focused her eyes on the door expectantly. She wished her boss would arrive. He would soon get to the bottom of this situation, find out exactly what was wrong with his wife. One thing was certain—she had not liked the peculiar looks exchanged by the two ambulance men when they had first seen Madelana Amory.

Rosita bowed her head. She focused her thoughts on the lovely young American woman whom she had grown so fond of in the last eight months, *willing* her to be all right, to open her eyes, to speak to the doctors now examining her.

A Catholic like Maddy, Rosita began to pray under her breath. "Hail Mary, full of grace, the Lord is with thee, blessed art thou amongst women, and blessed is the fruit of thy womb, Jesus . . . Hail Mary, full of grace, the Lord is with thee, blessed art thou . . . Hail Mary, full of grace . . . Hail Mary . . ." She went on repeating these words over and over again. Praying helped Rosita, gave her solace in times of trouble. Moreover, she was devout, believed her prayers would be answered by her merciful God.

Suddenly she lifted her head with a start as the door was flung open. "Oh Mr. Amory, thank goodness you're here!" she cried at the sight of Philip, jumping up, going over to him.

Philip took hold of her hand. "Thanks for phoning me when you did, Mrs. Ordens, and for acting so promptly. I'm grateful."

"Have you seen Mrs. Amory yet?"

"Very briefly, with Doctor Hardcastle. He's examining her himself. Naturally, he's concerned about the baby. And after he's conferred with the doctors in Emergency, I'm sure he'll be able to tell me what has caused her condition."

"She is unconscious then?"

"I'm afraid so."

Rosita Ordens sucked in her breath quickly. "I do wish I'd tried to waken her earlier, that I—"

"Don't blame yourself, Mrs. Ordens," Philip interrupted swiftly. "That serves no purpose, and you did what you believed was right. After all, she did appear to be merely in a deep sleep. I also thought that myself."

Rosita Ordens nodded glumly. Her worry knew no bounds.

Philip went on, "Ken's outside with the car. He'll drive you back to the house. I'll phone you the minute I have more news."

"Please do, Mr. Amory. I'll be anxious until I hear from you. So will Alice and Peggy."

"I know." He escorted the housekeeper over to the door. "Ken's parked in front of the main entrance . . . he's waiting for you."

"Thanks, Mr. Amory." Rosita slipped out of the office, knowing her employer wished to be alone.

Philip sat down, sank at once into his troubled thoughts. His mind raced, seeking answers. It was not natural for anyone to fall into unconsciousness in the way Maddy had. Something serious had induced this state in her—he was convinced of that. Radical action was needed. He would bring in a team of specialists, send his private jet to get them if necessary, wherever they were. Yes, he would do it immediately. *Now.* Suddenly he stood up, then sat down again, his nerves on edge. He pushed back the awful panic swarming over him once more. He must stay calm, handle things with cool intelligence. Yet he could hardly contain himself. He wanted to rush back to Emergency to be with Maddy, to look after her, to stay with her until she was her normal self. But there was no point, not at this moment. He was helpless, could do nothing. And she was in the best hands for now. Philip believed in allowing the experts to do their jobs. He was not going to play doctor.

After what seemed like an eternity to Philip, but was in reality only twenty minutes, Malcolm Hardcastle entered the office.

Philip was on his feet immediately, striding across the floor. He stared sharply at the gynecologist, searching his face, his own anxious and full of questions. Urgently he asked, "What caused Maddy's condition, Malcolm?"

Taking hold of Philip's arm, the doctor led him back to the group of chairs. "Let's sit down for a minute."

Philip was astute, and when Malcolm did not give him a direct reply he was instantly alert for trouble. Fear for Maddy gripped him. "What do you think happened to my wife between last night and this morning?" he asked fiercely, his blue eyes flaring.

Malcolm did not know how to break the news. After a split second of hesitation, he said, very quietly, "We're fairly certain that Maddy's had a brain hemorrhage."

"Oh my God, no!" Philip gaped at the doctor. He was stunned, shocked. "It can't be so . . . it just can't be!"

"I'm so sorry, Philip, but I'm afraid all the signs are there. Two very respected brain surgeons have now seen Maddy since she was admitted. I've just consulted with them, and—"

"I want a second opinion! Specialists brought in!" Philip interjected, his voice rising harshly.

"I guessed you would. I asked Doctor Litman to try and contact Alan Stimpson. As I'm sure you know, he's Australia's most renowned brain surgeon and considered to be one of the best in the world. Thankfully he lives in Sydney." Malcolm put his hand on Philip's arm, added in a most reassuring tone, "And even more fortunately for us, he happened to be at St. Margaret's Hospital out here in Darlinghurst this morning. Doctor Litman managed to catch him just as he was leaving to go back to the city. He should be joining us in a matter of seconds."

"Thanks, Malcolm," Philip said, calming down somewhat. "And excuse me for being snappish. I'm fraught with worry."

"That's understandable, and you don't have to apologize to me, Philip. I know the strain you're under."

There was a knock, and the door opened to admit a tall, slender, sandy-haired man with a freckled face and sympathetic gray eyes.

Malcolm Hardcastle leaped to his feet. "That was fast, Alan. Thanks for coming. I'd like to introduce Philip McGill Amory. Philip, this is

Doctor Alan Stimpson, whom I was just speaking to you about."

Philip, who had also risen, greeted the renowned surgeon. They shook hands, and then the three of them sat down together.

Alan Stimpson was a direct man who believed in getting to the crux of the matter at once. "I've just spoken to Doctor Litman, Mr. Amory, and I will examine your wife in a moment." His gaze was steady, level, as he went on, "However, I hadn't realized the baby's birth was so imminent, that the child is actually now two weeks overdue." He glanced at Malcolm. "Have you explained to Mr. Amory how dangerous a brain scan would be to the unborn child?"

Malcolm shook his head. "No, I haven't. I was waiting for you."

"Could you elucidate further, please?" Philip said to Alan Stimpson, his alarm increasing. He clasped his hands together to stop them trembling.

"There would be danger of radiation from a brain scan, Mr. Amory. It would most probably injure the unborn child."

Philip was silent briefly. Then he asked, "Do you have to do a brain scan on my wife?"

"It would enable us to ascertain the true extent of the cerebral damage."

"I see."

Doctor Stimpson continued in the same gentle tone, "However, before we make a decision about that, I must give Mrs. Amory a very thorough physical examination. I will then consult with my colleagues, and we'll decide on the best course of medical action to take."

"I understand," Philip said. "But I hope some fairly fast decisions are going to be made. Surely time is of the essence?"

"It is," Alan Stimpson replied. He stood. "Please excuse me." When the brain surgeon reached the door, he glanced back at the gynecologist. "I'd like you to be at this examination, Malcolm, and consult with us, in view of your patient's pregnancy."

Malcolm jumped up. "Of course, Alan." He turned to Philip. "Hang in there . . . and try to stay calm . . . take it easy."

"I will," Philip muttered, but he knew that this was the last thing he would be able to do. His gaze turned inward as he dropped his head into his hands, worrying about Maddy, becoming more anxious than ever for her. He was reeling from the shock. He could not believe this horrendous thing had happened. She had been so well last night. He felt as if he was living in some horrifying nightmare to which there was no end.

Ten minutes later Philip jerked his head up, found himself looking at the worried face of his brother-in-law, Shane O'Neill, who stood framed in the doorway.

Shane exclaimed, "I came as soon as I heard! I was out of the hotel. Barry tracked me down. He said to tell you he hasn't been able to contact Daisy yet."

"Thanks for coming," Philip murmured, relieved to see him.

"Barry told me the housekeeper found Maddy unconscious this morning. What happened, Philip? What's wrong with her?"

"The doctors think she's had a brain hemorrhage."

"Oh Jesus!" Shane was aghast. He stood staring at Philip, disbelief washing over his face.

"It occurred during the night most probably," Philip thought to add. His voice was hardly audible.

Shane took the next chair. "But she seemed perfectly normal last evening at dinner! Do they *know* what caused the hemorrhage?"

Philip shook his head. "Not yet. But Doctor Stimpson is examining her right now. He's one of the world's foremost brain surgeons. We're damned lucky he wasn't abroad, that he was actually out here at a nearby hospital in Darlinghurst this morning."

"I've heard of Alan Stimpson," Shane said. "He has an extraordinary record, has performed some miraculous brain operations. From what I've read about him, there's nobody better."

"Yes, he *is* brilliant." Philip turned to Shane. "I don't know what I'll do if anything happens to Maddy," he blurted out shakily. "She's the most important thing in my life . . ." He bit off the end of the sentence, unable to continue, averted his head so that Shane would not see the sudden tears glittering in his eyes.

"Maddy's going to be all right," Shane asserted, his voice confident, strong. "Let's not dwell on the worst, but think of the best instead. We've got to take a positive attitude, Philip. And you're not going to lose her. We must hold that thought."

"Yes . . . I'm glad you're here, Shane. It does help."

Shane nodded.

A silence developed between the two men.

All of Philip's thoughts and his mind and his heart were with his wife in Emergency. He kept envisioning her face. It had been pale, still, devoid of expression when he had seen her a short while before. He could not forget the limpness of her hand when he had held it in his. There had been something so lifeless about Maddy. His mind balked at the idea that she might slip away from him. He refused to contemplate this.

From time to time, Shane looked at Philip. His heart went out to his brother-in-law. But he did not say a word, not wishing to intrude on Philip's privacy. It was obvious that he wanted to be quiet, to be left alone. He was faraway, his handsome face ringed with worry, and his bright blue eyes, so like Paula's, were filled with growing anxiety.

Shane sat back. Silently he offered up a prayer for Maddy.

When Daisy came into the office a little later, Shane was on his feet and across the room to her immediately. She was white, and there was a stricken expression on her face. Shane put his arm around her protectively.

She looked up at him questioningly. "What has happened to Maddy?" she asked tremulously, clutching at him.

Shane explained in a muted voice, "It looks as if she may have had a brain hemorrhage."

"Oh no! Not Maddy! Philip—" She flew across the room to her son, sat down in the chair Shane had just vacated, reached out her hand to him, wanting to give him comfort.

"I'm all right, Ma," Philip said, taking her hand in his, squeezing it. "The doctors are with Maddy now . . . Malcolm Hardcastle, two doctors from the hospital, and Alan Stimpson, the famous brain surgeon."

"He's wonderful," Daisy said, relieved to hear that this man was in charge medically. Her hopes for Maddy soared. "I've met him several times through the Foundation . . . he's the very best. You could not ask for a finer doctor to take care of Maddy.

"I know, Ma."

Daisy swung her eyes to Shane, hovering nearby. "Barry is very anxious . . . he hasn't heard from either of you. You must call him, Shane, let him know what's going on. He can then get in touch with Jason, who went to Perth last night."

"Oh God, yes, I did forget to phone him," Philip muttered. "I'll do so now, and I'll call Mrs. Ordens at the house. She and the maids are as concerned as we are."

"I'm sorry, Mr. Amory, but there is little question that your wife has suffered a cerebral hemorrhage," Doctor Stimpson told Philip forty minutes later. "Her condition is very grave."

Philip, who was standing near the window, thought his legs were going to give way under him. He sat down heavily in the nearest chair. He was unable to speak.

Shane had been introduced to the two doctors

by Daisy a moment before, and he took charge, addressed the brain surgeon. "What's your recommendation, Doctor Stimpson?"

"I would like to do the brain scan as soon as possible, and then trepan her skull. That operation would at least relieve the pressure of the blood clot on her brain. Also, I should point out that without the trepanning of her skull she might never regain consciousness. She could be in a coma for the rest of her life."

Philip stifled an anguished cry. He clenched his hands, digging his nails into his palms. *Maddy never to be conscious again.* The thought of this was so appalling, so terrifying he could not—would not—countenance it, let alone accept it.

Alan Stimpson, compassionate, saw the agony on Philip's face, the mixture of pain and apprehension now flickering in those startlingly blue eyes. He was silent, waiting for the other man to marshal his swimming senses.

At last Philip whispered, "Please go on, Doctor Stimpson."

"There is the complication for the baby, Mr. Amory. If your wife were only a few weeks or even a few months pregnant, I would recommend aborting the child. Obviously that is not possible at this late stage of the pregnancy. And . . . well, she could go into labor at any moment. Therefore, the child must be delivered by caesarean section. I recommend that this be done without further delay."

"I can perform the caesarean immediately," Malcolm said.

"Will that endanger my wife's life?" Philip asked quickly.

It was Alan Stimpson who answered him. "Quite the contrary . . . I'd say she could be in more danger if Malcolm doesn't perform the caesarean. Also, in another sense it would be very helpful, in that I could perform the scan and the operation without fear of doing injury to the unborn baby."

"Then go ahead with the caesarean. Now," Philip answered rapidly, wanting no further procrastination. "But I would like Maddy sent to a private hospital . . . if she can be moved, of course."

"We can arrange to transfer Mrs. Amory to St. Vincent's private wing next door," the surgeon said.

"Then let's do that." Philip rose to his feet. "I want to go to my wife now, to be with her. And I'll accompany her next door."

36

At a few minutes past two o'clock that afternoon, Malcolm Hardcastle performed a caesarean section on Madelana Amory.

The child he delivered was perfect. But the mother did not know this. She remained in a coma.

Malcolm brought the news to Philip.

He was waiting impatiently with Shane and Daisy in a private room adjacent to the one he had taken for Maddy at St. Vincent's Hospital.

"You have a baby girl. A daughter, Philip," Malcolm announced.

Philip was pacing the floor.

He stopped, pivoted to face the gynecologist.

"Is Maddy all right? Did she come through it all right?" he demanded, his wife his first priority.

"Yes, she did. And her condition is the same as it was when she was taken to St. Vincent's this morning. I'm afraid she still hasn't regained consciousness. On the other hand, she has not taken a turn for the worse."

"Is that a good sign? Hopeful?" Shane probed.

"Yes . . . she seems . . . quite stable."

"Can I see her?" Philip asked.

"Not just yet . . . she's in Recovery."

"But when?" he asked again in the same soft yet demanding tone.

"In an hour. Now, about your daughter . . . she's perfect, just beautiful, and she weighs seven pounds ten ounces."

Philip remembered his manners. He grasped Malcolm's hand tightly. "Thanks for everything you've done, Malcolm. I'm grateful to you, relieved that the baby's all right."

"Can we at least see the child?" Daisy looked at Malcolm, then shifted her gaze to her son standing next to him. "I'd like to welcome my granddaughter into the world."

"Of course you can see her, Mrs. Rickards."

The four of them left the room together, walked down the corridor to the glass-windowed hygienically controlled nursery where new babies were taken immediately following their births.

"There she is!" Malcolm was exclaiming a few seconds later. A duty nurse, catching sight of the noted gynecologist, had already lifted a baby from a crib and was bringing her over to the window for them to see her.

"Oh Philip, she is beautiful," Daisy murmured, her eyes lighting up. "And look, she's got a little tuft of reddish blond fluff on top of her head. I think we're going to have another redhead in the family."

"Yes," her son responded laconically, staring at the baby through the glass. He wished he could be more enthusiastic about the child. But he was so sick at heart about his wife nothing else seemed to matter to him.

Eventually, he brought his gaze away from the nursery window, drew Malcolm to one side. "What happens next? When is Stimpson going to do the brain scan?"

"Shortly. Now, why don't you go outside and get some air? Or take your mother and brother-in-law for a cup of tea or coffee."

"I won't leave the hospital! I won't leave Maddy!" Philip exclaimed. "Perhaps I can persuade them to go. But not I, oh no. Again, thanks for everything you've done for my wife and my child, Malcolm," he said as he turned away.

Later, when they had returned to the room in the private wing of the hospital, Philip suggested to Shane that he accompany Daisy to the Point Piper house, to relax and take some sort of refreshment. "You don't have to keep vigil with me," he muttered, throwing himself into a chair.

"We do," Shane shot back quickly. "We're not going to let you go through this alone."

"We're staying, Philip, and that's flat!" Daisy said in a voice that was as resolute as her mother's had ever been. "My God, Shane and I couldn't stand it, being away from you and from Maddy. We're worried enough as it is without being isolated at the Point Piper house, not knowing what's going on."

Philip did not have the energy to respond, never mind argue with Daisy or Shane.

For a time he nervously paced the floor, then the corridor outside, his agitation increasing. In an effort to stem his spiraling anxiety, he returned to the room, phoned his offices in the McGill Tower, spoke to his secretary, Maggie, and to Barry, his assistant. He made the occasional comment to his mother and Shane, but for the most part he was silent, stood staring morosely out of the window.

He was accustomed to being in control and

master of his own fate. All his adult life he had been a man of action, a decision maker, a mover, a doer. He was not used to standing idly by in an emergency, no matter what the emergency was. But at this moment, perhaps the most crucial in his life, he had no alternative. He was not a doctor, and therefore he could do nothing to help the woman he loved beyond all reason. His frustration mounted, drew level with his fear.

Just before three o'clock he was permitted to see Maddy in Recovery. She was unresponsive, unaware of his presence, still in a coma. He returned to the private room filled with fresh anguish and distress and a burgeoning despair.

Daisy and Shane endeavored to comfort him, to reassure him, but they were not very successful.

"I know there is no wisdom at a time like this," Daisy said, going to Philip, taking hold of his arm, filled with compassion for her son and concern for her daughter-in-law's well-being. "But we must try to be brave and have hope, darling. Maddy is strong. If anyone can pull through this, why she can."

He looked down at Daisy and nodded, then turned away from her so that she would not see the pain and heartache flooding his face.

Alan Stimpson arrived at four and quietly

told them he had performed the brain scan on Madelana.

"Your wife did have a massive brain hemorrhage, as I originally thought when I first examined her, but I wanted to be absolutely positive," he reported.

Philip swallowed. His worst fears had been confirmed. His voice shook slightly when he asked, "Have you any idea what might have caused the hemorrhage?"

Alan Stimpson was silent for a split second. "It may very well have developed because of her pregnancy. There have been similar cases."

Appalled, Philip had no words.

"I want to operate, to trepan her skull now, Mr. Amory. I thought you would wish to see her before she is prepared for surgery."

"Yes, I do." Philip glanced at his mother. "We ought to have sent for Father Ryan. Maddy would have wanted her priest here, no matter what the outcome of the operation. Could you call him for me, Mother?"

Unnerved though she was by this sudden request, which underscored her own considerable fears for Maddy, Daisy nodded. "Yes," she said as steadily as possible, "I'll do it now, darling."

"There is every chance the operation will be successful," Alan Stimpson said confidently, looking with swiftness from Daisy to Philip.

"And I will do everything in my power to save her life."

"I know you will," Philip said.

The two men were silent as they walked down the corridor together. The brain surgeon showed Philip into the anteroom, which was a few steps away from the operating theater, and closed the door softly behind him.

Philip walked over to Maddy.

He stood gazing down at her, loving her with all his heart. How small and defenseless she looked, lying there on the narrow hospital bed. Her face was chalk white, the color of the sheets. Earlier, Alan Stimpson had told him they would have to shave off her hair. That beautiful chestnut hair. He did not care as long as they saved her life. It was fanned out on the pillow around her face. He touched it, feeling its silkiness, and then he bent, kissed a strand.

Seating himself on the chair, he took her hand in his. It was listless. He brought his face close to hers, kissed her cheek. Against her hair, he whispered, "Don't leave me, Maddy. Please don't leave me. Fight. Fight for your life, my darling."

Finally lifting his head, he stared at her for the longest moment, hoping and praying for a flicker of understanding, a sign that she had heard him.

He knew she had not. She was so very still.

He kissed her again and left. He felt as if his heart was cracking in half.

"My watch has stopped," Daisy said to Shane. "What time is it?"

Shane glanced at his wrist. "Almost six. Shall I go and rustle up a pot of tea?"

"Yes, I think I could use a cup. What about you, Father Ryan?"

Maddy's priest, who had arrived a little while ago, lifted his eyes from the prayer book in his hand. "Thank you, Mrs. Rickards, that's very kind. I'll join you."

"Philip?"

"I'd prefer a cup of coffee, Ma, if—" he began and stopped short when Alan Stimpson entered the room.

The surgeon closed the door behind him, leaned against it. He was dressed in his green cotton surgical gown and pants, had obviously come straight from the operating theater. He remained standing by the door, not speaking, his eyes riveted on Philip.

Philip stared back at him. There was such an odd expression on the surgeon's face, one he could not quite fathom . . .

Alan Stimpson said, "I'm sorry, so very, very sorry, Mr. Amory. I did everything within my skill to save your wife . . . but I'm afraid she just died on the operating table. I'm so sorry."

"No," Philip said. "No."

He reached for the chair he was standing behind, gripped it to steady himself. The knuckles of his tanned hands turned white. He swayed slightly.

"No," he repeated.

Father Ryan rose, helped Daisy to her feet. Tears had sprung into her eyes, and she clamped a hand over her mouth to hold back the sob rising in her throat. She moved rapidly toward Philip, followed by Shane and Father Ryan.

Daisy's heart was breaking for her son. She dared not contemplate the effect Maddy's death would have on him. He had worshiped his wife. Life is not fair, Daisy thought, her eyes brimming. Maddy was too young to leave us.

Philip sidestepped his mother, Shane, and the concerned priest, shaking his head violently from side to side as though denying the surgeon's words. His blue eyes were stunned, uncomprehending. He got hold of Alan Stimpson's arm. "Take me to my wife," he rasped.

Stimpson led him back to the small anteroom near the operating theater where he left him alone with Maddy.

Once more Philip stood gazing down at her. How peaceful she looked in death. There was not a trace of pain or suffering on her face. He knelt beside the bed, took hold of her hand. It was icy. Irrationally, he tried to warm it.

"Maddy! Maddy!" he suddenly cried in a low voice raw with agony. "Why did you have to die? I have nothing without you. Nothing at all . . . Oh Maddy, Maddy . . ."

He bent his head and his scalding tears fell on his fingers, which were tightly holding hers, and he stayed there with her for a long time until Shane came and led him away.

37

He took her back to Dunoon.

After a short private service at St. Mary's Roman Catholic Cathedral in Sydney, he flew her body to the sheep station at Coonamble. He sat next to her coffin the entire way. Shane accompanied him.

His mother and Jason followed in Jason's corporate jet, bringing with them Father Ryan and Barry Graves.

Once Philip's plane had landed, he had her coffin driven up to the manor where it was placed in the long gallery amidst the portraits of his ancestors. It rested there overnight.

The following morning dawned bright and

clear with a sky vividly blue and spotless, and in the brilliant, shimmering sunlight the gardens and grounds of Dunoon looked magnificent. But Philip saw nothing. He was numb with shock, doing the things he had to do automatically, by rote, and for the most part he was oblivious to those around him.

To carry her coffin on the last stage of its journey he chose as the pallbearers Shane, Jason, Barry, Tim, the station manager, and Matt and Joe, the grooms, who had become devoted to her in the brief time she had lived there.

At exactly ten o'clock on Saturday morning, the six men shouldered her coffin and carried it out of the manor. They followed Father Ryan down the winding path that cut through the spacious lawns and flower gardens and led to the little private cemetery beyond. It was in a sheltered glade surrounded by trees and enclosed by an old stone wall. Here Andrew McGill, the founding father, was buried along with his wife, Tessa, and all of the other Australian McGills who were descended from them, their graves marked by simple marble headstones.

Philip had chosen the plot next to Paul for his wife.

The first day he had ever set eyes on Madelana O'Shea, she had been gazing at Paul's portrait, had later said that she thought it was the great man himself suddenly sprung to life when she had seen *him* hovering in the doorway of the gallery. Maddy had often teasingly remarked that he looked like a riverboat gambler, just as his grandfather had, and she had been as fascinated by Paul McGill as she had been by Emma Harte.

And so he thought it appropriate, very fitting, that her final resting place was with his grandfather. In the most curious way, it was oddly comforting to him to know that they lay close together in this patch of earth.

The priest and Philip and the pallbearers finally came to a standstill by the open grave. It was in a corner of the cemetery, shaded by the lovely golden elms and lemon-scented eucalyptus trees she had come to love, just as she had come to love Dunoon and the glorious land upon which it stood, and which had so reminded her of her native Kentucky.

Daisy was waiting with Mrs. Carr, the housekeeper, the household staff, and the other men and women who worked on the sheep station, their spouses and their children. Everyone was dressed in black, or wore black arm bands on their most somber clothes, and the women and children carried sprays of flowers or held single blooms in their hands. And as they stood with their heads bowed, listening to Father Ryan conduct the Roman Catholic burial service, they openly wept for Madelana, whom they had held in great affection, and who had lived with them at Dunoon for far too short a time.

Philip's grief had turned inward.

It was frozen inside him, and he was dry-eyed throughout the ceremony. He stood stiffly, his body rigid, his hands clenched at his sides. There was a grim moroseness about him, and his vivid, cornflower eyes were hollow, empty, his handsome face thinner, wiped clean of all expression. He was a forbidding figure, and there was an aloofness about him that held everyone at bay.

When the final prayer for Maddy's soul had been offered up by Father Ryan, and her coffin had been lowered into the earth, he accepted the whispered, heartfelt condolences of his employees, then strode swiftly back to the manor.

Shane and Daisy hurried after him. He spoke not at all until they were inside the house. Turning to them in the great hall, he muttered, "I can't stay here. I'm going, Ma. I have to be by myself."

Daisy looked up at her son. Her face was drawn, white, her eyes red from crying. She touched his arm gently. "Please don't let it be like it was when your father was killed in the avalanche, Philip. You must get the pain out, you must grieve for your Maddy. Only then will you be able to function properly again, go on living."

He looked at Daisy as if not seeing her. His eyes pierced right through her, focused on some distant image that was visible only to him. "I don't want to live. Not without Maddy."

"Don't say such a thing! You're a young man!" Daisy cried.

"You don't understand, Mother. I've lost everything."

"But there's the baby, your daughter, Maddy's daughter," Daisy said swiftly. She was wretched, heartsick, and her feelings were only too transparent on her troubled face.

Once more Philip stared right through his mother. He made no comment, swung around, crossed the entrance hall, and left the manor without a backward glance.

Daisy watched him go, filled with the most enormous pain for her son. She began to weep quietly, turned to Shane. There was a dreadful helplessness about her. She did not know what to do.

Shane put his arm around her, led her into the drawing room. "Philip will be all right," he assured her. "He's in shock right now, not thinking straight."

"Yes, I know that, Shane, but I'm so afraid

for him. So is Paula," Daisy said tearfully. "She told me so yesterday when she phoned from London. She said, 'He mustn't let his grief fester inside him like he did when Daddy died. If he does, he'll never recover from Maddy's death.' I know exactly what she means. And she's right of course."

Daisy sat down on the sofa, fished around in her bag for her handkerchief, wiped her eyes, blew her nose. She glanced at Shane standing by the fireplace, added pointedly, "Perhaps we made a terrible mistake, stopping Paula from flying out here."

"No, Daisy, we *didn't!* It's much too long a trip for her to make for only three or four days! Philip was the first one to say so. He was quite adamant that she stayed in England."

"She might have been able to help him. They've always been close, Shane, you *know* that."

"True, she might," Shane agreed, softening his tone. "On the other hand, I don't think that even *her* presence would have diminished the shock, eased his suffering. It's the terrible suddenness, the unexpectedness that has so thrown him, quite aside from his awful pain. And that's perfectly understandable, when you consider that less than a week ago Maddy was in blooming health, awaiting the birth of their child. Everything was wonderful for them, and they were so much in love. And then *wham!* Overnight she's dead. He's been hit between the eyes, he's literally staggering from this tragedy, Daisy. But he *will* recoup. He has to . . . he's no alternative. We just have to give him time."

"I don't know," Daisy said doubtfully, "he worshiped Maddy."

"That he did," Jason said, striding into the drawing room, hurrying to be at Daisy's side. "And he'll suffer for a very long period. But Shane *is* correct, darlin', Philip will recover. *Eventually.* Somehow we all do, don't we?"

"Yes," Daisy whispered, remembering David.

Jason seated himself next to her, placed an arm around her comfortingly. "Now, sweet'art," he went on, "try not to worry about him."

"I can't help it." She looked at Shane. "Where do you think he's gone?"

"Most likely to Sydney . . . to be by himself. Like an animal in pain, he wants to lick his wounds in private."

Jason volunteered, "Philip has a huge conglomerate to run and he's very conscientious, Daisy. You'll see, he'll be at the helm on Monday, as usual, and if I know him as well as I think I do, he'll throw himself into business with a vengeance."

"And the work will be his salvation," Shane interjected quietly. "He'll use it as an antidote to grief yet again, as he did when David was killed, and it'll help him to keep going until the healing process starts."

"I hope he *will* come to grips with his sorrow, and that he'll make some sort of life for himself in the future," Daisy said.

She looked from her husband to her son-in-law with a worried frown. "Philip can be so odd. He's been an enigma to many people for years, including me at times." She sighed, and then unexpectedly her eyes filled again. "Poor Maddy, I loved that girl so very much. But then we all did, didn't we? And she was like a second daughter to me. Why did *she* have to die?" Daisy shook her head, and before either man could comment, she continued softly, "But it's always the good ones who go, isn't it? It's all so unfair . . . *so unfair.*" Tears spilled from Daisy's eyes, trickled down her cheeks.

Jason drew her into his arms. "Ah, me darlin', me darlin'," he murmured, wanting to soothe her, to calm her. He was at a loss, had no words. He knew only too well that words were cold comfort at a time like this.

After a moment or two, Daisy took hold of herself, sat up straighter, blew her nose, patted her eyes. Her expression was one of sudden resolve, and she said in her bravest voice, "We must be as strong as we possibly can to help Philip pull through this tragedy."

"He knows we're here for him," Shane said, giving Daisy his most cheerful smile, trying to be as reassuring as he could. "Take heart."

"Yes, yes, I will." She swiveled to face Jason. "Where is Father Ryan?"

"He's in the library with Tim and his wife, and some of the others. Mrs. Carr is serving coffee and cake and drinks for those who prefer something stronger."

"How rude of us! We should be there!" Daisy announced, immediately rising. "We must stand in for Philip." She hurried out.

Jason followed on her heels with Shane in his wake.

Privately, Shane was desperately worried about Philip, despite his encouraging words to Daisy. He could not wait to leave Dunoon on Monday morning. He was impatient to get back to Sydney, wanted to be close to Philip, to keep a watchful eye on him.

No one ever knew where Philip had gone that weekend after he had left Dunoon with such abruptness on the day of Maddy's funeral.

When Shane had tried to reach him later that night at the Point Piper house, Mrs. Ordens had said he was not there. Nor was he at the penthouse in the McGill Tower, according to José, the Filipino houseman.

Whether or not these two were lying on behalf of their employer, Shane could not quite determine; he did not even try very hard, knowing that if Philip wanted to hide behind the domestic help he would do so. He could be as stubborn as Paula. It was a family trait inherited from Emma Harte.

And then on Monday morning, Philip had walked into his suite of offices in the McGill Tower as he always did at seven-thirty precisely, and called Maggie and Barry into his inner sanctum for their usual early morning confab.

There was an air of such cold containment about him, and he appeared to be so formidable in his iron-clad grief, both Maggie and Barry dare not make a consoling gesture toward him, or venture any kind of personal comment whatsoever.

As Jason had predicted, Philip threw himself into work, and with a fury that defied description. As the days passed, his hours grew longer and longer. He rarely went upstairs to the penthouse before nine or nine-thirty in the evening, where he ate a light supper prepared by the Filipino houseman. He then retired to his bedroom, rose the following morning at six, was back in his office at seven-thirty, never once deviating from this relentless schedule. He had no social life, no contact with any persons other than his employees. In fact, he shunned everyone who was not directly involved with him in business, including his mother and Shane, to whom he was the closest. They became increasingly troubled by his behavior, but were helpless to do anything.

Barry Graves, who was with Philip most of the time during business hours, kept expecting him to make some sort of reference to Maddy, or to her death, or to the child, but he never did. And, to Barry, he appeared to become colder and more introverted as time passed. There was a sheathed anger in him that Barry knew would have to erupt in some form or another before very long.

Finally, in desperation, Barry called Daisy at her Rose Bay house one afternoon, and spoke to her confidentially, and at length, about her son and his concern for him.

The minute she hung up on Barry, Daisy telephoned Shane, who had just returned from a two-day trip to Melbourne and Adelaide, where he had been visiting the O'Neill hotels.

"I have to come into Sydney today . . . in a short while, in fact. May I pop in to see you, Shane?" Daisy asked.

"Of course," he said. "That'll be fine." He glanced at the clock on his desk. It was exactly five minutes past three. "Come by in about an hour. We'll have tea together and a nice chat, Daisy dear."

"Thanks, Shane, I appreciate it."

Promptly at four, his secretary showed his mother-in-law into his private office in the Sydney-O'Neill Hotel. Shane rose, went around the desk to greet her.

After kissing her on the cheek, he held her away, eyed her closely. "You look lovely, as usual, Daisy. But troubled," he said soberly. "About Philip," he added, leading her over to the sofa in front of the wall of plate glass overlooking Sydney Harbour.

Daisy made no comment.

They sat down together. She reached out, took hold of his hand, stared into his face. She had known him all his life, since the day he was born, and she loved him like a child of her own.

She said, after a moment, "You've always been such a good friend to me, Shane, not to mention a wonderful son-in-law. You were a great comfort to me when Mother died, and I don't think I'll ever forget how supportive you were at that most awful time in my life—when David was killed. You've been a rock for me, and for Paula, too. Now, yet again, I must ask you to help me, to do something else for me."

"You know I'll do anything I can, Daisy."

"Go to Philip," she said, leaning closer to Shane with some urgency. "Talk to him. Try to get through to him. Make him see that he'll become ill if he goes on like this."

"But he won't see me!" Shane exclaimed. "It takes me all my time to get through to him on the phone! You know I ring him every day. Maggie literally has to force him to take my calls. It's one hell of a tussle, I don't mind telling you. And when I ask to see him, beg almost, he hides behind pressure of work, business meetings, and the like."

"Oh yes, I know, I'm having the same problems with him myself. And encountering the same type of resistance. But I believe you're one of the two people who *can* get through to Philip. The other is Paula, but she's not here. So it has to be you. Please, please do this for me, and for Philip. Help him to help himself," she pleaded, her desperation surfacing.

Shane was silent, ruminative.

Daisy said swiftly, "Go over to the penthouse tonight! Force your way in! Actually, that won't be necessary. I'll phone José, alert him that you're coming. He'll let you in, and once you're inside the penthouse, Philip will see you, I'm sure of that."

"All right," he agreed. "I'll go. I'll do my best."

"Thank you, Shane." She tried to smile without success. "Barry's been helpful," Daisy now explained. "But there's only so far he can go with Philip. He's awfully worried about him. He says Philip's full of anger. Rage, really. Rage that Maddy died. He doesn't seem able to accept it, or place her death in any kind of perspective."

"It's been the worst shock to him . . . a very severe shock."

Daisy opened her mouth, closed it, bit her inner lip. Then she said softly, "Oh Shane, he hasn't even been to see the baby since Jason and I brought her to our house from the hospital, or asked me about her either."

Shane was not altogether surprised to hear this. "Give him time on that one," he said and paused thoughtfully. He chose his words with care when he added, "He may well blame the baby for Maddy's death, and therefore himself, since he is the father of the child. Remember what Alan Stimpson said—that Maddy's pregnancy might have caused her to have the brain hemorrhage. I haven't forgotten how appalled Philip looked on hearing those words."

Daisy nodded. "Neither have I, and I'd thought of that, too. Blaming himself, I mean." She sighed heavily. "Barry says Philip sinks into the most awful depressions. Maddy's death is a terrible scar on his heart, one that will take months to heal."

If it ever does, Shane thought gloomily, although he did not voice this opinion to his mother-in-law, seeing no reason to worry her unduly. Instead, he said, "Now, tell me about the baby, Daisy."

Instantly her face changed, lit up. "Oh Shane, she's the most adorable little thing. Actually she reminds me of your Linnet and Emily's Natalie. She's definitely going to be another Botticelli redhead . . . she's a real little Harte through and through."

Shane smiled and nodded and listened, giving Daisy every ounce of his attention. He knew how important it was for her to speak about her new granddaughter, the long-awaited heiress to the great McGill empire. Poor kid, he thought suddenly at one moment, she's come into this world under a cloud and carrying a rotten burden . . . her mother's death. Shane knew then that he had to do everything within his power to make Philip accept and love the baby. For both of their sakes. The father needed the daughter just as much as the daughter needed him.

After Daisy finally left, Shane waded through an enormous amount of paperwork that had been accumulating over the past week. He then penned a quick but loving note to Paula, and wrote postcards to Lorne, Tessa, Patrick, and Linnet. He finished just before six o'clock, when he went into a meeting with Graham Johnson, managing director of the O'Neill hotel chain in Australia, and three of the other top executives in the company. The main subject on the agenda was the new O'Neill hotel currently under construction in Perth.

At seven-thirty Shane brought the meeting to a close, and he and Graham walked over to the Wentworth for dinner. When Shane was in Sydney, he always made it a point to visit other hotels in the city. He liked to take stock of the decor, food, drink, service, and conditions in general, in order to make comparisons between the competition and his own hotel. He had always liked the Wentworth, and he and Graham spent a pleasant couple of hours together over a delicious meal of roast baby lamb with the most succulent vegetables, and an excellent bottle of local red wine. For the most part they spoke about business, covering various aspects of the new hotel in Perth. Shane agreed to fly out to

Western Australia with Graham the following week, before returning to London.

It was ten o'clock when the two men exited the hotel. Graham took a taxi home, and Shane strode off in the direction of Bridge Street where the McGill Tower was located. He needed the walk and the fresh air, after being cooped up in the executive offices of the hotel all day; also, he wanted to be certain Philip had finished dinner and was relaxing when he arrived at the penthouse. Daisy had suggested that he get there around ten-thirty and he had taken her advice.

A little while later, as he approached the black-glass skyscraper, Shane steeled himself for the impending encounter with his brother-in-law. He knew it was going to be difficult—painful, emotional, and upsetting. Riding up in the elevator, he asked himself what kind of wisdom he could offer Philip in his pain and sorrow, and he realized that he had none. All he could do was talk to the other man with compassion, give him his understanding, his support, and his love.

As prearranged by Daisy, the houseman, José, let Shane into the apartment as soon as he rang the doorbell.

The Filipino showed him into the beautiful cream-and-white living room that floated high over the city. It was dimly lit tonight, permitting the spectacular view to dominate. Bowing politely, the houseman said, "I tell Mr. Amory you here, sir."

"Thank you, José." Shane strolled over to a chair and sat down.

A split second later José was back, bowing again. "Mr. Amory says please wait."

"Yes, all right. Thanks again."

The Filipino smiled and bowed and hurried out on silent feet.

After fifteen minutes had elapsed, Shane grew restless, wondering what was keeping Philip. He got to his feet, walked over to the bar set against the far wall, poured himself a small cognac. He carried this back to the chair, where once more he sat down to wait. Sipping the drink, he mentally prepared himself for Philip, seeking the right words to use, the proper approach to take with him. One thing was vital. No matter what else he accomplished tonight, he must persuade Philip to go to Daisy's house with him tomorrow. To see the baby. He had made that promise to Daisy, and he himself knew how important it was that Philip put aside any feeling of blame, all guilt. Shane was convinced the baby was the key to Philip's well-being. Once he accepted her, he would love her, and only then would he begin to recover from his grief for Maddy, the loss of her.

It was another fifteen minutes before Philip finally emerged from his study. He stood hovering in the entrance to the living room, silently staring at Shane, his demeanor morose.

Shane rose at once, took a step forward, then stopped abruptly with a quick intake of breath. It took all of his self-control not to exclaim in concern when he saw his brother-in-law's appearance. Philip had lost weight, and there was an air of exhaustion about him, but it was his face that so appalled. It was ravaged. The cheeks were hollow, gaunt, the bright blue eyes dulled and red-rimmed, the purplish shadows beneath resembling dark bruises. The most startling thing of all, perhaps, was his black hair. It had turned pure white on either side of his temples.

There had never been any question in Shane's mind that Philip had taken Maddy's death badly; he had merely miscalculated the extent of his agony. The man was lacerated inside, suffering more horribly than even Shane had imagined. He understood then that whatever exterior equanimity Philip may display to the world it was utterly fraudulent. His cold containment and aloofness, so described by Barry, were his only defenses against total collapse. All this instantly became clear to Shane as he regarded Philip, and his heart went out to him.

Shane moved forward, and the two men clasped hands with their usual familial warmth.

Philip said, "I almost sent you away." He let go of Shane's hand, shrugged wearily, walked to the bar where he poured himself a large vodka, added ice cubes from the silver bucket.

"But there was no point—I suddenly realized that," he went on without turning around. "I knew you'd be back tomorrow or the day after and that my mother would come. And Jason. And then it occurred to me that one of you might have the insane idea of dragging Paula out here, so I decided I'd better see you . . ." Philip did not bother to finish his sentence. His voice was drained. He was worn out from lack of sleep, and his tiredness became apparent as he lethargically ambled over to the sofa and sat down. His usual vitality and vigor had fled.

Shane observed him quietly for a moment, then murmured, "It's been three weeks since Maddy was buried, and in that time you've seen me only once, Daisy only once. Your mother is worried about you, Philip, and so am I, for that matter."

"Don't be! I'm okay!" Philip said snappishly, with more spirit than he had displayed thus far.

"That's not true! You're not okay!" Shane shot back.

"Oh for God's sake, I'm fine."

"I don't think you are. And, very frankly, you need your family around you at a time like this. You need me and Daisy and Jason. Don't shun us, please. We want to help you, Philip, to comfort you as best we can."

"There is no comfort for me. I'll survive— everyone survives, I suspect. But the sorrow will stay with me forever . . . she was so young, don't you see? One expects old people to die . . . that's the life cycle. When we bury the old, time heals the pain eventually. But when we bury the young, the pain never, ever goes away."

"It will, please believe me, it will," Shane answered in his most compassionate voice. "And Maddy wouldn't want you to be like this. She would want you to take strength from—"

"I don't want you to make one religious statement to me, Shane!" Philip exclaimed with a flash of irritation.

"I wasn't going to," Shane replied gently.

Philip let out a long wearisome sigh, leaned back against the sofa, closed his eyes.

A silence drifted between the two men for a short while.

Suddenly, Philip got to his feet, went over to the bar, plopped more ice into his glass. He gave Shane a most penetrating stare, said in the bleakest of voices, "I can't remember anything about the past year, Shane. That's the most horrendous thing. It's . . . it's . . . *blank.* She's gone as if she never existed in my life." His voice broke, and he said hoarsely, "I can't remember *her* . . . I can't remember Maddy."

"That's the shock," Shane was quick to say, speaking with assurance, knowing this was the truth. "Really, it's only the shock, Philip. She'll come back to you."

Philip shook his head with vehemence. "No, she won't. I know she won't."

"The body is dead, but you have the spirit," Shane told him. "She's alive in you. Her spirit is in you, and in the child. Only her body's gone. Please believe that. Maddy is in your heart and in your memories, and she will be with you always. And there is the child."

Philip made no response.

He moved away from the bar, slowly crossed the room to the window, moving like an old man. He stood looking out. He had listened carefully to Shane, had absorbed his words. Now he was trying to come to terms with them, to accept them. Were they true? Was Maddy's spirit in him? Would she be with him always?

He sighed. He found no solace in anything Shane had just said to him. He had acknowledged the finality of death days ago, had acknowledged that his Maddy was gone from him forever. She had meant everything to him. She had been his life. Maddy had made the pain inside him stop, and just thinking about her had given him the happiest feeling, had warmed his heart. Now he could not even recall her face in his mind's eye. He had to look at a photograph to remember her. He did not understand why this was so. He had loved her so very much.

He snapped his eyes tightly shut, rested his aching head against the glass. He had killed her. He had killed the woman he loved more than life itself through the very act of love . . .

Shane said something, and Philip opened his eyes, but he did not answer. He had not been listening to his brother-in-law.

He stared at the night sky. How magnificent it was tonight, a deep midnight blue, velvet smooth, cloudless, filled with diamond stars and the bright, winking lights of the city's many skyscrapers. And off toward the eastern suburbs the sky was a curious amethyst spreading into the most vibrant of golds and a warm, glowing red.

It will be a beautiful day tomorrow, Philip thought absently. *Red sky at night, shepherd's delight, red sky at morning, shepherd's warning.* How many times had his grandmother said that to him when he was a little boy growing up. Emma had always been fascinated by skies and the light in them. Unexpectedly, the beauty of this evening's sky brought a lump to his throat and he did not comprehend exactly why. And then he remembered. Maddy, too, had forever commented about the clarity of light, cloud formations, the changing colors of the day as it moved into night.

Suddenly Philip stiffened, stepped closer to the window, frowning, his eyes focused on a dark cloud mass moving up above the skyscrapers several blocks away. How odd it looked. He couldn't quite make out what it was. "Oh my God!" he exclaimed a split second later. "Oh my God!"

Shane was on his feet, hurrying over to him. "What's wrong? Don't you feel well?"

Philip swung around, grabbed Shane's arm, pulled him over to the window. "Look! Over there! The black smoke, the red glow. Oh Christ, Shane, you've got a fire! The Sydney-O'Neill is on fire!"

Shane tensed. The breath caught in his throat as he followed Philip's gaze. He did not know the Sydney skyline as well as his brother-in-law, and it took him a moment to distinguish the smoke, find its source. He knew at once that it *was* his hotel going up in flames. He had just located the huge expanse of glass window wall that fronted his famous Orchid Room.

Without a word he pivoted, shot across the floor.

Philip followed, fast on his heels.

Together they took the elevator down, staring at each other speechlessly and in horror. As the elevator doors slid open, both men hit the lobby simultaneously, raced out into Bridge Street.

They began to run in the direction of the Sydney-O'Neill, the sound of their pounding feet drowned out by the screaming sirens of the three fire engines hurtling past them at breakneck speed.

38

As Shane ran on, heading for the hotel, he was not sure what to expect when he got there. Disaster, obviously, but to what extent and degree he was uncertain.

Only a hotelier understood the true horror of a hotel fire and its nightmarish consequences. So all of Shane's senses were alert to the greatest possible danger, endless problems of the most appalling kind. There would be panic, fear, chaos, and every type of injury. Smoke inhalation, burns, broken bones, trauma, shock. And death.

Rounding the corner of the street, he came into full view of the Sydney-O'Neill, his favorite hotel in the international chain. What he saw brought him to a complete standstill. "Oh God! No! No!" he gasped out loud. He was momentarily stunned, rooted to the spot.

His hotel was an inferno.

Flames, black smoke, heat confronted him. Helicopters circled and hovered over the top of the burning building, lifting people off the roof. Fire engines were in full operation with swarms of fire fighters manning hoses from the ground and from ladders; others were using ropes and ladders to rescue those trapped on some of the high floors.

There were ambulances and police cars parked at various strategic points. Doctors, paramedics, and the police were doing everything in their power to help those in need. Three ambulances carrying the injured sped past him, their sirens wailing as they headed to the nearest hospital.

Shane pulled his handkerchief out of his pocket, wiped his damp face. He was sweating profusely from running, the sudden intense heat, and fear for those who might still be trapped in the hotel. The scene before him was appalling, just as he had anticipated. Everywhere there was broken glass, debris on the ground, blinding smoke that was lethal in itself, the raised voices of police and hotel staff shouting orders, the sounds of crying and moaning from those in distress. A group of hotel guests, many of them in their night clothes, looked unnerved and frightened as they huddled together near a police car. Shane was about to go over to them when he saw two of the hotel's porters assisting them. They were taken over to the ambulance set up as a first-aid unit; here they would be treated for minor injuries, shock, and trauma.

Covering his mouth with his handkerchief, Shane pushed his way through the people milling around—hotel staff and security guards, police officers, paramedics, and ambulance drivers. He had to get closer to the hotel, knew he must take command of the situation immediately.

A policeman stopped him. "You can't go any nearer than this, sir. It could be dangerous."

"Thanks, officer, for your warning. But I'm Shane O'Neill, the owner of the hotel. I must get through, do what I can to help."

"Go right ahead, Mr. O'Neill," the officer said, suddenly recognizing him. He gave Shane a sympathetic look as he let him pass through the wooden barricade that had been erected.

Almost at once Shane spotted Peter Wood, the night duty manager. He grabbed his arm.

Wood swung around almost violently. A look of relief spread across his grimy face when he saw it was Shane. "Mr. O'Neill! Thank God you're okay! We tried to ring you when the first alarm went off around eleven o'clock. We realized you weren't in your suite. But we didn't know whether you were somewhere else in the hotel. We've been as worried as hell, keeping our eyes peeled for you."

"I was out of the hotel," Shane said. He gave the night manager a hard stare. "Do you know how many casualties there have been?"

Peter Wood shook his head. "Not exactly. But I'd say about fifteen people injured." He paused, dropped his voice. "And four dead, I think."

"Oh Jesus!" Shane drew Wood to one side as several guests were being shepherded to safety by a hotel security guard. When they were out of earshot, he asked, "Do we know what started this?"

"No. But I have my own ideas."

Shane peered at him swiftly, frowning. "You're not suggesting arson?"

"No, no. Why would anyone want to set the hotel on fire?"

"A disgruntled employee, perhaps? One who'd been sacked recently?"

Wood said very firmly, "No, Mr. O'Neill, I'm sure it's nothing like that. If you want my opinion, I believe it was an accident."

"I see. Where did it start, Peter?"

"On the thirty-fourth floor." Wood gave

Shane a pointed look. "You were lucky, Mr. O'Neill. You had a narrow escape."

Shane stared at Wood, the full impact of the manager's words suddenly hitting him. His own suite was on that floor, along with a number of other private apartments leased out on a permanent basis. There were rooms and suites for hotel guests on the thirty-fifth floor, and situated on the thirty-sixth floor, at the very top of the building, was the famous Orchid Room.

Shane exclaimed, "I can only thank God that I closed the entire thirty-fifth floor and the Orchid Room for redecoration last week. Otherwise this disaster would have been ten times worse if we'd had guests on the thirty-fifth floor, not to mention two hundred people dining and dancing in the restaurant tonight."

"Yes, we've all been saying the same thing."

"I presume most of the guests have been evacuated to emergency facilities in other hotels?"

Wood nodded. "To the Hilton and the Wentworth. We're lucky in another sense, sir. The O'Neill was not filled to capacity this week."

Philip ran up to them at this moment. He was out of breath, perspiring. "I've been looking for you," he said to Shane, then turned, nodded to Peter Wood. "What can I do to help?"

"Not very much," Shane replied. "From what I can see, the actions of my staff and the various agencies called to the scene have been tremendous. It *looked* like chaos when I arrived a few minutes ago, but it's not. They seem to have things under control." He glanced toward the hotel, his expression pained. Two of the middle floors were still burning, but reinforcements had been brought in; additional fire fighters were tackling the blaze with renewed energy, would soon have it put out.

Philip said, "Perhaps I can—"

Neither Shane nor Peter Wood heard what he said next. His voice was drowned out by a thunderous explosion that sounded like several huge kegs of dynamite going off. It rent the air, made all of them jump. They swung to stare at the hotel. Shock and apprehension flooded their faces.

"What the bloody hell was that?" Philip cried.

"Windows blowing out from the intense heat within the shell of the hotel," Shane said, shuddering. He dreaded to think that there might be more casualties.

"But I don't see any broken glass falling," Philip muttered, looking baffled.

"Neither do I," Shane said. "But I'm sure that's what it was."

Peter Wood volunteered, "It's probably the

windows on the other side of the building, Mr. Amory, the rooms facing Sydney Harbour."

A young woman wearing a dressing gown, her face streaked with dirt, hurried up to them. She appeared distracted, afraid. "Please help me," she said, tugging at Philip's arm. "Please, please help me. I can't find my little girl. She's lost. I can't find her. I know we got her out. I know we did." The woman's face crumpled. She began to weep hysterically.

Philip put his arm around her. "I'm sure she's in a safe spot. Come along, I'll help you to find your child."

"She's only four," the woman sobbed. "A baby, just a baby."

Philip attempted to comfort her as he led her off. His own agony, his all-consuming grief were forgotten in the horrendous tragedy of the fire.

By four o'clock in the morning the fire was out.

All of the injured, numbering some twenty-five, had been taken to the emergency room at St. Vincent's Hospital and to other hospitals in the city. The dead, totaling nine men and women, were in the morgue.

Fire fighters, police, and hotel staff were bringing complete order to the area. Shane had been in command for several hours, handling everything with cool authority and decisiveness.

The Sydney-O'Neill was a smouldering ruin, blackened by smoke, a burnt-out hulk against the skyline. Shane and Philip stood together in the rubble as dawn broke, looking up at it, both of their faces grim.

"What a horrible tragedy this has been," Shane murmured, turning to his brother-in-law. "So many injured and dead. It should never have happened. All I can think about are the families of those who died." He sighed heavily. "Well, I'm glad you were able to help that young woman. She was quite demented. Where *did* you find her little girl?"

"In one of the ambulances, being looked after by a paramedic. She wasn't injured, thankfully. Just scared after becoming separated from her mother." Philip took hold of Shane's arm, wanting to console him. "I'm sorry this disaster had to happen to you, Shane. You're suffering terribly because of the loss of lives, and for those who have been injured. But quite aside from that, I know how much you prided yourself on your safety systems."

When Shane was silent, Philip added, "I understand what this particular hotel meant to you. I'm so very sorry. I'll do anything I can to help you."

"Thanks, Philip." Shane rubbed his tired face, shook his head with weariness. So much for Blackie's dream, he thought, remembering how excited his grandfather had been about building the Sydney-O'Neill. It was he who had found and bought the land on a visit to Sydney with Emma years before, he who had decided it would be the flagship hotel in the Antipodes. Blackie had not lived to see it constructed, but he had approved of the first architectural blueprints before he died. Now his dream had gone up in smoke in the space of a few hours.

"I'll build it again," Shane said, as if making a promise to his grandfather.

"I know you will," Philip answered. "Now, come on back with me to the penthouse to clean up. You're going to need clothes and the like. It's a good thing we're about the same size."

Later that morning, showered, shaved, and wearing his brother-in-law's clothes, an exhausted Shane set up headquarters in the boardroom of the McGill Corporation.

It was here that he held his first meeting, began the investigation into the cause of the fire at his hotel. Present with him were Peter Wood, the night manager who had been on duty when the fire broke out; Lewis Bingley, the general manager; Graham Johnson, managing director of the O'Neill hotel chain in Australia, various executives from the Sydney-O'Neill, and Fire Chief Don Arnold, who had been in charge of the fire fighters the night before.

Once introductions had been made, greetings exchanged, Shane went straight to the heart of the matter. "We're looking to you for information at this moment, I'm afraid, Chief Arnold," he said. "I understand that you and your men have talked at length to many members of the hotel staff. Have you any idea how the fire started?"

"Through carelessness on the part of someone staying in the hotel," the chief said. "From what we found on the thirty-fourth floor, where it began, and from what we've since discovered, we're certain it was started by a cigarette. One that most probably fell into a sofa in a suite on that floor. One of the private jobs you lease out. In this instance, the suite leased to the Jaty Corporation."

"Could you go into a few more details, please, Chief Arnold?" Shane asked.

"Sure thing. One of the room service waiters came forward in the early hours of this morning. He told me that he remembered noticing an ashtray perched on the arm on a sofa in that particular suite. That was when he went to remove the dinner trolley around eight o'clock. I believe that the ashtray remained on the arm of the settee, that it was used several times before the couple occupying the suite went to bed. The ashtray later fell into the sofa, and a cigarette, which was not quite out, set light to the sofa. More than likely, it smouldered for a couple of hours until it actually burst into flames. Only seconds after waking, the two people in that private suite were dead."

"How do you know that?" Shane asked quietly.

"Two of my firemen found them huddled in the bedroom. They were not burnt. They were poisoned by the fumes from the foam stuffing in the sofa. It's so highly flammable that within seconds it creates the kind of inferno you had in your hotel last night. And those flames are so hot, so very intense, they can punch a hole in a wall or a ceiling, and shatter windows. The foam also gives off the most fatal fumes, chiefly cyanide and carbon monoxide."

Shane was horrified. He looked at Lewis Bingley, and exclaimed sharply, "Regulations against the use of foam in furniture were passed by the British Government in 1981. I've had foam banned in all my hotels for the past year. How come it was used here?"

Lewis Bingley shook his head. "We followed your instructions, Mr. O'Neill, we really did.

There is no foam in any of the furniture used in the hotel. You know we replaced all the furniture."

"But you just heard what Chief Arnold said! That sofa in the Jaty Corporation suite was upholstered with foam!"

The general manager pursed his lips nervously. "I can only think that it crept past us. *Somehow.* You see, Mr. O'Neill, the president of the Jaty Corporation used his own interior decorators, and they furnished the suite for him."

"Were they told of our new regulations?" Shane demanded.

"Oh yes. But they apparently ignored them," Bingley muttered.

"That is outrageous!" Shane exploded. "And in any case, we were remiss for not going back, checking that the decorators had heeded our warning about the foam." He tried to quiet his boiling anger, turned to the fire chief. "Who were the couple who died in the suite? Have they been identified yet?"

"The son and daughter-in-law of the president of the Jaty Corporation."

Shane shook his head sadly. His face was grave, troubled. "That's your analysis of how the fire began. But what happened next, Chief Arnold?"

"I think the sequence of events went like

this." Don Arnold then explained, "To quickly recap, the cigarette set the sofa alight. The foam smouldered, eventually burst into flames. That would have been around ten forty-five, ten-fifty, in my estimation. The flames had such intensity they blew out the windows within seconds. The sudden, new supply of oxygen created a wall of fire that burned right through the doors of the suite. Fuelled by the oxygen, the fire gained murderous force as it roared along the corridor of the thirty-fourth floor. It all happened in the space of minutes. Ten or fifteen, I'd say. Fire travels with the speed of light."

Shane nodded his understanding. He was unable to speak for a moment. He was shocked by what he had just heard. Negligence, he thought. First on the part of the decorators and then on the part of my management. They should have had that private suite checked once it was furnished. This tragedy might well have been avoided if they had. He sighed under his breath again. He had to hold Lewis Bingley accountable.

"One thing's for sure, Mr. O'Neill," Chief Arnold was saying, "your safety systems are the very best. The smoke detectors, the fire doors, and the sprinklers all worked like clockwork. If the hotel hadn't been as perfectly maintained for safety as it was, you would have had an even worse disaster on your hands."

Jason said, "This place gives me the joes."

Shane stared at him. "What do you mean?"

"It makes me depressed. It's so damn gloomy, the shades drawn, the lamps turned low." Jason eyed the half empty bottle of scotch on the coffee table. "And drinking in the middle of the afternoon, that's not you, Shane. Come on, mate, the booze ain't going to get you anywhere."

"I'm stone cold sober. But frankly, I feel like getting drunk. Bloody pissed to the gills, if you want to know the truth."

Jason shook his head. "You've had kronk mozzle, Shane, real bad luck. But you ain't no jackeroo. You know things like this can happen."

"I can't believe the hotel burned to the ground," Shane began and stopped. He sprang up, began pacing the floor as he had been doing off and on for days. *"Negligence! Sheer bloody negligence!"* he fumed. "If I'm not breathing down their necks every minute of the day, things start to go wrong—"

"You shouldn't be in business if you don't want the agro. And aggravation *is* the key word these days, mate. Still, I know what you mean.

663

The fire's been a bleedin' horrible tragedy. I can well understand why you're angry."

Shane exclaimed, "I pay the best wages, big bonuses, they get all kinds of benefits and God knows what else, and they can't check out the furniture in a bloody private suite. It's criminal, Jason. Criminal. You know as well as I do that the fire would never have happened if they'd been on top of the situation. Those poor people would not have died or been injured, if my managers had done their jobs properly. That's what makes my blood boil. So much pain and suffering for all those concerned. And I'm going to be up to my eyeballs in lawsuits and lawyers, not to mention insurance company investigators. Now *they're* about to start their own investigation into the fire."

"Well, that's to be expected, Shane," Jason was quick to point out. "And you *know* that. Anyway, they're going to come to the same conclusions as the fire chief, I'm sure. And look, there's no reason why you can't start making plans for the rebuilding of the Sydney-O'Neill, get the architects working on the blueprints already."

"I don't think I'm going to rebuild."

Jason was shocked. "You have to build a new hotel, Shane! You owe it to your grandfather. More importantly, you owe it to yourself."

Shane made no response. He sat down heavily on the sofa, dropped his head in his hands, this gesture full of weariness and despair.

Jason looked down at him, suddenly worried. He had never seen Shane like this, disheveled and unshaven, still wearing his pajamas and dressing gown in the middle of the afternoon. What was wrong with these young guys? Didn't they have any balls? First Philip had fallen apart after Maddy's death, and now Shane looked as if he was about to go to pieces, too.

Jason cleared his throat. "You were so abrupt with Daisy on the phone earlier, she asked me to come over to see what was going on here. She wants you to come out to Rose Bay for dinner tonight."

Shane lifted his head, shook it. "I have to work." He shoved the pile of folders on the coffee table in front of him. "I have all this paperwork about the fire to deal with."

"It's Saturday. You've got to take a break sometime. And by the way, where's Philip?"

"I honestly don't know, Jason. And if you'll forgive me, I really can't worry about him right now. Frankly, I've got enough problems of my own to contend with."

"Yes, I know. That's why Daisy and I want you to come over for dinner. It'll do you good to get out, to be with people."

"No, I want to be alone. And really, it's best that I am. I've a lot to do. And a lot of thinking to do."

"You know you can come over any time, if you change your mind."

"Yes. Thanks, Jason."

Shane picked up the bottle of scotch and poured himself another drink.

Jason shook his head sadly as he left the study, crossed the foyer, and quietly let himself out of the penthouse.

39

Alone, he rode across his land.

He was mounted on Black Opal, his ebony-colored stallion. Keeping pace at his side was a riderless horse. It was Gilda, the roan he had given Maddy after their marriage. Before leaving the stables he had strapped on Maddy's favorite silver-chased saddle, and turned the stirrups backward to symbolize that her owner would never ride her again.

It was the first time he had been back to Dunoon since he had buried Maddy here four weeks ago.

When he had arrived on Friday night, Tim and everyone else on the sheep station had welcomed him warmly, and it was apparent they were glad that he had at last returned. So was he.

Maddy's death had torn him apart, and he was filled with an unendurable sorrow. He had been afraid that it would be too painful to come here. They had been so happy together at Dunoon. But now, as he rode through the lovely, pastoral countryside on this Sunday afternoon, he felt a certain kind of peace settling over him. He knew that in part it was due to the tranquility, the gentleness, the stillness that abounded here.

He followed the Castlereagh River for a long time, then branched off, crossed several meadows, and took the winding track that led through the green hills of Dunoon. When he reached the crest of the steep incline, he dismounted, walked over to the great oak, stood gazing out across the extraordinary landscape.

How beautiful it looked after two days of rain. Everything was green and shimmering. It was the end of August, almost the end of winter. In a few weeks it would be spring; already the weather was superb, mild for this time of year. Philip lifted his eyes. The sky was a bright, polished blue, radiant with sunlight. The very perfection of the day seemed to underscore his

sadness. It was a day to share . . . with someone . . .

Philip turned away, went and sat down under
the oak, propped himself against its ancient
trunk. Taking off his flat-brimmed hat, he threw
it to one side, endeavoring to relax. His thoughts
were scattered, chaotic still, his mind fogged by
pain. But perhaps here he would be able to find
a little ease.

This was his special place; it always had been
since his childhood. Maddy, too, had grown to
love it up here on this high land. She had said it
was like being part of the sky. He smiled to himself at the remembrance, then recalled the morning he had met her in the portrait gallery, not
quite a year ago.

They had ridden out here, had sat for a while
under this leafy old tree. He had said some extremely personal things to her, which had even
startled him at the time. But she had not seemed
to mind. She had looked at him for the longest
moment, her lovely, intelligent gray eyes so
quiet and unwavering, but she had made no
comment. And at that precise moment he had
known he would marry her.

Madelana had been unique among the women
he had ever met. From the outset of their relationship there had been a strange familiarity
about her. It was as if he had known her, been

separated from her, then reunited with her again. He realized now that he had felt this way because he had been looking for someone like her all his life, that she was the woman he had idealized in his mind. He had found her finally, only to lose her . . . so quickly.

Maddy had had such inner grace. That, perhaps, had been the source of her radiance . . . she had been an incandescent being. A fragment of a poem by Rupert Brooke flashed through his mind . . . *All about you was the light that dims the greying end of night, . . . and, in the flowing of your dress, undiscerning tenderness.*

Philip sighed and closed his eyes, allowed himself to drift with his myriad thoughts, and slowly the memories came flooding back. He began to remember every little thing about their relationship . . . every single moment he had ever spent with her was suddenly crystal clear. He recalled the hours, the days, the weeks, the months. Each and every detail was precise and exactly in place, as if a reel of film was being projected before his eyes. And on that hillside, where he had been taken by Emma Harte as a boy, he found his Maddy again. He saw her as she had been the instant he had first set eyes on her in the gallery, her image intact. He smelled the fragrance of her hair, heard the laughter and joyousness in her voice, felt the gentle touch of her hand on his. And the tears came then, and he wept for her, and he remained on the hillside until the light began to fade.

And as he rode back to the manor, down through the green hills of Dunoon, the riderless horse at his side, he felt her presence everywhere, and he knew he would never lose his Maddy ever again. She was in his heart, and she would be a part of him for as long as he lived. Shane *had* been right. Her spirit *was* in him.

He flew back to Sydney late that night. Early on Monday morning he went out to Rose Bay.

His mother was startled to see him standing in the middle of her living room, and her surprise showed as she hurried to greet him.

Cool sunlight was pouring in through the windows, illuminating Philip's face most painfully. Daisy felt herself flinching inside and her heart shriveled. He looked as if he hadn't slept for weeks. His face was a study in desolation. There was a haggardness about him that startled her, as did the streaks of white in his black hair. It seemed to Daisy that he was a shadow of the man he had once been, his looks gone, his vigor and energy vitiated completely.

She wanted to take her son in her arms and comfort him, but she did not dare. He had pushed her away, held her at arm's length since

Maddy's death, and she had respected his wishes, had had no alternative but to leave him alone in his sorrow.

And so she was further surprised when he took a step forward, wrapped his arms around her. He held on to her tightly, as he had done when he was a small boy needing consolation, and she clung to him, loving him with all her heart. Neither spoke. This long embrace was enough; words were not needed. And Daisy understood deep within herself that the healing process had started for him. And she thanked God.

Eventually he released her and said, "Well, Mother, I thought I'd better come out to see you . . ."

"I'm so glad you did, Philip."

"I'm sorry for the way I've behaved, Ma. I realize I've been impossible, difficult with you, and with everyone else for that matter. But very simply, I couldn't help myself."

"Oh darling . . . I understand, truly I do. You've been suffering so very much."

"Yes." He hesitated a moment, then continued slowly, "Seeing Maddy's young life cut tragically short has been heartbreaking for me, and I honestly thought I would never be able to sustain the loss of her. It's been pure hell, Ma. But then last night, flying back from Dunoon, I began to realize there was also a degree of self-pity in my grief. I was not only mourning for Maddy, but mourning for myself as well . . . and mourning for the life we'll never have together now."

"That's only natural," Daisy murmured softly, her vivid blue eyes filling with sympathy and understanding.

"Yes, I suppose it is." He moved away from her, edged toward the door, then swung to face her suddenly. There was a little pause before he blurted out, "I've come to get the baby."

Daisy looked at him swiftly. Her heart lifted. "Fiona's with the nanny. The young Englishwoman Maddy engaged before she—" Daisy cut herself off, looked at Philip uneasily.

"Don't be afraid to mention Maddy's death, Ma. I've accepted it."

Daisy could only nod. She was reluctant to speak in case her voice trembled.

She led the way upstairs. "This is Mr. Amory. My son," Daisy said to the nanny as they entered the room.

"Yes, I know, Mrs. Rickards. We met when I went for the interview with Mrs. Amory."

Philip shook the nanny's hand, murmured a greeting, then strode over to the crib in the corner of the bedroom which was serving as a nursery.

He stood staring down at the baby.

He had not seen her since the day she was born. She was already a month old. After a few seconds, he bent down, reached into the crib, picked her up somewhat tentatively, looking trepidatious, as though he thought she might break in half.

Holding her away from him, he gazed into her small face. A pair of solemn gray eyes stared back at him unwaveringly. Maddy's eyes, he thought, and choked up. Bringing the baby to his chest, he held her tightly in his arms, close to his heart, one hand on her head protectively. This was Maddy's child. His child. A wave of love for the baby swept through him.

Slowly, Philip walked across the floor, still holding Fiona in his arms. He paused at the door, swung around.

"I'm taking my daughter home," he said. He glanced at Daisy. "Don't look so worried, Ma. It's all right. I'm all right." A small smile glanced across his mouth. "And *we're* going to be all right. We have each other."

40

"I tried to stop you coming over, Emily," Paula said as her cousin hurried into the study of the house in Belgrave Square. "But I was too late. Your housekeeper told me you'd just left."

Emily paused in the middle of the antique Aubusson carpet. She squinted across at Paula, who was sitting on the sofa in a pool of September sunlight. "Don't you want me to go with you to Heathrow after all?"

Paula shook her head, looking regretful. "I just hung up on Shane a short while ago. He doesn't want me to fly out to Sydney. So I've canceled my trip."

Emily was amazed. "But why doesn't he want

you to join him? You said he was all for it the other day, when you suggested it, urging you to come, in fact."

"He was, and *I* believe I *should* be with him at a time like this, but he now says he can handle things by himself, insists he's over the shock of the fire. Anyway, he thinks I ought to be here with the children. You know he's always had a bee in his bonnet about one of us being at home for their sakes."

"Winston feels the same way. But then so do we," Emily reminded her. She eyed Paula carefully. "Let's not forget that Grandy taught us to be responsible parents. She said that when we had children we should put them first, consider their needs above all else. In fact, she was adamant about it, most probably because she so frequently neglected her own."

"Emily! That's not a nice thing to say!"

"But it's true. And Grandy said so herself. She was so busy empire building, her kids took second place. Except for your mother. Aunt Daisy was the lucky one. Probably because Gran had made it by the time she was born."

Paula had the good grace to laugh. "Yes, you're right as usual, Emily." She let out a long sigh. "As much as I really want to be with Shane, I'm afraid it has to be his decision." A wry little smile touched her mouth. "Still, I can't help wishing I'd missed his phone call this morning. You see, I do think he needs me, despite what he says, if only for moral support."

"Then why not just *go,*" Emily suggested.

"Come on, Dumpling, you ought to know better than that!" Paula laughed hollowly. "Shane would be furious with me—you know how bossy and dictatorial he is—and the trip would then serve no purpose whatsoever."

"I suppose you'd better do what he says," Emily agreed, knowing how difficult Shane could be at times. She sat down in the chair opposite Paula, glanced at the breakfast tray on the antique Georgian coffee table positioned between them, saw that it was set for two. "It was jolly nice of you to include a cup for me," she said, smiling at her cousin. As she lifted the teapot and poured, she contemplated the basket of fancy French breakfast rolls. "You don't want that brioche, do you?"

"No, I seem to have put on weight in the past week. But you shouldn't eat it either," Paula warned.

"I know I shouldn't," Emily said and promptly reached for it. She looked thoughtful as she munched on the brioche. After a sip of tea, she sat back, said slowly, "Look here, Paula, perhaps Winston ought to go to Sydney. At least he would be able to keep Shane company, and I'm certain he could be very helpful in innumerable ways. He's leaving Toronto this afternoon and he'll be in New York tonight. Instead of going to Rochester to look at that printing plant, he could fly to L.A. From there he could continue on to Sydney, take that night flight you always rave about. I'll phone him right now."

"It's four o'clock in the morning in Canada!"

"So what. This is an emergency."

"No, it isn't, Emily, not anymore. Besides, I don't think Winston should go. Shane will be fine, he's a very strong person. He was just badly shaken up by the fire. And frankly, who wouldn't be? He was devastated that so many people were killed and injured. He kept repeating that every time he called, and you know he's hardly been off the phone to me since it happened. I think he went into a depression for several days—at least, that's the impression Mummy gave me. But he's pulled out of it now; I can tell by the tone of his voice. As I said, I'd prefer to go, to be with him, but I must do what *he* thinks is best."

"Yes," Emily said slowly; then she added, "And of course he does have a lot of strength— you're correct there. If anyone can cope, it's Shane."

"I *know* he can, Dumps. And remember, it's

not as if he's alone. There's my mother and Jason, and Philip, of course."

"Is Philip better then?" Emily asked.

"Yes, I'm glad to report. Shane told me Philip went over to my mother's the other day and took the baby home with him at long last."

"Thank goodness for that! I was getting a bit worried, I must admit. I had visions of Aunt Daisy and Jason having to raise Fiona. Imagine, at their ages!"

Paula smiled faintly at this remark. "Shane believes the disastrous fire and all it entailed shocked Philip out of his frozen state, brought him back to reality."

"I'm sure he's right. Shane's got a lot of insight into people, knows what makes them tick." She shook her head sadly. "Poor Maddy . . . dying in that way, so suddenly. It's been hard for me to accept."

"I know what you mean." Paula fell silent, thinking of Maddy. There was a dull ache in her heart for her sister-in-law. She missed her terribly, and her own grief had still not entirely abated. There were times when her eyes would fill up, even at work, and she had to excuse herself if she was with people, hurry away to be alone, to regain her composure. Maddy had been a most unusual woman and she had affected all of their lives.

Paula settled herself against the cushions, gazed off into the distance. Her eyes held a faraway look.

Emily watched her, but said nothing, not wishing to intrude on her at this moment. She knew Paula was thinking of Madelana, whose death had so shocked her, upset her so badly.

Out of the blue, Paula murmured in a voice suddenly turned gloomy, "I'm beginning to think there's a curse on this family."

Struck by the seriousness of her tone, Emily sat up in the chair and gaped at her. "Paula! How superstitious of you! You sound positively Celtic . . . some of Shane's Irishness must be rubbing off on you!"

"Well, just consider the past year, Emily. There's been the regurgitation of that old deception in Ireland, which ultimately led to the death of the estate manager. It was all very upsetting for Anthony and Sally, having to relive Min's death. And Anthony's felt responsible for Michael Lamont's stroke ever since it happened."

"It's better Michael Lamont keeled over from a stroke and died, rather than face a trial for murder."

"Good God, Emily! You fair take my breath away at times, some of the things you say!"

"But it's true, and I'm not a hypocrite."

"I know that, but you're so *blunt.*"

"Like Gran."

"Yes, like Gran," Paula agreed. There was a short pause before she continued softly, "Then there was Sandy's fatal illness, his shooting accident, followed by Maddy's brain hemorrhage and subsequent death, and last week the Sydney-O'Neill went up in smoke. Surely that's enough to make anybody think there's some sort of curse on them. Anyway, look at the terrible things that happened to Grandy throughout her lifetime. And what about the avalanche that killed Daddy, Jim, and Maggie? And there's my little Patrick, who was born retarded." Paula gave Emily a pointed stare. "It's as if we're being punished for something."

Not wishing to encourage Paula in these sudden, dire thoughts, Emily exclaimed dismissively. "Oh pooh! I don't believe that! We're a big, sprawling family—like the Kennedys. All sorts of awful things happen to people during their lives, but when there are a lot of you, as in our case, disasters only appear to be so much more numerous than in a small family. And despite everything, *I* happen to think we've been lucky . . . and in so many countless ways."

"Granted we're all fabulously successful and

rich, but we've had more than our fair share of tragedies."

"And I suppose we'll have many more."

"My God, Emily, you sound like Job's comforter."

"Oh sorry, darling, I don't mean to; nor do I mean to make light of the dreadful things that have recently happened in Australia. But I won't subscribe to superstition, and I'm surprised at you. Cursed indeed." Emily grinned, shook her head as if highly amused. "I can tell you this—if our Gran were alive, she'd have a real belly laugh."

"What do you mean?"

"She'd pooh-pooh you, too. She often said that we write our own scripts, live in what we ourselves create, and that we're ultimately responsible for everything that happens to us."

"*I* don't ever remember hearing her say that." Paula stared at Emily, frowning. Her eyes were puzzled. "Are you sure it was Grandy who said it?"

"Oh yes."

Paula nodded, and then she changed the subject.

But later that night she was to recall those words, and as she acknowledged their basic truth she did so with growing apprehension.

Paula spent the rest of the morning and most of the afternoon out on the floor of the store in Knightsbridge.

As she walked back into her private office, just after three-thirty, her private line began to shrill. Hurrying to the desk, she leaned across it, snatched up the phone, half expecting it to be Shane. Sydney was ten hours ahead of London, and he frequently rang her before going to sleep.

Her voice was therefore light, cheerful, as she said, "Paula O'Neill here," and clutching the phone to her ear, she walked briskly around the desk.

"It's Charles Rossiter, Paula."

"Hello, Charles! How are you?" She was disappointed, but she kept her voice gay.

"Er . . . I'm fine, thank you."

"You got my message then?"

"Message?" he sounded vague, slightly impatient.

"I telephoned you this morning, to let you know I'm not going to Sydney after all. So we can still have lunch on Friday, as we'd originally planned."

"Oh yes, of course I received it—"

There was a sudden pause, a hesitation on the part of her banker, and Paula said, "That *is* why you're calling, isn't it? To confirm our lunch?"

"No, actually, it's not."

She caught an odd note in his voice. "Is there some kind of problem, Charles?"

"I'm afraid so."

"But I thought those new documents were in order, and that—"

"It's nothing to do with your usual banking business with us, Paula," Charles interrupted. "Something very urgent has come up. I think you must come down to the bank for a meeting this afternoon. Say at five o'clock."

"Why, Charles? What's going on? You sound very mysterious."

"I received a telephone call a bit earlier this afternoon from Sir Logan Curtis. I'm sure you've heard of him, and of Blair, Curtis, Somerset, and Lomax."

"Of course. They're a very prestigious firm of solicitors, and Sir Logan is distinguished as one of the foremost legal brains in the country."

"Quite. Sir Logan requested a meeting today. Here at the bank with me. He wishes you to be present."

"Why?" she asked, surprised.

"Seemingly he represents your cousin, Jonathan Ainsley. The latter is visiting London from Hong Kong, where he has apparently lived for the past ten or twelve years. According to Sir

Logan, it is actually Ainsley who wants the meeting with us. To discuss a matter of business he has with you."

Paula was so startled she almost dropped the receiver. She was speechless for a moment, before exclaiming, "I have no business dealings with Jonathan Ainsley! As you are well aware, Charles. You've been my banker for years. My cousin draws dividends from Harte Enterprises, of course, but that is his sole involvement with the family. And with any of our businesses."

"Not according to Sir Logan."

"But you know otherwise!" she cried, her voice rising shrilly. "Sir Logan has been misinformed."

"I don't believe so."

"Charles, what on earth do you mean?" Aghast, she sat down in the chair.

"Look here, Paula, I'd really prefer not to go into it any further over the telephone. Quite aside from the confidentiality of the matter, I just stepped out of our annual board meeting to phone you, after I'd made the decision to accede to Sir Logan's request for a meeting. I'm very pressed. I must go back to the boardroom at once. However, I will say this, it is *imperative* that you are present."

"I don't understand."

"Whatever Jonathan Ainsley's business is with you, seemingly it could affect this bank, the other banks you deal with in the city, and the Harte stores."

"I'm more puzzled than ever! You must explain in greater detail!"

"I'm afraid I can't, Paula," Charles exclaimed, trying to keep his voice down. "I'm not being evasive. Please believe me, I'm not. Sir Logan gave me only the broadest outlines. He, too, did not wish to have a protracted conversation about confidential business over the phone. However, he did stress the importance of the matter to all of us. That's why I'm agreeing to the meeting. It sounds critical. Furthermore, I deem your presence to be crucial."

"I'll be there, Charles. At five sharp."

"Good. One more thing . . . I must forewarn you, Paula, Jonathan Ainsley will be in attendance this afternoon."

"I see," she answered grimly.

After she had said good-bye and hung up, Paula leaned back in the chair, pressed her fingers to her eyes. She was so stunned it took her a few minutes to gather her scattered thoughts, to get her mind working properly again.

She focused her concentration on her cousin. *Jonathan Ainsley,* she thought. *Why has he come back? What does he want?* She had no answers for herself. But she did remember the threat he had made against her years before, and her blood ran cold.

41

It was exactly five minutes to five when Paula walked into the Rossiter Merchant Bank in the City.

Charles Rossiter's private secretary was waiting for her in the reception area and took her into Charles's office at once.

The chairman of the bank, who was an old family friend, hurried to greet her, kissed her on the cheek.

"Have they arrived?" Paula asked as they drew apart, stood regarding each other worriedly in the middle of the room.

"Yes, about fifteen minutes ago. They're waiting for us in the boardroom."

"Do you know more about all this now, Charles?"

"A little. Sir Logan discussed it with me briefly."

"Jonathan Ainsley owns shares in Harte's, doesn't he?"

Charles nodded.

"He bought some or all of my ten percent which I put on the market recently, didn't he?"

"Yes. *All of it.*"

"I thought so. I figured that much out on the way here," Paula murmured, giving the banker a bleak little smile.

"He wants a seat on Harte's board of directors."

"He can't ask that! Owning ten percent of the shares doesn't give him the right to ask that! He can go to hell!"

"He's demanding it, Paula. And in my estimation he's out to make trouble for you."

"Obviously, Charles. Otherwise he wouldn't have bothered to come all the way from Hong Kong. Now, shall we go in? Get it over with?"

"Yes, let's do that," Charles agreed, escorting her across the room. He opened the side door which led directly into the oak-paneled boardroom of the bank.

Sir Logan Curtis, small, gray-haired,

younger-looking than she had expected, came forward as they walked in.

"Mrs. O'Neill, I'm Logan Curtis," he announced before Charles had a chance to make the introduction. He smiled as he offered her his hand.

Paula took it. "How do you do," she said in a businesslike tone. Out of the corner of her eye she could see Jonathan seated at the conference table. He did not rise, neither did he greet her, and she did not acknowledge him.

Sir Logan said, "Your cousin wishes to speak with you privately, Mrs. O'Neill. We will withdraw, leave you alone together." He glanced pointedly at Charles Rossiter as he walked over to the door.

The banker, who did not appreciate being pushed around in his own boardroom, was suddenly seething inside. He turned to Paula, "Is that all right with you?" he asked, his expression one of concern for her.

"Yes, of course, Charles," she responded evenly.

Charles Rossiter could not help admiring her coolness, her extraordinary poise under the circumstances. Nevertheless, he felt bound to add reassuringly, "I'll be next door in my office if you should need me, Paula."

"Thanks, Charles, you're most considerate."

She smiled at him as he slipped out and closed the door quietly behind him.

Alone in the room with her cousin, she turned slowly, walked toward the conference table.

Jonathan's eyes did not leave her face. He was elated, knowing he had the upper hand, enjoyed playing cat-and-mouse with her. He had waited a long time to get his revenge on Paula O'Neill, and now at last it was within his grasp. Earlier, he had resolved not to get up or ask her to sit down. He was not going to pay tribute to this cold, calculating bitch, who was the reincarnation of his diabolical grandmother, Emma Harte.

Paula came to a stop a few feet away from the table. She returned his stare unflinchingly. Her blue eyes were cold, steely.

Jonathan spoke first. He said in his smoothest voice, "It's been a long time since we faced each other across a conference table. I do believe the last time was twelve years ago, when the saintly Alexander gave me the sack, and you kicked me out of the family."

"I'm perfectly certain this meeting wasn't arranged in order that you and I could reminisce about old times," Paula snapped. "So let's get to the point, shall we?"

"The point is that I have—"

"I know you hold shares in Harte stores," she

said sharply, cutting him off. "Ten percent. I also know that you think you're entitled to a seat on the board. The answer is *no,* you're not. And now that you have my answer, I will leave."

Paula pivoted, walked back to the door. Her superior intelligence and shrewdness told her that he had more up his sleeve, so she was not surprised or perturbed when he said, "I haven't finished with you, Paula. I have something else to say to you."

She paused, turned to look at him. "What is it?"

"Over these many years I've been purchasing Harte shares through various nominees. Altogether, I now hold twenty-six percent."

Although this startled her, she managed not to show it. She kept her face still, her eyes steady, decided to make no comment. She watched him alertly. Instinctively, her guard went up.

Jonathan went on, "Furthermore, I also have the voting power over another twenty percent—" He paused for dramatic effect, and a smug smile slowly spread itself across his face. "Just think, Paula, forty-six percent in my hands! And you only have forty-one percent now." He laughed triumphantly. "I actually control more shares in the Harte stores than you do!" A gloating expression slid into his crafty eyes. "How unwise of you to put yourself in such a vulnerable position . . . just to buy the Larson chain in the States."

The shock Paula felt was so enormous she thought her legs were going to give way under her. But she managed to keep herself upright and steady, despite the tremors running through her whole body. She dare not allow any reaction to show.

Keeping her voice low, composed, she remarked, "And whose twenty percent do you control?"

"The shares left to James and Cynthia Weston, by their grandfather, the late Samuel Weston."

"They are minors. Those shares are in the control of their solicitors, executors of their grandfather's estate. And traditionally Jackson, Coombe, and Barbour have always voted those shares with me, as Sam Weston did when Emma Harte was alive."

"Allegiances can change, Paula."

"I find it hard to believe that Jackson, Coombe, and Barbour would involve themselves with you."

"Believe it . . . it's true."

"You're bluffing."

"Not at all." He rose, strolled down the other

side of the room. Halfway to the door he stopped, swung around. "It's only going to take me a week or two to buy the five percent I need to get control of Harte's. You'd better start packing your things, lady, and clear out of your office. I'm moving in." He gave her a cold, penetrating stare, his bitter loathing for her surfacing. "I'm putting you on notice. I am going to make a takeover bid for Harte's. And I promise you, I will succeed. I will be the winner this time! And *you* are going to be the loser, Paula O'Neill!"

She did not deign to answer him.

He slammed the door behind him as he left the boardroom.

Paula sank into the nearest chair.

She was filled with an internal shaking, and she clutched her bag in her lap to keep her hands from trembling. It seemed to her that all her strength had drained away.

Charles Rossiter appeared in the doorway. He rushed across the room to her, his face as white as hers, his expression grave, his eyes reflecting his apprehension.

"I knew we had trouble brewing this afternoon when I received that phone call. But I didn't anticipate that it was going to be this bad," he cried. "Sir Logan Curtis just briefed me fully on Ainsley's intentions. I'm flabbergasted."

Paula nodded, unable to speak for a moment. Her composure was shattered.

Charles peered at her. "Let me get you a brandy. You look awful."

"Thanks, but not brandy, Charles. I don't like it. Do you have vodka?"

"Yes, I'll go and get it. I need a drink myself."

He returned in a moment with a bottle and two glasses from the bar in his private office. He poured, handed her a glass. "Just knock it back. It'll do the trick."

She did as he said, felt the sting of the alcohol in her throat, then a warm sensation. After a moment, she said slowly, wonderingly, "I find it difficult to believe that a staid, old-fashioned firm of solicitors like Jackson, Coombe, and Barbour have done this. Thrown their lot in with Jonathan. *Could* he be bluffing, Charles?"

"I doubt it. Anyway, why *would* he? Besides, having Sir Logan Curtis at his side was a maneuver on his part to show you—*to show me*—that he is absolutely above board, very legitimate, and that everything he is trying to do is perfectly legal. Sir Logan told me he is rich, a tycoon in his own right, head of a big company, Janus and Janus Holdings, in Hong Kong. He and his wife have been staying at Claridge's for some weeks. No, Paula, I am afraid this is no bluff."

She exclaimed irately, "But why would Arthur Jackson go against me? Agree to vote those shares he controls with Jonathan's?"

"There is no question in my mind that Ainsley has offered Jackson a fabulous inducement to vote with him, something very beneficial to those children. Ainsley must have some sort of agreement with the law firm, Paula. He wouldn't have come here today if he hadn't been holding all the cards."

She nodded miserable, knowing he was correct.

Charles continued, "He wanted to undermine your reputation as C.E.O. of Harte's with our bank, of course, shake our confidence in you. That's why he asked for the meeting to be held here. Clever devil, isn't he? However, I just want to say this . . . *I* am behind you, Paula. This *bank* is behind you. As we were always behind your grandmother."

"Thank you, Charles." She stared at him morosely. "I'm in a mess."

"Yes, you are." He paused thoughtfully, added, "The mere *rumor* of a takeover bid for Harte's could be disastrous for you."

"I know." Abruptly, she jumped up.

Charles was taken aback. "Where are you going?"

"I have to get some air. I'm going back to the store."

"But surely you want to talk with me further, work out some sort of strategy, Paula."

"I'd prefer to do that tomorrow, Charles, if you don't mind. I feel the need to be alone right now, if you'll excuse me."

She sat at her desk in her office at Harte's in Knightsbridge, the world's most famous department store, her special territory, her citadel.

She was unable to move or think or focus on anything except the terrible problems facing her. She felt as if she had been bludgeoned about her head and her body. Her brain was still reeling, and from time to time waves of panic swept through her, blocking all rational thought.

For the first time in her life, Paula O'Neill was afraid.

She was frightened of Jonathan Ainsley, of the power he had over her, so suddenly, so unexpectedly. His specter loomed like a black cloud. And she detested the feelings of helplessness, of powerlessness, but she was fully aware they would not readily disappear.

He has me cornered, she thought, endeavoring to quell the nausea rising in her again, as it had been doing off and on for the past hour. *He's going to ruin me, as he threatened he would all those years ago. And I've no one to blame but myself.*

The queasy feeling intensified and she ran into the bathroom in the adjoining dressing area. Leaning over the washbasin, she retched and retched until she thought there was nothing left inside her. When she finally straightened, looked at herself in the mirror, she saw that her face was the color of putty; her eyes were red, watery, her cheeks streaked with mascara. After cleaning them with a damp tissue, she filled a glass with cold water, drank it gratefully. The vodka made me sick, she told herself, all the while knowing this was not so. It was nerves and fear and panic that were having such a dire effect on her system.

Returning to her office, she moved quickly toward the desk, then came to a halt in the center of the room. The portrait of her grandmother hanging over the fireplace caught her attention, brought into focus as it was by the picture light on top of the frame. Aside from the lamp on her desk, this was the only illumination in the shadow-filled room. Consequently, the portrait stood out in bold relief. Walking over to it, she stood staring up at the beloved face of Emma

Harte, captured with such lifelike precision in oils.

Oh Grandy, what have I done? How could I have been so stupid? I've jeopardized all that you built, put myself in jeopardy. You asked me once to hold your dream, and I've done just the opposite. I've let you down. Oh Gran, whatever am I going to do? How can I regain the advantage to prevent the stores from falling into the wrong hands?

The beautiful face in the portrait gazed back. The smile was benign, but the green eyes were watchful and shrewd.

If only she were alive, Paula thought, suddenly choking up. Tears came into her eyes. She felt so alone.

Patting her eyes with her handkerchief, she sat down on the sofa, continuing to study her grandmother's face. She began to twist the hankie in her hands fretfully, asking herself how the brilliant Emma Harte would have extricated herself from an appalling situation such as this.

But no sudden insights or clever solutions came to Paula, and in her anxiety she began to shred the lace hankie into tiny pieces. She was strung out, paralyzed by apprehension. She leaned back against the sofa, closed her eyes, trying to compose herself, hoping to bring some order to her turbulent and disturbing thoughts.

The chiming of the hour made Paula sit up swiftly. She glanced at the clock on the chimney piece. To her astonishment it was nine o'clock. Where had the time gone? Had she dozed? She realized she had been sitting on the sofa for over an hour.

Rising, she went to the desk, picked up the phone, instantly dropped the receiver back into the cradle. There was no point in calling Shane. He had enough to cope with right now. Her news would only distress him. Far better to wait until tomorrow or the day after to tell him, when she had worked out some sort of strategy. And she would most certainly have to do that: find a way to block Jonathan Ainsley's takeover bid for Harte's. *She could not let it happen.*

Unexpectedly, the feeling of claustrophobia she had experienced in the boardroom of the Rossiter Merchant Bank gripped her again. She felt as if she was suffocating, had the sudden pressing need to escape this room, to be outside, to breathe in fresh air.

Snatching up her bag, she flew out of the office, took the staff elevator down to the ground floor. And with a brisk goodnight to the security guard on duty, she left the store.

The air was crisp on this Wednesday evening, rather chilly for September. But Paula welcomed the coolness, found it refreshing. Certainly it seemed to revive her as she hurried away from the main thoroughfare of Knightsbridge, headed in the direction of her house in Belgrave Square.

Ever since she had left the bank in the city, she had felt dazed, unnerved, and panicked. But slowly, as she walked, these negative feelings were starting to lift. She had no idea what she would do, how she would proceed with Jonathan Ainsley, but she did know it was going to be an all-out war between them. And she was determined now to fight him with everything she had, do everything in her power to win. She could not afford to lose. Her cousin would be a calculating, cool, and devious adversary—she had no doubt about that. His threat had not been an idle one. He was in deadly earnest, would stop at nothing. He wanted the Harte stores. Equally as important, he wanted—no, *needed*—to ruin her. Manifold emotions were tangled up in his drives. And not the least of them was his overwhelming jealousy of her, which he had harbored since their childhood.

Unexpectedly, it occurred to her that there were several possible ways to outmaneuver Jonathan. But would they work? She wondered if one of them was even legal. She was not sure. She would have to check Harte's papers of incorporation tomorrow. She made a mental note to call John Crawford, her solicitor, when she got home. She was obviously going to need legal counsel.

Her brain was functioning again. This realization gave her a great sense of relief. Her mind began to race, and so intent was she on her mental machinations, she was unaware that she had bypassed her house until she found herself crossing Eaton Square.

She knew at once exactly where she was going: to see Sir Ronald Kallinski. Her Uncle Ronnie, her wise rabbi. He was the only one who could help her, guide her as Emma Harte would have guided her had she been alive.

42

Wilberson, Sir Ronald Kallinski's butler, opened the door of the Eaton Square house a few seconds after Paula rang the bell.

A look of surprise crossed his face when he saw her standing on the front steps. "Why, Mrs. O'Neill, good evening," he said, inclining his head politely.

"Is Sir Ronald at home, Wilberson? I must see him urgently."

"But he's entertaining guests this evening, Mrs. O'Neill. A dinner party is in progress."

"This is an emergency, Wilberson. Please tell Sir Ronald I'm here." Before the butler could stop her, she had walked right past him into the marble entrance hall hung with antique French tapestries. "I'll wait in here," she said firmly, pushing open the door of the library.

"Yes, Mrs. O'Neill," Wilberson said, sheathing his annoyance but looking pained as he hurried across the vast foyer and knocked on the dining room door.

It was only a matter of seconds before Sir Ronald hurried into the library to join her. Paula's unannounced arrival at nine-thirty in the evening had startled him. But his surprised expression changed to one of concern when he saw her face.

"You look frightful, Paula! What on earth is wrong? Are you ill?"

"No, I'm not, Uncle Ronnie. And I do apologize for bursting in on you like this. But something awful has happened. I'm in serious trouble and I need your help. There could be a takeover bid for Harte's. I could lose the stores."

Sir Ronald was thunderstruck. He understood at once that she was not exaggerating. It was not in her character to do so. "Excuse me for a moment, Paula. Let me explain to my dinner guests that I have an emergency, and ask Michael to hold the fort for a while. I'll be right back."

"Thank you, Uncle Ronnie," she said, and sat down on the leather Chesterfield sofa.

When he returned, almost immediately he

took a seat opposite her. "Begin at the beginning, Paula, and don't leave anything out," he instructed.

Slowly, precisely, with her usual attention to detail, she told him everything that had happened that day. She had a prodigious memory, was able to repeat every conversation verbatim. She started with Charles Rossiter's phone call to her and finished with her confrontation with Jonathan Ainsley at the bank.

Sir Ronald had been listening to her attentively, his chin resting on his hand, nodding from time to time. When she had finally given him all the facts, he exclaimed angrily, "My father had a name for a man like Jonathan Ainsley!" He paused, leveled his gaze at her, pronounced with contempt, "A *gonif.*"

"Yes, he *is* the biggest thief alive." Paula cleared her throat. "But actually, I've only got myself to blame. I set myself up for the likes of him." She sighed, shook her head. "I forgot that Harte's is a public company, forgot that I had stockholders. I believed it was mine, believed that no one would ever challenge me. I was over confident. Relaxed in too many ways. And that's always when the sharp knives come out, isn't it?"

He gave a slight nod, sat scrutinizing her closely. He loved her like a daughter, admired and respected her more than anyone he knew. She was daring, brilliant, and intuitive in business. It had taken a lot of guts to say what she had just said, to admit her mistakes. Nevertheless, he had been stunned at the outset of their conversation, when she had told him she had liquidated some of her Harte stock. It had been an error of the worst magnitude.

"I'll never understand why you sold that ten percent, Paula," he found himself saying with sharpness. "Never, as long as I live. Very flawed judgment on your part."

She looked down at her hands, fiddled with her wedding ring. When she finally looked up at him, she gave him a faint smile of chagrin. "I know. But I wanted to buy a chain of stores with my own money . . . So that it would really be mine."

"Your ego got in the way."

"That's true."

Sir Ronald exhaled heavily, adopted a softer tone. "But then nobody's infallible, Paula, least of all business executives like us. People seem to think that we're cut from a different cloth, that we're a special breed, with immunity from human frailties. They think we must be hard-headed, passionless, without any weaknesses to be able to wheel and deal, make fortunes the way we do. But none of it's true." He shook his head, finished, "In your case, some sort of genuine emotional need got in your way. And it distracted you."

"I think I had to prove something to myself."

A costly way of doing it, he thought, but said, "Recriminations and regrets are a waste of valuable time. We must turn disadvantage to advantage, make certain you come out the winner. Let's examine your options."

She nodded. His words reinforced her own attitude, which had grown more positive since she had been with him. "I could go and see Arthur Jackson, at Jackson, Coombe, and Barbour, appeal to his better instincts, get him to reverse his decision to vote the shares he controls with Jonathan's," she said. "I might even be able to find out what inducement Jonathan used, come up with a—"

"Telephone Jackson, by all means," Sir Ronald interrupted. "But don't be surprised if he turns a deaf ear. He's not beholden to you, and he doesn't have to tell you anything."

"Uncle Ronnie, he's behaved unethically!"

"It may seem that way, but it's not necessarily so. Arthur Jackson is the executor of Sam Weston's estate. He has only one obligation. To those children whose interests he protects. If he can strike a lucrative deal, or make additional income for them, he will."

"I think that's what he's done with Jonathan, don't you?"

"Most likely. Ainsley's always been a crafty operator. He's probably offered to pay a big cash dividend out of his own pocket to the Weston estate, as long as the law firm votes the stock they control with his." Sir Ronald rubbed his chin, pursed his lips, ruminated. Then he added, "I'll do a little fishing tomorrow. I have ways and means of finding things out. There are no secrets in our world, you know. Hold off on your phone call to Arthur Jackson for the moment."

"Yes, I will. Thanks, Uncle Ronnie." She leaned forward eagerly. "Is there any reason why I can't launch a bid to take Harte's private? Buy out my stockholders?"

"Yes, one very good reason. I won't let you."

"But it *would* be legal?"

"It would. But to take your company private, you would have to offer money publicly, in the open market, to your stockholders. And you would immediately expose yourself to every predator and corporate raider in the City and in Wall Street." He shook his head with great vehemence. "No, no, I won't permit you to do that, Paula. There would be other takeover bids, possibly hostile ones. And anyway why should your stockholders take your money? They may prefer to take Sir Jimmy Goldsmith's money or Sir James Hanson's or Carl Icahn's or Tiny Rowland's . . . or *Jonathan Ainsley*'s. You'd all be bidding against each other, accomplishing nothing except pushing up the price of the shares."

Her face changed ever so slightly and she glanced away, biting her lip. After a moment she looked at him and asked in a tired voice, "Then what *can* I do, Uncle Ronnie?"

"You can start looking for a few small stockholders who among them hold ten percent of the Harte shares. Perhaps four or five, maybe even as many as twelve. Track them down, buy them out—at a premium, if necessary. You've already got forty-one percent. You only need fifty-one to have control."

"God, I'm so stupid, Uncle Ronnie! What's wrong with me tonight? I keep losing sight of things. Obviously I'm not thinking straight."

"That's understandable, you've had a nasty shock. Also—" He paused thoughtfully before continuing, "I think there's one other thing you *must* do, my dear."

"What's that?"

"You must dispose of Jonathan Ainsley."

"How?"

"I don't know at this moment." Sir Ronald pushed himself to his feet, walked over to the window, stood staring out into Eaton Square, his analytical mind examining various possibilities. Eventually he swung around. "What do we know about this *gonif?*"

"Not much, I'm afraid, since he left England and went to live in Hong Kong."

"Hong Kong! So that's where he ended up after Alexander turfed him out. A very *interesting* place, Hong Kong. Now, tell me what little you do know."

Paula did as he asked, repeating the information Charles Rossiter had given her, which he, in turn, had learned from Sir Logan Curtis.

"Start digging, Paula," Sir Ronald told her, "and dig deep. Do you have a particular private investigating firm you use for business matters? If you don't, I can recommend one."

"No, that's all right, thanks. I use Figg International and have for years. They handle all of my security at the stores, provide guards—you know, the usual thing. They happen to have a private investigating division with offices and agents all over the world."

"Good. Hire them immediately. A *momzer* like Jonathan Ainsley must have more than one skeleton in his closet—" Sir Ronald bit off the end of his sentence when the library door flew open.

Michael walked in, and when he saw Paula he exclaimed, with a laugh, "Oho, so you're the emergency!" Instantly, he realized how serious Paula and his father were and continued in a more sober tone, "From the way you both look, it *must* be an emergency." His eyes rested on Paula. He took in her extreme pallor, her tired eyes. "What's wrong? It's not something to do with the fire in Sydney, Paula, is it?"

"No, Michael, it's not," Paula said quietly, then glanced across at his father.

Sir Ronald said, "Jonathan Ainsley has returned, and he's in London. To make trouble for Paula."

"How can he do that?" Michael demanded.

"Uncle Ronnie will explain."

Once his father had acquainted him with the facts, Michael went to sit next to Paula on the sofa. He took hold of her hand affectionately. "Dad's made some excellent suggestions, but what can *I* do to help you?" he asked.

"I honestly don't know, Michael, but thanks for offering. Right now I'm going back to the store. I must start checking the records, go over the computer printouts. I must find those crucial stockholders. And as fast as possible."

"I'm coming with you to help you," Michael announced.

"Oh, you don't have to, honestly. Uncle Ronnie has guests. I've interrupted your dinner party."

"You can't do a job like that alone," Michael protested fiercely. "You'll be at it all night."

"I was going to phone Emily."

"Good idea. Let's call her from here. We'll meet her at Harte's. The three of us can handle it together."

"But—"

"Do let Michael go with you, my dear," Sir Ronald interjected. *"I* will feel better, knowing he's at the store with you."

"All right." Paula rose, kissed him on the cheek. He hugged her to him, and she murmured, "I can't thank you enough, Uncle Ronnie."

He smiled down at her. "We're *mishpocheh,*" he said.

43

"*Know thine enemy,*" Paula said. "That's what this is all about, Jack, why I asked you here."

Jack Figg, managing director of Figg International, nodded quickly. "I get the picture."

"The situation is critical. I wouldn't have dragged you to the store at eleven-thirty at night otherwise."

"That's no problem. I'd come out at any time for you, Paula."

Jack Figg, who ran the biggest and most successful security and private investigating company in Britain, sat back in the chair facing her. He pulled an Asprey leather jotting pad out of

713

his sports jacket and said, "All right, Paula, *shoot.* Give me as many facts as you can."

"That's just it, I don't have very many. However, it's my understanding that Jonathan Ainsley has lived in Hong Kong for about twelve years. That's when he left England. He owns a company called Janus and Janus Holdings. More than likely it's to do with real estate; that's always been his area of expertise. He's married, but I don't know to whom. Charles Rossiter told me that they're presently staying at Claridge's. Oh, and he mentioned that the wife is pregnant." Paula lifted her shoulders in a shrug. "I can't tell you more than that."

"Hong Kong is obviously our jumping-off point. But I'll also have him watched here, so we know what he's up to."

"That's a good idea, and, as I just said, the situation is *critical.*"

"I understand. And no doubt you needed the information yesterday."

"No, five years ago, if the truth be known," Paula answered quietly.

Jack Figg gave her a knowing look. "But actually, how long *do* I have?"

"Five days—at the most. I'd like your report on my desk by Monday."

"Good God, Paula! You're asking for miracles! I can't deliver in that short a time!"

"Jack, you have to—otherwise the information will be worthless to me. It'll be too late." She leaned across the desk, her face tense, her blue eyes focused intently on him. "I don't care how many agents you put on. It can be a hundred, if necessary—"

"If I do that, it's going to cost you a lot of money," Jack interjected.

"Have I ever haggled with you, Jack?"

"No, of course you haven't—it's not your style. But digging deep, doing a complete profile of this nature can become very expensive. Very quickly. Especially when there's a time element involved. To gather the kind of information you want, I have to turn Ainsley inside out. I *will* have to put a lot of operatives on. It'll also be necessary to move a number of my agents from other Far East countries into Hong Kong. That in itself will send the costs skyrocketing. Then there'll be all kinds of payoffs, bribes—"

Paula cut in, "I don't need to know the details, Jack. Just do it. *Please.* Get me as much information on Jonathan Ainsley as you can. I need ammunition against him in order to defend myself. There's got to be some skeletons in his closet."

"Maybe not, Paula. He might be as clean as a whistle."

She was silent, knowing this was true.

715

"But I hope he's not," Jack added swiftly, "for your sake. And look, I'll try to get back to you on Monday. However, it could be Tuesday."

"Do your very best, Jack."

"I'll get to it tonight," he promised, impatient to start working the telephones and the telex machine. He stood up. "The Far East is already open for business."

After Paula had walked Jack Figg to the staff lift and thanked him once again, she hurried into the office where Emily and Michael were working on the records of Harte's shareholders.

"Any luck yet?" she asked from the doorway.

"Not yet," Emily answered. "But never fear, we're bound to come up with some names before too long. How did it go with Jack Figg? Is he on the job?"

"He is. And I have a lot of confidence in him. If there's anything to find, Jack will find it."

"Oh, I'm sure there's *sleaze* in Jonathan Ainsley's life!" Emily exclaimed. "He always was weird and mixed with a strange bunch when he lived here. Like that awful Sebastian Cross."

Paula felt a cold little shiver run through her. "I'd rather not think about *him,* if you don't mind."

"Why should *he* bother you! He's dead. Anyway, don't stand there looking like a sucking duck. Come and help us."

"Of course." Paula joined them.

Emily gave her a batch of computer printouts. "Start on these, but before you really dig in, let me get you a cup of coffee and one of the sandwiches I brought with me. You haven't eaten all night, Paula."

"I'm not hungry, darling. But I will have a cup of coffee. Thanks, Dumps."

Paula concentrated on the top sheet, running her eyes quickly down the page of names. Harte's had hundreds of small stockholders who held nominal amounts of shares, as well as those others who had acquired larger blocks over the years. Suddenly, her heart sank. This *was* an endless task, as Michael had said earlier. It might even take longer than one night—several days perhaps—to find the people they needed. Jonathan had boasted that he was quickly going to buy up the five percent he needed. But it was not a boast. She knew he fully intended to do exactly that.

"I bet Jonathan has his stockbrokers and all kinds of flunkies skittering around, trying to buy Harte shares!" she exclaimed, voicing her thoughts, looking at Michael.

He returned her glance. "I'm sure he is. But

you have the advantage, Paula. You have the inside information—these records."

"Yes," she said dully, starting to read again.

Emily brought coffee for the three of them, sat down next to Paula. "Cheer up, lovey. We'll get the results soon. As Gran used to say, many hands make light work. But oh boy, do I wish Winston and Shane were here to help us."

"Oh, so do I, Emily. I miss Shane so much and in so many different ways. I can't wait for him to get back from Australia. I feel as if half of me is missing when he's not here."

"Are you going to phone him tomorrow, tell him about this?" Emily inquired.

"I think I have to—he'd be hurt if I didn't. I only hope it doesn't upset him too much. I couldn't bear that. Poor darling, he's had too much to contend with lately."

It was the gentle tone, the loving nuances, the look of longing in her eyes that stabbed at Michael. *She worships Shane,* he thought with a flash of insight. *He is her life.* At that precise moment Michael knew what a fool he had been to think she would ever entertain any advances from him. The mere thought of what he might have done in a foolish moment caused him acute internal embarrassment.

He dropped his head, pretended to concentrate on the sheet of names to hide his sudden discomfiture. His sexual desire for her had not waned in the past year. He had constantly fantasized about her, but how ridiculous he had been —he saw that now. She was happily married to his friend. How could he have ever thought that she would be interested in him, or any other man for that matter. It had always been Shane since their childhood.

Michael felt as if a veil had been lifted. He saw everything with sudden clarity. He understood then what she had been doing earlier in the year . . . she had been persistently pushing Amanda at him. He ought to have recognized that months ago in New York, known that Paula was out of his range. But he had been so caught up in the fantasy in his own head, he had been blind to many things, most especially reality.

"Here it is!" Emily shrieked. "I've found a shareholder with quite a substantial number of shares."

"How many?" Paula asked, hardly daring to breathe.

"*Four* percent. Gosh, she must be a fairly wealthy woman."

"Who is she?" Paula asked excitedly, her voice echoing Emily's enthusiasm.

"A Mrs. Iris Rumford of"—Emily traced her

finger across the printout—"Bowden Ghyll House, Ilkley!"

"A Yorkshire woman," Michael said quietly. "Perhaps this is a good omen, Paula."

On Saturday morning at ten o'clock, Paula sat opposite Mrs. Iris Rumford in the handsome drawing room of her lovely old manor house in Ilkley.

It was obvious to Paula that Mrs. Rumford was a woman of considerable means, and she had been graciously received and offered coffee on her arrival minutes before.

Paula had accepted a cup, and the two women had exchanged pleasantries, discussed the weather. Now, as she finished her coffee, Paula said, "It was very kind of you to see me, Mrs. Rumford. As my assistant told you, I wanted to talk to you about your shares in Harte's stores."

"Yes. And it's my pleasure, Mrs. O'Neill. Anyway, it was the least I could do, in that I had tea with your cousin, Jonathan Ainsley, on Thursday."

Paula almost dropped the coffee cup. She put it down carefully on the end table. This was the last thing she had expected to hear, and she gave Iris Rumford a sharp look. "He also came to see you about your shares in Harte's presumably?"

"Yes, Mrs. O'Neill. He did. He offered me an excellent price for them, went very high actually."

Paula felt her throat tighten, and she swallowed several times before saying, "And did you accept his offer, Mrs. Rumford?"

"No, as a matter of fact, I didn't."

Paula relaxed. She smiled at the older woman. "Then I can make you an offer for them, can't I?"

"You could, yes."

"Name your price, Mrs. Rumford."

"I don't have a price."

"But you must know how much you want for your shares."

"No, I don't. You see, I'm not all that keen to sell them. My late husband bought them for me in 1959." She gave a funny little laugh. "I'm sort of sentimentally attached to them. Harte's is my favorite shop in Leeds. I've always patronized it."

Paula held herself still, pressing back her annoyance. She had obviously come here on a wild goose chase. But she could not afford to antagonize this woman; she needed her too badly. Paula said, "Well, of course I'm glad you like the store, that you're a satisfied customer. But look here, I do wish you would consider my offer. I will purchase your shares at the same price Mr. Ainsley quoted to you."

Iris Rumford studied her for a moment, frowning slightly, as if she were trying to make up her mind about something. Then she said, "Is there going to be one of those big battles? The kind I read about in the financial pages of the Sunday *Times?*"

"I sincerely hope not," Paula exclaimed quietly.

Unexpectedly, Iris Rumford pushed herself to her feet.

Paula also rose, realizing the conversation was suddenly at an end.

"I'm sorry, Mrs. O'Neill," Mrs. Rumford murmured. "Perhaps I should not have let you come to see me. I've wasted your time, I'm afraid. You see, I thought that I might sell my shares, but now I've changed my mind."

"I'm truly sorry to hear that." Paula stretched out her hand, trying to be cordial.

Iris Rumford shook it. "I can see you're angry. And I can't say I blame you. Forgive my vacillation. And please excuse the indecisiveness of an old lady."

Paula said, "It's all right, really it is. But if you should change your mind again, please ring me."

All the way back to Leeds, Paula fumed.

She was baffled and irritated by the woman's odd behavior, as well as being disappointed. Had Iris Rumford just wanted to be important for a brief moment in her life? Or was it a case of simple curiosity on the part of a lonely old woman? Had she merely wanted to meet Jonathan and herself? Paula wondered how Jonathan Ainsley had found Iris Rumford, how *he* knew that *she* owned a block of Harte shares.

She sighed with some exasperation as she pressed her foot hard on the accelerator, and headed the Aston Martin in the direction of Leeds. Going to see Iris Rumford *had* been a waste of time.

Paula spent most of the day working in her office at the Leeds store.

Several times she went out onto the floor, but mostly she kept herself busy with paperwork. And she strove not to think about Jonathan Ainsley, the possible takeover bid, or dwell on the frightening prospect of losing the stores to him.

When she did become tense, she reminded herself that in the last forty-eight hours her stockbrokers and Charles Rossiter had between them managed to acquire another seven percent of Harte shares on her behalf. They had bought them from nine small stockholders Emily and

Michael had pinpointed on the computer printouts.

Only three percent, that's all I need now, she kept saying under her breath whenever she needed to lift her sagging spirits. The words consoled her.

At four o'clock she placed a pile of papers in her briefcase, locked her office, and left the store. She usually stayed until six, even on Saturdays. But Emily was coming over to Pennistone Royal for dinner that evening, and Paula wanted to spend an hour with Patrick and Linnet before she arrived.

It was a lovely September afternoon, very sunny, and Leeds had been busy all day. The traffic was heavy on Chapeltown Road as shoppers returned to the outskirts after a day in town. But Paula was an excellent driver; she dodged in and out between the other cars, was soon on the open road going to Harrogate.

She was approaching the roundabout in Alwoodley when the Cellnet phone in her car rang. Reaching for it, she said, "Hello?" half expecting it to be Emily.

"Mrs. O'Neill, it's Doris at the store."

"Yes, Doris?"

"I have a Mrs. Rumford of Ilkley on another line," the switchboard operator said. "She insists it's very urgent. Apparently you have her phone number."

"I do, Doris. But it's in my briefcase. Please give her the car number, ask her to phone me at once. And thank you."

Only a few minutes after Paula had hung up, the car phone rang again. It was Iris Rumford, and she got straight to the point. "I wonder if you could come and see me tomorrow? To discuss those shares again."

"I really can't, Mrs. Rumford. I have to drive to London tomorrow. In any case, since you don't want to sell, there doesn't really seem to be much point, does there?"

"I might reconsider your offer, Mrs. O'Neill."

"Then why don't I drive over now?"

"All right," Iris Rumford agreed.

"You don't know who I am, do you?" Iris Rumford was saying to Paula an hour later.

Paula shook her head. "Should I? Do I know you?" Her brows knitted together in perplexity. She fixed her gaze intently on the other woman. Iris Rumford was thin but sprightly, with silver hair and a ruddy complexion, and she looked to be in her seventies. Paula was certain she did not know her. "Have we met?" she asked with another frown.

Iris Rumford sat back and returned Paula's

penetrating stare. At last, she said slowly, "No, we haven't met. But you knew my brother. Or at least, you were acquainted with him."

"Oh," Paula said, lifting a black brow. "What was his name?"

"John Cross."

This name so startled Paula that she almost exclaimed out loud. She managed to say in a normal tone, "We met when he owned Cross Communications." As she spoke, Paula thought of his late son, Sebastian, once her deadly enemy and Jonathan's best friend. She realized immediately how Jonathan knew about Iris Rumford and the stock she owned in Harte's.

"You were very kind and courteous to my brother at the end of his life," Iris Rumford continued. "He told me about you when he was dying. He respected you, thought you were very fair. It was your other cousin, Mr. Alexander Barkstone, that I met briefly, when my brother was in St. James's Hospital in Leeds." Iris Rumford looked into the fire. There was a short pause. "You and Mr. Barkstone . . . well, you're different from Jonathan Ainsley . . ." She brought her eyes to Paula, half smiled.

Paula waited, wondering what was coming next. When Mrs. Rumford made no further comment, she said, "Yes, I do believe we are. I hope so. But sadly, Mr. Barkstone is now dead."

"I'm sorry to hear that." The old lady gazed into the flames again. She muttered, "It's funny, isn't it, how people in families can differ so very much. He was wicked, evil, my nephew, Sebastian. I never had much time for him. John, of course, idolized him, the only son, the only child. But he killed my brother, drove him into his grave with all that wickedness. And Jonathan Ainsley was just as wicked. *He* hammered quite a few nails into my poor brother's coffin. Bad lot, Sebastian and your cousin."

Suddenly, Iris swung her silver head, focused her eyes on Paula once more. "I wanted to meet you, Mrs. O'Neill, to judge for myself what kind of person you are. That's why I asked you to come this morning. You're a sincere woman—I can tell that from your eyes. Anyway, I've never heard anything bad about you hereabouts. Mostly they say you're like Emma Harte. She was a good woman. I'm glad you take after her."

Paula had no words. She held her breath.

"And so, if it will help you personally, I *will* sell you my Harte shares."

For a moment Paula thought she might burst into tears. "Thank you, Mrs. Rumford. It would help me, very much so. I would be most grateful if you sold them to me and not to my cousin."

"Oh, I never intended to sell them to him. I

just wanted . . . well, wanted to look him over again, satisfy myself that I'd always been right in my judgment. Also, I got a bit of satisfaction from dangling the carrot in front of him and then snatching it away." She shook her head. There was a shrewd glint in her wise old eyes. "When you both phoned me about selling the shares, I got a feeling he was out to make trouble for you. Well, never mind, he'll get his comeuppance one day."

"Yes." Paula leaned forward, said, "I told you this morning I would purchase the shares at the price Jonathan Ainsley had offered. That still stands, of course."

"Good Lord, that doesn't matter! I wouldn't dream of holding you up, Mrs. O'Neill. You can have them at market value."

44

Paula stood in front of the fireplace in her office at Harte's in Knightsbridge, below the portrait of Emma. It was three-fifteen on Tuesday afternoon, and she was waiting for Jonathan Ainsley.

Generally she wore black to work. Today she had chosen a bright red wool dress, simply tailored with long sleeves. She thought the color was appropriate. It was strong, defiant, bold, and it echoed the way she felt.

She had turned disadvantage to advantage. She was about to demolish her enemy.

But when Jonathan appeared a few minutes later, she realized that he misguidedly believed *she* was going to capitulate to *him*. Everything about him indicated this. He sauntered in, looking sanguine, his demeanor arrogant, his smile superior.

He halted in the middle of the floor.

Adversaries, they did not greet each other.

He said, "You sent a message. I'm here. You have something to say to me?"

"You've lost!"

He laughed in her face. "I never lose!"

"Then this is a first for you." She lifted her head slightly, the gesture one of confidence and pride. "I've acquired additional Harte stock . . ." She paused for effect. "I now hold fifty-two percent."

This information threw him. He recovered himself. Displaying no emotion whatsoever, he sneered, "So what. I have forty-six percent. I'm the *second* largest stockholder and entirely within my rights in demanding a seat on the board. I shall do so formally today. Through my solicitors. I also intend to proceed with my takeover bid." His eyes swept over her coldly. "This will be my office in the not too distant future."

"I doubt it!" she shot back. "Furthermore, you don't have forty-six percent. Only twenty-six."

"Have you forgotten that I control the shares held in trust by Arthur Jackson for the Weston children?"

"I forget nothing. And I am absolutely certain Arthur Jackson will not be doing business with you after today."

"Don't be so ridiculous!" His expression turned smug. "I have an agreement with him, with the law firm. A written agreement."

Paula took a step forward, reached for a manila envelope on the coffee table, stood holding it in her hands. She tapped it with a bright red fingernail. "When Arthur Jackson finishes reading this report, which was delivered to him an hour ago, I feel quite confident he will be shredding the agreement."

"What report is that?" he asked, his expression now one of disdain.

"An investigation into your life in Hong Kong."

He threw her a look of contempt, said with scorn, "You have nothing on me. I'm clean."

Paula studied him thoughtfully. "Funnily enough," she said after a short pause, "I'm inclined to believe you. But nobody else will."

"What are you implying?"

Ignoring this question, she continued, "You have a partner in Hong Kong, a silent partner, one Tony Chiu, son of Wan Chin Chiu, who died last year. The older man was your mentor, your advisor, and also your silent partner from the moment you arrived in the crown colony.

Pity the son's not as honorable and reliable as the father."

"My life and my business in Hong Kong have nothing to do with you!" he spluttered. He was irate, trying to hold himself in check.

"Oh yes it does. It has a great deal to do with me when you are trying to take over Harte's."

"And I will take it over!"

"No you won't!" Her eyes narrowed, and she proceeded in a soft but deadly voice, "It was very interesting to discover that Tony Chiu has a sideline. A very profitable sideline. He's alleged to be the biggest dealer of opium in the Golden Triangle, with a huge network spreading through Laos and Thailand. Convenient, isn't it, that he can apparently launder the drug money through Janus and Janus Holdings without anyone being the wiser about what he's up to. What a wonderful front for him. But I wonder how the Hong Kong Government and the Hong Kong police would react, what they would do about it—if they knew the real facts."

He gaped at her. "You're lying!" he screamed. "That report you're clinging onto for dear life is a pack of lies! Tony Chiu is not a drug dealer, he's a respectable and *respected* banker. And he certainly has not been using my company to launder drug money. I would know about it. He could not do a thing like that and hide it from me."

She smiled sardonically. "Don't be naive. You have Chinese employees who are his men, placed there by him even when his father was alive. He handpicked them in readiness for the future, for the time he would take over his father's banking concerns. And those men are his spies in your organization."

"Bullshit!"

"Your wife, Arabella, knows all about it. She is his business partner, has been for years. And he's financed many of her businesses at various times, including the antique shop she now owns in Hong Kong. She, too, is his spy. That's why she married you. To spy on you."

Jonathan was livid with rage, unable to speak coherently. He wanted to hit Paula O'Neill in the face for saying such unspeakable things about Arabella. He took several deep breaths, gasped angrily, "Someone with a vivid imagination has written a piece of fiction for you. *It's all lies, lies, lies!"* His breathing was ragged as he finished, "He is my silent partner. We are never seen together. My wife does not even know Tony Chiu."

"Why don't you ask her?"

His lip curled and his pale eyes filled with hatred for her. He shifted his gaze to the portrait of Emma Harte above her head, and his loathing for the two of them intensified. "You bloody bitch!" he hissed. "You're just like that old cow used to be! I piss on her grave! I piss on yours!" he cursed.

His words denigrating her grandmother incensed Paula. She went in for the kill. With meticulous care, she said, "The beautiful Arabella Sutton, doctor's daughter from Hampshire, is not quite what she seems to be. No doubt you are aware she lived in Paris for years. But did you know she was a 'Claude girl'?" Paula laughed coldly, taunted, "Don't tell me a sophisticated man like you doesn't know all about Madame Claude. She ran the most successful, indeed the finest, sex operation ever known in Paris. And until 1977 . . ."

Jonathan gaped at her. He was dumbfounded.

". . . Arabella Sutton, *your wife,* was one of Madame Claude's call girls. She went by the name Francine."

"I do not believe you," he shouted. "Arabella is—"

"Believe it!" she shouted back. She flung the envelope at him. It landed at his feet. "The report and copies of certain official documents attached to it will make interesting reading for you."

Jonathan saw it out of the corner of his eye, but he made no move to pick it up.

Paula said in an icy voice, "Instead of trying to knock my house down, go and put your own in order."

He opened his mouth to say something, then closed it. He glanced at the envelope at his feet. He longed to show her what he thought about her report by walking away from it. But he could not. His overriding desire, his consuming need to see the official documents she had just alluded to got the better of him. He bent down, picked it up, swung around, and strode to the door.

"I've won!" Paula called after him. "And don't you ever forget it!"

He halted, looked back at her. "We'll see about that," he said.

Paula walked back to her desk, sat down, reached for the phone, changed her mind. She sat thinking for a while. There was one more thing she had to do to ensure complete success, but it required her to be utterly ruthless, more ruthless than Emma Harte had ever been. She was still balking at the idea. She glanced over at the portrait of her grandmother, then brought her eyes back to the photograph in the silver frame on her desk. It was of Shane and the children. They, too, were Emma's heirs. She had to protect Harte's for them, no matter what it took.

Without any further hesitation, she reached for her private phone, dialed Sir Ronald on his direct line.

He picked up the phone after two rings. "Kallinski here."

"Uncle Ronnie, it's me again. Sorry to keep bothering you today."

"You're not, my dear." There was a slight pause. "Has he left?"

"Yes. Shaken, but not conceding anything. In fact, he was obviously determined to keep on fighting me. And so I will dispose of him in the way we discussed. A copy of the report will go to the authorities in Hong Kong. But honestly, Uncle Ronnie, I—"

"No regrets I hope, Paula."

"It makes me far more ruthless than Grandy ever was."

"That's not true, my dear. Emma could be *extremely* ruthless, too, when there was something for her to be ruthless about . . . such as Harte's, the business empire she built from nothing, and those she loved."

"Perhaps you're right."

"I know I am," Sir Ronald murmured, speaking in a softer voice. "I told you last night that

Jonathan Ainsley will never be off your back. He'll always keep trying to get the stores. That's the nature of the man."

When she remained silent at the other end of the phone, Sir Ronald added, "You have no option but to stop him now. To protect yourself."

"Yes, I realize that, Uncle Ronnie."

He sat in the corner of Claridge's foyer, where afternoon tea was being served. But he scarcely heard the rattle of tea cups, the violins, or the varied background noises. He was reading far too intently to notice anything.

Jonathan had read the report twice.

At first he had wanted to dismiss it as pure invention, a vindictive interpretation of the facts on someone else's part, and especially the sections about Tony Chiu. But now he was finding this difficult to do. There was too much genuine information included to dismiss the entire thing as bogus. He had been amazed to read a whole page about his affair with Lady Susan Sorrell. That had been such a clandestine relationship he could hardly believe his eyes when he had come across her name. He was convinced Susan would not have talked about their sexual relationship when it was in progress. Or after it finished. She was terrified of gossip and of invoking her husband's wrath. Divorce from her rich banker was the last thing she wanted.

He came out as clean as he had insisted he was to Paula O'Neill, despite the information about Tony, which disturbed and alarmed him. If it *was* actually true, then he could be implicated in something he knew nothing about. Janus and Janus could be in jeopardy, as he might be himself. It could turn out to be serious. He would have to fly back to Hong Kong as soon as possible, start his own investigation there.

The thing which truly distressed him, however, was the detailed account of Arabella's past. This was backed up with photostats of documents relating to her years in Paris. Her whole life in France had been tracked and meticulously recorded in these pages of typescript. There was no longer any question in his mind that she had used the name Francine and that she had been one of Madame Claude's girls. Quite aside from the documentation, there were so many other things which made him give credence to the report. There was her sexual expertise and knowledge, her overall attitude toward a man, which smacked of the courtesan's trade, her sophistication, her worldliness, her elegance . . . Madame Claude's girls had all been like her.

Carefully sliding the papers back into the envelope, he got to his feet, hurried out to the lift.

There was nothing productive he could do about Hong Kong at this moment, but he could go upstairs and confront the woman he was married to.

As he rode up in the lift to the tenth floor, his suppressed anger bubbled up in him, spiraled into a terrible fury. He was ashen-faced and shaking inside when he entered the suite. He went in quietly, but she heard him and came out into the foyer, smiling.

"Jonathan darling, how did it go?" she asked, coming over to him, kissing him on the cheek.

Jonathan was devastated by what he had just read about his wife, and he could hardly bear for her to touch him. He had to hold himself rigid in order not to react to her kiss or to strike her.

He had loved her, had considered her to be his most perfect possession. She was soiled now, damaged, worthless.

Again she said, "How did the meeting go at Harte's?"

"So-so," he said noncommittally, controlling himself even though the rage boiled inside him.

Arabella looked at him oddly, detecting a sudden coldness in him; then she immediately dismissed this as irritation with Paula O'Neill, his *bête noir.*

Turning, she walked back into the sitting room where she had been reading, settled herself on the sofa. Her knitting bag was next to her, and she opened it, took out the baby's jacket she was making, began to ply the needles.

Jonathan walked in after her, put the envelope down on an end table, went over to the bar, where he poured himself a neat vodka.

He stood sipping it, regarding her, thinking how heavy with child she looked this afternoon. The baby was due any moment, and as much as he wanted to confront Arabella head on, he knew he must restrain himself. He did not want her anymore, and he would divorce her as quickly as possible, but he certainly wanted his child . . . his son and heir.

He said conversationally, "Did you ever know a man in Hong Kong called Tony Chiu?"

If Arabella was startled by this question, she did not show it. "No, why do you ask?" she murmured, all calm contentment.

"No special reason. His name happened to come up at lunch with my solicitors today. I thought you might have run across him in your travels, know something about him."

"I'm afraid I don't, darling."

He finished the vodka, reached for the envelope, and crossed the room. Taking the chair facing her, he said, "You lived in Paris for years . . . but you never want to go there. Why is that?"

"It's never been my favorite place," she said, lifting her eyes from the knitting, smiling at him lovingly.

"Then why did you live there for almost eight years?"

"My work was there. You know I was a model. And why all these questions about Paris, Jonny darling?"

He said slowly, "Are you afraid to go to Paris?"

"Of course not. And why are *you* being so strange? I don't understand you."

"Are you afraid you'll run into some of your old . . . paramours, is that what it's all about, *Francine?*"

Arabella gazed at him. Her pitch-black eyes were full of innocence. "I don't know what you're getting at, or why you're calling me Francine." She laughed lightly, shook her head.

"Because that's the name you used when you were a call girl."

"What on earth are you saying?" she cried, looking at him askance.

"Don't deny it! The documentation is all here, courtesy of Paula O'Neill. You can read it for yourself," he said, pinning her with his eyes. "It's an investigation into my life, and they've done quite a number on yours, too."

Arabella had no alternative but to take the documents he was thrusting at her.

"Read them."

She was suddenly terrified. She saw the dark gleam in his eyes, the cold implacability on his face. He could be cruel, dangerous when crossed; she knew that, knew all about his temper. She did as he said, scanning the pages swiftly, not wanting to read them, knowing the papers were damning. But words jumped out at her; she took in the general contents, and her heart tightened in her chest.

She handed them back to him. Her face was the color of chalk. Tears glittered in her eyes. "Darling, please, you don't understand. Let me explain. Please. My past has nothing to do with today, with now, with you, with us. It happened so long ago. I was very young. Only nineteen. I left that life behind me long ago, Jonny darling."

"I'm going to ask you one more time," he said. "Do you know Tony Chiu?"

"Yes," she whispered.

"Did he back your antique jade business in Hong Kong?"

"Yes."

"Why?"

"We've been in business before at different times. He's a bit of an entrepreneur."

"And he put you on to me, didn't he? Set me

up as a target for you. He wanted you to ensnare me, to marry me so you could keep an eye on me. For him."

"No, no, that's not true. Oh Jonny, I fell in love with you! I did! You know I did."

"Admit you set me up. I know everything," he railed at her.

She began to shake. Floundering, she cried, "Yes, I did try to ensnare you that night at Susan Sorrell's, when we first met. But very soon after that, I became involved with you. I didn't want to do anything but love you. *Truly.* You must know that from our time at Mougins, from our extraordinary intimacy there, the way we became almost one person."

"I can't believe anything you say," he exclaimed, going to pour another drink.

She watched him go, return to the chair. Once he was seated again, she said, "I told Tony I couldn't give him any information about you. *That I wouldn't.* And that decision was reinforced more strongly than ever when I became pregnant with our child . . . I love you," she repeated, meaning this, her eyes riveted to his face.

"And are you involved in the drugs with him?"

"I don't know what you mean," she cried, truly baffled.

"For God's sake, don't keep denying things!" he shouted. Something in him snapped. He jumped up, took hold of her shoulders, shook her violently. "Whore," he shouted at her, "tart, *putain.* I loved you—no, adored you. I thought you were the most perfect thing, the most beautiful woman in the world, without blemish. But you're nothing . . . dirt."

Arabella began to weep uncontrollably. "You've got to believe me, Jonny. I love you with all my heart, and I've told him nothing—"

"Liar!" he screamed at her.

She reached out to him, grabbed his coat sleeve.

He shook her hands off him, his face filling with contempt and hatred. "Don't touch me."

Suddenly Arabella's face twisted and she brought her hands to her stomach. "The baby! I think the baby's coming. I'm having a contraction. Oh please help me . . . help me, Jonny. Get me to the hospital. *Please,"* she begged.

Arabella was in labor by the time he got her to the London Clinic. She was taken to the delivery room immediately.

Jonathan went to wait in the lounge reserved for expectant fathers in the famous private clinic. An hour and a half later his son was born. A nurse came to inform him of this, explaining that he could see his wife and child shortly.

He did not care about Arabella. His only interest was in his son. The heir he had always wanted. He would take the child away from her as soon as he could. Women like Arabella—whores—were not interested in children. The boy would be brought up as an English gentleman. Suddenly his mind turned to schools. He would send the boy to Eton, where he had gone, and then to Cambridge University.

Settling into his thoughts, he sat quietly, waiting patiently to see his child. He realized he was excited, that he looked forward to holding the baby in his arms. His father and mother would be happy. This was their first grandchild. Perhaps he would call the boy Robin. After the christening, the reception would be held at the House of Commons. As a leading politican and member of Parliament, his father could easily arrange that.

He switched gears, contemplated Paula O'Neill, considered the problem of the Harte stores. More than ever he was determined to go through with his plans to wrest control of the chain from her. He must. There was his son and heir to consider now.

A nurse came to fetch him sooner than he expected. He followed her down the corridor to the private suite he had booked for Arabella a month ago. The nurse showed him in, disappeared, murmuring she was going to get the baby.

Arabella was in bed, propped up against the pillows. She looked pale, exhausted.

"Jonny," she began, reaching out her hand to him. Her eyes were imploring. "Please don't be like this with me. Give me another chance, for the sake of our child. I've never done anything to hurt you. Never. I love you, darling."

"I don't want to talk to you," he snapped.

"But Jonny—" She broke off as the door opened. The same nurse walked in, this time carrying the baby wrapped in blankets and a lacy cashmere shawl.

He hurried over to the bed as the nurse placed the baby in Arabella's outstretched arms. They looked down at their child together.

Jonathan stiffened. The first thing he saw was the epicanthic fold of the eye, the little bit of skin covering the inner corner that was unmistakably oriental.

The shock on his face mirrored the stunned expression on hers. Arabella looked up at him speechlessly.

"This is not my child!" Jonathan shouted, his rage exploding. "It's Tony Chiu's! Or some other Chinaman's, you bloody whore!"

He pushed past the incredulous nurse, half stumbled, half ran out of the suite, wanting to put as much distance between himself and Arabella as he could.

The uniformed chauffeur turned on the ignition and the stately, silver-gray Rolls Royce pulled noiselessly away from the Claridge Hotel, rolled off on its way to the London airport.

Jonathan leaned back, sank into the glove-soft leather of the seat. His rage was monumental, would not abate. He could not get over the shock of Arabella's past, her duplicity, her treachery, and the knowledge that she had been sleeping with another man whilst married to him. An oriental man. There was no way she could ever deny that. The baby was living proof. *Tony Chiu,* Jonathan thought for the umpteenth time. Her old friend and benefactor was the most likely candidate.

He glanced at his briefcase next to him on the back seat, and his mind zeroed in yet again on the report. He was not sure how much truth there was in the information it contained about Tony Chiu's activities. But if the man was laundering money through Janus and Janus, he was going to put a stop to it. Immediately. And somehow he would find a way to even the score with his Chinese partner.

Jonathan could not wait to get back to Hong Kong. He glanced at his watch, saw that it was only nine-thirty. He had plenty of time to catch the midnight flight that would take him to the British Crown Colony.

Slipping his hand into his pocket, he automatically curled his fingers around the pebble of mutton-fat jade. He brought it out, stared at it in the dim light of the car. His eyes narrowed thoughtfully. It no longer looked the same. Somehow it had lost its luster. But it *was* his talisman. He laughed hollowly to himself. Some talisman. It had brought him no luck recently. Only bad joss. Very bad joss.

Rolling down the window, Jonathan flung the pebble out into the street, watched it roll away into the gutter.

The car sped on. He sat back, smiled to himself. He was glad to be rid of the jade piece. Now, perhaps, his luck would change.

748

EPILOGUE

We are each the authors of our own lives . . .
there is no way to shift the blame
and no one else to accept the accolades.
Paul McGill in *A Woman of Substance*

They sat together on the rocks at the Top of the World.

It was a glorious Saturday afternoon in late September. The sky was the color of speedwells and glittering with sunlight, and below them the implacable moors were softened by wave upon wave of purple heather. Somewhere in the distance there was the sound of rushing water as a stream tumbled down over rocky crags, and on the lucent air there was the smell of heather and bracken and bilberry.

They had been silent for a while, lost in their own thoughts, enjoying being together again, being up here where it was so peaceful.

Shane put his arms around
.ose to him. "It's wonderful to
with you," he said. "I'm lost
art."

her head, smiled at him. "I feel the

ad we came up to the moors today,"
ent on. "There's nowhere like them in
.ole world."

randy's moors," Paula said. "She loved
n, too."

"Especially up here, at the Top of the World."

"Grandy once said that the secret of life is to endure," Paula murmured and looked at him quizzically. "I hope *I* will."

"Of course, you will, my darling. *You have.* In fact, you've not only endured, you've prevailed. She'd be very proud of you. Emma always wanted you to be the best. And you are."

"You're prejudiced."

"I am indeed. But that doesn't make my statement any less true."

"I almost lost Harte's, Shane," she whispered.

"But you didn't. And that's what counts, Paula."

He jumped off the rocks, took hold of her hands, helped her down. "Come on, we'd better get back. I promised Patrick and Linnet we'd share their nursery tea."

752

EPILOGUE

They walked through the heather, h[o]
hands, buffeted forward by the wind as
headed for the car parked on the dirt r[oad]
Paula stole a look at him, loving him, relie[ved]
and happy that he had returned from Austra[lia.]
He had arrived in Yorkshire last night, and [he]
had not stopped talking since, full of his pla[ns]
for rebuilding the Sydney-O'Neill Hotel.

Paula came to a sudden halt.

Shane also stopped, turned to look at her.
"What is it?" he asked. "Is there something
wrong?"

"I hope not," she replied, starting to laugh.
Her eyes were bright with happiness. "I've
wanted to tell you since last night, but you
haven't given me the chance—"

"Tell me what?" he probed.

She leaned into him, looked up into his face,
that face she had known and loved all her life.
"We're going to have another baby. I'm almost
three months pregnant."

He pulled her into his arms and hugged her,
then held her away. "That's the best welcome-
home present I've ever had," Shane said, smiling
at her.

And he continued to smile all the way back to
Pennistone Royal. •

ding
they
oad.
ved
ia.
he
s

About the Author

...aylor Bradford is one of the most pop-
... beloved authors in the world, a writer
...uly knows how to be the best. In addition
...e Harte family novels that began with *A*
...nan of Substance and continued in *Hold the*
...eam, she has written the acclaimed interna-
...onal bestsellers *Voice of the Heart* and *Act of*
Will. She lives in New York City with her husband, Robert.